"I WANT HIM. WANT THE WAY HE MAKES ME FEEL LIKE THE CENTER OF THE UNIVERSE. THE UNIVERSE OF US."

I want to be part of a whole again, not a limping shell. I want…

The light is blocked out, and his lips are on mine. My hands steal to the sides of his face, and I take him in: a sweet kiss that makes me want to cry.

There must be a term stronger than *wanting*, but it's lost in his gentle touch. Like our first kiss, that day in the homestead house when we looked at each other and realized we were doing more than playing house all those years; we were practicing.

The want pulls my brain from reason. This must be how addicts feel. My fingers slide down the stubble on his soft cheeks. I know the topography of his face better than my own. I'll pay the penalty later. I need this. I'm taking this. Not sure I could stop now, anyway.

He slants his head, and when he opens his mouth, sweet turns hot. He seems as desperate as I feel, tasting, testing, pushing. We can't get close enough. His hands cup my butt and he lifts and turns me, so I'm standing on the running board. We're the exact same height. I know, because we tested it out before he bought this truck. I'm squeezed between the truck body and his, yet still, it's not enough. Wrapping my fists in his shirt, I pull him closer and melt into his mouth. Tonight's memory is going to have to last me the rest of my life.

Praise for Laura Drake and Her Novels

THE SWEET SPOT

"Drake is a fabulous new voice in romantic fiction; this is a first-class Western!"
—***New York Times*** **bestselling author Linda Lael Miller**

"Poignant, heart-wrenching, hopeful…this realistic contemporary zeroes in on issues of trust, communication, healing, and forgiveness. A cut above the rest."
—*Library Journal*

"A sensitive, honest look at a family destroyed by loss… Drake's characters are so real, so like us, that you will look at your own life and count your treasures."
—*RT Book Reviews*

"Lovers of western settings will enjoy debut author Drake's detailed descriptions of bull riding and cattle ranching."
—*Publishers Weekly*

NOTHING SWEETER

"Drake writes excellent contemporary westerns that show the real American West—not a dude-ranch fantasy…This one's not to be missed."
—*RT Book Reviews*

"A sweet, passionate, at times heartbreaking romance set in picturesque Colorado with two very strong-willed protagonists, each recovering from their own recent setbacks."
—*HarlequinJunkie.com*

SWEET ON YOU

"*Sweet on You* is a wonderfully written book and one I wholeheartedly recommend to fans of just about any genre."
—The Romance Review

"A bittersweet romance contemporary that deals with grief, heartbreak, and forgiveness. Drake's ability to work past the trite and hit on the cusp of the matter with beautiful prose and a genuine empathy for her couple made that book a winner for me."
—Smexy Books

ALSO BY LAURA DRAKE

The Sweet Spot
Nothing Sweeter
Sweet on You

THE Last TRUE
COWBOY

A CHESTNUT CREEK NOVEL

LAURA DRAKE

FOREVER

NEW YORK BOSTON

Copyright © 2018 by Laura Drake
Excerpt from *Home at Chestnut Creek* © 2018 by Laura Drake
Cover design by Elizabeth Turner Stokes
Cover photograph by Rob Lang
Cover copyright © 2018 by Hachette Book Group, Inc.

Forever
Hachette Book Group
1290 Avenue of the Americas
New York, NY 10104
forever-romance.com
twitter.com/foreverromance

First Edition: December 2018

Forever is an imprint of Grand Central Publishing.
The Forever name and logo are trademarks of Hachette Book Group, Inc.

The Hachette Speakers Bureau provides a wide range of authors for speaking events. To find out more, go to www.hachettespeakersbureau.com or call (866) 376-6591.

The publisher is not responsible for websites (or their content) that are not owned by the publisher.

ISBN 978-1-5387-4643-1 (mass market) ISBN 978-1-5387-4641-7 (ebook)

Printed in the United States of America

10 9 8 7 6 5 4 3 2 1

OPM

To the sisters of my heart:
All the lost young girls like me,
who found themselves in a library.

THE *Last* TRUE
COWBOY

CHAPTER 1

CARLY

Addiction sucks. I should know. Papaw has his White Lightning. Nana has her Bingo-jones. My addiction has sad green eyes and my name tattooed across his left pec.

But my wedding-dress dreams *always* come in second to his rodeo. There's even a term for it: Rodeo Widow. Except to earn that title, I'd have to be *married*.

Squinting through the windshield glare, I shift the knob on the steering column to third and press on the gas, but the speedometer doesn't budge. Dang it, at this rate I'm going to be late for the breakfast shift. Papaw bought the truck new about the time I was born, and Nana named it "Nellybelle." Said she stole the name from a car on some TV show—Roy Somebody. All I know is, I'm stuck driving the beater, so Nana can drive the Camry to Bingo.

I'm less than a mile from the paved road when clanking starts under the hood. It sounds like the hammers of hell in there. I take it out of gear and lurch to the side of the washboard road and watch the dust billow up in the rearview mirror. "Now that's just craptastic." I'm no mechanic, but I've been driving since before I could reach the pedals. I know what a thrown rod sounds like. Nana would say, "Nellybelle's sleeping with Jesus." My luck she'll want to have a funeral.

I grab a rubber band from the glovebox and lasso my hair into a thick ponytail. My hair is more strawberry than strawberry blonde, meaning if it takes longer than ten minutes to catch a ride, I'll look like Elmo. With freckles. Luckily, Papaw left a gimmie cap behind the seat. I slap it on, throw my purse strap over my shoulder, open the door, and slide into the hot morning.

Once I hit the blacktop, odds are somebody will stop. One good thing about living outside of Unforgiven, New Mexico, all your life is that sooner or later someone you know is bound to come by.

I hear it before I see it. Quad Reynolds's truck materializes through the heat-haze off the blacktop. It's almost as ancient at Nellybelle (may she rust in peace).

He pulls alongside me and yells out the window, "Where's your car?"

Now the Reynoldses aren't among Unforgiven's best and brightest, and given a population of 1,500, that's not a high bar. Quad was the first of his clan to get a high school diploma, mostly thanks to kind and long-suffering teachers passing him along year to year like a white elephant gift. People can't help what they're born with (or without), but Quad has had a thing for me since third grade. He's also got body odor and dandruff so bad his eyebrows flake. I stuff my hands in my back pockets and walk up to the window. "I broke down. Can you give me a lift to town?"

"Heck yeah. Climb in." He unhooks the bungee cord that holds the passenger door shut. "Wait." He holds the door closed with a hand on the window frame. "You're not gonna make me eat those foldy-overy things again, are you?"

Exasperation puffs from my lips. "They're crepes, and no one made you eat them the first time. Besides, I took them off the menu." Mostly because no one ate them. I keep trying changes to the menu to improve business, but so far, the only thing that's gone over is Ratatouille. And only because I told them the name is French for "hash."

"Oh good." The door moans when he pushes it open.

I climb into the cab, right into his yearning look. "When're you going to throw over that no-account cowboy and fall for me, Carly Sue?"

"Believe me, I'm considering giving him up."

"Well, I'm available, but you better hurry 'afore some woman snatches me away."

Not going there. I'm no mean girl. "I'll take it under advisement, thanks." I turn so the springs quit pushing on my butt bone and so the bungee doesn't scrape my shins.

He drapes an arm over the steering wheel, and the breeze washes me in the smell of day-old sweat. "Where is Austin now, anyway?"

"Let's see. What day is it?"

"Thursday. No. Wait. Friday."

"He's in Las Cruces. Three-day rodeo at the county fair this weekend."

He shakes his head. "That boy can ride. I'll give him that."

Yeah. That's the problem.

Austin and I fell in love in first grade. I looked across the craft table and recognized a piece of me, staring back.

Something about him just clicked with me. It was the same for him, and like two jigsaw pieces, we snapped together. We never have come undone. Until now.

This time, I mean it.

Quad's truck rolls into the sleepy-with-morning town. The street curves around Soldier Park, with its peeling bandstand and obligatory Civil War cannon. The Civic Theater is finally playing last month's blockbuster for anyone who hasn't made the fifty-mile trek to Albuquerque. Austin took me to The Civic on our first real date, in junior high. I don't remember what movie, because we ended up making out in the balcony the whole time.

A few pickups are parked in front of the Lunch Box Café, owned by our main competitor and archnemesis, Dusty Banks. He puts the grease in "greasy spoon," but I guess some people enjoy that. We cruise past too many windows blotted out by paint or covered in butcher paper.

Unforgiven has faltered for years, tripping and stumbling to the edge of default. Doubly unlucky, we're not only at the end of a defunct railway spur, but we're on Route 66—the abandoned part.

Quad pulls up in the last angled parking space outside Chestnut Creek Café. It's the end of the road, literally. The converted railway station has been my second home for every one of my twenty-nine years. Papaw bought it back in the '50s, when the spur shut down, and named it after the place where he asked Nana to marry him (he hides his romantic streak well). He cooked, and Nana worked the cash register. Nowadays, Papaw works more at his side business (the still) and Nana keeps the local Bingo parlor in business. But hey, they earned a rest. They'd planned to turn it over to my mom and dad, but a drunk driver on Interstate 40 crashed that dream when I was just a baby.

"Thanks for the ride, Quad." I reach for the bungee cord but he's quicker, leaning over my lap, giving me a close-up of his "ambiance" and his bald spot. I hold my breath until he's on his own side again.

"You bet. Now, get out in that kitchen and rattle those pots and pans." He chuckles and slaps his thigh, raising a cloud of red New Mexico dust.

I don't bother to remind him that I'm not the cook. I just slide out and hold the door shut so he can re-hook the bungee.

The gingham curtains and the old-fashioned gold lettering on the glass door raise a faint haze of pride in my chest. The bells on the door jingle as I step inside and the café wraps itself around my heart, welcoming me with breakfast babble and the smell of bacon. I inhale a deep breath of home.

"Hey, Carly." Moss Jones raises his coffee cup in a salute, his grizzly-brown beard full of crumbs.

"Mornin', Moss."

Lorelei, my friend and our longtime waitress, swishes by, balancing four plates and three orders of toast. "You're late, Carly Beauchamp."

"Yeah, tell me about it." I push through the swinging door to the kitchen and head for my office. "Hey, Fish."

The name on our cook's driver's license is Joseph King, but he'd rather be called by his Navajo name—Fishing Eagle. He's got a dozen eggs, a rasher of bacon, and a boatload of hash browns crowded on the grill and a spatula in each hand. "Carly, can you grab me more bacon?"

"Sure." I pull open the door to the walk-in refrigerator.

"And some more eggs?" His voice is muffled by the heavy door.

I've just finished that when Lorelei sticks her head through

the serving window. "Fish, you got those grits for table five?"
She sorts tickets on the order wheel. "Hey, Carly, would you
mind setting me up for coffee?"

"Sure." I push back through the swinging door to the dining area. I'm the manager and heir-apparent, but most days
that washes out to being the gofer. After grabbing a cup for
myself, I pull coffee and filters from under the counter and
start scooping and stacking enough set-ups to last through
lunch.

Conversation flows past me like a river.

"We even went down to the courthouse in Albuquerque,
but they didn't know, either. I'm gonna—"

"So, I tell him, if you think you're going to the bar
tonight, you've got—"

"Last week's rain washed out the road. I can't even get to
my field, much less—"

My phone blats the opening notes to Blake Shelton's
"Austin" and my hand jerks, slinging coffee across the
counter. "Crap on a cracker." I'd let it go to voice mail but
I've been dodging his calls for two days and if I don't answer soon, he'll sic Nana on me.

Nana loves Austin. And she's not alone. Every girl in Cibola County adores him. Every mom wants to adopt him.
And no dad wants him anywhere near his daughter.

Acid scalds my stomach lining. I pull my phone from the
pocket of my jeans, mash the button, and prop it between my
cheek and shoulder. "Hey."

"Hey, Tigger."

In two words, I'm opening to him like a morning glory to
the sun. I've read that twins have a special language that only
they understand. Austin and I are like that. We're hard-wired
into each other's feelings like a Vulcan mind-meld, without
the weird face-touching thing.

In those same two words, I know he's hungover. I can see him partying with his buds at some trashy bar the night before. I should—I've been there for enough of them. But that was in the glory days, when Austin was winning buckles and I was Cibola County Rodeo Queen. We lived for the road, sex, fair food, sex, and the dream we could make a living on barrels and rough stock.

That bubble burst when I had to come home and help Nana and Papaw with the diner. Yeah, I miss it, but you've got to grow up sometime. But Austin still hasn't. To be fair, he *is* making a living at it, if you consider having just enough money for rodeo dogs, gas, and his next entry fee "living."

Which reminds me. "Don't you 'Tigger' me. We need to talk, Austin Davis."

"Aw, come on, darlin'. Don't be mad. You know I can't stand it when you're upset."

His drawl flows over me with the sweetness of Sunday morning sex. He knows I love his voice. It eases through my cracks, loosening my muscles and my resolve.

"I'll be home for Sadie Hawkins on Friday. We'll talk then."

The litany he's recited too many times burns the sweetness to ash. "I'm serious. I can't go on like this." I drop the coffee scoop to hold the phone in both hands, as if he could feel the painful squeeze. "The girl gets to ask for Sadie Hawkins. I'm not asking you." I click the end button, wishing for the old days, when you could end a call with a satisfying slam.

In high school, the Student Council thought it'd be fun to include the whole town for Sadie Hawkins Day. Every year since, it's a blowout party in the town's square. Austin and I have been to every one of the past fourteen of them.

Streaks are overrated.

My ears prickle as I realize the diner is filled with an un-natural silence. I turn. Every eye in the place is lasered on me like I'm some rare zoo animal. My face blazes, which only makes me madder. I hate to blush. Redheads don't do it well.

"Aw, come on, Carly," Moss says, too loud in the quiet room. "You say that ever' time."

I slap a hand on my hip. "Really?" God, the nerve.

"Really," June Stevens says from booth number three.

Several heads nod.

Dropping the phone in my shirt pocket, I stomp for the kitchen. "This place has the privacy of a glass outhouse." My palms hit the door with a hollow boom and I stride for my office. At least that door has a satisfying slam.

* * *

An hour and a half later, morning work done, I'm sitting, drinking coffee and cataloging my troubles...the biggest of which has a bad-boy grin and one really fine butt. If I sit here any longer, I'm going to tip into sulkiness. And I'm not a sulker. It's time to tackle the trouble I *can* do something about. Wheels.

The café is hopping with the early lunch crowd, and Lorelei has a reinforcement. Sassy Medina, a new-to-town girl with a pretty smile and good references.

Lorelei spies me and hustles over. "Would you hold the fort for a few, Carly? I've got to run down to O'Grady's for tomatoes and we're almost out of Spam."

"Sure. Just be sure Jerry gives us the discount."

She rolls her eyes. "Thanks. I've only worked here seven years, so I'm likely to forget that."

"Yeah, yeah, just go." Grabbing a half apron from under

the counter, I tie it on and drop a book of order tickets in the pocket. Coffee pot in one hand, sweet tea pitcher in the other, I go on refill patrol.

At the first table, my second-grade teacher, Ms. Simons, says, "You stand your ground, Carly. Austin will wise up and marry you. You just wait and see if he doesn't."

The high-schoolers in the booth at the window titter and ask if Austin is officially available for the dance. As far as I'm concerned, he is.

At the counter, the town drunk, Manny Stipple, explains with beery sincerity why Austin deserves another chance.

At twenty-nine, my biological clock has stopped ticking—it's tap dancing on my ovaries. Every girl from my high school class is married and having babies, except me. Well, me and Rose Hart, but she wears men's clothes and is taking hormones to grow a beard. She goes by Roy now.

I'm just about to lose it when my posse spills through the door, trailing strollers, diaper bags, and toddlers. Julie, Jess, and I ruled the homecoming court, and we've managed to stay close through marriages (theirs), kids (theirs), and break-ups (mine). We were all great friends, but Jess and I—we had a special bond. Back in junior high, she decided it wasn't fair that I didn't have a sister, so she stepped up for the job. We've been tight ever since. I love me that Jess.

They take booth number one and settle, passing out crayons and goldfish. I drop menus on the table and we chat while they decide. Jess rubs her stomach as she studies the daily specials on the board above the order window.

"Jess, are you preggers again?"

"Can you believe it?" She smiles at me with a glow reserved for pubescence and motherhood.

My biological clock bongs a funeral dirge.

She eases her toddler over, scoots down, and pats the bench next her.

Lorelei walks in the front door, her arms full of bags.

"I want to hear all the nasty details, I promise. But right now, I've got to fix a problem. Can I borrow someone's car?"

Jess's perfectly plucked brows draw together. Even in motherhood, she keeps herself up—if you ignore the spit-up stain on her silk shirt. "Take mine." She reaches in her diaper bag, pulls out her keys, and tosses them to me.

"Thanks, hon. I'll be back before you're done with lunch." Her son wails, and she waves me off.

I unlock the door of the SUV, shift a stuffed Minion to the passenger seat, and climb in. The hot air is infused with eau de Kid. Discarded juice boxes and crumbs litter the floor. My mood falls like a rock tossed into a dry well. It's not that I need a vanful of kids to feel complete. I have a full life. But dang, my dreams aren't all high-and-mighty. All I want is to raise a big family in a small town, with the love of my life. Cutting Austin loose will mean cutting loose of all my dreams. But I'm sick of hoping and praying and attempting long-distance mind manipulation.

Maybe I can convince him to come home, take over his dad's ranch, and start our business.

Yeah, that's the maybe I hoped for last year.

And the year before that. And…I blow out a breath. I'm not getting anywhere sitting here, sweating and counting spilled goldfish. I fire the engine, put the car in gear, and head out of town.

Floyd's Super Clean Used Cars sits all by itself, two miles out of town on the road to Albuquerque. Cars are cheaper in the big city but I don't have that kind of time. Turning into the almost-deserted lot, I park and head for the '50s-style glass-fronted building. Metallic air conditioning greets me, along with a gum-snapping salesman. Ignoring his howdy, I stride for the back office to rustle us up a new truck. Who am I kidding? Rustling is about the only way we could afford a new one. If I don't find a way to compete with the Lunch Box... *One problem at a time.*

The owner hasn't changed a bit from our high school days. Well, except for the paunch. "Jeez, Floyd. Really?"

He drops a nasty girlie magazine in a drawer and his cowboy boots from the desk. "Hey, Carly." His eyes scan the parking lot. "You looking to trade in the mommy-mobile, huh?" He drops a wink. "Austin know about this?"

I cross my arms. More crap I do not need. "You know very well that's Jess's car."

One corner of his mouth lifts. "Ah, so it is. What can I do you for, Carly?"

"I need to buy a used truck."

"What happened to Nellybelle?"

"She took a dump on the way to work this morning."

Floyd stands, sweeps off his cowboy hat, and lays it over his heart. "Please extend my condolences to your dear Nana."

"Cut the crap, Floyd. I need wheels." I do some quick math in my head to figure what I can afford. "And none of that south-of-the-border stuff you slap a cheap paint job on to make it look saleable."

He puts on a hurt look. "Darlin', you know that when I do have the occasional 'international trade,' I save it for the tourists."

Except the only tourists in Unforgiven are ones who made a wrong turn on the way to Albuquerque. And they sure aren't looking to buy a car. "Just show me what you've got."

He leads the way to the almost-empty lot. "We're a little short on inventory. We had a big blowout sale here last

week. You prob'ly heard my commercials on the radio."
He puffs out his chest and steps to a dusty compact with
burnt paint.

I heard them. But again, not a mean girl. "That won't
work. You know it's too small to carry Papaw's...product."

"And fine product it is, too. Been known to sample it a
time or two myself." He wanders to a battered Dodge Cara-
van that, from the look of it, could be the first specimen that
came off the assembly line.

"It'll hold six, with room left over for a golden retriever."
He gives me the sleazy salesman grin and waggles his bushy
eyebrows.

The sticker on the window is in my price range, and I'm
desperate. But I haven't fallen that far yet. If Austin sees
me in that, he'll think...well, I don't want to think what
he'll think. What the whole *town* will think. *Poor Carly,
wannabe mommy.* My face blazes hotter than the 102-degree
air. "Floyd, this will not do. I'm not looking for anything
special, just a better-than-beater truck that'll get me to work,
and Papaw can borrow now and again for deliveries. How
hard can that be?"

He takes off his hat and scratches his head. "Honest,
Carly, that's all I've got right now. Next shipment of used
cars isn't for two weeks."

"I don't have two weeks, Floyd." I hate the whine in my
voice, but I really am desperate.

He squints into the sun. "I do have something. But it's not
what you're looking for."

Neither is the Mommymobile. "Let's see it."

I follow Floyd's waddle to the shop behind the showroom. "If you're gonna try to sell me something you're
working on—"

"Nope. Just storing it to keep it out of the weather." He

strides to a sheet-covered mound in the center of the bay, lifts the edge, and pulls it off with a magician's flourish.

"That's not a car."

"Damn, Carly, your powers of observation are downright acute." He drops the cover in a corner and slaps the dust off his hands. "This here's a 2005 Honda Shadow Spirit VT750."

The motorcycle is low to the ground, but it's not a cruiser; you'd sit almost upright on it. It's got chrome pipes running down the side and a cushy seat that steps up to a tiny passenger seat with a short sissy bar. But it's the paint job that makes me fall in insta-love. An eye-popping royal blue, with lighter blue flames rippling down the tank. Thoughts zip through my brain like summer heat lightning.

My grandparents would have a fit. I get it; my parents died on a bike.

He names a price lower than I'd have guessed.

It sure wouldn't work as Papaw's delivery van. But it's cheap enough that maybe he could buy a truck, when Floyd gets more inventory.

"It's got low mileage." Floyd must see something on my face, because he's got a greedy gleam in his eye. "Prettier'n a speckled pup, ain't it?"

I nod. My brain flashes to the picture on the wall outside my bedroom. I've seen that photo every day since I've been old enough to toddle down the hall. A frozen moment, of parents I don't remember. My dad, in greasy jeans and a white T-shirt, sitting on a Harley with ape-hanger handlebars, grinning at the camera. My mom, draped around him wearing shorts and a halter top. When I was little, I got the happy. As I got older, I got the sexy. My mom is smiling, but her nails make indentations in the T-shirt—like she wanted to rip it off and do him, right there.

They died on that motorcycle. But even that was romantic—they went together, her arms wrapped around him. Neither had to face a long life of being alone. The thought makes me shudder.

That photo whispers to me at night, telling me bedtime stories of speed and laughter and love. When I think of my parents, it's that stop-action moment that I feel in my gut. Young, full of the future, and mad for each other. That's what I want.

That's my dream.

I found the guy, but that dream depends on Austin to make it come true. Here sits a dream I can make come true, all by myself.

But Nana and Papaw...No, you know what? I've worried about what people would think all my life: I've worked my butt off, being what everyone expected Carly to be: Austin's girl, the dedicated granddaughter who quit rodeo to take over the diner. Well, everyone is going to have to stand back—I'm going to put what *I* want first for once.

Floyd is still standing there with his face and his stomach hanging out.

"You'd give me more off, if we bought a truck too, right? A volume discount?"

He rolls his eyes to the rafters. "Lord, I give to your church every Sunday, but I hadn't planned my business to be nonprofit."

I give him my best Rodeo Queen smile. "If money's tight, maybe you should drop your magazine subscriptions." Floyd's a negotiator, but he's got nothing on the grandkid of a Cajun bootlegger.

His fat mouth twists. "Oh, all right. Fifteen percent off the bike for a package deal." He squints across the bike at me. "You got a license to ride, Carly?"

"Yep." I got it back in high school, and never dropped the endorsement. I pull my wallet from my back pocket. "How much you want to hold it?"

Floyd holds up his hands. "I've known you since kindergarten. Your word is good enough for me."

* * *

That evening, Lorelei is driving me home. We've passed Nellybelle's corpse and are almost to our turnoff when my phone blares "Austin." I check the time, then power off the phone. He must be getting desperate if he's calling this close to his event. I look up to see a flash of pity crossing Lorelei's face.

"Friday is Sadie Hawkins. You may ride over with Nana and Papaw, but you know darned well that when Austin shows up and bats his eyes, you'll end up two-stepping the night away—first in the town square, then in his bed." She turns into the long dirt drive that leads to my house.

I rest my arm on the open window and let the breeze blow out my thoughts. "Not this time."

She doesn't roll her eyes, but it's a near thing. "So, what, you gonna dump Austin and go out with Quad?" She pulls in the dooryard.

"Nah. When Austin really understands how important it is to me, he'll agree to make this his last season."

"If you say so. I'll be by in the morning to pick you up for work."

"Thanks, Lorelei, I appreciate the ride." I slide out, slam the door, and wave as she backs up.

The screen door shushes over the worn green linoleum that's been here so long there's a thin spot next to the sink. The smell of liver and onions smacks me in the face.

Nana is at the stove, poking the contents of a cast-iron skillet like she's got a live rattlesnake in there. If it weren't for the liver smell, I'd half believe she did. Nana's always been quirky and outspoken, but the past few years, as she puts it, her "give-a-shit gave up the ghost." She now says whatever she's thinking, to whomever. We had her tested; it's not Alzheimer's. It's more like Old Folks Tourette's.

She removes the perpetual cigarette from the corner of her mouth, taps the ash on the coffee can ashtray on the counter, then returns it to her lip. "Well com'ere an' give me a hug, sugar."

She watches me cross the floor with the forever squint she's gotten avoiding smoke from that cigarette. Her gray hair is pulled into a messy bun on the top of her head, stray bits standing straight out, defying gravity. Nana's hair used to be red, like mine. They say she was a looker in her day.

"What's the matter?"

Ducking the cigarette, I put my arms around her short frame. Her skin is like biscuit dough, white and pillow-soft, and she smells of smoke, onion, and sweat. The smell of love, and home. "You won't want to hug me when I tell you that Nellybelle died." I kiss her cheek.

"I heard." She rocks me a few seconds, then releases me. "Ah, fuck it. The old nag outlived her usefulness ten years ago." She turns back to the stove. "Now go wash up. Dinner's in fifteen. Emma Jean's pickin' me up, an' I can't be late to Bingo."

Instead, I head for the office where an ancient desktop computer perches on the rolltop desk. It takes forever to fire up. Papaw refuses to replace it, or to get faster internet service, contending that it's bad enough that they make him pay for TV when it used to be free. With Papaw, all change is seen as a conspiracy.

When I finally get to Google, I type, "Motorcycle riding tips."

Luckily, I won't have to start from scratch. My memory flashes film clips from high school, when Austin taught me how to ride the county dirt roads on his little off-road Yamaha. He'd yelled "Shift!" in my ear until I figured out the sound of the revs winding up. And when it got hot, we'd stop at Chestnut Creek to skinny-dip and wind up each other's revs. We had no responsibilities. No expectations. Life rolled out in front of us, and we screamed along, flat-out, never thinking ahead.

God, I miss those days.

I jot several websites on a scratch pad from Haley Feed &Tack, fold the sheet, and put it in my pocket. I'll do research at the diner tomorrow, where they don't haul in pixels via mule team.

By the time I've set the table, Papaw is washing up at the kitchen sink. "I'm gonna have to use the Camry tomorrow to pick up a load of corn at the feed store."

Nana sets the bowl of mashed potatoes on the table. "Last time you did that, we had that squirrel 'pocalypse in the trunk."

"I'm gonna buy it in bags this time. Can't fit as much in that way, but…" He crosses to the fridge, opens the door, and roots around for ketchup.

I pour three glasses of iced tea. "I stopped by Floyd's, but he had a blowout sale last weekend, and didn't have anything worthwhile. He says he'll have some trucks in next week."

Papaw plops the ketchup in front of his plate and lowers his long, thin frame into the chair with a grunt.

His knee must be bad today. Probably not a good time to bring this up, but he'll know soon anyway. I set the gravy boat on the table and sit. "Looks good, Nana." In keeping with our mealtime hierarchy, I pass the platter of fried liver to Papaw.

"Thank you, missy."

Nana fills hers, then passes each plate to me.

Papaw says grace.

Might as well get it over with. "I bought a motorcycle at Floyd's today."

Forks still.

Papaw peers over his half-glasses at me. A stray sunbeam hits his gaunt cheek, silvering his whiskers, aging him. Or maybe it's just highlighting what I haven't wanted to notice. When did he get so old?

"What in tarnation you gonna do with that?"

"Time I had my own vehicle." I try to cut my liver, but my knife screes across my plate. "It's used, and cheap. Floyd cut me a volume discount, so we can still afford a used truck."

"Ladies don't ride motorcycles." His voice cuts better than my knife.

My back goes up. "This one will." No one has a say in *this* dream. Besides, he makes me sound like I'm a flighty teenager. I've come up with a practical solution to a problem. A great solution.

I bite the inside of my cheek to keep the words in. I can fight with Nana. But Papaw is so close-lipped and prickly, I can never be sure enough of his love to fight with him.

"What does Austin have to say about this?"

Pawpaw always takes Austin's side. "He has no say in this."

"Oh."

If I hadn't been watching close, I'd have missed his eye twitch.

"I mean it." The words bounce off the walls, louder than I'd meant.

"I ain't disagreein' with you, missy."

"You may not have noticed, but I'm all grown up now. And if I want to ride a motorcycle, I'm danged sure gonna do it, and no man is going to tell me different."

Papaw wipes his mouth on his napkin. "Lord help us, you sound like your daddy."

His quiet sadness cools my temper. I reach out and touch his hand, suddenly aware how frail his bones are. "Don't worry. I don't plan to become a statistic."

"Neither did they." A stringy muscle works in his jaw. "Don't promise what you cain't deliver, missy."

CHAPTER 2

CARLY

"Keep dawdlin' and we're gonna miss the whole thing," Papaw bellows from the living room.

"Cool your jets, Slick. Perfection takes time." Nana yells back.

I set the rhinestone comb in her hair, and when it tries to fall out, I secure it with a bobby pin. "You look beautiful." I kiss her cheek, inhaling her signature scent; lilac dusting powder.

We both look at her in the oval mirror over her dresser. Despite my curling iron and enough hairspray to kill the ozone layer, stray hairs still float around her head, but at least they're slightly curled hairs. I managed to talk her out of her puffy slip, so her red, white, and blue square-dancing skirt stands only at half-mast. The tan support hose and black or-thopedic shoes make her legs look even bonier. But the eyelet cotton blouse sets off her cornflower-blue eyes, and when she smiles, a pretty, younger woman peeks out at me.

She winks at the mirror. "Let's go knock 'em dead."

"Word, Nana." We fist bump, and head down the hall.

Papaw is pacing. "Product's loaded. We gotta go." Seeing Nana, his long face lifts into a shy smile and he fingers the brim of his hat in his hands. "You look real nice, hon."

"Why, thank you, Leroy." She pats her hair.

"What about me?" I give a Vanna White flourish.

Papaw frowns. "Women oughtn't go to a dance in britches."

"These are my favorite jeans. Cost me half a week's wages."

"Then you got robbed. Didn'tcha see the holes in 'em?"

I know a useless argument when it's coming at me. "Let's go. We're going to be late."

"Where's that man of yours? He should be pickin' you up at the door."

"Sadie Hawkins is girl's choice. I'm going stag." I step past him and out the screen door, but I catch the worried look they exchange. The ride to town is mostly quiet.

When Papaw turns onto the town square, my lips and my heart rate slide up. The shadows hide the worn paint and empty stores. The high school kids have dressed the trees and the bandstand in white twinkle lights, changing the am-biance from neglect to magic.

Pat and the Squeaky Wheels are tuning up on the band-stand. Pat Stark owns the auto repair shop in town, and only hires mechanically inclined musicians. They may have a few screws left over after an engine rebuild, but they can flat-out *play*. Pawpaw cruises by slow, then parks behind the diner.

I scoot out of the backseat, then wait while he walks around and hands Nana out. I follow, smiling at their clasped hands. This could be Austin and me, in some future, forty years from now. Our kids will be grown and gone, but we'll still have each other. The love I've stuffed down the past week rises like warm dough, encasing my heart in softness. I get impatient with him, but I know in the bedrock of my being that he's the only man for me. *Soulmates.* It sounds like a sappy bathroom-stall-etching, but it fits.

* * *

AUSTIN

I'd recognize my baby anywhere, even from the back. Hair the color of a strawberry roan's mane, and that smokin' body, slid into my favorite jeans, the ones with the pocket bling that flashes when she rolls her hips. She's standing at the edge of the dancers, watching her grandparents, a shimmer in her eyes and a smile on her lips.

I slide up behind her. "Sweet, aren't they?" I put my arms around her rib cage, and drop my chin on her shoulder. "We started this gig back in high school, and we'll look like that at our fiftieth Sadie Hawkins Dance." Her perfume wraps around me, the same one I've given her every Christmas since high school. It blends with her own scent, so potent I go insta-hard.

She stiffens under my hands. "I'll probably still be single then."

"Aw, come on, Tig. We're gonna get married." I sweep an arm over the crowd. "The whole town knows it." I cup my hands around my mouth and whistle loud enough to be heard over the band. Heads turn. "Hey! Y'all know I'm gonna marry my Carly, right?"

Cups of beer and voices are raised in a chorus of *Hell yeah's*, along with a few wolf whistles.

I love it when she blushes. "Stop." She slaps my bicep. "You'd have to ask *me*, not the whole town, you fool."

"Oh yeah, I forgot that part." I put on my most charming smile and hope she lets the subject slide. A little distraction would help. I grab her hand. "Come on. I want to dance with my girl."

She may be peeved with me, but like every other time we've danced, the world clicks off, and it's just her and me. The fairy lights are pretty, and I spin her every few steps until she's smiling again. When I move wide to avoid the Hansens, she moves with me, perfectly in sync, just like always. I love dancing with Tig.

But when she looks up at me, there's a wrinkle in between her brows. "Austin, we need to talk—"

"I have a surprise for you," I whisper in her ear. I don't think to do surprises often, but when I do, they're memorable. The last one involved some of Victoria's Secrets, on top of the water tower. Oh yeah. Memorable.

"What is it?"

"What, and ruin the surprise?" I nip her ear, and she squeaks. "You're gonna have to miss church, though. I'll pick you up at eleven. You just be ready for a picnic." I tuck her head back on my shoulder.

The surprise won't be what she wants. But I can only hope it'll be enough for now. She's wanted me to come off the road for years. To get married, then start our family, and our rodeo rough-stock business. It's what I want, too. Just one more year on the circuit. I mean, a man has to stockpile a bunch of stories to tell his grandkids when he's too old to do more than rock on the porch, right? Rodeo is what I was made for. It's all I've wanted to do since I could walk. And I'm good at it. I've put away a nest egg—maybe not as big as some, and maybe not as much as we'll need, but I'll fix that in the coming year. I'll win it all. *Then* we'll get married.

Because I've got the world's best prize, waiting at the end of the rodeo road. My Tig.

The music ends, and with one last spin, I lead her away. "I'm thirsty. You want a beer?"

"I could drink one."

We get in the snaking line for the Elks' beer booth.

"Hey, Austin, you going to ride Ruidoso this year?" Steve Seaver asks from halfway up the line.

"I'll be there."

Manny Stipple, just ahead in line, breathes a fog of alcohol over me. "Didja bring home a buckle from El Paso dis year?" Clearly, he's been to see Carly's Papaw.

"Nah, not this year." I shore him up with a push to his right arm. "Sure you haven't had enough to drink, sir?"

"Pssssht." Manny waves me off, nearly dumping himself in the dirt. "You may be a good rider, but I get the buckle in drinkin', ever' time."

I pull my hand back but stand ready to catch him if he falls. "I wouldn't dispute that for a minute, Mr. Stipple."

"Heyyyyy, Auuuustin," a group of junior high school girls chorus, strolling by.

I tip my hat and they giggle behind their hands.

Tig tucks her hand under my arm, and I lay my hand over hers. I'm about the luckiest guy on the planet. Home, at a dance where I know everybody and my girl on my arm. I take in a deep breath of spring, beer, and Carly.

It doesn't get any better than this.

Two hours and two beers later, we've made the rounds of

all our friends and I've danced with Carly's Nana and just about every old lady from hereabouts. I cut in on Carly and Jake Parsons, just before "Amarillo by Morning" ends. I lead her off the dance floor, her face flushed, her eyes sparkling in the lights. I lean in and whisper, "This is nice and all"—I nuzzle her neck—"but I'd really like to spend some alone time with this wild redhead I know."

She flips her hair off her shoulder. "Who you callin' wild, cowboy?"

"I ride wild for a living, remember? I should know." God, she's adorable. I put an arm around her neck and pull her to me. I've been wanting a kiss forever. And trust me, Carly can kiss. I mean, I've never kissed another girl (except that time in sixth grade), but I don't need to. Carly pours herself into a kiss, holding back nothing, giving everything. Makes me want to pull her under a tree and do what comes naturally.

She wants it, too, because she shoots a look over her shoulder to be sure no one is watching, then grabs my hand and tugs. We're running through the shadows, laughing. We both know where we're going—and in my bed, we'll get there.

* * *

CARLY

Hours and hours later, in Austin's iron bed in the apartment above the defunct Tanya's Togs, I stretch amid the rumpled sheets, a pillow under my shoulders. I'm sleepy, sated, and a bit smug. Every time with Austin is as amazing as the first (without the parking brake in the small of my back). He has a laser focus, and just remembering the things he does makes a blush of heat radiate from my girly parts. Since Austin is my first and only, I'm not an expert, but surely no man could be better. Most of the time I'm afraid I'll faint from unending orgasms.

The streetlamp lays a strip of light across the bed, spotlighting the delicate skin at the apex of his thigh. I love that place. I want to spend more time on that place. I sigh. "I've got to get home."

Austin's forearm drops onto my rib cage, and his fingers curl around the outside of my breast. "Nah." His voice is slow and sex-drugged.

"Nana will worry." I glance out the window at the black sky. "I've got to at least text her. The dance has been over for hours."

He groans when I sit up and reach for my phone on the nightstand. *I'm with Austin. I'll be home in a couple of hours.*

Within seconds, her answer buzzes in my hand.

Well, duh.

I drop the phone on the orange crate nightstand. "Well, maybe I have a *little* time before you need to take me home."

He grabs me from behind, and I fall back into him, laughing.

* * *

CARLY

Late the next morning, I run to answer the knock on the screen door.

Austin looks fresh and sexy, though I have good reason to know there's no way he got more than four hours' sleep.

"Wow, you look like one of those New York magazines." He cocks his head. "You did catch the picnic part, right?"

I smooth my new halter dress over my thighs. I fell in love with the yellow daisies, and how the silky fabric felt on my bare skin. I've been waiting for a special occasion to wear it for the first time. I'm praying for special today. "Don't you like it?"

"No." His hands slide across my bare back. "I love it."

He gives me a long kiss, and my body wants to pick up where we left off.

"I just don't want to get it dirty."

I drop my sandals, toe into them, and lift the pie safe from the counter. I got less sleep because I stayed up to bake. Oh, speaking of that . . . I hand him the thermos of coffee. We're both going to need that. "I'm ready. Where are we going?"

"I want to show you something." He takes the pie from me and sniffs the plastic top. "Is this what I think it is?"

"What, and ruin the surprise?" I feed him his line from last night as he hands me up into his truck, and I scoot over to the middle. I'm greeted by the smell of fried chicken. "Perfect. I love The Prairie Chicken."

He runs around and hops into the driver's seat. "I was hoping you'd think it was homemade."

"If it were, it'd be by your momma." I roll up the window so my hair doesn't get messed up, since it decided to cooperate today. Well, as much as it ever does.

"Hey, I can cook." He puts the truck in drive and starts down the long dirt road to the highway.

"Shoe-leather steaks on a grill is *not* cooking."

"The guys never complained."

"That's because they had a six-pack each before you fed them."

He drops an arm over my shoulders. "Then it's a good thing my future wife is a great cook."

"Flattery may get you an apple pie, Cowboy."

"Remind me to be sweet more often." He kisses my cheek.

"I've been meaning to talk to you about that." I stay in the moment to keep from getting ahead of myself. I steal a glance; he's focused on the road, his hand relaxed on the steering wheel. There's no reason to think this is going to be my engagement day. Except, *wouldn't* he try to act like it's any other day, so not to spoil the surprise?

He would...*if* he's planning a surprise. Otherwise, he's just everyday relaxed.

Just in case, I try to memorize the day. It's perfect. Monsoon season assures that it won't get too hot, and the rain last week has brought out delicate little daisies and Indian paintbrush at the side of the road.

We ride, each in our own thoughts, until Austin turns off at the dirt road at the edge of his parents' land. In the distance is his family's weathered-to-gray, two-story homestead house. It housed three generations of the Davis clan, until his parents married and built a modern ranch house, a mile at the other end of the property.

"I thought we could have a picnic out here and not be disturbed."

How romantic! My heart kicks in my chest.

We gather the food, and Austin snatches a blanket from behind the seat. "Mind the railing. I fixed the steps, but haven't gotten around to that yet."

I take the steps, his hand warm on my back.

I've been out here before, of course. We used to play house here when we were little. Well, I played house. Austin played cowboy, coming home to me after his "cattle drive" and Indian wars. The house is snug, but hasn't been lived in for twenty-five years. The old-fashioned wallpaper is faded and peeling in places. The rooms are empty and full of the smell of dust and filtered sunlight. They echo as we walk in. I may just be sentimental, but I've always felt safe here; as if the decades of happiness seeped into the walls, and they now exhale it over me. I shiver.

Austin spreads the blanket on the floor of the front parlor. "Do you mind if we eat first? I'm starving."

"This is not a news flash, Davis. Since when are you not hungry?" I sit on the blanket and unpack the food.

He drops down beside me. "Well, someone made me miss dinner last night."

He nuzzles, making me giggle. "That wasn't me, you horndog. And I didn't get to eat, either."

"But now that I think about it, I'm hungry for more than chicken." He kisses my neck.

"Chicken is highly overrated," I murmur against his throat and undo the buttons of his shirt. His hand slides up my leg and he discovers my surprise: no underwear.

He groans. "Oh, you're killing me, Tig."

I lay back on the blanket. "I can stop." I slide the edge of my skirt up my thigh. "Anytime."

"Don't you dare." He sits back on his heels and unbuttons his Wranglers.

"Whoa there, boy." I put a hand on his chest when he leans down. "Protection, remember?" The pill has always made me sick, so, like it or not, he's a condom man.

He groans, then struggles to get a hand in the jeans puddled at his knees. He takes care of business, and he's over me again, hard and ready.

I wrap my legs around his waist and pull him into me, too hungry to wait any longer. The tension that has built all day coalesces to a ball of crackling static inside me, shooting down my nerves and exaggerating the friction of every small movement. His hands are flat on the floor on either side of my head, and he watches my expressions change as he moves. The ceiling over his head is the one I'll see every morning I wake. His face will be the first I see—

Thoughts are blown away by the lightning strike of my orgasm. Seeing it, he's caught up as well, and we cry out together.

It takes some time for us to recover but when we do, we fall on the food until there's nothing but crumbs and a couple leftover pieces of pie. Austin groans and stands. "That was the best meal I ever ate." He chucks me under the chin. "Both of them. But now, it's time for the surprise." He extends a hand to help me up. "You ready?"

I shouldn't have eaten so much. My stomach is full and jittery—not a great combination. I let him help me up, then I brush a few crumbs from my dress, so he won't see my hands are shaking. I know I shouldn't get my hopes up, but it's too late now. He takes my hand and leads me up the stairs. At the top of the landing he turns left, into the master bedroom.

"Ta-da." He sweeps his arm.

I scan the room. "What?"

"I replaced the windows."

Now I notice the stickers on the new glass, and the old wood is replaced by vinyl. "Oh. Nice. Good job."

"Tigger?" He walks over to the window. "You really want me to come off the road?"

My heart bongs off my breastbone. "I *need* you to, Austin."

"Well, okay then. You've got it."

"What?" The word spirals in pitch and volume, following

my tripping heartbeat. I take a deep breath, trying to seal in the moment, to save it between the pages of my memory like the carnation in my high school scrapbook the year he and I were Homecoming King and Queen. I memorize his words, the light in the room, the moment.

I walk over and, not wanting to miss a nuance, put my hands on the sides of his face and raise it, so the light from the new window falls on the hard planes I know better than my own. His mouth is smiling.

His eyes aren't.

My muscles jerk taut in an attempt to protect my soft organs. I want to stick my fingers in my ears to block his words.

"After next season." His smile falters. Even a rough-stock rider loses nerve, sometimes. "Think about it, Tigger. We'll be thirty. A nice, round number to begin our lives together. We can still have ten kids by the time we're forty. More, if we have a couple twins, like my uncle—wait, where are you going?"

Bitterness tastes like ashes at the back of my throat. "Why do I get my hopes up? I'm like Charlie Brown with the football, in *Peanuts*. We've done this at least once every year since we were twenty. Do the math, Davis."

I'm done. Done with the hoping. The wishing. Done with not asking, because I'm afraid to hear the answer. "I get antsy, and you act like you don't notice. Like you don't know why. Then I get bitchy, then bitchier, until we're...here."

There will be no surprise sparkly ring. That's a daydream I wove, trying to hope it to reality. Like when I was thirteen, and inked *Mrs. Austin Davis* on all my school notebooks. "God, I'm a fool. Another year. Then another. Until you're thirty-eight, broken down, and hurting. Those are the years I get?"

"No. I just told you. One more year." He takes a step toward me. "I promise."

"The same promise, last year." I hold up a hand. "No. It's not even about the year. It's that you expect me to sit here and wait for you. See, you're *my* dream. My first and only dream." I push down on the emotion that's bubbling like a lava lamp in my gut. I. Will. Not. Cry. "It's obvious I'm your second." The words fall out, to clunk like chunks of cement to the floor. I hadn't known that saying them out loud would make them so...real. But there they lie, and I can't take them back. They wouldn't fit inside anymore anyway.

He spreads his arms, like he's the offended one. "As long as I'm winning, I'm making money for our future."

"Don't you even try to tell me you're doing it for 'us.' You don't always win, and life on the road is expensive. You'd bank more money working for your dad here on the ranch." I have to try once more, to make him understand. Because I can't give up until I know for sure where I fit. I step back into the room. "Austin, please, listen. It's like all I am is 'Austin's Girl.' I thought I was your partner. We were going to build a business together. A family. A *life* together. Now I get it. My role is 'Austin's Cheerleader.'"

I make a fist and shake an imaginary pom-pom. "Go, Austin." My voice comes out flat.

"If I wanted a cheerleader, there's plenty of buckle bunnies out there. I want you, Carly. You just have to trust that I know what I'm doing—"

"See? That's exactly what I'm talking about. It's your job to decide, my job to trust." I throw up my hands. "Why do I bother? We've had this discussion so many times..." I turn and walk to the doorway.

"Seventeen." His mumble comes from behind me.

I whirl to face him. "Oh, I get it. I'm a crapbird for bring-

ing it up. Well, you won't have to dread this, ever again."
The anger drains out of me in a rush, leaving nothing but the
bitter taste of sadness that's trying to crawl into my throat.
"I finally get it. You've made it clear as the glass in that new
window." I walk to the door. "I'm done. Don't come asking
me to marry you, Austin Davis, because the answer is going to be no. Forever. And you can take that to the payout
window."

He opens his mouth, then closes it.

I go down the staircase, my bare feet leaving tracks in the
dust.

His boots clunk down the steps behind me.

I toe into my sandals, grab my pie safe. "I want to go
home." I push open the screen, walk down the steps, crawl
into the truck, and belt myself in the passenger seat.

A minute later, he locks the door of the house and rounds
the front of the truck.

Dead silence takes on new meaning on the drive home. I
hold my anger close, blowing on the embers when they start
to cool. It's the only way to keep myself from crying, and to
hold onto one shred of my dignity.

I use the time to reload what ammo I have left. When he
pulls up to my door, I hit him with it. "I'll have you know
that I'm done putting my dreams on hold for you. I have my
license, and a motorcycle down at Floyd's in my name."

"You what? What do you want a motorcycle for? It's
dangerous."

I throw him a huge eye roll. "Says the guy who rides two-
thousand-pound bulls for a living."

"Yeah, but I'm a man."

I shouldn't be surprised. I was raised on old-fashioned
country attitudes, and you can't get much more country than
Unforgiven. Still, it rankles. "You know, the sad thing is, you

don't see anything wrong with what you just said." I know this is just an immature attempt to hurt him, but when you're dying inside you use whatever you can.

He frowns across the gulf of seat between us. "Tigger, I don't want you doing this. Really, I don't."

"You lost the right to call me that, Austin Davis." I raise my chin. "And you have no say in it. I'm going to go find out who I am, without you. I'm done with being who everyone expects me to be. I'm a single woman, and this is the twenty-first century. I'll do whatever I please. And you?" I flick my nails at him. "You're in the rearview mirror." I push open the door and take the long step down. "Hit the road, Austin. That's what you're *really* good at."

I walk away and don't look back. I just wish I could have done it without the internal whimpering.

I'm glad Nana and Papaw are having lunch in town so they aren't here to witness the meltdown. I pace the twelve steps across my room, revelations going off like self-esteem claymores.

Twenty-five years gone, loving a man who loves the rodeo more.

I've got to be the last one in town to know this. Everyone must think Austin has me wrapped around his finger...or some other dangling appendage.

Has he?

Well, if he does, that ends today. I probably should feel some pride for finally standing up for myself and chasing my own dreams, but I don't.

I am destroyed.

CHAPTER 3

CARLY

Two weeks later, Papaw's new truck backfires through the turn onto the town square, demonstrating why I named it "El Fartito." The only thing *new* about it is the owners. It's only five years younger than Nellybelle but it runs, and I don't have to bum rides to work.

A flicking glance in the mirror takes my heart out of gear. A longer look makes it hammer like Fartito at sixty.

A dusty red F250 is two inches off my bumper. Behind the wheel, green eyes, a country-boy smile. Austin. He wasn't due back until—crap. Today *is* Monday. He may not recognize the truck, but he sure knows my hair: the color, the texture, how it tastes.

His grin spreads and he raises his index finger from the wheel in the universal country greeting.

I feel the tug of the gravitational pull in that grin. My stomach rises like the first time I jumped off the cliff into the quarry lake.

Give him another chance. The voice in my head is a little girl's. A little girl who believed in the tooth fairy, bedtime stories, and happily ever after.

Well, that chick needs to strap on some big-girl panties. A wave of *pissed* rolls over me. I do this every time. My resolve is firm, right up 'til Austin enters my orbit. I lock my eyes forward and flick him a one-finger salute of my own.

He blats his horn and my fingers go white on the wheel. There's no ditching him; he knows where I'm going. Can probably even guess I've been on a supply run. My jaw snaps tight so fast my teeth click.

Buggers on a bun.

I pull into a spot in front of the diner and turn off the ignition. The truck bounces, chokes, and wheezes for thirty seconds before, with one last fart, it dies. Blood flash-floods my face. A glance in the rearview mirror confirms that I look like a baked tomato. I'm so not ready for this.

Austin steps to my open window, rests his arm on the sill, and smiles in at me. "Damned fine vehicle you got here, Tigger. Floyd palmed it off on you, didn't he?"

"Don't you diss El Fartito, Davis." I can't think with those radar-love eyes zeroing in on me. I duck my head, grab my purse and the grocery bags, and push open the door, forcing him to step back. I slide to the hot asphalt.

"Don't I at least get a hug?" He opens those well-muscled arms.

I want to touch the soft curl falling on his forehead. I want to trace those lips with my tongue. I want to run. "Get. Lost." I duck around him and hoof it for the diner.

The bell clanks when I pull open the door. The dinnertime

babble settles over me. My heart settles to a more normal cadence. This is *my* turf.

The bell clanks again.

Lorelei's standing at the cash register, hand on hip.

The deep, too-loud voice comes from behind. "Carly Beauchamp, are you telling me you got no sugar for a cowboy who brought you home a Champion's buckle?"

The diner falls silent as the O.K. Corral before the shooting started.

Can skin burst into flame? I pass the bags to Lorelei. "Give it to a buckle bunny, Davis. You've got nothing I want."

"Aw, come on, Carly, don't be mean," Moss chimes in from his seat at the counter.

The teenagers in booth four sing a soprano chorus of "Hey, Austin."

Ignoring my personal peanut gallery, I ask Lorelei, "Everything okay?"

"Um. Fine." She's looking over my shoulder.

"You don't need anything?"

"No. We're good."

"Your Nana raised you better than to ignore folks, Carly." My junior high principal's voice hasn't grown less commanding over the years.

"I don't recall putting my love life to a vote." I turn to glare at the room in general and my nose almost brushes Austin's shirt. I take a step back. If I leave now, it's going to look like I'm running. And Carly Beauchamp doesn't run. I put my palms against his chest and push until he backs up. I cross the floor, hit the swinging door to the kitchen, and head for my office.

I don't hear it swing closed.

Fish's voice comes from behind me. "Hey, Austin, when did you get back into town?"

"Just now. You still teachin' the kids drumming?"

"Oh yeah. You'll have to come out—"

The rest is cut off by my slamming office door.

I haven't even caught my breath when it opens and Austin peeks in, waving a white napkin. "Can we parlay for ten minutes?"

And give him time to change my mind? "No."

The door opens wider. "Aw, come on, Tigger, five minutes, and promise I won't bother you no more."

I narrow my eyes. "Swear?"

"Swear." He licks his finger and makes a cross on his chest.

At my nod, he steps in and closes the door behind him. The room gets too small. Austin Davis isn't a big man, but his personality fills a room. He's cocky, irritating, too good-looking, charming, and damn it, his cologne is working on my lady parts.

He slips his fingers in the front pockets of his jeans. "Carly, you've been the only woman for me since the first grade. There is not a buckle bunny that could ever turn my head, and you know it." He tips his head to the side and gives me his most winning smile, which takes a blowtorch to my frozen heart. "You're my girl."

"Not anymore, I'm not." I look down, so his puppy-dog eyes can't influence me.

"Your beautiful face is the last sight I hope to see before I die. Don't you know that by now?"

His voice flows over me, his words making inroads in my resolve. Afraid my voice will give me away, I shake my head. Instant gratification versus long-term happiness has started a war, and the heavy artillery barrage has begun. In my gut. In my brain.

"Do you want me to get down on one knee out there?" He

points to the dining room. "Because I will. I'll drive out and ask your Papaw for your hand right now. Just say the word."

This would be so much easier if he was the loser I make him out to be when he's gone. But when he's standing in front of me, those arguments are as see-through as my Victoria's Secret undies. "See? This is why I can't do this." I put my hands in my curls and pull. "It isn't about being in love. It isn't about being engaged. Hell, half the town already figures we are!"

He rests his hands on my folded arms. "Aw, come on, Tig."

I jerk my arms away and take a step back. "Not going to happen."

He hooks a finger in his belt loop. "It's gonna happen. We'll get married as soon as—"

"I know, I know. I've heard it a hundred times. I'm what you'll do when you can't do what you want to do anymore."

"Now I never said th—"

"This no longer works for me, Austin. I feel like a parting gift on some game show." My voice cracks like hot tea over ice. "I know all about your dreams. What about *mine*?"

"Our dreams are the same, Tig. We'll buy some quality bloodlines—bulls and horses. In ten years we'll be sitting pretty, supplying rodeos in three states with the best bucking stock around. C&A Rough Stock, that's us." He takes a step, but my hand stops him. "By then, there'll be babies—boys I can teach to ride, and beautiful little girls with hair of fire and freckles, to steal cowboy hearts." I see his belief in the depths of those green eyes. "I *love* you, Carly Beauchamp."

I know he loves me. I'm tired. I'm hurting. I'm weak. I miss the one person I can totally be myself with. My body has missed him. All I want to do is set down all my worries for a while.

But then I'd have to live the rest of my life knowing that when it came down to it, I didn't matter as much as what my husband *really* wanted. And I've had a long two weeks to think about that. I can't do it. "We. Are. Done. Look me in the eyes, Austin Davis. Can you see that I mean it?"

He looks. Close. Then he nods.

I point at the door. "Get out. You come sniffing around, I swear I'll get Pawpaw's shotgun and load your butt with buckshot."

With one more "forgive me" look, he walks out.

I'm blazing hot. He led me along for nine years. Nine years I can't get back. I've cut myself loose, with no safety net, and now I'm falling. How dare he just assume I'm going to blindly follow, my hands in the back pockets of his Wranglers, until he decides to turn around and deal with me? The nerve. The arrogance. The... buttwipe. I fume, calling him names in my head that Nana would wash my mouth out for.

When the edges of my anger at him burn off, there's plenty left for me. I'm not some empty-headed buckle bunny. I went along. I lived in hope, in denial, for nine years. Sure, I pitched a fit once a year, but it was just a rock in the stream of Us. We came back together on the other side, with barely a ripple.

Did I ever really believe it would be one more year?

Yes, I did. For maybe the first five years. After that, I dreaded our annual Come to Jesus meeting as much as he did, because of what might be on the other side. Oh, those agonizing weeks, when the frustration and anger would build.

Every year it got harder—the stakes got higher. On one hand, he was getting older, so odds were better that he'd end his career. But hitting that rock all those years left damage, below the surface. Every "next year" hurt more. Until this year, when I couldn't help but see what I'm sure everyone saw a long time ago.

He doesn't want to end his career. I'm always going to be second.

And that tells me I was in denial about a lot of things. We're not equal partners in this relationship. That he never loved me as much as I loved him.

And that I was in love with the guy I wanted him to be, not the real Austin Davis.

Even as I think it, I realize that I've thought this before. I thought it, and quickly buried it, down in the deep dark. I didn't want to know.

I'm sure he loves the Carly he thinks I am, and I can't really blame him, since I've worked hard to be that Carly.

She's the only Carly I know, too.

Is there another me under here? God, how can I have gotten this old, and not ever considered that?

My insides feel shredded, clawed to strips. I need maternal advice. In the old days, I'd've called Austin's mother, but that's out now. I pick up the phone to call a lifeline. I admire the heck out of Cora Jenkins. She's older than my mom would be, but we got to be fast friends back when I was running barrels on the rodeo circuit. Her husband owned the food truck that supplied the rodeo, and when he died of a massive heart attack leaving her bereft and broke, Cora took over. She was alone and lonely, and I was overdosed on testosterone from hanging with cowboys 24/7. I'd bring a bottle of wine, and we'd talk about anything and everything until the wee hours of the morning.

A half hour later, I hang up calmer. Cora's down-home savvy, support, and sympathy are like a shot of novocaine to my aching soul.

There's a tentative knock at my door. "Carly? It's me."

I sit upright and pull out order forms so it looks like I'm working. "Come on in, Lorelei."

"You know better than to let those idiots out there get to you. They're all jealous because of what you and Austin—" She steps in and shuts the door behind her. "Whoa. You look like late August roadkill. What is it, hon?"

"I broke up with Austin. Forever." And if she tells me I always say that, I'm going to lose it.

There is no private life in a small town. Especially when you own the place everyone comes to gossip. The town has had a front row seat to every one of Austin's and my breakups. Some years they last a week; some years, a month.

But this time is different. I have a hard head, but the lesson has gotten through, this time. I'm done for good.

She hikes a butt-cheek on the desk and takes my hand. "Oh Carly, I'm so sorry."

My breath rushes out, which, as it turns out, is the only thing holding me upright. My head drops onto the desk. "At least you believe me."

"Hon, anyone with half a brain would know to look at you. Was it the rodeo?"

I'm half glad I don't have to explain, half mortified that I don't. I really was the last one to figure it out. I nod.

"Well, you know what? You're worth ten little boys like that, Carly Beauchamp. He'll never grow up, and you deserve better."

"I know you're right. So why does it feel like I'm going through DTs?" I hold out my hand. It's got the shakes.

"Cold turkey is always best." She pats my back. "What you need is distraction. You want to come out to the Rooster with me on Friday night?"

The Rowdy Rooster is Unforgiven's only bar, and it lives up to its name. Most Saturday nights end in a brawl. "Nah.

By then, the word will be out, and all I'd get are pity dances, or come-ons. Thanks anyway."

"You're probably right."

An idea pops into my brain, fully formed. "I need to go where I don't know anyone. Where I wouldn't have to explain, or hear...maybe I'll hit a bar in Albuquerque."

"Not alone."

"Why not?"

Lorelei's brows go up and her eyes get big. "Carly, Albuquerque may be only fifty miles away, but it's a big city. You don't know what could happen."

"Yeah, that's the draw." I'm full up with people telling me what I can and can't do."

"No, it's not safe. Promise me if you want to go, you'll call me. I'll go with you."

"I'm not ready yet, anyway." I pick up a pen. The order isn't going to place itself. "How are we doing for tea? I was thinking of trying some of that Passion Fruit instant stuff."

Lorelei's mouth opens in horror.

"I'm kidding, I'm kidding." I sigh, trying to duck a vision of the ceaseless stretch of days ahead.

CHAPTER 4

CARLY

A month. That's how long it's taken for the steam to build to the point that I have a constant whistling in my ears—a pressure cooker ready to blow. I've tried, truly. Tried to settle into the bombed-out shell of a life I have left. Tried to shore up the brave façade that crumbles every night when I'm alone. Tried to wait out the gossip, and the comments.

Where's Austin?

When's he coming home?

Really? Broken up? Again?

Nana doesn't say so, but I know from her sideways looks that even she thinks we'll get back together.

But what they don't know is, this time is different. I've always come in second place in Austin's life. I'm going to go find a life of my own to star in.

I hadn't realized that if you are with someone long enough, people see you as a single entity. Carly/Austin, Austin/Carly. They have a slightly unfocused look when they talk to me—like they're looking for someone who isn't there. Like they're not sure they know me anymore.

I'd be pissed, but I don't know me anymore, either. Who am I, all by myself? It's past time I find out. I lift my duffel and head for the door.

"I'll see you Saturday afternoon, Nana." The screen door slaps behind me.

I climb into El Fartito, who starts after blatting an opinion about a trip to Albuquerque. I roll down the drive, heading for I-40 and some distraction.

Maybe Austin convinced himself he's rodeoing for us. Maybe I could guilt him into coming off the road. But I think too much of dreams to dash his. Besides, what kind of marriage would that be? He'd eventually resent me for taking away the last of his glory days. And I'd always know I came in second.

What we have would crisp to cinders, and we'd end up like the Harrisons down the road—bitter and hateful, staying together out of fear and habit. Better that love dies a natural death than to burn alive. I know I'm right. Even if I don't want to be.

Besides, what good is my dream if it depends on someone else to make it come true? Hand-me-down, that's what it is. But I've realized that's not all. My job is a hand-me-down, too. It was supposed to be my parents'. I love the diner and I'm proud of it, but would I have chosen that if I'd had a choice? I took a semester of classes at the community college, but when Nana's filter broke to the point she was cussing out customers...It was silly, really. You don't need a degree to run a country diner.

Come down to it, my whole life is hand-me-down. The town, the house I live in...even my motorcycle rebellion is unoriginal.

Pathetic.

I've been naive and trusting. It's time to grow up. To toughen up, build up a layer of callus so I'm not so vulnerable. I need to see to my own needs, my own happiness, my own future. Even though I have no idea what that looks like, I know it's there. I'm going to find my hand-me-down dreams: a man who loves me more than what he does, a family, with lots of kids in a big old house—no, that's the old dream. Maybe I'll sell the diner. Move to Denver. Get a degree. Become a biochemical engineer.

Okay, so I'd have to be good at science for that. But when the canvas is blank, you can paint any picture, right? I mean, two months ago, I couldn't have imagined *this* reality, so...

I'm so sick of stewing in my own angst. It's time to face it: My old comfort zone is gone—vaporized. I've got to take a step forward before I freeze to immobility, stuck in hell. Papaw always says, "Do something, even if it's wrong." I never really knew what he meant by it.

I get it now.

I hit the entrance ramp and merge onto the Friday night river flowing to the city. I told Nana I was staying with a friend. I didn't tell Lorelei I was going at all. The whole point is to let off some steam where I'm not half of the C&A franchise. No heartbroken "poor Carly." Just an anonymous chick in a generic country bar.

This weekend is a beginning. Driving to Albuquerque and staying in a hotel by myself. This is research: excavating to find who Carly really is. I'm going out. I'm going to have a good time. A thrill of potential shoots through me.

It's full dark, sage-tinted wind blows in the window, and

Garth's on the radio. Something in me unwinds. It feels like freedom.

Forty minutes later, I'm cruising just off Central Avenue, looking for a dive country bar I've heard of…there! A fluorescent pink neon sign announces:

BUBBA'S FLAMINGO LOUNGE
HOME OF COWPUNK AND STEAMCHUNK

I have no idea what the heck kind of music that is, but Bubba's is rumored to have a good atmosphere, and there's a decent chain hotel right across the street. No way I'm driving home as drunk as I plan on getting. I steer Fartito into the hotel parking lot.

By the time I check in, change, do my hair and makeup, it's time. My Friday-night-tight jeans earn me two horn blats and a wolf whistle as I cross the street, my inlaid cowgirl boots clicking. My parched ego soaks up the male interest.

Like I said, pathetic.

The bouncer looks me over and doesn't card me. Yeah, fine, I've taken worse hits than that, dude. I step into the long dim room and my heart syncs to the beat of the long-haired, sleeve-tatted bass player, lifting my mood. If you're into local dives, this is the place. The seats are worn, the floor is sticky, and the vibe is laid-back. The crowd is an eclectic mix of drugstore cowboys and pierced oddballs.

I flip the curls off my shoulders and head for a tiny unoccupied round table against the wall. I order a Bock and ask for a menu from a harried waitress, then sit back and listen. The band seems a cross between punk rock and country. An electric violin wails, and the lead singer sounds like he gargles with lye. I'm surprised to realize my foot is tapping and my lips are stretched in a smile.

This could be just what I've been needing.

The waitress brings my beer, but has forgotten the menu. She says she'll be back. A wannabe cowboy stops by, tips his spanking new Stetson, and asks me to dance. I thank him and send him on his way. Once you've had a real cowboy...Besides, how *would* you dance to this? From what I can see, the kids on the dime-sized dance floor are just bouncing around like Red-Bull-charged Muppets on pogo sticks.

My radar pings. I glance around. Several guys are looking, but one at the bar is staring. Intense brooding blue eyes, slicked jet-black hair. In a black leather jacket, white T-shirt, worn jeans, and motorcycle boots, he doesn't fit the clientele any more than I do. He tips his chin at me, drains his beer, stands, and strolls over.

"I think there's a *real* country bar down the street." He smiles down at me.

I'm done being categorized by arrogant men. "Yeah, and I imagine there's a biker bar down there, too. Did you get lost?"

"My apologies, Miss. I usually have better manners." His smile slips, leaving a sexy half-smile. "I'm Brett Cummings." He does a quarter bow at the waist.

He's cute, in a dangerous kind of way. He's older— maybe early forties? But what rivets my attention is the sadness in his eyes. An echo of recognition vibrates through my chest. Loss touches loss. I am *not* looking for a guy. But that pain marks him as a member of my tribe. The ones who know that personal disaster can, and *does* happen.

He gives me time to look my fill. "If I promise not to underestimate you again, do you mind if I sit?"

"It depends. Did you ride here on a motorcycle, or is that a Halloween costume?"

"I've got a '16 Softail Fat Boy sitting under the security lamps around back. Want to see it?"

No way I'm going "out back" with a guy I don't know. I study his open face. If he's lying, he's good at it. I push out the chair across from me with my boot. "I have a 750 Honda Shadow."

His eyebrows go up. "Beautiful, smart, *and* a biker?" He turns the chair backward, straddles it, and sits, forearms draped over the back. "Now I am intrigued, Miss..."

"Carly."

"Can I buy you a beer, Miss Carly?" I nod, and he flags the waitress, who, for him, hustles over. "So, tell me how you came to be a rider."

I tell him. It's kind of nice. I'd never lie, but I'm also not caught in the amber of the Carly Beauchamp that Unforgiven knows. I'm free to be Carly 2.0.

By the time we finish the beer, he has me laughing at his motorcycle exploits. He's the lead mechanic at the Harley dealer in town, and teaches motorcycle maintenance at a local community college.

He asks where I'm from, and I just say a podunk town. He's originally from Kentucky, but moved here three years ago. He is polite, open, and interesting. After the next beer, I ask the question I really want the answer to. "So, Brett Cummings, where'd you get those sad eyes?" It seems Carly 2.0 says what's on her mind.

He *tsk*s and shakes his head. "That"—he spears me with a look—"is going to take something stronger than a beer. Join me?"

He orders Scotch, and I have a C&C.

"I moved out here three years ago to try to get my wife back." He looks at the amber in the glass like it holds the future. "See, she left me and came out here to live with her sister. Said I was a 'fun sponge.' That's newspeak for boring." He looks up with a twisted smile. "Need I mention that my wife was seventeen years younger?"

"Ouch. I'm sorry." I know from the "was" and the sad eyes, but I have to ask. "It didn't work out?"

He snorts, and tosses back the Scotch. "She wasn't living with her sister."

I wince. "A guy?"

"Zachary." His voice is all sing-song-sarcasm. "Cue the heavy sigh."

"Why did you stay?" Poor guy.

"She and Zachary moved to Hawaii. And I like it here. The dry air, the interesting people..." His smile is tentative, but his brows look hopeful. "I find you very interesting, Carly...Hey, I don't know your last name."

"I've got to hit the ladies room." I stand. My knees are pliable, and I grab the back of my chair. "Whoa. I need to eat. Grab the waitress, will you? I've been trying to get a menu for two hours."

"Okay, but when you come back, it's your turn to tell me your sad story."

"Prepare to weep." I wobble to the restroom, one doorway in a corridor that leads to the back door. I squint at it, then behind me. He can't see me from where he's sitting. I keep walking, and hit the security bar.

I get a whiff of the dumpster to the left of the door, and slap a hand over my nose. Sure enough, spotlighted under a sodium lamp sits a gleaming Harley. I let the door fall closed and take the few steps to the bathroom. He's nice. And I could use a friend. But no more than that. I need to make that clear, and soon.

Back at the table, another C&C awaits. Brett is relaxed in his chair. His face lights when I sit.

"I need to clear shomthin—" I shake my head. I need to slow down. I used to pack it away, but I don't drink much nowadays. "I need to let you know something, up front. You seem like a nice guy, Brett, but I just broke up with my one and only, and I'm not looking to date."

He raises his hands. "I'm good with that. I'm not sure I am, either. Friends then?"

"Yeah, I could use that, for sure." I look around. "Where's that danged waitress? I've got to eat something, or I'm going to be a puddle under the table."

He frowns. "Oh, I'm sorry. She said the kitchen closed a half hour ago." He snaps his fingers. "Tell you what. You tell me your story, and then I'll buy you dinner. There's a good barbeque place, just down the sidewalk."

That should be safe. It's not like it's a date or anything. "Okay, but I'm buying my own."

"Deal. So? Tell me." He tosses back the Scotch, and signals for another.

"Well, he's a rough-stock rider and the love of my life." I sip my drink. "I thought he was everything, but it turns out, I was dreaming…"

* * *

CARLY

Light. Wha…? Through a pounding undertow of confusion, I claw myself to the shore of consciousness and peel my eyelids open. Lasers pierce my skull and I hear myself moan.

Where am I?

Through slitted lids, the generic room slowly comes into focus. *Hotel room.* My curling iron and brushes crowd the business desk. *My room.* I hit the button on my phone. *At eight a.m.*

Last night… Sad blue eyes, and a sadder story. Dread swivels my head to my right. *Empty. Thank God.* But the pillow is dented, the covers disheveled.

No. This can't be.

My mouth tastes like that dumpster last night smelled. I run my tongue over furry teeth. Did I drink *that* much?

Something is tugging at me. Something important. I roll to one elbow and study the bed beside me. I pull a single black hair from the pillowcase. Surely, I didn't.

I wouldn't.

I shift and sit up. Something liquid slips from me. Something I know isn't my period, because I had it three weeks ago.

I *did.*

Oh, my sweet Jesus… Austin. I cheated on Austin! No, we're broken up. That fact brings no solace. I feel as cheap as a whore's perfume.

Austin. We were over, but he was still my only… I'll never be able to say that again. My heart squeezes in an acid bath of fresh grief. I'll think about that later.

Where is this… Brett? Maybe he went to get us coffee. I pull the covers up to my neck.

When I come to again, I check my phone. Ten.

Then I remember, in vivid technicolor detail. Making out, leaning against the hotel room door. Laughing, almost falling, when he opened it. Then the video speeds up; flashes of tossed underwear, an unfamiliar black furred chest, those piercing blue eyes below me, watching as I came…

Oh sweet Jesus, what have I done?

Horror blooms in my brain and spreads, shooting down nerve endings, waking my body with a live-wire crack of lightning. I try to hop out of bed but only manage to fall out of it. Pulling myself up by the bedsheets to kneel, then gain my feet. The floor rolls beneath me, and I lurch to the bathroom to heave everything, from my toes up, into the toilet.

One thing sure, Brett is in the wind. What kind of guy takes advantage of a clearly incapacitated woman? And then bails?

But I can't just blame him. *I'm* responsible for me.

I came here to discover who the new Carly is. Apparently, she's a slut. Another factoid hits my solar plexus. He didn't use a condom. Probably assumed I was on the pill, like every other single woman on the planet. But the pill made me sick, and…How am I going to live with this?

I can't think. I won't think. Not 'til I can handle it. I rest my hot cheek on the cool tile floor to rest.

I want to go home. But I can't go home like this, because look what I've done—and oh my God, what do I do now?

* * *

Two hours later, after buying a morning-after pill at a drugstore and downing it, I'm sitting in a Denny's a few streets from the hotel, inhaling coffee and choking down dry toast. Caffeine is helping resurrect my brain. I had to get as far away from that tainted hotel room as possible.

I guess I should be glad he didn't steal my credit card.

I'm calling that dickhead and giving him a piece of my mind. I pull out my phone, ignore the flashing voice-mail icon, and hit the internet. I find the Harley dealer, and while the phone rings, practice a rant in my head.

"Harley Davidson of Albuquerque."

"I need to talk to Brett Cummings."

"Who?"

"Brett. Your lead mechanic."

"I'm sorry, Miss. We don't have anyone by that name working here."

"Tall, black hair, blue eyes?"

"Our lead mechanic is Hispanic. And I'm sorry, but that doesn't sound like anyone who works here."

"Seriously?" My stomach begins an agitation cycle. "Is there another Harley dealer in Albuquerque?"

"No'm. Just us. Do you have a bike that needs work? I can—"

I click End. My thumbs fly, looking up community colleges in town. Fifteen minutes later, I give up. None of them have a Brett Cummings on staff.

The enormity of this smacks me in the face, reverberating through my body like walking into a door. Brett Cummings doesn't exist. He lied. Probably about everything. I pay the bill and climb into the truck, then just sit staring out the windshield. I can't go home. Not like this. I'm Nana's good girl. The *town's* good girl. The enormity of my error hits.

What if he had a *disease?* I scrub my hands over the skin of my arms, as if I can rub off the experience. Oh, I'm screwed, in more ways than I realized. This is not something you mess with. I'm going to have to see a doctor. I make a mental note to look up how soon STDs can be detected, and the number of an out-of-town physician.

A wave of revulsion swamps me. I want to douche with boiling alcohol.

I drop my forehead on my hands, fisted on the wheel. If a friend told me they'd done something like this, I'd chew them up one side and down the other. What was I thinking?

I wasn't.

Nana has always told me not to trip over something behind me. That's exactly what I did.

Nana. Suddenly I miss her with the fierceness of a lost toddler.

I'm going home. I'm not telling anyone about this. It was my stupidity and I'll live with it. I'll bury it deep, pretend this day never happened, and maybe someday, it will fade like a bad dream.

And I'll never, ever, go drinking alone again. Ever.

Which reminds me of another Nana-ism: *Forget the mistake. Remember the lesson.*

I take the backroads home, trying to convince myself I can do this; I can lie to my grandparents, to my friends, to the town and no one will know. Except I've never had much to lie about, so I stop by the side of the road and practice in the rearview mirror. After throwing up my dry toast breakfast and about a gallon of coffee, I start up again.

I roll back into Unforgiven, raising a shaky "howdy" finger off the wheel to cars that pass.

That old Robert Frost poem we had to read in high school floats through my mind. *"Home is the place where, when you have to go there, they have to take you in."* I have no doubt that Nana and Papaw will take me in. But they don't *know* what a fool I am.

But I put myself in that bar. Alone. Lorelei warned me. I knew better. And running from one thing doesn't absolve you from running into another.

Thank God Austin is on the road. I may be able to fool Nana and Papaw, but Austin knows me like I know myself. He'd look at me and know.

CHAPTER 5

CARLY

Four weeks later, sitting in an almost-empty waiting room in a clinic on the other side of Albuquerque, I'm inhaling cheap disinfectant and the smell of my own worry. I almost turned the truck around three times on the way here. But STDs are no joke, and I sure wouldn't put it past that loser to have given me a lovely parting gift. But I don't have time or energy to hate someone I'll never see again. I need all my attention focused on getting past what happened.

"Ms. Davis?"

Realizing the doctor in the doorway is talking to me, I jerk to my feet. They asked me for a name when I checked in. I couldn't use mine. Austin's just popped out of my mouth. Hearing the name that was supposed to be mine, in this place, sounds like . . . blasphemy.

Face flaming, I follow her as she ushers me into a tiny exam room. She begins by asking me questions, and I give her the multiple-partners/can't-be-too-cautious/online dating-sucks story I concocted on the drive here. I guess I'm not the only dumb bunny on the planet, because she asks me to strip in a bored voice as she hands me a rough paper gown.

I lie in the stirrups, jumping at every touch.

Afterward, she takes two tubes of blood, snaps off her gloves, tells me to get dressed, and hands me a plastic cup to pee into. She points me to the bathroom next door.

Back in the exam room I wait, feeling like packaged meat on an assembly line. I fidget. And worry. Five minutes. Ten.

At fifteen, the door opens, and the doctor steps in.

"Do I have anything?" My arms wrap around my womb, as if shielding it from the news. "STDs, I mean?"

She's reading her clipboard. "We won't know for two to three days. The receptionist will call you with the results." She looks up and studies me. "Are you aware that you're pregnant?"

"I'm not." My heart stutters to a gallop. *A mistake in the lab.*

"I assure you, you are. The urine test was positive. You're about four weeks along. We'll do a blood test as well, but—"

"No!" My voice bounces off the too-close walls. "That's impossible. I took the morning-after pill. I bought it at a drugstore. I threw away the receipt but..." *What, like a receipt will prove you're not pregnant*? My brain feels tased.

"Levonorgestrel is about sixty-five percent effective."

"What? I didn't know that. Why don't they tell you that?"

"Did you vomit within two hours of taking it? That lowers the efficacy as well."

"I…" I remember heaving my breakfast on the side of the road on the way back to Unforgiven.

Her look sharpens. "Will you be taking this pregnancy full term? Because if not, we can schedule—"

I don't hear the rest, because I'm out the door.

I drive, unaware of where I am, or where I'm going. I can use new math, old math, or a supercomputer—the answer is the same. No way this is Austin's baby.

And he's a whiz at math.

My brain scrabbles for a way out. I don't know why my town was originally named Unforgiven, but it sure hasn't changed much since then. Unmarried pregnancies aren't un-heard of, but our town square isn't the only thing behind the times.

I was voted Class Sweetheart, Student Council President, Rodeo Queen—the unelected Girl-Next-Door of the town. I've never stopped to consider the responsibilities that came along with that.

That Carly is history.

When this gets out (and it always gets out in a small town) I'm, at best, a fool. In the reality TV version, I'm a total loser.

Surely Jess and my posse would stand behind me. If I somehow can find the guts to tell them.

I know there's another option. But even if I could ignore my religion, all I've wanted my whole life is a houseful of babies. Could I really have an abortion? I don't know. But one thing's sure: That decision is only part of the future bearing down on me like the old 954 freight that used to run through Unforgiven.

A whiny voice in the back of my brain whispers, *It would solve your problems. You could go to Albuquerque to have it done. No one would ever know.*

Except me, of course. But could I live with myself?

You don't even know who the father is. He could have bad genes. Schizophrenia! No one would blame you —

Right. Except me.

But the voice is right about one thing. An abortion would solve my problems. Well, a bunch of them, anyway. But I can't make a decision that huge when I'm in a state. I'll think about it later.

A horn blats, and I realize the light I wasn't aware of stopping at has gone green.

The radioactive reality drifts down, burning everything, exposing the worst yet. Austin is lost to me forever. I didn't realize until just now, but somewhere, deep inside, I held hope that we'd get back together. He's an old-fashioned guy, with morals as rigid as the walls of the First Baptist Church. Even if he could accept (eventually) that I slept with another man, could he ever love the result of it?

Wait. Everyone's going to assume the baby is Austin's! OhGod-ohgod-ohmygod, I have to tell him. Before anyone guesses I'm pregnant. How do you start a conversation like that, especially with a proud, macho guy who rides one-ton crazed animals for a living? A small caterpillar of sympathy squirms in my chest. Austin may not be perfect, but he doesn't deserve this.

But an abortion...Internet photos I can't click away from fast enough hit my brain in living color.

Could I raise a baby alone? What the heck do I know about being a mother? Could *I* even love a baby that was conceived from the biggest mistake of my life? Would I always look at it and remember that night?

More fallout settles, and I moan. My worst fear, two months ago, was being alone. No Austin, no homestead house, no white dress. Living a future way different than I'd planned; a scary prospect when you've never even considered there was a Plan B, much less implemented it.

If only I could run away, to start over somewhere else. Like those people you read about who disappear and are presumed dead, only to be spotted years later, kicked back somewhere warm, sipping umbrella drinks.

If I'm going to borrow dreams, I'll take *that* one.

God, I know you won't give me more than I can handle, but this time, you've got me mixed up with someone else. Someone stronger.

My skin feels too tight from the emotion pushing up from the inside. I'm going to need to tell someone. But not face to face. Not yet.

There's only one person on the planet I can tell. I pull over and shut down the truck. When it stops farting, I hit speed dial.

"Carly? You usually call after dinner. What's wrong?"

Just hearing Cora's husky voice loosens every emotion I've tried like hell to keep in. "Everything." My voice comes out mangled and watery.

"Hon, what is it?"

The news rushes out of me like runoff in a storm drain after a downpour.

"Oh, Carly." I hear no judgment, only sympathy. "What are you going to do?"

"I don't see any way through this. I don't know if I could have an abortion, but I can't imagine being a single parent, either." I push the tears down until I'm steadier. "I can't tell my grandparents. I can't think. I can't breathe…"

"Have you thought about going away somewhere until the baby is born? You could give it up for adoption, then head back home. You sure wouldn't be the first to do it."

I don't know if I can give up a baby that's smaller than

my finger. When they put a sweet-faced bundle in my arms? No way. A sob breaks through. "God, I just wish I could get away from this unforgiving place. Maybe I'd be able to see what to do with a little distance."

"Then why don't you take a vacation?"

A pretty picture of that umbrella drink taunts me, until I remember. Pregnant women can't drink. "My spare cash wouldn't get me past Albuquerque." And besides, you can't outrun a guilty conscience. I've been trying for weeks.

I can hear a spoon clinking the sides of a cup. "Give me a minute. Let me think."

Silence for a minute. Or maybe it just seems that long.

"You know, *I* could use a vacation. My daughter has a three-month-old I haven't even met yet. You could take over managing my truck."

Oh, great. Now I'm just one of those hopeless women that Cora hires. "No, I'll just—"

"You'll just what? It would give you some time to recover a bit from the gut-punch. And you'd be earning money while you're doing it. Why not?"

My brain, which has been running in circles for hours, straightens.

Lorelei can handle managing the diner. But will she?

My mood lifts from the floor. I could even ride the motorcycle. Cora always has two women per truck; a cook and someone to work the window. I could let the cook drive the truck...Oh, Nana would have kittens if I rode that motorcycle out of town.

Freedom whispers in my ear, and I take my first deep breath since the doctor walked in that exam room. It won't heal my filleted heart, or solve any of my other problems. But maybe it could be a way to survive until the pain is bearable. "Do you really think I could?"

"I don't see why not. But one thing—no, two things you need to know before you decide."

My stomach drops. I wasn't aware that I'd already made up my mind to do this, but I must have. "Are they show-stoppers?"

"Depends on you. First, you know my truck is on the rodeo circuit. Odds are, you'll run into Austin."

I'm going to have to tell him. Sometime. Maybe it would be better on the road, where neither of us is on our turf. "I'll deal with that when I have to. What's the second?"

"My cook. She's good, and dependable, but a little… rough around the edges."

Cora has built her business into a fleet of five food trucks, and she only hires women who need help. Battered or pregnant, parolees or lost souls—she teaches them job skills that set them on a path to independence. No use pretending I'm better than them, when I'm so obviously not. "I'm used to dealing with employees. That shouldn't be a problem."

"Okay, but I think it's only fair to tell you: She's on parole."

* * *

CARLY

It's after the lunch rush the next day before I get the guts to call Lorelei to my office.

She sticks her head in the door. "You wanted me?"

"Come on in, have a seat." I take a six-inch pile of cat-alogs and circulars from the only other chair in my closet-sized office. "I've gotta get caught up on the danged filing."

Lorelei sits, fingers laced so tightly her knuckles are

white. "You're not going to lay me off, are you? Because I really, really need this job."

I'm so intent on my speech, it takes me a second to compute. "What? No! Where would you get that idea?"

"Well, I know the waitress at the Lunch Box has been talking to you, and she's been a head waitress longer than I have, and…"

"Are you kidding me?" I flick a hand to brush away her worries. "You've been with us seven years, and I depend on you. You really think I'd just dump you for someone dumb enough to work for Dusty Banks?"

Her blond bangs lift with her huge sigh. "No, I guess not. It's just that I get freaked out worrying about mom's medical bills and all. Sorry. I know you better than that."

Her mother had a stroke two months ago, but I didn't know they had money problems. "Well then, how'd you like to make some extra money for a couple weeks?"

She sits up. "You bet. Doing what?"

"I'm going on a working vacation, and I need you to manage the diner while I'm gone."

"Me?" The word comes out in a mouse's squeak.

"Why not? You double-check every order before I send it as it is. You know the shifts. I could teach you what you don't know in like two hours."

She tips her chin up and looks at me out of the corner of her eye. "What's going on, Carly? You never take time off. And isn't 'working vacation' an oxymoron?"

"Nothing, now I do, and you're probably right." I shuffle papers to avoid her probing look. "You remember me telling you about Cora, right?"

"The lunch truck lady."

"Yeah. Well, she wants a vacation to go see her grandkids and I told her that if I could get you to cover for me, I'd cover for her. Besides—" I look up. This part is easier because it's true. "I want to try out my new bike. And to get away from all the gossip and nosy Unforgivians."

Her look of pity is familiar—it's the one everyone gets when the subject of Austin comes up. "Can't say as I blame you. But if it's any consolation, he's hurting too, Carly."

I can't ask. It'll add ten more pounds to my guilt. But the little girl inside says, "How do you know?"

She looks at the papers on my desk. At her feet. At her clasped hands. "He texts me to ask how you are."

Make that fifty pounds of guilt.

"Look, I'm sorry. I didn't mean to be disloyal, I swear. But Carly, it's so sad to see a strong guy like that hurting...It's like seeing a dog flinch from your hand, you know?"

I must have winced, because she rushes on. "Look. Forget I said anything. I won't answer him again, I promise."

"It's okay, Lorelei. You won't know anything anyway, because I'll be gone. That is, if you'll cover for me." Her face lights up when I tell her the temporary raise she'll get. We spend a few minutes making plans.

"Sounds good. I'll stop by before I'm off, and we can go over the rest." She stops in the doorway. "Carly, I know it's none of my business, but..."

I brace myself. No good news ever starts that way.

"You should talk to him. You guys still love each other. It's obvious. You're miserable and he's a mess. You guys can work this out; I know you can." She steps out, and the door falls closed.

Maybe so—before the latest trip to Albuquerque.

Now, it's impossible to the second power. And if Austin hadn't tutored me through algebra, I wouldn't even know what that means.

* * *

AUSTIN

"Sheeite." At the last second, I cut the wheel of my F250 and make the turn into the Rexall parking lot, earning me a kid's-toy-car beep from the Mini behind me. I give him a "my-bad" wave. "You're not from around here, are you, dude?" Must be hard to see around all the big-ass trucks in town.

I came to town to get bandages, and I almost drove right past. My brain has been like that lately. Hell, I wouldn't have cut myself on that damned barbed wire if I'd had my mind on the job, instead of wondering what Carly's doing…how she's feeling. Does she miss me? I thought we'd be back together by now. We always have before. Maybe there was some invisible line I crossed that only women can see?

Sure would help if women came with instructions.

I stuff my wallet in my pocket and head in. The automatic door whooshes open and I walk into a wall of chilly air. Hopefully I can get in and get out. I'm tired, my muscles hurt, and I smell like my horse. And there's that bottle of Jack waiting at home.

I'm bent over in the first aid aisle when I hear a warm-honey voice. For a nanosecond sparklers go off, before reality kicks in. I peer over the display, heart hammering in my ears.

Carly is on the opposite side, discussing the stamp pad ink selection with Mr. Swalls, the druggist.

The bandage box crunches, and I force my hand to relax. I go still and just take her in. It looks like she just got off work. A book of guest tickets peeks out of the pocket of her stained half-apron. Her hair is pulled into a messy ponytail, the rest of the curls dancing around her face. Her freckles stand out against her pale skin. She looks tired. She looks wonderful.

She glances up, right into my eyes.

She looks *so* sad.

She snatches a bottle of ink off the shelf, thanks Mr. Swalls, and scoots down the aisle to the checkout stand.

No cashier. Score for me.

I hustle up behind her, fisting my hands to keep from touching her. "Carly."

She closes her eyes and just stands, leaning on the counter.

When I touch her hand, she jerks it away and whirls to face me. "Please. Austin, I can't do this. Not now. I can't handle it." Her voice cracks like a cold glass in hot water.

She doesn't look good. Her color is off. Something's wrong. "Are you okay?"

She hiccups a laugh, or hysteria. I can't tell which.

"Hell no." She shoots a panicked glance right, then left. There's no one around. She reaches in her purse and tosses a five on the counter.

"Carly, I just want you to know. I'm sorry."

She bolts for the door like I'm some kind of stalker.

I watch her go. I'm confused, worried, and heartsore. But mostly, I'm so sorry.

CHAPTER 6

CARLY

A week later, the outskirts of Unforgiven whiz by the truck's window. Good-bye.

The clinic called; no STDs. Turns out, what I worried about most now seems like nothing.

"You don't have to do this, you know." Nana takes her eyes off the road. "Nothing's better than home when you're hurting."

Of course, she's referring to my breakup with Austin. I don't have what it takes to tell her the rest. Not yet, anyway. Maybe I'll find the courage for that out on the road. I'd better, or this baby will, eventually. We're flying down the highway. Who knew this truck could do seventy-five? "Go, Fartito," I say under my breath.

"What?" She looks over at me and two wheels drop off the edge of the road.

"Nana!" I grab the wheel and push left. Fartito swerves into the oncoming lane.

The eighteen-wheeler bearing down on us blasts his air horn.

"Gimmie that." Nana snatches the wheel and we cross the double yellow into our lane again. "Been driving since I was thigh-high to a gnat's ass. I don't need no help. You jest sit there and think about what you're running from, missy."

Like I've thought of anything else. I close my eyes and try to relax. They say you have fewer injuries on impact that way. It would be my luck to get killed going to pick up what Nana calls my "murder-cycle."

"I know you're having a rough patch. But running never fixed nothing."

I snatched this chance out of the air like a horny toad with a fly. Cora booked a flight to her daughter's in Oregon for three weeks. It's all set. I'm going. "I'm not running, Nana. I'm not even getting a vacation. I'll be working the whole time." I try to keep the excitement out of my voice. Not that this trip will change anything, but I can use a break from familiar faces and prying eyes.

Nana's snort tells me she's not buying it.

Floyd's comes up on our left. Nana slows for the turn, enough so two wheels don't leave the ground. But it's a near thing.

Floyd reclines in a lawn chair in front of his showroom, squinting into the sun. His eyes widen when the truck slides to a stop six inches from his fancy boots. Dust billows up, obscuring him, but I can hear him coughing. "Holy NASCAR, Carly, what in tarnation—"

"Don't you 'holy' me, Floyd Hendricks!" Nana yells out

the open window. "I knew your momma when she was sneakin' shine in her tea 'til she was puttin' your diapers on crossways."

"Miz Nana." Floyd emerges from the dust cloud, coughs into his fist, and steps to the driver's door. "I didn't know it was you. Could I offer you some cool water on this hot day?"

She opens the door and takes the long step down. "Buzz off, Slick. I gotta say good-bye to my Carly."

Floyd holds up his hands and backs away.

I open the door, slide out, and walk to the truck bed where my leather jacket, helmet, and duffel sit waiting. I lift them out, smiling at the black helmet with the gaudy pink hibiscus on the side. Lorelei surprised me with it last night. I'm the one who should've gotten her a present; she'll be holding down the fort at the diner.

Leaving Austin tugs at my heart.

Homesick sours my stomach.

Hurry, the road whispers in my ear.

Nana stands, bat-wing arms outstretched, her stray hairs waving me good-bye.

I step into her arms and hug her tight. "Now, Nana, don't go all drama-queen on me. It's only a three-hour ride." I pull in the smell of the only mother I've ever known, and hold it in my lungs.

I feel her chest hitch. She's got to be thinking about my mom and dad's last ride. I pat her back to soothe, but I'm tired of ghosts. "I gotta go, Nana."

"All right, baby girl, but don't you forget." She steps back, grabs my chin, and looks me fiercely in the eye.

I'm only half-listening. The motorcycle is calling me. "What?"

"You're a Beauchamp. And Beauchamp women are

tougher'n cowhide." Eyes glistening, she waves me off. "I gotta get to Bingo. It's a twofer matinee, and I'm gonna kick that bitch Betty Jones's ass." She spins on her heel and climbs into the truck.

I pick up my stuff and stride for the garage, hearing the spray of gravel and the squeal of rubber when Nana hits the tarmac. I half want to run and wave her down.

Floyd is waiting for me, arms crossed, beaming like the mailman just delivered his "Cupcake of the Year" calendar. "I had 'em wash it up all pretty for you, and the first tank of gas is on me."

I set down my stuff. My bike reclines on its stand like Mae West on a fainting couch. A sunbeam from the high windows caresses it, fanning the cool blue flames on the tank. Something lighter than air fills my chest, making it hard to breathe.

I'm really going to *do* this.

"I'm really sorry about Austin, Carly." He studies his boots. "Sincerely I am."

I throw my arms around him and lay a big ol' kiss on his slab of a cheek. "I don't care what Nana says. You're the best, Floyd." I step back before he can get his arms loose.

"You'll be careful, right? If you end up roadkill, your Papaw is gonna come hunting my ass, and he's as good a shot as he is a moonshiner."

"You never miss a good chance to shut up, do you, Floyd?" I put up a hand. "Thank you. Really. Now go away, willya?"

He walks away, and I carry my stuff to the bike. Fear and excitement put a fine shake in my hands as I set the duffel on the passenger seat, and bungee it to the sissy bar. I shrug into my dad's butter-color suede leather jacket. I grabbed it from the closet this morning, figuring if I'm borrowing his dream, the jacket comes with it. It's too hot to wear, but the thought of my skin grating on asphalt rips an icy shudder down my spine. Heat, I can live with.

I throw my leg over and settle, liking how the seat cups my butt. I don my pretty helmet, thread the strap, and snug it up. Then I pull the bike upright and sit a few heartbeats, trying to absorb the moment.

In a very real way, I'm going home, and I can't wait. The excitement of the rodeo crowd, the smell of cotton candy, feeling a part of something bigger, taking a small part in the history of the American West. It's something I know, inside and out. Maybe I'll manage to settle there, to lose the off-footedness I've felt lately. Maybe by slipping back into the rodeo circuit, I'll find my way back to who I am.

Regardless, it feels good doing something instead of hunkering down in Unforgiven, waiting for the sky to fall. When I return, who knows how I'll be different. Adventures change you. The one to Albuquerque sure did. So do babies.

As of now, I'm responsible one hundred percent for my own safety. My own life.

Plus one.

I'm not even capable of making good decisions for myself. How could I be responsible for another? But I'm not going to solve the Rubik's Cube of my future, sitting here. I turn the key, pull in the clutch, and hit the starter. The engine roars to life, pulsing pure power between my thighs.

I spend the first hour of the trip white-knuckled terrified. I remember how to shift, and lean, but there was no traffic on the dirt back roads where Austin taught me to ride. I block out the picture of my instructor's green eyes. Maybe someday I'll learn to block the memory *before* the shiv slips between my ribs.

I pull over for gas at the edge of Albuquerque. I haven't

been here since that weekend. I shoot a look around at the patrons of the crowded gas station. The odds of seeing Brett...No, that's not his real name. I looked it up online, and there's not a Brett Cummings who resides in New Mexico. What would I do if I did see him? My whole body flushes like how Nana describes one of her hot flashes.

I'd stalk over, slap his face. No. I'd pull him aside, tell him "I'm pregnant," and ask what he was going to do about it. Oh, who am I kidding? I'd probably run to the bathroom, hide, and throw up. I'm not the bold, brassy Beauchamp woman I used to be. My confidence is shaken, and my self-esteem is whimpering in a corner. I throw my leg over and pull off my helmet.

The lady on the other side of the pump who's filling her truck gives me a thumbs-up. "You go, girl."

I just smile. At least I look badass on the outside.

Five miles later, I'm all alone on a straight road that leads through brush-covered plains. The sun warms my cold fingers. The fringe of my dad's jacket is playing in the wind. Scents come to me: sage, and dust, and clean, high desert air. I suck it in, and the sense of doom that's dogged me the past weeks recedes. Thank God for Cora. This is just what I've needed.

I let the wind blow all thoughts out of my head and relax in the moment. If only I could live cocooned in the Right Now. My lips stretch into my first smile in what seems forever.

Way too soon, but two hours later, a road sign for Comb's Corners flashes by. I take the exit and roll to a stop at the old-fashioned town square, with the stone county courthouse in the center. The lawn is covered in swap-meet sun shades that shelter tables of artwork and crafts. Brightly clad people swarm, lending a festival feel.

The food truck is parked on the street opposite me; Cora's

arm is waving out the window. I ease into the crawling parade of traffic around the square, keeping my feet down to
stay upright. I tuck in front of the truck, grateful for the bike;
God knows where I'd park a car.

I've just dismounted and pulled off my helmet when Cora
is there, enveloping me in a huge hug. "Thank God you
arrived safely." She backs up enough to see my face but
doesn't let go. "How are you?"

"This second? Great." The relief of having someone who
knows still love me hits me so hard it weakens my knees. I
soak up her hug. I hadn't realized how much I needed one.
"It's second to second, lately."

"Are you feeling all right? Have you told anyone?" she
whispers.

I shake my head. "I'm fine."

With one last squeeze, she lets me go. "Well, you're here
now. Come meet Nevada. I've just got time to show you the
ropes. Uber is picking me up in an hour for the airport."

She takes my hand and leads me to the truck. It's red,
with CORA'S CATERING in orange on the side. The long serving window is open and propped, providing shade. Baked
goods, chips, and cookies crowd the tilted shelf; the serving
counter is above it. I see the thin back of the cook at the grill,
and the message on her T-Shirt: OMG—NO ONE CARES.

"Nice shirt."

Cora darts a look at me. "Well, I did tell you she was
unconventional."

"I'm sure we'll get along fine."

Cora cuts through the waiting line of customers, opens
the rear door, and takes the two steps up. "She's here!"
Her voice is fakey-happy. "Nevada Sweet, meet Carly
Beauchamp. Carly, this is Nevada, the best cook in my fleet."

The blonde turns, wielding a spatula like it's a weapon.

She's shorter than me, and slightly built with a boyish figure, wearing a grease-spattered half apron over blue jeans. She's still young, but has the tough, skin-over-bones face of a long-term barfly. Nana would say she looked like she'd been "rode hard and put up wet." But it's the animosity blazing from her blue eyes that brings me up short. She looks me up, then down. "Yeah." And turns back to flip the burgers. She lifts a can with holes in the top and sprinkles something over the meat.

"What's in the can?" I say, just to be polite.

"You a cook?" She doesn't look up.

"I used to be."

"Then it's none of your business, now, is it?"

"Nevada." The word spirals up at the end, in a warning. Cora pushes past me. "Carly, why don't you help me get caught up with the line, then I'll show you what you need to know."

I'm stepping past when a snort of dismissal comes from behind, too soft for Cora to hear.

Lovely. Any delusions I harbored that this was going to be a relaxing three weeks fly out the serving window.

An hour later, a compact pulls up. The driver beeps the horn and waves.

"That's my ride. I've got to git." Cora unties her apron." Carly, text me or call me with any questions, okay? Nevada"— she waits until the girl turns—"you behave. You hear?"

The cook flicks me a look and her nostrils flare, like she smells something off. "Yes'm." She steps into Cora's hug. "You have fun. Hurry back."

Cora bustles past and snatches her purse and suitcase waiting at the back door. "I'm going to love me some grand-kids." She bustles down the steps, and the driver comes to help her with the suitcase.

I close the door and walk back to the serving window.

"Oh, this is going to be a certifiable riot," Nevada grumbles behind me.

Now there's something I can agree with. I pick up the order pad, pull the pen from behind my ear, and address the frazzled mommy who's next in line. "Can I help you, ma'am?"

CHAPTER 7

CARLY

By the time the blazing orange at the horizon has disappeared, I'm throbbing: my back, from handing food out the window, my feet, from standing all afternoon, my ears, from the techno-punk that Nevada has blasted from the boombox over the grill since Cora left. I asked her to turn it off—no response. I asked her to turn it down, and she complied, sort of. But the bass thump remained, a white noise irritant that I didn't recognize until my jaw muscles cramped from grinding my teeth.

When the last customer wanders away with hands full of chili dogs, I step outside, lower the metal sunshade, and lock it, transforming the restaurant back to a vehicle.

I take the steps back into the truck. Nevada is cleaning the grill. She looks worse than I feel. Grease-spattered shorts, filthy apron, her dirty blond hair flopping out of her ponytail.

"What do you say we grab a shower, then find something to eat that's not soaked in grease?"

She grunts, which I'm taking as a yes. "Where is the hotel you and Cora stayed last night? I'll meet you there."

She points to the front of the truck. "Maddy's Motel, a mile that way."

"Do you have a key?"

"Yeah."

The spatula scrapes across the metal grill—and my nerves. "I was asking if I could have one."

"You didn't say that."

I sigh loud enough for the passersby to hear. "Did Cora leave her key to the room at the motel for me? If so, where?"

She waves the spatula at the front of the truck. "Console between the seats."

"Thank you." I squeeze by, careful not to touch—I'd probably get thorns embedded in my skin. I snatch the old-fashioned plastic key with a flaking "10" in gold paint from the pile of junk in the console. Cora told me that she and Nevada roomed together, staying in cheap hotels to save money, but that I could choose better hotels and get my own room if I wanted. But I'm already beholden. No way I'm going all princess at Cora's expense. Even if it means rooming with a human cactus.

I climb over the passenger seat and out the door.

Nevada might make it a bit awkward, but this is a tiny blip on my radar—hardly noticeable compared to the massive blip coming at me, bigger every day. I drop my hand to the buttons of my jeans. No bulge yet, but someday soon...A bomb's tick-tick-tick echoes through me, flash-freezing my guts.

I put on my gaudy helmet, throw my leg over the bike, and fire the engine. Too bad there's only a mile to go. I'd love to hit the road and have the wind blow my worries away. I check traffic and ease out onto the circle.

Maddy's Motel is as shabby as its key. Turquoise cinderblock, with a red neon sign out front. I unstrap my duffel and walk to room ten where, for lack of a nail, the "1" has fallen upside-down. I push the door open with my boot and the hot, closed up-smell of cheap smacks me in the face, conjuring ghosts of countless rooms just like this—rodeo-road hotel rooms I shared with Austin. Back then, I hardly noticed the bare lightbulbs and scratchy sheets. Sepia stop-action memories flash: his bare chest, his hands, his boots next to mine beside the bed. I pull in a deep lungful of happier days, and almost choke on nostalgia that burns like a hit of cheap weed.

Lord, I wasn't asking for a Hollywood career. My dreams weren't big. Just to have a bunch of kids in a big, falling-down old homestead house, with the man you made for me beside me every morning. Why was that too much to ask?

But even as I think it, I know. God didn't ruin my dream. Austin and I did. Looking at it from the other end of disaster, waiting another year doesn't seem that horrible.

But the tail whip of truth follows close behind. It wasn't the year of waiting. It was being second. I've got to remember that, when missing him hurts. I want a guy who puts me at the head of the line, just like I do him. I dump my bag on one of the beds and head for the shower. Nevada will want one when she shows up.

I'm still waiting an hour later when she slams through the door. I turn off the farm report on the TV. "You okay? I was about to go looking for you."

She rolls her eyes. "I've been on my own since I was fifteen. I hardly think I need a mother hen to look after me."

I give her my best rodeo-queen smile, through gritted teeth. "Okay then. Why don't you hop in the shower, and we'll find something to eat?" I step to the rickety desk and pick up the cardboard flyer. "Looks like our choices are Friendly's Chicken or the Pizza Palace."

She drops a canvas sailor's duffel on the bed, pulls it open, and paws through the contents. "Already ate."

"What? Where?"

"Fixed myself a BLT in the truck."

The irritation that simmered all day boils over. "That's downright rude. You knew I was waiting for you."

She takes the one step to the bathroom and slams the door.

Okay, be that way. I snatch my helmet and shrug into my jacket. Friendly's it is.

* * *

Just before dawn, I'm washed onto the shore of wakefulness by a massive wave of nausea that propels me from bed at a run. Once I rid myself of last night's dinner, my stomach settles. I'd like to blame it on the greasy chicken, but more likely, it's thanks to the tiny bean in my belly that demanded I scarf it in the first place.

Might as well get a shower, since I'm up. I'm going to need all the together I can get, because today we travel forty miles to Santa Rosa for the Guadalupe County Fair. And *Rodeo*.

And Rodeo = Austin. My gut does a backflip and I hover at the toilet, hand over stomach, until it decides to settle again.

Two hours later, I bump over the grass, following the truck to the food zone of the midway: a corridor of trailers, tents, and trucks, whose placards advertise hot dogs, beer, funnel cakes, and fried pickles. I pull in behind the truck, drop the kickstand, take off my helmet, and sit for a moment, inhaling the smell of Rodeo: crushed grass, livestock, and fair food.

How could I have forgotten? The contestants milling, pinning entry numbers on each other's backs, the vendors calling to each other as they set up, the mic checks, the bustle behind the chutes. An undercurrent of potential builds until the air fairly crackles with it. My body reacts: my blood speeds up, my steps are lighter as my mood rises like the helium balloons the man next to us is blowing up.

God, I've missed this.

Nevada rounds the corner of the truck. Today's T-shirt says, SARC: MY SECOND FAVORITE "ASM." She stops and puts a hand on her hip. "You going to help, or sit there all day with a dorky look?"

I pull the key. "Cora did tell you I'm your boss, right? It would help if you showed a little respect."

She gives me a "whatever" flip of her hand and takes the steps at the back door of the truck. Some of my helium escapes.

When I walk in, Nevada is up front, in the driver's compartment. I grab a couple eggs and two pieces of bread. I eye the bacon, but my stomach says *nuh-huh.* I'm fiddling with the knobs on the grill when Nevada yells, "What do you think you're doing?" She barrels to the back and stands hovering. I can tell she wants to push me out of the way, but her fists remain at her sides. "You trying to take my job? Back off."

Her reaction is so over-the-top, it dawns on me—she needs this job, and she sees me as a threat. Well, that's an easy fix. "I don't want your job." I take a step back, hands up. "I don't know what Cora told you, but I *have* a job. My family owns a diner in Unforgiven, and—"

"Cora told me all about your perfect little life." She flips on the grill, spreads some butter, and cracks my eggs.

"Perfect?" God, if she only knew.

"Oh yeah. Rodeo queen, the town sweetheart, the local stud for a boyfriend. So, I've gotta wonder…" She drops the bread in the toaster, then turns and spears me with a look. "What are you doing here?"

"I'm…"

The light is dim because the sunshade is down, but I know she sees my blush when one side of her mouth turns up.

"I'm on vacation."

She turns back to flip my eggs. "Oh yeah, probably."

I squeeze past her to retrieve the cash box from the safe, and when I get back, she hands me my breakfast on a paper plate. "Thank you."

"Just ask from now on." She bends to check the supplies in the fridge.

I eat, then step outside to open the truck-wall-sunshade.

"Champ!" The voice cuts through the setup bustle.

My heart gives a soft skip at my rodeo nickname—a mashup of my last name and my barrel racing blue ribbons. Especially being yelled by that voice. I turn just in time to be swept up in Shane Dalton's strong arms. He spins me around, yelling in my ear, "Hot damn, Champ, the place just isn't the same without you!"

I put my head back and watch the sky go around, giggling like a teenager. "Put me down, you polecat!" Austin's best friend is one of mine, too.

"Who you callin' a polecat, you yellow-bellied sheep-herder." He smiles up at me, then sets me on my feet again.

It's a game we've played for years, hurling two-hundred-year-old insults at each other. "God, it's good to see you."

He ducks his head, hiding his face under the brim of his hat. "What happened, Carly? Austin is slinking around like a stray cur dog." When he looks up, the worry in his eyes is a jackknife to my gut. "What could'a happened so bad that would break you two up?"

The eggs are staging a revolt and the toast and coffee are joining forces. "Look, Dalton, I'll talk to you later, okay?" I spin and, my hand to my mouth, run. I make it to the grass behind the food truck before the eggs win the skirmish.

When I hoist myself back into the food truck, Nevada gives me a raised eyebrow stink-eye. To say that the atmosphere in the truck is better today would be an overstatement. But we do find a way to work around each other—a silent dance that gets a bit easier as the day wears on. She lowers the boombox thump a notch, and I'm careful to write legibly so she can easily read the orders.

Cora has a good reputation with the rodeo crowd, and there's a line all afternoon. I'm grateful because it keeps my mind off…everything.

The loudspeaker is a background drone to the customers' chatter and the grease pop on the grill until, an hour in, I hear what I realize I've been listening for all along.

"Okay folks, next up is a New Mexico boy, who needs no intro, because he made a name on the circuit years ago. Out of chute four, on Broomstick, Austin Davis!"

A roar rises from the local crowd. They scream and cheer for four seconds, then groan, and I swear I can hear their sucked-in-and-held breaths.

"Hey lady, can I get two cheeseburgers? Hey—"

"Shhhhh!" I'm leaning over the counter, trying to hear over my own heartbeat. I hate it when an arena goes quiet.

"He's okay, folks, just lost his air there for a minute. Let's give that cowboy a hand."

"Dude. Ya gonna take orders, or stand there with your boobs hanging out?" Nevada's grumble behind me makes me realize that the girls are trying to make a break for it.

The guy in front of me looks like he's forgotten his cheeseburger.

I straighten so fast my vertebrae pop. "Do you want fries with that, sir?"

* * *

CARLY

When night falls on a county fair, magic comes out with the stars. The rides are all dressed in fairy lights, and a veil of enchantment hangs over the midway, accented by screams from the Wild Mouse.

The after-dinner rush is over. Nevada didn't want a break, so I take one. I pull in the cool-air scent: popcorn, cotton candy, and memories.

See, I believe that everyone has a "Time of Their Lives." You can tell by listening to people talk. Billy Simmons, Unforgiven's all-state quarterback, still talks about the homecoming game of '87. Cora's was the summer she met her husband. Mine? That rodeo summer with Austin, the year I was Rodeo Queen.

I'd fall out of bed at dawn to feed and groom my gelding, Buttwipe. Oh, don't feel bad for him. Trust me, he earned the name. He was quicker than slicked snot, but he had the personality of a constipated octogenarian defending his lawn. He'd bite, kick, "accidentally" step on me. And I was his favorite person.

I'd meet up with Austin and we'd grab breakfast with our buds, laughing about the night-before bar antics. Then I'd doll up—hair and makeup, bangles and satin—and borrow a flashy paint pony to carry the flag in for the opening ceremony. Then I'd run for the horse trailer, to change for my event. Rodeo all afternoon, dinner on the Midway, maybe take in a few rides, then hit the bar. Drive to the next rodeo—repeat.

Those were the days. I'd hoped those wouldn't be The Time of My Life. I'd wanted that to be after we were married, and—

"Carly."

Though it's quiet, Austin's voice slams into me, stopping me faster than a tie-down roping horse. I turn on my boot heel. "Damn, Davis, you scared the pee out of me." He doesn't need to know I'm being literal.

"Sorry. I just didn't want you to get away from me again." He takes off his hat and works the brim.

I hate that, because I know an apology is coming. And I so don't deserve his regret...I have too many of my own. "Stop."

"What?"

He looks up, and those green eyes do what they always do—zap my brain like a power surge to a computer, making me forget everything I must remember. I look away. He isn't mine anymore, a fact we'll *both* know—when I get up the guts to tell him.

He drops his hat on his head, then cups my elbow. "I heard you were working Cora's truck for a couple weeks. Let's walk."

You do not want to do this, my more intelligent side whispers. My dumber side says, "I have to get back soon. Nevada's all alone." At least walking, I can focus on the fairy lights instead of him.

"I know you don't want to hear this, but I have to say it, even if it makes no difference."

His glance warms the side of my face.

"Could I ask you this one last thing, that you hear me out? Because I don't know how to live with myself if you won't."

Oh, this is going to hurt. For a long time. But I owe him a lot more than to listen, so this is the least I can do. Not trusting my voice, I nod.

"You were right. One hundred percent. I was selfish, and self-centered. I was avoiding growing up, buckling down and starting our business."

I hear him draw in a breath, and he stops at the edge of the sporadically lit contestant parking area where the dark hulks of pickups and horse trailers look like sleeping dinosaurs.

Here it comes. I tighten my muscles and straighten, to bear the weight.

"It wasn't because I was having more fun on the road, or because I didn't want to marry you." He reaches for my hand, then changes his mind and shoves his hands in his pockets. "I was afraid."

This is so not what I thought he was going to say that it takes me a second to process. "What?"

He nods. "I'm *good* at riding rough stock. Always have been. I don't get the credit; it's a God-given talent. But what if I'm not good at *raising* rough stock? The business end of it? We'll be married, and babies on the way, and there'd be bills, and obligations, and loans..." He shrugs. "It freaked me out. I kept going, one year, then two, and...well, you were there. Every now and again, I'd look around and see the kids on the circuit and realize there were less guys my age every year, and I'd freak out. I'd go home and tell you one *more* year."

I thought I was prepared. But this is so much worse

than I anticipated. If Albuquerque had never happened, I'd be falling in his arms right now. I'd be telling him it'd be okay—we're in this together, partners—and there's nothing to be afraid of, because...

I hear a sound, and realize it's a sob, and that it's coming from me. I put the back of my hand to my mouth to bottle it up.

"I had to tell you. See, it's not you, Carly; it's me. You were always my first choice. I just didn't trust that I was good enough to take it." He searches my face. He knows me as well as I know him; he sees what I can't say—that I can't say yes.

I want so badly to tell him why I can't. I'm not ready. I'm a coward. I just stand there, words clogging my throat, and watch him walk away.

CHAPTER 8

CARLY

I'm standing at the white board outside the truck the next morning, pen poised. "What do you want for today's special?"

"I don't care."

"Well, yesterday it was fish sandwiches. How about rodeo dogs?"

"How about a double serving of, I. Don't. Care." She reaches up to crank the volume on the boombox.

Slayer is screaming "Raining Blood." Great. I hate that I even know that song. I didn't, before being stuck in a tin can with a sullen, grown-up two-year-old for ten hours a day. I don't understand why she's so hostile. I find myself both wanting to find out the answer, and wanting to stay ignorant. I fill out the rest of the board, making specials of what we have left over. We're going to have to hit a box store and stock up before we leave town.

As I watch the early risers walk the grounds, a hollow feeling fills my chest. Funny, I'm back in my old world with people all around me, yet I've never in my life been so lonely. I'd love some distraction from the problems that my brain works over like well-worn worry beads. But everyone I know here is tied somehow to Austin, and I don't know how to answer their questions.

Homesickness hits. You can't know lonely in Unforgiven. You know everyone in town, and they know you. Even driving on a back road, people at least wave, and many will stop in the middle of the road for a good chin wag.

But then again, that's how gossip spreads. A flush of heat shoots up from my chest that has nothing to do with the rising temperature outside.

And I've *got* to talk to Austin. After his admission last night, my secret wears on my conscience like a hair shirt. I may not be the person I thought I was, but I'm not someone who can live with having Austin find out about the baby from someone else.

One impossible task at a time. I work like a robot, taking orders, checking the line from the window every few seconds, looking for broad shoulders and a Cattleman Creased Stetson. I've been speech-writing in my mind all morning, trying to come up with some way to explain, without having him hate me.

This is going to be a stunning shock to Austin. So far, most of my scenarios end up with tears (mine) and anger (his).

And I haven't even started on the explanation for Nana and Papaw.

There's a recurring theme here. I can't seem to make a freakin' decision. About anything. It's like I'm in one of those dreams where it's essential you do something, but you move in slow motion, and minutes tick away…

Life used to be so simple. Joking with the regulars at the diner, the comfortable routine with the staff. At home, setting the table for dinner with Nana and Papaw, with nothing more on my mind other than what's on TV that night. Counting the days until Austin came home, so we could fall into the bed over the store and make love all night. Best yet, though, spooning with my best friend, talking about nothing and everything, until I'd drift off, safe in his arms.

You think you appreciate it, at the time. I didn't, but I do now…

I'm tired. Tired of worrying. Tired of not liking myself. Tired of being whiny. Well, like Nana says, "You made yourself a shit sandwich. Now you get to eat it." Man, I miss her.

Luckily, business slows while the rodeo's happening. I give Nevada a break, and she's gone forever. By the time she climbs back in the truck, I've got my apron off. "Where the heck did you go?"

"Why? You got somewhere to be?"

Her smirk crawls under my skin. "I'll be back in a bit."

As always, she has a retort, but I'm out the door and don't hear it. The announcer is two riders into the bull-riding event when I sprint to the arena. It's only ninety degrees out, but the crowd is packed in the bleachers, raising the temperature and blocking any stray breeze. I find a slot and slide between a little girl and a cowboy wannabe nursing a beer.

He tips his hat. "Hello, pretty lady."

I give him a quick nod, then focus on the chutes.

"Next up is Shane Dalton. He rode Battle-axe for eighty-two points yesterday. Let's see how he does on Sit and Spin."

I cup my hands around my mouth. "Go, Shane! Stick on him!"

"You know that guy? Is he your boyfriend?"

My stomach flips. As much from the BF comment as the wash of beery breath from Mr. I-bought-the-buckle.

The gate swings open, and a red spotted bull comes out butt first. Shane's up on his rope, and balanced, ready for the bull's next move. It turns right. Bad choice for the bull. Shane matches the animal's timing, jump for jump. After four seconds, he starts spurring with his outside foot, big money chops, to impress the judges. When the horn blows at eight seconds, Shane pulls his hand out of the rope and the bull's next kick throws him off. The cowboy hits the ground running, and after a glance over his shoulder to be sure the bull isn't chasing, he pounds his fists into the air.

"How 'bout that, folks?"

The crowd cheers. I put my fingers in my mouth, curl my tongue, and let loose a piercing whistle. Shane hears it. He finds me in the crowd and points at me, laughing.

"The judges liked it, too. They score it an eighty-three and a half points!"

"Mommy, that lady hurted my ears."

I look down. The little girl is scowling at me, hands over her ears. "I'm sorry, sweetie. I promise not to do it again." I manage to sit, though my toes are tapping a hurry-up dance on the wood boards. I checked the day sheets; Austin's up next.

"Can I buy you a beer? Hey, whasyername, anyway?"

Great. Unfortunate taste in clothes, irritating, *and* drunk. The rodeo trifecta. "No, thank you."

Saved by the announcer. "Austin Davis bucked off yesterday, but he's back today, and knowing him, looking to take it out on his bull, Dust Devil. Out of chute two, let's cheer on a local favorite!"

I can't cheer. I never could. I'm suspended in frozen anticipation, holding my breath, sitting on my crossed fingers.

The wannabe bumps my elbow. "Hey, honey—"

"Shhhhhh," I hiss.

A massive black brahma rears in chute two, and the cowboys grab Austin's flak jacket to keep him from falling under the bull's hooves. With a hand tied to the animal, the chute is the most dangerous place to be. "Get out! Nod! Nod!" I mutter with the last of my breath and finally, he does.

The gate swings, and the bull takes off, running straight and crow-hopping across the arena. This is the worst kind of ride; the bull looks easy but isn't. Every jarring thump pulls Austin off his rope. His score is going to suck.

If he makes it to the whistle.

Even as I think it, Austin loses his spur hold, and his legs fly out behind him. His hand pops out of the rope, and he lands face-first in the dirt. The bull gallops off.

Getupgetupgetup.

After an agonizingly still moment, Austin pulls himself to his feet and his hat billows dust when he smacks it against his thigh. The bullfighters entice the bull to the exit gate.

"A rare second buck-off for Davis. Let's show some appreciation for the effort."

Austin takes his rope from one of the bullfighters and limps to the gate, the crowd's applause his only parting gift.

I want to catch him before—

"Hey, sweet cheeks. Whatyasay—"

My boot on his instep cuts off whatever drivel he was about to spout. I stand, and ignoring his wheeze, step down from the stands and jog for the contestant area behind the chutes.

When I find him, Austin's pulling tape off his wrists. "That bull was a pig. Totally not your fault."

He turns at the sound of my voice. "Yeah, I'll tell that to Shane when I don't have gas money."

"You need gas money? I've got—"

"I'm not taking your money, Tigger." His gaze is watchful, reminding me of Shane's "stray dog" comment. "What did you want?"

For things to be the way they used to be. "Are you staying tonight before heading out?"

"I am."

The look on his face freezes in place. Open and unafraid, he watches me close, his gaze flicking over my every movement. But his eyes, sad and hopeful and sweet, somehow form an arrow that pierces my chest. I'm going to hurt him. Bad. I wish I could walk away and never see him again, just so he could stay innocent.

But that's the coward's way out. "We need to talk. Can we meet after dinner?"

"Sounds good. And Tigger?" He steps into my personal space and runs a finger down the inside of my forearm. "I miss you."

I want to forget. To lean into him and share the weight on my shoulders.

But that weight is what is going to drive him away. "Good." I straighten my shoulders and take a step back. "See you then." I turn and walk away before I can change my mind.

* * *

CARLY

The long, dread-filled day is over. I walk in and out of yellow pools of sodium light in the contestants' parking lot. Did I, just this morning, wish I could talk to my best friend? Well,

I'm going to get the chance in a few minutes, and all I want to do is jog back to my bike and get the flock out of here.

Because, after tonight, I don't think I'll have a best friend.

I spent the day making a bullet-point list of items to cover in the conversation. By afternoon, the bullets zipped through my brain, faster and faster, until even Nevada noticed I was a mess. Well, I think she did; she just pointed to her T-shirt:

> Calm down.
> Take a deep breath.
> Hold it for like 25 minutes.

Now I'm hyped so bad a fine shake runs down my limbs, and I just want to get it over with.

I scan the rows of big-ass trucks that all look the same in the dark. Hey, maybe I won't find Austin...Nah. The only thing worse than this day would be waiting another day to tell him.

A shadowy figure leans against a truck two rows in, one boot up on the running board. "Austin?"

His head comes up and my heart, ignoring the memo, knocks my ribs in a happy dance. I keep my feet to a sedate pace. Why rush to disaster? Then he steps into the light, and I know why. Broad cheekbones, prominent jaw, and lips too full for a guy.

I've always loved those lips.

"Hey, Tigger." He leans one hand against the hood of the truck. "I should have asked you if you wanted to have dinner. Or we could—"

"No." It comes out too loud and echoes down the row. I swallow and start again. "This is good." Dark is best. I don't want to see his face in sharp fluorescence when I tell him.

"What's wrong?" He steps to me and runs his hands down

the backs of my arms. "You're shaking." He tips his head to look down into my face. "Are you okay?"

An unladylike snort of laughter explodes from my nose. "No. Not at all."

"Aw, hon." He leans his butt against the truck and gathers me into his arms.

I have no choice but to lean into him. Okay, I have a choice, but I ignore it, because his arms form a familiar circle of safety and comfort that I haven't felt in *so* long. I'll just rest here for a minute, then...

"Talk to me, Tigger. What can I do to fix this?"

His words slap me to reality. This is so wrong. I shouldn't be taking comfort from the one I'm fixing to take all comfort from. *Stop. Back away.*

But when I shake my head, my forehead rubs the front of his shirt, releasing the smell trapped inside. I take a deep breath of him: cologne, pheromones, and familiarity. A sticky wad of lonely gathers in my chest that's hard to breathe around. "Can we stay here, just for a minute?"

He tucks me in tighter and rests his chin on the top of my head. "You got it."

The words rumble through his chest and into mine. I'm not going to ruin these last stolen moments of peace. I lay my ear against his chest and let his heartbeat calm me. My breath settles into his rhythm; strong and even.

"I've missed you like half my brain is gone."

My head bounces with his chuckle, and I snuggle in closer.

"No, really. I was looking all over for my sunglasses today. Shane pulled them off my head and asked if I also forgot to tell him about my lobotomy."

"You've got more smarts in your boots than I have in my whole body," I whisper into his shirt, treating myself to a deep breath of Austin, trying to hold it in, soak it into the lining of my lungs, so I'll never forget.

What if…I know it would be stealing, for me to take one more night for myself before I tell him. Nana taught me better.

I feel his smile against my hair. His lips move down to my temple. His teeth catch my earlobe and he sucks on it.

Either a bull lowed in the pens, or I moaned. I'm not sure which. I want him. Want the way he makes me feel like the center of the Universe. The Universe of Us. I want to be part of a whole again, not a limping shell. I want…

The light is blocked out, and his lips are on mine. My hands steal to the sides of his face, and I take him in: a sweet kiss that makes me want to cry.

There must be a term stronger than *wanting*, but it's lost in his gentle touch. Like our first kiss, that day in the homestead house when we looked at each other and realized we were doing more than playing house all those years; we were practicing.

The want pulls my brain from reason. This must be how addicts feel. My fingers slide down the stubble on his soft cheeks. I know the topography of his face better than my own. I'll pay the penalty later. I need this. I'm taking this. Not sure I could stop now, anyway.

He slants his head, and when he opens his mouth, sweet turns hot. He seems as desperate as I feel, tasting, testing, pushing. We can't get close enough. His hands cup my butt and he lifts and turns me, so I'm standing on the running board. We're the exact same height. I know, because we tested it out before he bought this truck. I'm squeezed between the truck body and his, yet still, it's not enough. Wrapping my fists in his shirt, I pull him closer and melt into his mouth. Tonight's memory is going to have to last me the rest of my life.

Making out with someone who knows what you need before you do—who, when you do "that thing," reacts the exact same way, every time...it's the *best*.

Then somehow, we're up in the cab and I'm lying on top of Austin (he got the bench seats special for us, too). He grasps the front of my shirt, and there's a pistol-shot *pop-pop-pop* as the snaps come undone.

In a deep part of my brain the pheromones haven't fogged; reason is yelling *don't do it! You're making it worse! Don't*— Heat and hormones blot out the rest.

Austin dispatches my bra with a practiced twist of his fingers (I bought it with that move in mind). He takes my nipple in his mouth, makes that little groan in the back of his throat—and I'm lost. Lost to the fact that anyone could walk by. Lost to thought.

Lost to him.

My eyes closed, my hands work by braille, remembering and memorizing the soft hair on his chest, the dip at the curve of his hip, the hard length of him, straining the buttons of his Wranglers.

Things get frantic and we're laughing, trying to kick out of boots and straight-legged jeans in a tight space. It takes forever. But finally, he's there, his bare chest a rock-hard slab beneath my hands, his even harder cock poised at the perfect middle of my straddled legs.

"Slow down, cowboy. I'm going to make this last."

His cock surges against me and he groans.

Smiling, I nip my way down his neck, cup him, and roll his balls in my hand. He loves that.

He runs his hands down the length of me until he reaches my butt. He tries to guide me down. He looks up at me, his eyes full of lust...and love.

So much for slow. His look alone makes my twinkie twitch.

A smile quirks one side of his mouth. Because we both know this is going to be epic.

"God, I've missed you." I slide, slow, slick, and hot, down his shaft, my nails digging in his pecs, chewing my lips to stifle a scream.

"Shhhhh. Shh, baby." He pulls me to his chest and rocks me, knowing perfectly well that my clit is in hard contact with his pubic bone. He moves, slow and rhythmic like a rocking chair, but with the opposite effect. It winds me up. And up. We spiral together, him getting stronger, but not faster, until the pleasure is so exquisite it hurts.

He catches my mouth and pours in all the emotion he hasn't said. He bucks under me, once, twice. It pushes us both over the edge, and I moan into his mouth, "I love you. Always."

When the fog clears, we're sprawled bonelessly together, separated only by a thin layer of sweat. Coming down from a high like that is always hard, but this time I didn't pack a parachute. I open my eyes, squinting in the harsh glare of reality. When I push off his chest, his arms tighten around me.

"Not yet, Tig."

Yes, yet. It was "yet" an hour ago. A day ago. I snatch clothes from the floorboard, shrugging into them as fast as I can...like that'll make what just happened, not happen.

No, I don't wish that. I wish a zillion other things, but never that.

His hand brushes my waist. "Where you going? Come lie down for a minute."

I knew I'd pay for stealing. And as terrified as I am to tell him, I can't be sorry. "We need to talk, Austin. You know we do. But I can't tonight. I've got to..." I'm not compounding my sin with another lie. "I just can't."

"Okay, Tig. I'll see you Friday. We'll talk then. Now,

come back here. I want to have a deep conversation with your body."

It would be so easy. All I'd have to do is loosen my muscles and my self-control. I'm relaxing into him... but I can't. I've already taken more than was mine. I should have never allowed this to happen. But I'm weak. And in spite of what he's going to think when he hears the truth, he means everything to me. I do a push-up off him and pull on my last boot. "I'm sorrier than you know, but I can't." I open the door. The wanting makes me steal one look back and to put my hand, one more time, on the chest that is no longer mine. "Remember, I love you."

Yeah, there's a parting gift.

He's going to hate me.

CHAPTER 9

CARLY

Five days later, we wake in Roswell. I suggested that we make unscheduled stops here and there along the way: industrial parks, mall parking lots, municipal ball fields. We only got chased off twice, and we've upped the average bank deposit by a chunk. I'm proud, feeling like I'm repaying Cora in some small way.

After my normal routine of throwing up and getting a shower, I step out of the bathroom. Nevada is watching TV, sitting on her bed in a T-shirt that reads, WHEN I ASKED, "HOW STUPID CAN YOU BE?" IT WASN'T A CHALLENGE.

Cora really needs to think about putting that girl in a uniform. "I checked the propane on the truck yesterday. If we don't get them refilled today, we're in trouble."

Her gaze doesn't move from the set. "Duh."

I take a breath and let it out slowly. I need this break as much as she needs this job, so I'm going to give it another try. I sit on the other bed. She's watching one of those crappy shopping network shows. "I bought a 'jewel' necklace from them once. It was garbage."

She grunts.

"I don't know how they make it look so amazing. Maybe they're using the real thing for the taping, then ship you Taiwanese crap."

"I wouldn't know."

"You've never bought anything there? Then why are you watching?"

"Beats the pork futures report."

"Yeah. Just barely." God, I need coffee. But, though it still smells wonderful, since the pregnancy, it tastes like hot, rancid motor oil. I ignore my caffeine withdrawal and try to think of something we have in common to talk about. "You know, I just realized. I don't know anything about you." I sit and fold my legs on the bed. "I'll tell you what. I'll tell you something about me, then you tell me something about you."

No response.

I'll take a yes on that, because the only other option is pork futures. "I've lived my whole life in Unforgiven. My Nana and Papaw raised me since I was two, when my parents died in a motorcycle accident." I whip through the high points of my life: Student Council, Cibola County Rodeo Queen, manager of the Chestnut Creek Café, all without mentioning Austin. I wind down when I realize I'm starting to sound as fake as a Christmas letter.

"I mean, it hasn't always been easy. The diner isn't making enough money, and..."

Shutupshutupshutup. "Anyway. Your turn. Tell me something about you."

"Oh, let's see…" She puts her finger under her chin and looks at the ceiling. "I like long walks by a lake, my favorite color is lavender, and I think Justin Timberlake is *dreamy*." She drops the falsetto and scowls. "Oh yeah. And I don't like you."

"You know, I may have gotten a hint of that somewhere along the way. But why? You don't even know me."

Nevada stands, and takes the two steps to the bathroom. "Oh no. As of now, I know *way* too much about you."

The door slams loud enough to wake the people three doors down.

Why do I keep trying? In a couple weeks, I'll be back home, and I'll have lots more to worry about than this.

But I know why. I've got one of those Labrador puppy personalities—everybody likes me. Well, maybe not Ann Miner, the snooty president of the historical society, but she even looks down on the mayor. *And Austin, when he finds out.* I slept with another man, got pregnant, and then took comfort from Austin, and I have yet to find the guts to tell him.

Hardly the actions of a woman who claims to have loved one man her whole life.

The magnitude of my sin in the truck slams, rocking me. Holy cripes, could Austin think we're getting back together now? He wouldn't. Would he?

* * *

AUSTIN

I pull the truck into the cutoff for the fairgrounds on Friday. Roswell has always been lucky for me. I have three Champion buckles from here already and, as good as I feel, I'm gonna score another this weekend.

And I get to see Tig. I've been counting the minutes like some doe-eyed teenager with a first crush, and I don't care. She still loves me.

My life is getting back on track; I can feel it.

I hit the road late, so the parking area behind the arena is almost full. I pull in, shut it down, and head for the chutes to see who's around.

Metal rings with the sound of bulls' hooves as they're being unloaded. Ropers are in the arena, throwing loops, warming up their horses. I see some riders behind the chutes, but I don't want to stop and chew the fat. I'm keyed up as a hot barrel horse. Hey, it's eleven—I could eat. Smiling, I head for food truck alley, and the beacon of Cora's red truck.

Life. Is. Good.

Lexi Falls saunters by in her signature painted-on jeans and boobie buffet on display. She's a lackluster barrel racer, and all the guys know Lexi is mostly here to rub a polish on buckles. Not to be crude, but Lexi has been known to fall.

"Hey, Austin."

"Lexi." I touch the brim of my hat and keep going. I've got a lady to see.

"It seems congratulations are in order."

I turn and walk backward. "How's that?"

"I just saw Carly having morning heaves behind Cora's truck." A sly smile slithers onto her lips. "Y'all better schedule the wedding. I hear maternity bridal gowns are hard to come by." She turns, and hips rolling, motors on.

Carly, sick? I turn and jog for the red blob in the distance. What the heck is that she-cat jawing about? Carly's not pregnant. I'd be the first to know, if she was.

She's in front of the serving window, filling the wire shelves with small bags of potato chips.

I pull up a step from her and touch her arm. "Tig, you okay?"

She hunches her shoulders with a jerk, and the bag in her hand crumples. "A-Austin. I didn't expect you until—"

"You're sick?" When she doesn't move, I take her upper arm and turn her to me. She looks strained and her skin is pale, but that's how it has been, lately.

Her brows pull together. "I'm not sick; why do you ask?"

"Well, Lexi Falls just told me she saw you throw up, and—"

Her hair flies when she whips her head to the tough-looking girl in the truck. "I'll be back, Nevada, okay?"

"Whatever."

"Let's go somewhere and talk." She grabs my sleeve and walks off.

I follow. Worry rolls through me like the far-off rumble of summer thunder. "What's going on, Tig? Lexi somehow got the idea you were preg—"

"Shhhh! Hang on a second, will you?" She looks around, then heads for a barren, grassy area fifty feet behind the truck.

When we arrive, she spins to me. "I'm pregnant, all right? But you don't have to worry; it's not yours."

I fall back a step as much from her spitting tone as her words. "What are you saying? Of course it's mine. You don't have to worry, hon, we'll just get—"

"It's. Not. Yours." Color has drained from her face, except for two spots of red, high on her cheeks.

What alternate Universe is this? Tig was my first; my
only. And I'm her—no, I'm not. I can see it in the stubborn
line of her jaw, the ice in her unwavering look. The muscles
in my shoulders let go. I lock my knees to keep them from
letting go. "What the f—"

"I made a mistake, okay?" Her eyes slide away. "A huge,
impulsive, ignorant, moronic mistake."

"I think you'd better tell me. Now, Tig." My voice is
quiet, but there's iron in it.

"I was lost. I was mad. I was—conflicted. You didn't take
me seriously, that we were broken up. No one in town did,
asking all the time how you were, when we were getting
back together. When I told them we weren't, they'd get this
smug smile." She grabs her hair and pulls. "You can't imagine how that feels, to have finally realized who you are is not
who you want to be, but everyone around you is pushing you
to be the same...I was going insane. So, I took off for Albuquerque, to forget all that for a night. I met a guy in a bar,
and—don't you dare look at me like that, Austin Davis. You
wanted to hear, so listen."

I push down the pissed and nod.

She wraps her arms around her waist. "His wife had left
him, and we got to talking. I made it clear there'd be nothing
more, and he was fine with that. But I was drinking, and he
was drinking, and somehow..."

Her words speed up like a downhill roller coaster.

"The next thing I know, it's morning and I'm alone, remembering what happened. What I did."

When she looks up, her eyes are red, and filled with sadness. "I know it probably doesn't make a difference to you
now, but Austin, I'm so, so sorry."

"I—" I'm not sure what I was going to say, because another fact drops like a bomb in my head. "Last week. In the

truck. Tell me you didn't know then. That you didn't..." But I know from her flinch, she did.

She can't look at me. "I knew."

Red-paint anger splashes in my brain, behind my eyes. I see red, literally. "You let me believe, for an entire week, that we were getting back together. That we *were* back together. And now you tell me... Who *are* you?" I squint down at her. "It's like I'm in a '50s sci-fi movie, and an alien has taken you over. You look like my Carly, but you're not. You can't be, because my Carly would never—"

"You know what? Screw 'your Carly.'" She leans in, face flushing. "Your Carly is dead. No—I'm starting to think she never existed. She was some perfect girl we made up."

"What the hell are you talking about?"

"I'm not that perfect girl."

I glance down at her belly. "Well, that's obvious, isn't it?" I want her to feel the pain, the betrayal I'm feeling right now.

She's pulled the world out from under me.

Her face blanches with shock. Then her eyes narrow, and her chin juts. "You forgot one thing, Mr. High and Mighty. We were broken up. So, none of this is your business anyway."

"We'd have gotten back together. You know it. I know it. The truck episode last weekend proved it." I cross my arms over my open chest wound.

"No. I'm never going back to being 'Rodeo Barbie' again. I may screw up." She swallows. "A lot. I may not know who I am yet, but I promise you one thing, Austin Davis. I'm danged sure gonna find out."

This is useless. I look at her round face, peeking out from all that fiery hair. Those sweet freckles sprinkled across her turned-up nose. The spirit in those eyes. This is gonna be the hardest thing ever, seeing her down the road, because she's right. My Carly is dead, replaced by this…whoever this is. My anger burns down. The only thing left in the cold ashes is a blistered agony of pain. "Good luck with that."

* * *

CARLY

I watch Austin walk across the field and out of my life. I want to chase him down, to try to explain about that night in the truck. But what would I say? That I was grabbing onto what I needed?

It was like that song about seeking shelter against the wind. You are thankful for the shelter, but you don't consider past that. I'm a horrible person.

And his pain, and knowing I caused it, throws me into a new level of hell.

My feet drag the dirt on the way back to the truck. I'd rather hide under it than climb in, but that's not an option. I'd love even more to get on the bike and blow out of here. But I'm not in any shape to ride right now, anyway. Not that I care much what would happen to me.

I need to toughen up. I have a *baby* to think about. At least, today I do. I don't know about tomorrow.

Nevada is cleaning the grill when I step into the truck. She takes one look at me, lifts a paper plate of cinnamon toast, and hands it to me. "You've gotta be hungry."

Nevada offering more than sarcasm? I must look terminal.

"You look like you need a beer, and I'd get you one, but pregnant women aren't supposed to drink."

Emotional whiplash stops me in the doorway. "What?"

"Ex-con isn't spelled s-t-u-p-i-d." She turns back to the grill. "Let me guess. Your cowboy isn't going to make an honest woman of you?"

That hurts, but it's just a bee sting on top of a bullet wound. "Oh, it's lot's worse than that. We're never getting back together. And it's my fault." I sound like an overacting soap opera star, but heck, I kind of am. "I've made such a horrible mess of things, and there's no way to fix it."

She walks to the fridge, in the front of the truck, and throws over her shoulder, "Well, well. Maybe we do have something in common, after all."

* * *

CARLY

One good thing about working with someone who doesn't like you—they leave you alone to your thoughts. Well, thoughts and head-banging music. The first few hours are busy, thanks to the rodeo. Late afternoon, there are only a few people cruising the food zone. It's time. I untie my apron. "I need to run an errand. Can you handle this for an hour?"

She rolls her eyes. "Like I need you."

"Good." I slam the apron on the counter. "We've really got to address your attitude sometime." I don't wait for her retort; my nerves are crispy already, and it wouldn't be fair to take it out on her.

I put on my helmet and fire up the bike. Downtown, squinting at the building numbers, I pass alien souvenir shops and new age bookstores. The alleged UFO crash here in the '60s has kept this remote town crawling with tourists ever since. I wish it would have crashed in Unforgiven—we could use the business.

I turn in at the generic stucco building, the Roswell Pregnancy Center that I looked up last night. I need information.

I still haven't decided what to think of the little bean growing inside me. It's going to change my life in ways I probably haven't even thought of yet, no matter what I decide.

Could I live with myself if I went through with terminating this pregnancy? I don't need a law or a preacher to tell me it is a life. I *know* it. My body knows it. I haven't felt a kick, or even a flutter yet, but I feel different. And it's not about the sore boobs, or the hunger, or the nausea. It's...I don't have a word for it, except for life. Or the promise of it, running through me.

But what if I decide to have the baby, and can't bond with it, because of how it was conceived? Not only would I be giving up the Carly I was, but I'd be harnessed to a being that I have no feeling for, no bond with, for the rest of my life. A life sentence, pretending to be a mother. Kids are smart. A kid would know. I'd not only be messing up my life, but another's, too.

How do women, married or not, ever have the guts to have a baby? The massive responsibility of starting a life, then steering that person on a path...Hell, I can't even make good decisions for myself. Odds are, I'd really screw up a kid.

At the dentist they do x-rays, and cover you in a lead apron. The responsibility feels like the weight of that apron. My decision will change everything, but how can I know how I'll feel then, sitting where I am now? I can't.

But at least I can be informed. I drop the side stand, pull the key, tuck my helmet under my arm, and stride for the door.

The lobby is small, empty, worn, and green: walls, carpet,

and plastic furniture. I avoid the gaze of the matronly woman talking on the phone behind the check-in window and step to the racks of pamphlets hanging on the wall. The walls exude a musk of disinfectant, dust, and dread—as if the fear and worry of every woman who sat in these chairs has soaked into the walls. It makes me want to hold my breath.

The lady pushes the glass back. "Can I help you?"

"No, thanks, just looking." I pick pamphlets from their slots. Thankfully, I can pass over the STD ones. And I'm way late for the birth-control ones. *Pregnancy Facts. Your Body, Your Decision. Do I have to tell my parents?* Can you really make a decision this huge from reading a glossy tri-fold? That seems as unlikely as the events that brought me here.

Something about the place is giving me the willies. I glance out of the corner of my eye at the only door other than the one I came in. The door that lies at the end of one of my choices. My guts vibrate in a tsunami of *wrong, wrong, wrong.* My mind hasn't gotten the memo my body already knows. There's no way I'm doing this.

Suddenly and perfectly, I know.

A chinook warmth washes over the shelf of ice inside me. How could I ever have imagined that I could harm this little innocent thing inside me? It's a *baby.* I'm carrying a miracle of *life.* I may not be sure about half its DNA, but the rest is *mine.*

A video streams in my mind, of a nurse, handing me a burrito-wrapped bundle. I can see the look on my face: surprise, tenderness, bliss, and tears.

My baby.

Another blast of warmth hits—I don't care if I lose everything: my home, my job, my place in the world. This baby and I will make it. I'll see to it.

My body hums a frantic one-note song:

Getout-getout-getout.

I've got to get out of here.

I shove a half-inch stack of folded paper into my jacket and push through the door.

Back in the parking lot, I stand beside the bike, trying to catch my breath.

I've chosen the lesser of two bad choices. But the weight of the lead apron, at least for now, is gone.

For better or worse, kid, it's you and me.

CHAPTER 10

AUSTIN

Shit. The only thing I managed not to fall off today was a fence. I shouldn't be surprised; my brain sure isn't in the game. I heave my bareback rigging toward my gear bag, and get on one knee to unbuckle my spurs.

"Austin." Carly's soft, sad voice comes from behind me.

I stuff gear in my bag as fast as I can. "I've got to git."

"I know, but can I talk to you?"

Half my stuff hanging out, I pick up the bag. "I don't think so."

"Don't forget your bull rope." She points to the fence.

Crap. I tug the slip knot, throw it over my shoulder. She's blocking my way.

"Can I at least walk you to your truck?"

I shrug. "Free country."

She's tripping along, almost jogging to keep up. I sigh and slow down.

"I wanted to tell you I'm sorry."

I keep walking, threading my way through the lines of pickups. Where did I park my damn truck?

"Austin, please. Will you just hear me out?"

I reach my truck and toss my bag in the bed and turn. "Go ahead then. I've got to get on the road." Man, she looks wrecked. Dark circles under eyes that are dull and sad...unCarly-like.

"I was selfish. I admit that. I was tired, and lonely, and missing you so bad." She clasps her hands in front of her and looks at the ground, like a chastised schoolgirl. "I didn't go planning that. I just got caught up, and..."

Even with her hair falling in her face, I can see her blush.

"I couldn't stop."

She looks up, her mouth turned down, her bottom lip shaking. "I didn't even think about you thinking we'd be back together. Thinking doesn't happen much when we start—" She takes a breath and looks up, into my eyes. "What I'm trying to say is, I'm an idiot. I made a bad mistake. You can think I'm a flake, or whatever. But I can't stand that you think I'd hurt you like that. On purpose."

Damn me. I want to wrap her in my arms and tell her everything's going to be okay. But that's just because she looks so much like my Carly. To remind myself she's not my anything anymore, I grab the door handle. "Okay. I gotta go."

* * *

CARLY

We decided to stay the night, and the next morning a glance in the bathroom mirror gives me a start. My face is bloated; my eyes are pools of reddened sadness, the bags under them so dark they look like three-day-old shiners. And I don't want to think about trying to comb the hoorah's nest on top of my head.

Inside me, though, there's an odd stillness that holds the faintest whiff of peace. After all, yesterday, I told Austin. Badly, but I did it. I made the decision to keep the baby. Two things I thought I couldn't do, and I'm still standing. I know it's only the beginning of many things I must do that I don't think I can. Like telling Nana and Papaw. And Unforgiven.

And I'll have to figure out how to live without Austin. That's going to be hardest of all.

But the jitters aren't dancing this morning, and I have no trace of morning sickness.

The way things are going, I'll take what I can get.

I strip out of my T-shirt and underwear, and step under the cheap water-saver showerhead. How can the spray hurt when there's barely enough water to wet my skin? I soap my belly slow and soft. Only I would know there's a little pooch to it.

Mornin', baby. A smile rises in me. I don't have Austin, but I'm not alone.

Ten minutes later, I'm trying to repair the damage to my face with a makeup miracle.

Bang, bang, bang! "What, are you nesting in there? I gotta pee."

I pull the door open to Nevada's perpetual frown. "Well, good morning to you, too."

Arms full of clothes, she mumbles something and pushes past me.

I step out. "We need to make a grocery run on the way out of town. I saw there's a Costco—"

She slams the door on the rest, so I sit on my bed with my tiny travel mirror and finish my makeup. I've had about enough of Miss 'Tude. I've made allowances for what I'm sure was her crappy childhood. I've gone out of my way to try to get along. I even put up with her eardrum-stabbing music. I'm no longer the soft little yes-woman. I'm tough. "Honey, you may be all Homie, but you push a country girl too far, you gonna see some cat-crap crazy," I mutter, brushing on mascara.

She reappears in ten minutes in micro shorts and a ratty-looking T-shirt with BITE ME in faded letters.

"You know, Costco sells T-shirts and shorts with real legs on them."

"Do they sell cans of 'Give-a-shit'? Cuz I'm fresh out."

I shake my head. "I'll meet you in the Costco parking lot. You know where it is, right?"

"I know where it is. I don't know why you just don't give me the credit card. You afraid I'm going to steal from Cora?" She stands, feet apart, chin out, her hands fisted at her sides.

I lift my dad's jacket from the chair and shrug into it. The thought had occurred to me, but this probably isn't a good time to bring it up. I grab my helmet from the desk. "Let's go, I want to get on the road. We may be able to pick up some lunchtime business somewhere."

"You're gonna have to wait. Somebody was hogging—"

Nevada's not the only one who can slam a door.

* * *

CARLY

A half hour later, I'm sitting on the concrete in the shade of Costco, fuming. She doesn't do makeup. She pulls her dishwater mop into a ponytail, and God knows, she doesn't spend time on her wardrobe. She's dawdling to tick me off. And it's working.

Ten more minutes pass before the truck pulls in the lot and parks. I'd love to march over and chew her out, but I'm not giving her the satisfaction of going to her.

She walks right past me, ignoring the cart I'm standing next to, pulls out another, and pushes it through the doors when they *whoosh* open.

Okay, that's it. I leave the cart and stomp after her. "Just what the happy heck is your problem?"

"You want to do this now? Okay." She stops and plants a fist on her hip. "All your little 'countryisms.' Look, you want to say 'fuck'? Say it already." She puts her head back and yells at the beams, two stories up. *"Fuuuuuuck."* She turns to me and shrugs. "See? Not so hard."

I point to the glowering mother who has stopped her cart to put her hands over her toddler's ears.

She snorts. "Deal, lady. I'll bet he's already heard it from his father."

I put a hand on her forearm. "Stop it."

She jerks away. "Don't you touch me."

"Seriously. You're rude, crude, and you have no manners. I've never done anything to you, yet you've hated me since you first slapped eyes on me. You're going to tell me why, if I have to dogpile you in in the middle of this store until you do."

Her face is screwed into a red knot of distemper. "Little Miss Perfect." She hisses. "All the men fall all over you—"

"What are you talking about? They do n—"

"You don't see them watch you when you walk by? Like they're stray dogs, dying to have you pet them. They get all stumbly and tongue-tied around you. I don't get it—it's like they think you're girl-next-door wholesome. Shows what they know." She pushes the cart into the first aisle.

I stand, stunned for a moment. I've spent the past month and a half beating myself up, slinking around, feeling guilty. I'm not taking it from this one. A crimson fountain of rage goes off in my brain. "I'm not done talking to you, bitch!"

She stops. As does everyone else within hearing range.

"I made mistakes. But at least I'm not a felon."

Her face hardens like cement in the sun. I've gone too far, and I don't care. I stomp down the aisle until I'm even with her. "I don't give a flying bat booger what you think of me, Nevada Sweet. I'm your *boss*. Cora left me in charge, and you will show respect for that, if nothing else." I notice we're by the flour. I heft a ten-pound sack and heave it in the cart. "Now, *shop*, damn it."

She shoots me a look, but shuts her mouth.

She may be smarter than I gave her credit for.

* * *

CARLY

The bike vibrates beneath me. I'm following the truck, but staying back a hundred feet to avoid the buffet-zone right behind it. My thoughts are skipping like a rock tossed across a lake.

It may have been justified, and it sure felt good, but I'm

ashamed of my behavior in the store. I was taught not to lower myself to a bully's level. Nana would snatch me bald, if she knew.

Nana. Under my ribs, a hollow place bursts open and homesickness fills me. *I want my Nana.*

I'm exhausted. I'm heartsick. I want to go home. And this is only the beginning of a long road that's going to end with a helpless human in my arms, and a much longer road ahead. Alone is one thing, but this is like hanging off the side of a cliff, clinging to a branch that's loosening a bit more every day. That kind of alone.

I thought it'd be good to get away from Unforgiven's prying eyes and local gossip. Now all I want to do is go where everyone and everything is familiar. Even if they hate me when the news gets out, at least there's Nana and Papaw.

Unless they hate me, too. I imagine their matching looks of disappointment, hardening to disbelief when I tell them the baby isn't Austin's.

I've got to stop this. I'm not going to know for sure until I tell them. And to tell them, I have to be *home*. But Cora's not due back for another week. That week stretches unending ahead of me. I have no idea how I'll get through it.

Hey, maybe Cora's not having fun, either. She could be sick of diapers, and arguing with her daughter. Maybe she's as ready to come back as I am to go. It's possible.

I check the left lane, pull into it, and hit the throttle until I'm even with the driver's window. I hold up my hand, fingers touching my thumb; our signal for "I have to pee."

Eye roll, then Nevada points at the sign for the next exit, one mile up. I raise my thumb in agreement, and fall behind again.

We pull off the highway and into the first gas station we find.

After a snide comment about pregnant women's bladders, Nevada heads for the Stop-n-Go mart.

I pull my phone and hit speed dial.

"Hello?"

Cora's voice brings a flood of moisture to my eyes. It seems so long since I heard a friendly voice. "Hi, Cora."

"Oh Carly, it's so good of you to call—Brittany, do not eat the cookie dough. Don't you know it'll give you worms?"

I hear a chorus of pre-teen gross-out in the background.

"Sorry, Carly. We have a kitchen full of Brittany's friends, and my daughter went to the store to get more butterscotch chips."

"How's the baby?"

"Down for a nap, but I doubt that's going to last long with this bunch... Annalise, not in her hair!"

"Sounds like bedlam."

"Are you kidding?" I hear her smile. "This is heaven."

So much for being saved by the cavalry. I knew it was a long shot. "I'm happy for you." And I am. But... I shoot a glance at the store. "Look, Cora, Nevada is worse than difficult. She's rude, obnoxious, and insubordinate. We almost got in a knock-down in Costco. I don't know if I can—"

"Megan, mind the stove, hon, it's hot. Sorry. Have you tried sitting down and talking to her?"

"I threatened to sit *on* her to get her to talk to me, but she's a hard case. Won't you fill me in on what happened to land her in jail? It might help."

"I'm sorry, Carly, I promised her I wouldn't. I'll lose her respect if I go against her wishes."

"I get that. I just don't know if I can work this out."

"Come, Brittany love. Take the spoon and keep mixing this, will you?" I hear steps, and the noise recedes. "I know this is hard for you, Carly, but there's not much I can do from here. I did warn you, remember, but you—"

"I know, I know. I'll find a way to work it out, Cora, don't worry."

"Now, tell me how you're feeling. Morning sickness? Have you run into Austin yet?"

"Yes, and yes." The store door opens and Nevada walks out. "But it's a long story, and I've gotta run. You enjoy the family and I'll fill you in when I see you in Alamogordo, next Sunday."

"Okay, but Carly? Please be patient. She's hurting, too."

"I'll try. Thanks, Cora. Kiss the baby for me." I drop the phone into my jacket pocket by the time Nevada walks up. My stomach growls. Loud.

The corner of her mouth lifts. "You want me to fix you a hamburger?"

Wow. If that's her idea of an olive branch, I'm grabbing it. "I'll tell you what. We're close to stopping for the night anyway. I'll buy you dinner."

She looks at me like I'm a vacuum salesman standing on her doorstep. "Why?"

"I'd offer to smoke a peace pipe, but we'd probably be arrested for contraband, right here in the parking lot. It's a free meal that you don't have to cook. Are you going to turn it down?"

"Hell no. Lead on, moneybags."

We head to the pizza place that shares a space with the station's convenience store. I'm starving, but seeing the pooled grease on the slices under the heat lamp makes my stomach start an agitation cycle. I order a salad and garlic bread, instead.

Nevada orders two pieces with pepperoni and a soda from the pimply kid in a paper hat.

I pay, and we take one of the two plastic tables. The locals must feel the same way I do about the pizza; the place is deserted.

Nevada takes a big bite and grease runs down her chin.

I must have winced, because her face tightens and her chin lifts. "What, my manners not good enough for a Rodeo Queen?" She swipes her chin with a thin paper napkin.

"No. It's just the grease doesn't agree with the baby."

"Oh." It comes out small.

"Not everyone is judging you every second, you know."

"Yeah. Probably. In your world." She takes another bite.

I pick at my salad, picking my words as carefully. "We live in the same world. It's all in how you look at things."

"Look. I can tell you're trying to be all sincere. But I doubt your world growing up had rats and junkies and Johns, okay? You grow up that way, then tell me how I should see things."

She takes another bite, like she just told me we were low on coffee. I check the muscles of my face, to be sure my shock won't show. "Where did you grow up?"

"Houston. Third Ward. And I don't want to talk about it. I've had social workers in my life. I don't need another."

"Okay, fair enough. What do we talk about?"

"Dunno." She says around a mouthful of pizza.

Talking to Nevada is like juggling porcupines bare-handed. "What do you think of the rodeo? Have you watched it yet?"

She nods and swallows. "Cora made me, when she first hired me. I think it's stupid."

She's a city girl. I smooth my hackles. "Why do you say that?"

"A bunch of kids who don't know they can die, doing dangerous things with huge animals, for tacky jewelry and not much money." She shrugs. "What's the smart part about that?"

"I'd like to argue, but put that way, I'm not sure I can."

"Holy shit." She slaps her forehead. "Is this it? The end of the world? Did we actually find something we can agree on?"

"Nah, I love the rodeo."

When I smile, she smiles back.

CHAPTER 11

CARLY

We've made our meandering way to Ruidoso the past week, picking up extra cash by feeding people at industrial complexes, offices, and the random parking lot. Nevada was her normal attitudinal self, but we've worked together a bit better; which is to say she managed about ten minutes of conversation per day. But we haven't gone all roller derby, so that's progress, right there.

Friday morning in the lead on the bike, I take the road out of Ruidoso into the mountains, a section of Highway 48 known as the Billy the Kid Trail. The air is fresh and pine-infused, the scenery beautiful. My spirits lift.

Unforgiven tugs like a tether on my heart. One more rodeo. By Sunday, I'll be on my way *home*.

I've changed from the girl who scooted out of town like a scared bunny. I've felt the shift inside that the baby is only partly responsible for. I may not have it all figured out yet, but I feel forged; as though the fire has made me stronger, tougher. I don't need to be half of a couple franchise.

Next time, I'm going to choose a man who wants to be a *partner.*

In the tiny town of Capitan, Nevada passes me and pulls in at the Horse Head Motor Inn, a single-story cinder block from the '60s, painted baby-barf gold. The sign out front is missing most of its old-fashioned lightbulbs.

We park, and Nevada steps out of the truck.

I shut down the bike and pull my helmet off. "This place is sketchier than usual. You sure you don't want to drive up the road and see what else there is?"

She squints at the worn façade. "It does look more like a horse's ass than its head, but it'll mean less expense for Cora." She looks down her nose at me. "Not up to your queenly standards?"

There's that sweet temperament. "By all means, lead on." I throw my leg over, stand, and pull the key. I guess I should be happy that she wants to do right by Cora, but my back hurts just imagining the mattress in a place like this. I check us in, and the measly nightly rate about guarantees the bed is going to be bad.

The huge fluffy thunderheads that gathered as we ascended have morphed to flat-bottomed steel wool, parked on our heads. "We'd better get everything in before those things let loose," I yell over the wind to Nevada on the way back to the truck. "It's gonna come a gully-washer."

"Golly, Elly May, wonder if'n they got a ceeement pond in this here place?"

"Oh, hush up, city girl." I roll my bike under the overhang

in front of our window. It'll save me a wet butt later. I unstrap my duffel from the sissy-bar, and open the door with the key on an old plastic fob.

The smell of stale Lysol smacks me in the face. The room is small and boxy, and a bare lightbulb with a long pull chain hangs in the middle of the ceiling. Linoleum, cinderblock walls, vinyl curtains, and paint-by-number artwork over the beds. The bathroom fixtures are chipped and rust stained, and I refuse to look too closely at the shower grout.

My cozy bedroom back home calls to me, with the bed under the window covered in the quilt Nana made by hand. I sigh and toss my duffel on the saggy bed. It squeals. Great.

Nevada slams through the door. "The gully-washer's here." Beyond her, rain drums the broken asphalt parking lot.

"That should make for a mud-fest rodeo." I untie the top of my duffel.

"Nah, they'll cancel." She sits on the bed and bounces. It squeaks like a stepped-on rat.

"You're kidding, right? In rodeo, anything less than a full-on lightning storm is considered entertainment. For the audience, it is, anyway." I pull out a change of clothes. Not my good ones.

"Seriously?"

"Hey, the projects aren't the only dangerous places, you know." I'm learning that if I'm to survive her razor-sharp snark, I've got to give as good as I get. "I'm going to grab a shower. We'll head to the rodeo grounds in an hour. It's about two miles out of town, and I want to snag a spot on some grass, so we don't get bogged down."

"Can hardly wait."

I wear flip-flops in the shower, in case of athlete's foot, or worse. At least there's hot water. When I step out, I rub the mirror twice, but it keeps fogging and the fan just makes noise. I pull on my clothes, open the door, and walk into the room. "I'm going to have to wait to do my hair. It's a sauna—What are you doing?" But I can see plainly what. She's leaning over my bed, pawing through my duffel.

Her face goes red and her eyes widen—the picture of "busted."

The raw emotions of the past days gather, swirling into a black whirlpool of anger in my chest. "Oh, I get it. You pick crap hotels to save Cora money, but you feel free to steal from me." I take the three steps to the bed to snatch my duffel from her, ripping the cord through her fingers. "I should have known. Once a thief, always a—"

"Don't you say that!" She bounces off the bed, right into my face. "I am *not* a thief!"

"Says the felon. Then why were you pawing through my things?"

"Because I . . . I just wanted to . . . Oh, fuck it. You believe what you want. I don't give two shits and a gully-washer what you think of me. You hear me?"

"They can hear you at the rodeo grounds!"

"Don't you dare yell at me."

"What are you going to do, beat me up, city girl?"

"Don't tempt me."

"No, you know what? How about I just call the cops?"

She flinches.

"Yeah. Then I'll call Cora, and let her know she's been wrong about you."

As if her tension was held by her stare, her shoulders slump and her chin drops to point at the floor. "I wasn't stealing. I did that one time, but I had a good reason. And I paid for it."

I cross my arms. "Tell me about what happened, back

then. Depending on your answer, maybe I won't call the cops." She doesn't need to know I wouldn't.

Her bed rat-squeaks when she drops onto it. "I'd just started working as a maid in one of the nice hotels on the north side of Houston. A cherry job." She shoots a look around the room. "I lived in a rented room, worse than this. I was eating dinner at a cheap diner when I saw her. A teenager; not much more than a kid, really, hanging out in front, trying not to stare at the people eating inside. She was dirty, had a ripped-up backpack and a windbreaker that wasn't made for Texas in December."

My bed squeals when my butt hits it.

"She looked sad, pissed, and scared. I know what that's like. I went out, brought her inside, and bought her a meal. While she wolfed it down, she told me she was from Dallas. Her mother had a new boyfriend that was bad news, so she took off. She didn't have to tell me what 'bad news' meant. Her darting eyes and shaky hands did that." Nevada tucks escapees from her ponytail behind her ear. "She was trying to get to Lafayette, where her grandma lived, but she ran out of money. I took her to my room, let her take a shower and sleep on my floor. I wanted to give her the money she needed, but I'd just started working, and every penny I had went to rent the room and buy me one meal a day.

"I'm an honest person. I *am*." She glares at me. "But the guests at that hotel, they were rich. I was cleaning this guy's room and found his wallet in the bathroom. It was stuffed with cash. He wouldn't notice if I just took enough to buy a bus ticket to Louisiana and maybe a couple of candy bars to tide her over. It was a worthy cause, after all. I stuffed a fifty and a twenty in my pocket, and was putting the wallet back when the guy walked in. He pressed charges, and they charged me with stealing the whole fifteen hundred dollars in his wallet. I did twelve months."

"What happened to the girl?"

She shrugs.

From the little I know of Nevada's childhood from her "rats and junkies and Johns" comment, she saw herself in that girl. Her tough-chick façade is to cover a scared kid who had to grow up way too fast.

We sit in silence for a time, until I remember. "So why were you going through my things?"

"Makeup." It comes out like she's a little girl, caught in the act.

From her squirm, this is harder to admit than grand larceny. "What?"

"Look, it's not a big deal, okay? I just wanted to see what brands you use, so I could, you know..." The rest is unintelligible.

"So you could what?"

When she looks up, her face is pink, heading for scarlet. "Buy some."

"Well, heck, why didn't you just ask?"

She shrugs. "Because you'd laugh at me, and make a big deal about it."

"Do I look like I'm laughing?"

She studies my face. Closely. "No."

"You might find that not everyone is out to put you down, or make you feel bad, if you'd stop snapping at them long enough to listen."

"Where I came from, they did."

"Well, good on you, for being smart enough to get away from that place. You want to give the rest of the world a chance?"

Her jaw takes that familiar hard line, and I realize I've

pushed too far. I pull out my two makeup bags, unzip them, and dump the contents on the bed. "What do you want to know?"

She looks at the pile like it could be harboring a rattler. "Everything?"

"Nevada Sweet. Do you mean to tell me that you've never worn makeup?"

"When there's not enough money for food and the rent"—she waves her hand at the pile—"all this is unimportant."

Sweet Jesus. "Okay, let's see. You and I have different coloring, so not everything I have will work, but . . ." I dig through the pile for pastel eyeshadow samples I got at a makeup party once.

"You're not putting all that glop on me, are you? I don't want to look like I'm turning tricks behind the food truck."

I put a fist on my hip. "Does my makeup look the least bit whorish?"

"N-n-no."

"Then shut up. And follow me. There's not enough light in here to see a shadow from a spook. The bathroom light is garish, but we'll make do."

A half hour later, I'm looking in the mirror at a fresh-faced, All-American girl. "Are you sure you won't let me show you how to do the false eyelashes?"

"Oh hell, no. I'm good."

"You're better than good. The cowboys are going to be drooling on the counter of the lunch truck." I pat her curly high ponytail. "When we go to buy you makeup, we're getting you some Shimmer highlights."

"I don't know . . ."

"And I do. That's why you asked me for help."

She sticks her tongue out at me in the mirror.

"We could stop by a mall when we get to Alamogordo. You know, to update your wardrobe."

"Stop right there. I like my clothes. If you don't, you can bite me."

"It was worth a shot." I check my phone. "We'd better get a move on if we're going to catch the lunch crowd."

When we step out in the parking lot, the showers have ended. The air is washed clean and smells good enough to bite down on. But there are pools of water everywhere. "It's going to be a goat rodeo."

"What? Those guys are way too big—"

"No, city girl." I can't help my chuckle. "A goat rodeo is a screwup. A fubar. A—"

"A cluster-fuck."

I know now. She uses tough as a primer, to cover the gaps in her education, manners, and her soft spots. "You've got to work on your vocabulary."

She smiles. "You want to ride in the truck? We're coming back here tonight, and that way, you won't trash out the bike."

"Brilliant idea, Sweet."

We park, and Nevada heads to the back, for the grill. I stop her with a hand on her arm. "You go open the window. I'm cooking today."

"No, you're not."

"Yes. I am." I plant a fist on my hip. "You think I can't do it? I cut my teeth as a short-order cook at the diner."

"It's my job." She manages it with her teeth clenched. She'd make a pretty good ventriloquist.

"Not today, it's not. I'm the boss, remember?"

Grumbling, she takes the steps out the back door.

An hour later, I flip a burger and mentally pat myself on the back. I've seen the cowboys eyeing her backside at the grill. Now that they've gotten to see her face, they're swarming.

"Hey, Nevada, come go out with me tonight."

"Screw off, dude. I don't date cowboys."

"How come?"

"Why waste your time on a guy who probably won't be alive on Monday?"

Another jumps in. "I'm a team-roper. We never get hurt. Will you go out with me?"

"No."

I sneak a look over my shoulder. She's smiling.

Score! No woman I ever met could resist a charming cowboy.

Including me.

I know Austin's routine. He's over shooting the bull with the guys, stretching and getting ready. If he bought lunch, it was from another vendor—I haven't seen him. "Longing" is a pale shadow of a word compared to this thing...this feeling that I don't have a name for. Like a magnet in my chest, pulling, always pulling. I haven't found a way to turn it off, or ignore it. It's there all day, every day. But especially at night; like in the dark, it goes searching. It finds him and pulls him into my dreams.

I swipe sweat out of my eye with the back of my wrist. I survived the fallout from that night in Albuquerque by putting the past behind me and facing forward; time to do that again.

* * *

AUSTIN

Shane cinches my bareback rigging on the broomtail in the chute, turns, and claps me on the shoulder. "Go get him, Dude."

The rodeo dog I had for lunch churns in my stomach. I know better than to eat before I ride. Too late now. I climb the chute and settle on the fidgety gelding.

Focus or die.

I shove my hand in the rigging, banging my fingers closed with my other fist. I scoot up, lean back, rest my spurs on the point of the bronc's shoulder, and nod.

The horse rears out of the chute, and I'm balanced, lying back, until the first jarring thump of his front hooves. Then I pull my knees up... *Toes out, toes out*... Mud slaps me in the face; my neck explodes in a burst of pain from the whip. The bronc duck-dives away, heading right for the fence. There's a roar. I don't know if it's the crowd, or it's in my head. My hand is loosening, every buck, every—

Clang!

I lift my face out of the mud, thankful my knees hit the metal fence before my face did. *Get up. Never let them see you*... The world wobbles, and my knees follow. Black dots dance at the edge of my vision. Someone grabs my elbow. "I'm okay. I'm okay. Leggo."

I swipe mud out of my eyes. When my knees firm up, I limp for the gate.

I'm too old for this shit. Bareback is the hardest event on a cowboy's body. The best ride, you're a rag doll, flopping around.

"Shit, Austin. You okay?" Shane knows better than to help if I don't ask, but he's hovering.

"Yeah. God, it's a mud bath out there."

"Bad luck that arm-jerker headed for the damned fence."

"No shit." I put my hand to my neck, and roll my head. No permanent damage, but this is going to hurt like a mother tonight. "You'd better get ready; you're up in a few."

He walks off, and I limp for my gear bag. Twenty-nine is

ancient for this event. I need to quit bareback. But if I do, my chances for purse money go down.

But wait…My brain kicks in. Without Carly, I've got no reason to save anymore. All the joy has gone out of my dream of starting a rough-stock business. C&A is nothing without the "C." Maybe I'll just go to work for Dad, like he's wanted me to, forever.

The sunny future I had planned now looks like a long, gray day. Forecast—icy rain. When I hunker beside my bag, my knees pop. Goddamn, that hurts.

Screw it. Ice and Jack Daniels will fix anything that's not broken.

* * *

CARLY

"Aw, come on, ladies." Jake Straw, a bullfighter, stands leaning on the counter while we clean up. Well, him and five other cowboys. "There's a beer truck, and a live band tonight. You don't wanna miss this."

Yeah, I do. After being on my feet all day, all I can think of is a hot bath, and bed. It's got to be the bean that's sapping my strength; I'm usually raring to go about now.

"I can vouch for most of these guys. They're gentlemen." He looks over his shoulder. "'Cept Skank Lewis…He's a little sketchy."

"Hey!" Skank's offended shout raises a laugh.

"But luckily, I fight two-thousand-pound bulls for a living. I can protect you."

I snap at his arm with a dishtowel. "Quit oozing all over that counter. I just cleaned it."

"Aw, Carly, you don't mean that. You tell Nevada how sweet I am, willya?"

Nevada is watching them out of the corner of her eye. They're watching her butt sway as she cleans the grill.

I step over to her and lean in. "These are nice guys. You wouldn't have to worry about any of them."

"Huh," she chuffs. "Do I look like I'd be scared of a couple of good ol' boys?"

"Then go. Have a good time. I'll finish up here."

She shoots a look back at the guys. "You're not coming?"

"Nah. I want a bath and a nap, and I don't even care which order they're in."

"You sure?"

"Sure." I turn back to the window. "Someone who is *sober* will need to drive Nevada back to the hotel. Do you think any of you can promise that?"

Pete Stevens raises his hand. "I can. I'm not old enough to drink yet."

"Okay, Nevada says she'll come. But she's a city girl, and doesn't know all y'all's ways. So, anybody gets out of hand, you're gonna answer to me, y'hear?"

"Yes'm, Carly."

"We're perfect gentlemen."

Nevada steps up beside me. "I can about guarantee we're not going to have a problem." *Snick!*

She holds up a switchblade and the light flashes off the wicked steel.

The guys take a step back.

I hiss at her, "Jesus, Nevada. Put that pig sticker away. You'll scare them off."

Her smile is mostly mischievous, with a sliver of scary as she pushes the blade back in.

Oh, she'll do just fine.

CHAPTER 12

CARLY

So, did you have fun last night?" I've managed not to ask until we're getting set up at the rodeo. I keep my eyes on the counter and wipe. I know if I make a big deal of Nevada coming in at one a.m., she'll close like Unforgiven after the sun goes down.

She sniffs. "Considering I was two hundred miles from any kind of civilization, surrounded by a bunch of dumb cowboys, it was okay."

"Sweet, you witch. You're not going to give me any details?"

"Nope." She turns her back, displaying today's T-shirt slogan: WHAT DOESN'T KILL YOU, DISAPPOINTS ME.

I shouldn't expect miracles.

The announcer begins his sound check. I glance to the arena, watching for broad shoulders and long legs. There are lots of them over there, but not the ones I want to see. The magnet in my chest pulls hard, and I rub my knuckles over my breastbone to ease it.

"You got heartburn? I hear that when you're—" Nevada shoots a look around. "you know...that you get that a lot."

"Nope."

She follows my glance. "You want to go watch today? I can handle it."

"Nah, but thanks." I turn back to rearranging cellophane-wrapped sweets. This trip has been too drama-filled and painful to be a visit to my glory days, back before I knew the yoke of responsibility, or that, someday, I'd need more than this.

I sigh, and move on to filling the chip clips.

We lived in the moment back then, not sparing a thought that those days would someday end. But they have; at least for me. I don't belong here anymore. I may not know what the future looks like, but this is my past—I feel the fact solid as a chunk of quartz.

I try to remember that last rodeo Austin and I shared, but find that I can't. All of them coalesce into a sum of the moments I remember. You often don't know when something is the last of its kind. I can't decide if that's a blessing, or a curse.

And that makes me sad.

I'd love to go find Austin. To see him, just once more in his element. This element that used to be ours. But we've said everything. And that makes me empty.

Will I look back someday and see Austin as my past as well? I don't want to believe it, but before this trip, I didn't think I wouldn't fit in at the rodeo, either.

Looking back now, I can see that this time on the road has

been an interlude. A time to say good-bye to the old, accept today's reality, and—dread, like a bolt of electricity, shoots down my spine. Tomorrow, I go home.

To tell Nana and Papaw, about who their granddaughter really is. To decide how I'm going to tell the town.

To face whatever happens next.

* * *

CARLY

By two o'clock the rodeo is over, and Nevada is standing by my bike waiting for me to get ready. A dusty four-by-four pulls up to the food truck and Shane rolls down the window. "Hey, Carly. Yo, Nevada, you going to be at the Roundup in Clovis next weekend?"

Her high ponytail swings with her head shake. "Don't know. Don't look that far ahead."

His smile droops. "Well, maybe I'll see you there. Buy you a rodeo dog?"

She sighs and sweeps an arm over the truck. "Do I look like I need you to buy me a hot dog?"

"N-no, but—"

"*If* I'm there, you can explain this bulldogging thing to me. I don't get it."

His smile cranks to blinding. "Be proud to. See you there." He floors it, kicking up mud and fishtailing his way to the main road.

Nevada watches until his truck disappears. "God, they're immature."

"Yeah." I check the bungees holding my duffel to be sure they're tight. "But they're damned cute, aren't they?"

"Marginally." She pulls a map from her back pocket. "Now what's this hairball idea you have?"

I show her on the map. "We'll go back to Ruidoso, then take 70 south to 244, to 82 and take it west."

"Why are we taking the long way to Alamogordo?"

"It winds back through the mountains. I hear it's just gorgeous."

"But way longer."

"Come on, city girl. We've got until noon tomorrow to drive seventy-five miles. You need to take a back road now and again in life."

"Oh, all right, if it'll make you shut up about all the Rocky Mountain High shit."

"You won't say that after you see it." I throw my leg over and settle on the seat. "And thanks for the ear worm."

She tips up her nose. "Oh, that's a song?" She walks to the truck, tosses the map on the passenger seat, and pulls herself behind the wheel. "Lead on, biker chick."

The main road snaking through Ruidoso is packed with tourists. Since the truck usually breaks trail, I'm doubly careful, watching for traffic pulling out. But when we hit 244, the divided road becomes two wide lanes that lead up into the mountains.

The bike seems to float over the pavement and easy, sweeping curves make my right wrist itch to bury the throttle. But a glance in the rearview of the truck lugging along nixes that. There's almost no traffic, so I'm able to take in the towering Ponderosa pines, the brick-colored soil, the cotton-ball clouds. The fringe on my dad's jacket flips in the brisk wind, but the sun is warm on my shoulders. I smile, realizing I'm humming a tune from the guy with the floppy hair and round glasses. What *was* his name?

We pass the entrance to the Inn of the Mountain Gods,

the Mescalero Apache Ski resort and casino. There's a funny kind of irony there. We used to tempt them with trinkets. Now they tempt us with chips. I hope they're making a mint off the tourists. We crest the long, steep hill and the road levels out. Nevada flashes her lights, then pulls off the road. I pull over, shut down the bike, and walk back to her. "Isn't it beautiful here?"

She's frowning at the dash. "The truck is overheating."

I look in the window. The temp gauge is pegged in the red. "Did you have the A/C on?"

She rolls her eyes and *tsks*.

"Just checking." I pull off my helmet. "It's probably from climbing that huge honking hill. We'll have to wait until it cools. Should be fine."

"Hope so." She looks around. "We're in the butthole of nowhere."

"Nah, not yet. Didn't you see the casino back there?"

"Proves my point. They only gave the shitty land to the Indians."

"My Nana would say, you'd bitch if you were hung with a new rope."

She frowns. "Huh?"

"Never mind. I'm starving. I'm going to make a sandwich while we're waiting. You want one?"

A half hour later, the little bean is fed, the engine has cooled, and we're back in business. A handful of miles up, I take the turn onto 82. It's a small two-lane road that winds through trees and mountain meadows so green they hurt your eyes. Tiny creeks bisect them, root beer–colored water tumbling over rocks and deadfall. When I sweep around a corner, fifty feet into the meadow, a doe raises her head. I point so Nevada doesn't miss seeing it, then slow a bit. That's as close as I want to get to a deer. I'm sure she'd agree.

Five minutes later, I'm singing at the top of my lungs when I glance back. No truck. Jesus on a skateboard, what now? I pull over, check both ways, duck-walk the bike into the opposite lane, and head back the way I came. She better not have hit that deer...

The truck is on the side of the road, steam shooting from under the hood, water spraying below. This can't be good. I ride slowly past, repeat the duck-walk maneuver, and pull off the road ahead of it. This is more than a fifteen-minute stop. I put my helmet on the gravel next to the bike, shrug out of my jacket, and hang it on the sissy bar.

Nevada yells out the window, "Where the hell did you go?"

I walk to the front of the truck. "I was communing with my Zen. Pop the hood."

Steam billows when I open it. "Oh, shitsky."

Nevada stands next to me. "It must be bad. That's the closest I've heard you come to swearing." She glances at me. "Well, except for the Costco Conflict."

I give the engine compartment a quick glance. "The only way Cora's baby is getting out of the mountains is on the end of a tow chain."

She peeks in. "How do you know?"

"The water pump is trashed. Can't you see?"

"I don't know a water pump from a breast pump. How do you know?"

I unhook the support arm, and drop the hood. "I grew up on a farm. You learn to fix things with bubble gum and cat hair."

"Well, we've got the gum. No cat hair, but maybe you could go ask that deer..."

"Very funny. I'll go get my phone and look up the nearest tow. Maybe we'll get lucky, and there's one in Cloudcroft."

"I've gotta pee."

"Well, have at it." I retrace my steps to the bike.

"There's no bathroom." The small voice comes from behind me.

I stop. "You're kidding me, right? You have like eight zillion trees here, and no traffic. Go in the woods, city girl."

She eyes the trees. "But what if there's bears?"

"Oh, for cripe's sake. If there are, they're only little black bears. They're not going to bother you."

"You mean there *could* be bears?"

"Where's all that tough now? Take some napkins from the truck and go take care of business. If a bear comes, you can scare it off with your sarcasm." I point to the trees. "Go."

She snatches some napkins from the console and minces her grumbling way into the woods.

By some miracle, I'm able to get two bars, but that's where our luck runs out. The closest tow service is—

"IIIIEEEeeeeeee!"

My head snaps up at the *Psycho*-scream and my feet are beating pavement for the truck, my heart trying to crack my ribs. From the terror in that yell, this is not a drill.

I find the trail in the wet grass that Nevada made going in and follow it, full tilt. Barely inside the tree line, she almost barrels into me, running as fast as a human can with their pants around their ankles.

I grab her shoulders to keep her from falling. "What? What is it?" I don't see claw marks, but the terror in her eyes isn't faked.

"I'm bit! A rattlesnake bit me!" She whips her head to look behind her.

"Where? How do you know it was a rattler?"

"Back there." She points back into the trees. "I may have never seen one before, but even I've seen a Western movie. I know the sound."

"I mean, where did you get bit?"

She turns her back, so I can see the puncture wounds on the back of her right thigh, about three inches below her butt. "Oh, shit."

She whips around and grabs my arm. "I'm gonna die, aren't I?"

"You're not going to die." But this is not good. We're fifteen miles of mountain roads from Cloudcroft, and it's so tiny, I doubt there's medical help there. No vehicles have passed since we've stopped. "What the hell were you thinking? You never pee in the woods without looking around first." My fear comes out garbled, more like anger.

"How the fuck am I supposed to know?" She reaches to pull up her shorts, then thinks better of it, and throws her hands in the air. "Why didn't you tell me?"

"Every woman on the planet knows that."

"Well, I don't, dumbass! I'm from the Houston projects. All the snakes there have two feet."

My mind clicks through the scenarios. Most of them don't end well. "Jesus F. Christ, Sweet, if you'd actually open up and *communicate,* someone might—" .

"Are you saying this is *my* fault? You're the hick, you should've—"

"Hey, I'm not the one with holes in my butt. You're responsible for your own booty. I can't think of everything!"

"Everything? Really?" She leans in, her face inches from mine. "Since when do you think of anything besides yourself?" She lays the back of her hand against her forehead. "Woe is poor widdle homecoming queen me! Life didn't turn out like I planned. Boo the fucking hoo." She's breathing hard and if looks could do it, I'd be dead meat.

"That is so mean. I'm struggling, and you—"

"You entitled, self-centered, spoiled..." She sputters,

clearly too pissed to form words. "You know what? Never mind. If I'm gonna die, I'm not going out fighting about your 'problems.'" Her air quotes almost scratch my face. "I don't need you. I don't need anyone. Fuck off." She pulls up her shorts and marches for the road.

I stand stunned for a moment, then take off after her. "Stop. Hey, Sweet, stop!"

She's standing beside the truck, hands on her knees, breathing hard.

An extra dose of adrenaline slams into my bloodstream. I've got to get her to a doctor. Fast.

"There's a knife in the truck. Do you have time to sterilize it?" she says, panting.

"What?" I'm so busy clicking through solutions, I don't get it.

"I've seen the movies. You have to cut it open and suck out the venom."

That pulls a surprised chuckle from me. "Don't believe everything you see on TV. I've read that it doesn't help, and opens you up to infection." I pat her back. "Besides, I don't like you near well enough to do that."

She manages a shaky smile, but panic has eaten through her toughness, and for the first time since I've met her, she looks like the scared young woman that she is. The best thing to do is keep her calm. A racing heartbeat is going to spread the poison faster.

"Come on." I guide her forward with my hand on her back. "You get pillion seat."

"Do you know how to do this?"

I grit my teeth. "On-the-job training." Twisty, late-afternoon-shaded mountain roads aren't the best place to learn to ride two-up, but I don't have much choice. I *have* to get her down the mountain. Now.

By the time we get to the bike, she's shivering. Whether from shock or venom, I have no way of knowing, and it doesn't really matter anyway—there's nothing I can do about it here. I hand her Dad's jacket. "Put this on." I unhook the bungees and grab my duffel. "I'll be right back. I'm going to put this in the truck and lock up."

I jog to the truck, disastrous scenarios piling in my mind like leaves in a gutter. This is dangerous for all *three* of us. I could drop the bike on any one of the curves on the way down the mountain. We could hit a deer. Nevada could lose consciousness and fall off. I could—*shut up, Carly. This is not helpful.*

I dump my duffel, grab Nevada's wallet from the console, then lock the truck and jog back to the bike. I can't let any of those things happen, that's all. There's too much at stake, and it's all on me.

Nana's scratchy voice echoes in my mind: *Suck it up, Buttercup. Life is a bitch, so if it's easy, you're doing it wrong.*

Sucking it up, Nana. Sucking it up.

"Are you sure you can do this?" Nevada's voice is shaky.

"Yes." I check the back of her leg, being careful not to touch it. It's swollen, and angry red. "How does it feel?"

"Hurts like a mother."

"Yeah, I've heard that."

I wish she had on long pants, and something more substantial on her feet than tennis shoes. But if we go down, a little skin is going to be the least of our worries. I lift my helmet, then hesitate. "I'd let you wear it, but if I get a bug in my eye…"

"Can we just go? I'm getting really dizzy."

That is not a good symptom. My stomach jitters like a drunk with DTs. I pull on the helmet. "Okay, there's only three things you have to remember, but they're really important, so listen up."

"Trust me, I'm listening."

I bend over and drop the passenger foot pegs. "If I stop, you keep your feet on the pegs. I'll handle the rest. But most important"—I touch her arm, to get her to look at me—"you have to stay right behind me. If I lean, you lean. No more, no less than I do. You're my shadow, okay?"

She nods, and her eyes close. "You said three."

I finish cinching the helmet strap, throw my leg over, and settle. "The sissy bar will help keep you secure, but you've got to put your arms around me and hang on. You hear?"

I hit the kickstand with my heel and it retracts. I make sure my feet have good purchase in the gravel, and tighten my hands on the grips. "Okay, throw your leg over."

The suspension dips, and while she gets settled, I try to slow my mind. I've got to think clearly and ahead at the same time. I feel her fumbling for the foot pegs, then her arms come around my waist. Good. The closer she is, the easier it'll be for her to lean with me, instead of fighting it.

I fire the engine, and check the empty road for cars. "We're off in a cloud of turkey turds. Just hang on."

CHAPTER 13

CARLY

This sucker rides like a dump truck, two-up. "You okay?" I raise my voice to be heard over the wind.

"Fuck, it hurtsss."

Nevada is slurring and shaking like an aspen leaf. She's also about cutting me in two, hanging on. But better that than—*Deer!* "Braking!"

Go, momma. Get out of the friggin' road!

Nevada's staying right behind me, but her weight exaggerates everything. Maybe if I speed up just a...yeah, that helps. The bike wants to stay up. All I need to do is—

"Unnnhhh."

"Going as fast as I can. Just hang on."

More damned curves. Only twenty more miles, but we've

gotta get out of these damn twisties. It's taking too long. "Hey, you alive back there?"

"Nhhhhhhh."

"Come on, city girl, where's all that tough now? Hang on, damn it. Tighter. Hear me? Tighter!" If she passes out, we're going down. Now I'm shaking. Concentrate. Concentrate. One curve at a time…One curve… "Hey. Sing with me. Rocky Mountain High…Nevada. Damn it, sing!"

She's getting wobbly. This is not good.

Breathe, Carly. Breathe. You can do this. You have to do this. Hang on, Bean. I'm not letting anything happen to you. I won't.

Finally, I can see the valley. The twisties are loosening. Easing more to sweepers. Maybe I can inch up the speed, just a bit… "Nevada, come on, homie, sing!"

Friggin' R.V.'s. Ant pulling a sugar cube. Get out of the way! Jesus, lady, get a car you can drive!

Thank God, the edge of town. But the speed limit dropped. God, this is never going to end. Red light, red light…easy, easy. Ugh. At low speeds, the extra weight wants to pull us over. "Hey, feet up. Feet up, remember?"

A blue "H" sign. *Thank you, God. Easy, easy.* She's getting wobbly on the shifts. "Hey, city girl. Hang on. We're almost there." Can't be more than another mile or so…get off here. *Yikes! Almost didn't make that turn.* Luckily, no one in the other lane. Slow turns are the worst.

Where the heck is this place? How are people supposed to—there!

I pull up at the Emergency Room entrance. "Don't you move, Nevada. You'll dump us, sure. Hear me? Nevada? Hey! Hey, somebody, help!"

Two guys in scrubs jog out of the electric doors, one pushing a wheelchair.

"She's been bitten by a rattlesnake. Back of the right thigh, about an hour and a—Hey, easy, I'm gonna drop the bike!"

"It's okay. I've got her." He lifts Nevada off and the suspension lightens.

"Jesus." She's so pale I can see the veins in her closed eyelids. She looks like death. I'm so glad I couldn't see her when I was riding; I'd've freaked out. "Is she breathing?"

Her limbs are floppy, and he practically pours her into the wheelchair. "Yeah. We'll get her in. You park and meet us. What's her name?"

"Nevada. Nevada Sweet." My hands are shaking so bad I can hardly pull in the clutch. It takes me twice to get moving.

Since I'm not family, they won't let me in the treatment room. I call to have the truck towed to Alamogordo. I think about calling Cora, but decide to wait for an update. No sense worrying her before I have to. I think about calling Nana, but home seems a zillion miles away—another lifetime. Besides, if I broke down on the phone, I'd scare her to death.

I sit and wait. And wait. I watch the comings and goings of others in crisis mode. Why did I waste time fighting with her? I'm easygoing, but that girl is like a jet catapult—she can take me from zero to supersonic with a few words. She can't die. No one dies of snakebites anymore.

Do they?

"Who came in with Nevada Sweet?" A nurse in scrubs stands at the door to the inner sanctum.

I'm there before I give the order for my feet to move. "I did. Is she okay? Can I see her?"

"Follow me."

Beyond the door is one big room, sectioned off with a sea of sky-blue curtains. She leads me to the one against the back wall. I can't see any of the other patients, but their disembodied whispers and moans are ghostly. A shivering starts up in my gut. Anyone around rodeo knows shock when they see it. Or feel it.

The nurse pulls back the curtain. Nevada is in bed, wearing a hospital gown, an IV tube winding down and ending in her arm. Her eyes are closed, her skin as pale as the sheet.

My feet stop at the curtain. They won't go farther. "Is she going to be okay?"

"Yes. Another half hour, things would have been much worse. She's responding to the antivenin, but slower than we'd like. We're holding her overnight for observation." Someone calls out, and she leaves me.

Eyes still closed, Nevada says, "I'm not dead yet. You can come over."

I step to the bed and try to take her hand, but she shakes me off.

"I told you I'm not dying. Back up off me." But a ghost of a smile quirks her lips.

"I'll call Cora in a few, but is there anyone else you want me to call? Your mom? Someone else?"

"Nah. I'm good." Her chin lifts, but there's the finest quiver to her lips.

"I'm so sorry, Nevada. I can't imagine what I was thinking, standing there arguing when I should have had you on the bike and gotten you out of there right away."

"Yeah, but you also saved my life, so I guess I have to forgive you."

Now that I know she's going to be okay, exhaustion hits so hard I've got Gumby knees. There isn't a chair. "Scoot over."

She moves her legs, and I perch on the edge of the bed.

She fingers the edge of the sheet. "I was scared."

"God, so was I." We're quiet for a bit, listening to the comings and goings on outside the curtain, and inside our heads. "You know, you'd better be nice to me now."

She snorts. "Yeah, like that's gonna happen."

I buff my nails on my shirt. "Well, you know, a rumor could start on the rodeo circuit, that you got snake-bit on the butt."

Her mouth drops. "You know that's not true."

"Didn't say it was true. Just that it could be a rumor." I smile down at her.

She almost smiles back, but then drops her head on the pillow. "Go away, willya? I'm beat."

"Oh, sorry. I should have thought of that." I hop off the bed. "I'll go call Cora, and check on the truck, and... Nevada?"

She opens her eyes.

"I'm sorry."

"Get outta here. Can'tcha see I'm tired?"

"Going."

I walk back to the admitting area and keep going, until I'm standing beside a concrete bench, in the sunshine. Traffic comes and goes in the parking lot, and past it, on the street. I sit and dial Cora.

"Carly, I was just fixing to call you. I leave for the airport within the hour. So far, my flight's on time. Pick me up outside the terminal, okay?"

"That's why I'm calling. Change of plans."

"Why? Is everything all right? Are you sick? Is the baby—"

"I'm fine. In fact, we're all fine. Or we will be, soon enough."

"What happened?"

I give her the five-minute version of the day's events.

"Oh my God."

"They're only keeping her overnight to be cautious. But I'm afraid you're going to have a hell of a tow bill."

"I couldn't care less about that. I'm just grateful you're both all right. You were very brave, Carly. I'm so glad you were there with her."

Brave. Not Hardly. Nevada nearly died by argument. "You'll need to get a cab to the hospital. I can't carry you dragging your roller suitcase behind on the bike."

"That would sure be a photo for the paper, wouldn't it? No problem. I'll see you tonight. I can't wait to hug you both."

I hang up. So much has happened in ten hours. My heart is sore, my nerves are crispy, and I'm shaken. Without planning, my thumb hits speed dial to a person who I *know* loves me.

"Carly-girl. I was just telling Irma...you remember Irma, from Bingo?"

Through the babble in the Elks Hall, Irma yells, "Hi Carly."

"Damn, Irma, It's not like an orange juice can and a string. You about blew out my eardrum. Anyway, Carly, I was just telling her that my baby is coming home tomorrow."

Tenderness fills my head in a liquid rush. "I'll be there, Nana. I just called to tell you how much I love you."

"Aw, now that's sweet. I love you right back, Carly-girl. I'm gonna make—wait. Oh, fuck me! Bingo! I've got a Bingo over here!"

Irma's shrill voice joins Nana's, calling for verification of the win.

I can just picture Nana standing up, waving her card. "I'll see you tomorrow, Nana. Enjoy." I hang up, lean my back against the sun-warmed cement, and take in the last rays of the sunset. Packing up the truck this morning seems a month ago. So much has happened. So much to think about.

Something is different. Something happened on that terrifying ride down the mountain, like things shifted inside—settled. I search, looking for what it is, what it means.

I close my eyes and turn my focus inward. I hear my breath, my heartbeat, blood coursing through my veins. That same blood is nourishing another human being.

This new Carly is more than a screwup. Nevada is safe, because of me. The baby is safe, because I did things right. Could I have what it takes to be a good mother? Right now, it feels like I do. My hand steals to my belly.

You in there, Bean? You rest easy. Momma's got you.

I love you.

"Are you okay, lady?" A stooped little man with a four-pronged cane is standing in front of me, his white brows arched like concerned caterpillars.

I swipe at my face and smile. "I'm more okay than I've been, but not as okay as I'm going to be, thanks."

CHAPTER 14

AUSTIN

W hen did bar bands get so danged loud?"

"Dude, lighten up. You're about as fun as a dislocated shoulder." Shane smacks the back of my head.

"Well, bail then. By the way, that hottie at the table against the wall is checking out your ass."

"Where?" He whips around to face the room. "Oh. Nice. She's bound to be more fun than you. Later, bud." He threads between crowded tables.

I throw back the shot of Johnny, and watch Shane in the mirror over the bar. He leans over, whispers in her ear, and they make their winding way to the dance floor. The crowd is packed in, the band so loud I can feel the bass thump in my chest. I signal the bartender for another, and she nods as she shakes a martini. And I do mean shake. The tied-up T-shirt with the collar cut to cleavage is a lazy man's dream—no imagination necessary. And her Daisy Dukes have more than one guy at the bar wiping his mouth.

I shouldn't have come. Shane and I make some extra cash working stock for a rough-stock supplier out of Portales when we're in the area. I should be back at the bunkhouse, repairing tack. I'm not in the mood for any of this.

"You're Austin Davis, aren't you?" The bartender pours, then sets the bottle beside my glass.

"Yes'm."

She looks me over like I'm a sirloin in the H-E-B meat case. "I'm Daisy."

Of course you are. "Howdy." She has blond hair that looks like it got rumpled in somebody's bedsheets. She's tiny, with big blue eyes and a chest that Mother Nature had only a small hand in.

"They say you're a great rider." The edges of her mouth curl in a grin that tells me she's not talking about livestock.

She'd know better than to ask, if she knew me. I'm a one-woman man. Or I have been up 'til now.

She drops her chin to look at me through those long eyelashes. "Wanna help me close up tonight?"

I throw back a shot, and she pours another. "Well, that's a serious proposition. Can I take some time to give it proper consideration?"

"I sure *do* hope you take your time, cowboy." She gives me a naughty wink and walks away.

Something tells me she knows the bottom of her cheeks are flirting with the edge of her shorts.

Well, why the hell shouldn't I sample the local wares? I'm a single guy, even if it was never a status I aspired to.

That night in the truck has taken up way too much of my head lately. Now I know why Carly didn't remind me to use protection like she usually does. Did. She may not have done it on purpose, but the fact that she didn't even think about me that night, made me finally understand how she's changed. How far apart we are. The old Carly never would have done that. She always thought of other people's feelings.

Even if I could find a way past that—somehow—there's the baby.

Carly and I are not only broken up; we're blown to hell.

So why not take a little comfort where I can get it? I watch Shane slow dancing with the brunette whose name he's probably forgotten already. That doesn't keep him from practically making out with her on the dance floor. All the unmarried cowboys do it; new town, new bar, new babe. And I've got nothing to stay true to anymore.

Still, something in my chest squirms at the thought of hooking up with a stranger. How weird would it be having that little blonde beneath me, instead of Carly? Well, there's no reason not to find out. It's gotta happen sometime. Why not tonight? I throw back another shot, fill my glass, and wave the barkeep over.

Three hours, two band sets, and uncounted shots later, Daisy locks the door behind the last bleary straggler. Shane, with the brunette pinned to his hip, shot me a thumbs-up on his way out.

After the hours of jangling noise, the silence echoes in my head. Or maybe it's the booze. I wobble when I step off the barstool. I should'a stopped a while ago.

Slow it down. Pay attention.

My chute-procedure mantra calms, and it makes me smile to think about using it in this situation. I take a deep breath and walk over to where…um…Daisy-as-in-Dukes is counting out the till.

"Hey."

"Shhhh." Her lips move, counting.

She is pretty, in a young, cheap kind of way. "You're over eighteen, right?"

She bands a stack of ones, then her eyes roll. "Hello. I'm a bartender. You gotta be twenty-one to do that." She tips her head and squints at me. "Not the quickest horse in the race, are ya?" She bends and drops the cash in a safe, giving me a shot of her butt cleavage, closes the door, and spins the combination lock.

Never thought about the fact that she'd be sizing me up, too. My ears get hot. "Never knew anyone who got smarter, drinking Johnny Walker."

"Now that is a nat'ral fact." She smiles and sidles around the bar, and into my arms. There must be risers back there, because the top of her head barely reaches my armpit. She looks up at me, vampire-red lipstick gaudy in the neon light. She inhales deeply. "Damn, you smell good."

"Thank you, ma'am." Her breasts are even more impressive, smashed against my waist. Below my belt buckle, interest peaks. I lower my head to kiss her, but can't reach. "Hold on a sec." I put my hands around her tiny waist and lift her to the barstool. That's about right. Just about as tall as Carly—*Shut up. Not now.* "There. That's better." I bend to kiss her, and just before our lips meet, I think about getting that lipstick all over my face.

She sucks me in. Big, sloppy kisses. I mean, she's all over me, breathing heavy, her legs wrapping around the back of my thighs to pull me closer. I can't breathe. I back up. "Whoa there. We got all night."

"Maybe you do. I've gotta get home and let the babysitter go." She shucks the T-shirt over her head. No bra. Yep, implants. I've got to know. Guys talk, but...whoa. They're not hard, but they're not...right.

She's all over me again. I put my hands on the sides of her face, to try to control her mouth. I feel like I'm being eaten alive. Her hands fumble at the buttons of my Wranglers. My cock is ready, but the thought of putting it…I get a visual of a shark's mouth with rows of razor sharp teeth, and I stumble back. No. Nuh-huh. I can't do this.

"What's the problem, big man?"

"You're 'mazing, Maisy. It's not you. It's—"

"Maisy? It's *Daisy*, you hick." Her face is painted with disgust. And lipstick smears. "You should'a told me this was your first time."

I snort. "It's not. I just—"

"Like I said, I don't have time. I gotta get home." She snatches her T-shirt from the bar and shrugs it on, pulling at it until she's sure her doctor's artwork is displayed. She hops off the barstool, walks behind the bar, grabs a buckskin purse, and heads for the door.

Her lightning shift of mood has me on my heels.

She's holding the door, frowning. "Let's go. I gotta lock up."

Two minutes later, I'm standing outside the bar, watching her old Camry peel out of the parking lot, wiping my mouth on a cocktail napkin. Is this how women feel after a one-night stand? Is this how Carly felt?

Dirty. Used.

But unlike Carly, I dodged that bullet. I taste the bitterness that rises with the Johnny Walker in the back of my throat.

* * *

CARLY

I open my eyes to the crack in the ceiling that's been over my bed since I was a little girl. I kind of like that crack. I lock my fingers behind my head and look around my room in the barely dawn light.

It's well used and nothing fancy or special, but it's home. Where I've always belonged.

The frilly white little-girl dresser that Nana's been trying to get me to let go of since junior high is covered in tatted lace, jewelry boxes, and perfume bottles. My tiny closet, with clothes jammed so tight some stick out, and my shoes stuffed in a hanging rack on the door. The school desk where I did every bit of my thirteen years of homework. The bulletin board above it, with rodeo ribbons, mementos, and photos. So many photos. Austin and me, on the homecoming float in the parade. Me, in Nana's lap in the mine-now office at the diner. Both of us are smiling. I'm missing a front tooth. Me and Austin, riding his favorite horse, my arms around him, my head on his shoulder. Austin's senior picture.

I couldn't even look at that board before I left. Now, it's time. I slip out of bed and cross the room. One by one, I unpin the Austin photos, then go to the dresser and pull the ones stuck into the edges of the mirror. I don't stop to study them. I don't need to—I know every fold in his shirt, the tilt of his hat, every smile. When I'm done, I have a handful of memories. The Old Carly's memories. I stop and look around the room again. It seems different now. Like a time capsule, when I step into it, and I'm the little-girl Carly. The Homecoming Queen Carly. The C in C&A.

But I also know, outside this room, the other Carly waits. The one I'm not comfortable with, because I don't know what she'll do next. Last night, when I got home, I slipped into this room, and the old Carly, like a cozy pair of slippers. But this morning, the slippers don't quite fit.

Maybe because they're the size I was back then—not now.

I look down at the photos of that Carly's life. I can't throw them away. It'd be like erasing the past. My heart thuds, slow and sad. I love my past. I wish I were still living my past.

No, that's wrong. I was ignorant in my past. I was in love with a dream man I made up in my head, not the real thing.

The new Carly urges me to hurry up. We have things to do.

The closet. I go on tiptoe, take down a shoebox already stuffed with memories, put the photos in, mash down the top, and put it away. My stomach growls. Loud. I put my hand over the small bulge. "Hang on, Bean. I'll get you something—"

"Coffee's on, missy. Daylight's burnin'!" Papaw's gruff wake-up call from the kitchen has been the same my whole life, too.

Thank you, Lord, for bringing us home safe. Someday, I'm sure I'll appreciate the lessons of this summer, but that day is a long way off.

At least I have Nevada to show for it. We're friends, whether she wants to admit it or not. Note to self: Call Nevada and Cora today.

I step into my moccasin slippers and shuffle to the bathroom, kissing my fingers and touching my parents' photo on my way by. *Thanks for letting me borrow your jacket, Dad.*

When I step into the kitchen, Nana is stirring oatmeal on the stove and Papaw is reading *The Patriot.* I wonder if it's ever occurred to anyone else that *The Unforgiven Patriot* was an unfortunate name for our local paper. Unless there's a part of town history that I don't know about.

"Mornin'." I kiss Nana's cheek.

"Morning, hon." She puts the spoon down to hug me. "Good to have my girl back home."

"Not as good as it is to be home. About a week in, all I wanted to do was click the heels of my ruby slippers, but I forgot to pack them." I pour coffee from the ancient percolator and sit at the table. "Any new news, Papaw?"

The paper crinkles when he lays it aside. "Same old, same old. Looks like Tractor Supply has a special on chicks. You still want some, Momma?"

"Be good for Sunday dinners."

I don't believe it for a minute; Nana's last batch of chickens died of old age.

"'Sides, I miss having the little peckers around the place."

Coffee shoots up my nose, and I cough into my paper towel. Man, I missed this. How could I have ever thought leaving home would be the answer to anything?

Nana sets her chipped blue bowls of oatmeal in front of us.

Distance has made me aware of how precious home is. How much I have. Their dear, lined faces, heads bowed for grace. They've worked hard their whole lives. I'm acutely aware that I'm a Trojan Horse. What I have inside is going to disrupt their staid lives. How can I ask them to accept a baby, when for weeks, I wasn't sure *I* could? How do I tell them that Austin isn't the father...?

Stop it. Doesn't matter how. I just must do it. "Um. Y'all have any plans tonight? I thought we could sit and catch up."

"You know where I'll be."

Yeah, Papaw, in the La-Z-Boy, in front of the TV, as always.

"I've got Bingo at noon, so I'll be home." Nana sips her coffee. "I want to hear all about your trip. Oh, and I'm making your favorite for dinner tonight."

"Meatloaf? Can't wait. I've eaten enough rodeo dogs to last me the rest of my life." I force-feed myself oatmeal. When Bean is satisfied, I take all our dishes to the sink. "Gotta get ready for work. See you at supper."

They nod, their faces in the paper. Such a normal morning. And yet, today, I see how precious normal is. I step to the table and put a hand on each shoulder.

They look up, startled.

"You know how much I love you, right?"

Papaw just grunts. Nana smiles and pats my hand. "And we love you, child. Now go get ready, before those hungry bastards call here, looking for you."

An hour later, I unlock the front door and step into my second home.

"Carly." Lorelei runs across the floor to hug me. "God, I'm glad you're back."

"Looks like you held the fort—the place is still standing."

"Pure luck, I'm telling you. Moss threatened to boycott until you got back, and that danged greengrocer tried to raise prices on me."

"And yet, the building still stands." I smile and pull her into a hug. "Thank you. I didn't even know how much I needed a vacation."

She lets out a huge sigh. "Thanks. I'm just so glad to see you. You make running this place look easy, but I can testify, it's not."

"I think that's one of the nicest things anyone's ever said to me." I put my hand on her back. Time to do the next thing I think I can't. "Now, come on back to my office. I need to talk to you."

Her shoulder tenses.

We push through the swinging door to find Fish, sprawled on the floor, digging paper goods from under the counter.

"What in the world are you doing?"

His head pops up. "Hey, Carly. Inventory. It's good to have you back." He goes back to counting.

I close my hanging jaw, grab Lorelei by the bicep, and march for my office. When we're behind a closed door, I ask. "I've been trying to get him to help with inventory for*ever*. How the heck did you do it?" I take catalogs from the guest chair, and indicate she should sit.

"I told him I'd buy him a TOP CHEF apron and one of those tall white cook hats."

"Wow, that's it? I'da thought—"

"And that I'd clean the grill, for two weeks in a row." Her lips pull back from her teeth in disgust. "And the deep fryer."

The two smelliest, greasiest, back-breakingest jobs in the kitchen. "Ugh. You took one for the team, there."

"Yeah, tell me about it. I ruined a pair of jeans last night."

"I know a couple of high school band kids who are trying to raise money to do a march-in at Disneyland in September. I'll get them to do it."

"No, I promised."

"Lorelei. I owe you big-time. This is the very least I can do." I hit the button to fire up the computer.

"Then I'm not going to argue." She leans forward and parks her elbows on the desk. "Now, tell me everything. You were awfully cryptic when you called to check in. Was it great? Did you run into Austin a bunch? What happened?"

"You may be sorry you asked." I check the clock. We've got a half hour before we open. I can trust Lorelei. And she needs to know. "Do you remember when we talked about going to the bar, after I broke up with Austin?"

Her brows draw together. "Yeah, but what's that got to do with your trip?"

"Only everything."

I give her the short version.

She grabs my hand when I wind down. "Jeez, Carly. I don't know what to say." She dabs at her eyes. "You thought you had a lot of drama before. And now . . . What are you going to tell your family? What are you going to tell the town? I mean you can hide it for a while, but not forever." Her gaze targets my not-quite-flat stomach.

I take a breath and remind myself this Carly needs to be courageous. "Well, I told you. That's a step, right? I'm talking to Nana and Papaw tonight. I haven't decided about the town, yet. I'm only tackling one thing at a time." I grab her hands. "But Lorelei, I'm going to have a *baby*." Joy bubbles up and I squeeze. "Do you know what a blessed miracle that is?"

She smiles back.

"Now, let's get it together. We've got hungry Unforgivians to feed."

The day flies by. Customers stop me every few minutes to chat, asking where I've been, how I'm doing, what Austin's up to. I tell them about riding the open road on my bike—the food truck and other distractions, so they don't notice I ignored their last question.

A month ago, their nosiness would have bothered me. Today, it feels like being neighborly. Well, except when Quad Reynolds asks me out. I let him down easy.

Before I'm ready for it, it's time to go home. I linger, cleaning the counters and stacking coffee setups, until Lorelei shoos me out.

Maybe I could take the long way home. Via Phoenix.

What if the old adage is wrong, and home *isn't* the place where, when you go there, they have to let you in? Losing Austin meant losing my future. I never considered I could lose more. My grandparents' respect means everything.

I've never given them reason to be disappointed in me. Well, there was that D in algebra. Austin tutored me after that, so there was never a repeat performance, but the memory of their faces is scratched on the basement wall of my brain.

And that disappointment is cookie-stealing compared to this.

As if sensing my mood shift, El Fartito slows. "Nope. I'm going home. For good or bad. This won't be really real until I tell them." I put my foot in it, and the engine whines a protest. "Yeah, me too, Bud. Me too."

The day that flew by slows. Dinner takes forever, and Nana wants to know why I just pick at my favorite meal. By the time I'm done washing dishes, Nana and Papaw are settled in the living room, glued to Pat and Vanna, and the spinning of that danged wheel is wearing through my last nerve.

My muscles are tight to the point of humming by the time I put down the dishtowel, walk to the living room, and snap off the wheel, mid-spin.

Papaw frowns. "Hey, I was fixin' to solve that puppy."

"I'm sorry, but I need to talk to you."

Nana pats the couch cushion beside her. "You've been like a mouse in a snake cage since you walked in the door. Come tell us."

I step to the couch, but sink down to the floor, pull up my knees, and wrap my arms around them. You know, in case I have to protect my guts. There's no way to ease into this. "I have to tell you something that... You're going to... First, I want to say ..."

"Spit it out, missy."

Papaw's gruff voice turns my words to ice cubes in my throat. I have instant brain-freeze.

Nana touches my shoulder. "Stop it, Leroy. Can't you see she's shaking like a leaf? What'sa matter, darlin'? You know you can tell us anything."

"I don't know if I can. I only know that I have to." I try to pull air into my locked lungs. "I'm going to have a baby."

Silence falls like an anvil.

I can see a muscle working through Papaw's silvered whiskers. "And why isn't that Davis boy here, asking for your hand?"

"It's not—" I inhale saliva. I choke, and for a few terrified seconds I'm afraid I'm going to pass out. Nana slams her fist into my back and surprise gets my lungs working again.

Papaw takes a step toward the mantel, for the double-barrel shottie that hangs above it.

I wanted to break the news easy, but only shock is going to get through his anger. "The baby is not Austin's." I saw a show once, about what happens to the balloons after the Macy's Thanksgiving parade. Like them, Papaw deflates, folds over, and drops onto the couch.

In the not-so-distant past, being pregnant with Austin's child would have been the worst scenario I could imagine. Now, it would be the best. "I wish it weren't true, but Austin isn't the father."

There it is. That dreaded disappointment. But this is much worse than an algebraic D. They're older. And aging as I watch. Nana's shoulders hunch, and the hand that reaches for Papaw's is shaking.

His angry eyes laser into me. "I think you'd better tell us what the Sam Hill is going on, missy."

"Nana, remember the weekend I went to Albuquerque to visit Paige, from high school?"

She nods.

"I didn't. I mean, I went to Albuquerque, but I rented a

hotel room." I'm determined to be as gentle as I can, but I'm not weaseling out of my own culpability. "No one took me seriously that Austin and I were broken up. I was frustrated. I was hurting. And I just wanted to get away from people who knew me so well. To be someone else, just for a night."

They sit, faces frozen in seriousness, looking like that painting of that farmer couple with the pitchfork. It hurts to hold their stares, but I owe them that.

"I went to a bar. I met a guy who'd broken up with his wife. I only wanted to talk. That's all he said he wanted." I bite down on my lip to make it stop wobbling. "But I was drinking, and…" I drop my head to avoid his gaze. The new Carly may be brave, but no one is brave enough to look their grandfather in the eye and tell him she…has needs. "The next thing I know, it's morning and he's gone."

"What?" Papaw jerks to his feet.

I hold up a hand. "Wait. Let me get it all out. Then you can…" I don't want to know what words come after that. I'm afraid to even think them, for fear they'll become real. "I had myself tested. I don't have any diseases."

Nana's hand covers her heart. Her skin is corpselike.

"But I am going to have a baby."

Papaw's butt hits the couch again. "Who is this…person? What does he have to say for him—"

"Leroy." Nana pats his hand. "Let the girl talk."

Papaw's jaw snaps closed. He's taken on all the color that drained from Nana; his face is flushed an unhealthy, dusky red.

"I don't know where he is." Hell, I don't know *who* he is, but brand me for a coward, I'm not telling my Papaw that. "I drove around for hours, trying to figure out how I could come home and face you." I sniff. "I finally convinced myself that I could put it behind me, and it would all just go away."

I wrap my arms around my waist, as if to keep Bean from hearing. "I thought about an abortion—"

Nana's gasp forces me to look up. Tears are sheeting down her face, and her mouth is open in a rictus of pain. "Nana...I'm sorry," I wail, and throw myself against her legs and wrap my arms around them. "I'm so, so, so sorry."

The pressure of her hand on the crown of my head soothes my pain enough to go on. "Y'all hadn't even planned on raising me. You should be relaxing and enjoying your retirement, not listening to a baby crying at two a.m." I force my shoulders down. Almost done. "I'll move into town. There's space for rent over The Civic—"

"You will not." Papaw's soft words are spoken hard. "You are our blood. A Beauchamp."

I feel like I can breathe for the first time since I walked in the door. Nana talks game, but Papaw is the one who makes the rules around here.

"You don't owe us nothing, missy." He's looking past me, his head moving side to side. "I always hoped you'd set up the diner to run on its own, then move on. Go to school. Do...whatever you wanted with your life. Pick out your own shoes and walk in 'em—not just step into your parents'." His gaze drops to me. His eyes are tired, world-weary, and sad. "Have you told Austin yet?"

"Yeah, I did. It didn't go well."

"Never mind. You will have this baby, and we will live as we always have. I'll hear no more about it." He stands and steps past me. "Come on in the kitchen. I'll make coffee, and we'll figure this out."

Nana watches him go, her eyes shining. "That's why I fell in love with that man."

Then she looks down at me. "C'm'ere, sugar."

I rise to my knees and have to stop myself from crawling

into her lap. Her arms come around me, and I drop my head to her shoulder. She pats my hair. "It's all gonna work out fine, Carly-girl. You'll see."

"Fine" is beyond my ability to imagine. But I'm so happy that my baby will get to know these amazing people who raised me. I have huge shoes to fill. I'll do my best to not look like a little girl, playing dress-up in Nana's heels.

CHAPTER 15

My reaction time is for shit. I should have never bucked off that last bull." A week later, I reach across the sticky table at The Pancake Palace to snag the syrup. "I've had slumps before. This feels different."

"Quit worrying. You'll ride your way out of it. You always do." Shane shovels in waffles smothered in peanut butter, jelly, and honey.

"God, you're giving me diabetes just watching you eat that."

"You should talk. You want me to have the waitress bring in an extra bucket of syrup?"

"Nah, I'm good."

He studies me as he chews. "Do you think it has something to do with you and Carly breaking up?"

Shane knows that Carly and I are done, but not the details. None of his business. And really, none of mine, anymore. "I don't know. Could be, I suppose." I take a mouthful of coffee to wash down the wad that's only part pancake. "All I know is, rodeoing is less fun, every week."

"Who are you?" He waves a broad hand in front of my face. "Alien? Walking Dead?"

I shrug. "I'm thinking about hanging this season up after this weekend." I can't bring myself to say—hell, think—that it'll be for good.

He stops, mid-chew. "Serious?"

"Well, I'm sure not winning, so it means I'm taking money out of savings to fund my riding. And that's back-asswards." Every dollar I take out proves Carly was right, telling me it's time to quit.

The truth is, I'm afraid it *is* time. It takes me twice as long to warm up before a ride, and way longer than that to heal. I'm the oldest guy in the bar, most nights. How could I not have noticed that?

But it's more than all those things. Rodeo has been my home for so long, and suddenly it's like I'm trying to squeeze myself into a little kid's chair—I just don't fit.

But rodeo is all I know. And with nothing and no one waiting anymore...I feel as lost as a maverick calf.

"So, what're you going to do, go home?"

"Yeah. Dad has been wanting me to take over so he can semi-retire."

He snorts a laugh. "Like your dad is ever going to retire."

"That's what I thought. But he and Mom are talking about wanting to travel: Grand Old Opry, San Francisco, even an Alaskan Cruise."

"Wow. Things are changing, huh?"

"Yeah, and you know how much I hate change."

"But going from the lights and the crowd, to Unforgiven..."
He mock-shudders. "I'm glad I'm younger'n you. When I do
decide to hang up the riggin', I'm not going back to that dead
burg. I want to go where there are some people."

My back hits the cushioned booth. It never occurred to
me to go anywhere else. "Where?"

"I don't know. Montana?"

"Oh yeah, because when you think population, Montana
is the first place that comes to mind."

"True. Maybe Colorado."

"All they got there's hippies, potheads, and Hollywood
types, playing rancher."

"You got a point. Luckily, I got time to think about it." He
takes a hit of his glass of milk. "But won't it be weird? Unforgiven is too small for you to not bump into Carly every
time you turn around."

"Tell me about it. Maybe I'll just become a hermit. A
modern-day mountain man."

"You'd look like crap in a beard. Besides, you like people."

"There's that." The rodeo may be the past, but all I see
of the future is endless days, following some shit-smeared
cow's butt. Forever.

Dang, Carly. Why couldn't you have just waited?

Truth hits like a wasp sting. I'm a total ass. She did wait.
Nine years' worth. Trying to hang on to something that was
over anyway, cost me everything.

I don't have to remember Carly's face; it's etched on the
back of my eyelids. Her rusty-red corkscrew hair that gets
into everything I own. Tawny freckles that make her look
like a naughty little girl. Those clear green eyes, looking into
me—seeing the person I always *meant* to be.

And so clearly, am not.

* * *

CARLY

I'm in my office at the diner the next day, sitting in front of my computer, trying to work out how to be a liar. After talking to Nana and Papaw last night, I've decided not to tell anyone about the baby until I can figure out how to do it and not hurt the diner. Or myself. It's not a secret that will keep for long, but I'll appreciate the reprieve for as long as I can get it. I need some drama downtime.

It's weird, going about my day, talking to people I've known all my life, knowing something they don't—something that will change how they see me. I'm ashamed of myself now, for privately looking down on girls who got in trouble in high school. Guess I bought into the stigma. The new Carly won't be as quick to judge; she's going to look deeper.

I thought this would be the best time of my life. I sure never expected to be doing this alone. I wonder how Austin's doing. Is he still mad? I force my mind from that worn track.

I smile as I type into the search bar: "bassinets."

Ten minutes later there's a knock on the door. I jump and turn off the screen. "Come in."

Lorelei sticks her head in. "Have you placed the order yet? We need some coffee filters, and Fish says he needs more dish detergent."

I wave her in. "I have it ready, but haven't placed it yet. Close the door behind you, will you? I need your opinion." I press the button, and the screen comes to life.

"Ohhhhh, cuteness!" She leans over my shoulder. "This is really happening, isn't it?"

"Yep. What do you think, yellow flowers or blue sheep bedding?"

She points. "Click on that Dory mobile. No, the one in the right corner."

There's a commotion from the dining room. Both our heads come up when a wavery, high-pitched voice cuts through the babble. Lorelei beats me to the door, but I'm right behind her when she pushes through to the diner.

Nana stands, fists on hips, in full cry. "Don't you flirt with me, you drunken rooster. You've been trying to get in my whities for decades. I'm married, and a *lady*, you douche-nugget."

Wobbling on a stool at the counter is Manny Stipple, wearing a bowl for a hat. Pea soup drips down his face to plop into his lap. Luckily, he is far enough into today's alcohol allotment that he just sits staring at Nana with bleary adoration.

Of course the diner is packed with an ogling early lunch crowd. My stomach drops.

Nana is in lecture mode, her pointer finger leading the way. "If Leroy was here, you'd be on your ass on the floor, and you know it. You Stipples never had a manner between you." She sniffs. "And, when *is* the last time you brushed your teeth?"

We'd forgotten to give Sassy, the new girl, "Nana training." If Lorelei had been here, she'd have sounded the alarm, and then headed Nana off at the door. I make it to Nana's side and grab an elbow. "Nana, what do you need?" I tighten my grip on her elbow and sidle for the door. She has no choice but to follow. I tip my head at Lorelei, hoping she knows it means to get Manny cleaned up, and a free lunch.

"What're you assholes staring at?" Nana's slightly fuzzy chin juts. Not much gets by her, and surely not a diner full of staring patrons. "If one of you had any upbringing at all, you'da helped a lady who's being accosted by a perv."

"Come on, Nana, let's get some air. Have you seen the new potato peelers at the dime store?" I push open the door and practically drag her out.

"Dickwads." She throws over her shoulder.

I don't relax until the door falls closed, and we've crossed the deserted street to the park, where I lower her onto a bench beside the cannon and release her. "What's up, Nana?"

She glances around to be sure we're alone, then takes my hands. "I couldn't go on and on around Leroy, but I wanted to tell you how excited I am that I'll live to see another Beauchamp generation."

Nana doesn't show love easy, but when she does, it's wide open. Gratitude rushes to my eyes. I have to blink it back. "It's sure not how I'd planned it, but I'm starting to actually get excited about a baby."

"I hate that you felt like you had to go through this alone." She pats my hand.

"Can I ask you something?"

"Child. After last night, I'd think you'd know you can talk to us about anything."

I'm not sure how to put my jumbled thoughts into words. "I had my life all planned out. I knew exactly what, and who, I wanted. When that fell apart, I was so torn up I didn't want to look ahead. Then, after...after Albuquerque, all I could do was think about getting through, day to day. When I did think about the future, I didn't see past when the baby will be born.

"Papaw got me thinking last night." I look at my sensible shoes. "But how could I even consider any new dreams? I have responsibilities. I'm going to have a baby. I've got the diner to run. What the heck would I do with a college degree, even if I could get one?"

"You're kidding, right?"

Nana's tone pulls my head up.

"It's not like when I was young. You girls nowadays can do anything you put your mind to, and if somebody doesn't like it, you can tell 'em to kiss your booty." She tips her head and squints up at me. "I'm just sorry you never asked us. You don't have to feel stuck. Hell, if you want to sell the diner, you just go ahead and do it. Your dreams can be whatever you want 'em to be, hon."

"You and Papaw were counting on me. I wasn't going to let you down. But the baby—"

"Hell, if you've got class, I'll take the baby to Bingo with me. Those old broads would love it. Don't you worry about that. You just decide what you want to be, then you go bust your ass gettin' it."

"I'd never sell the diner, Nana. But Lorelei has proved that she's more than capable of running it." Could I? Could I really? And if I could, what would I choose? I'm not sure. "God, you're a treasure, Nana."

"And I love you, too, darlin'." She sobers. "Are you sure it's over with you and Austin?"

"I'm sure. He loved me as much as he could, but it turned out to be only the parts he liked." And even if he could forgive me, the baby was a major part he didn't like. I sigh. "How did you manage to stay with Papaw all these years? He's a great guy, but you have to admit, he's not the most evolved man on the planet."

Her little eyes get a twinkly, far-away look. "Ah, he puts up with my failings, so I can't be too hard about his. The toughest is when you're young. You're busy working for what you want, and your focus is on what you don't have.

"But as you get older, all that crap fades. You see, under all that, friendship and companionship are what you always wanted. Spending your remaining years with someone who knows you better than you know yourself, you relax in their hands, knowing they'll be there for you. Forever."

"Guess you have to pick that kind of guy from the get-go." My heart gives a heavy thud of regret. I look down at Nana's hands, blue-veined and knobby, but strong and sure.

"Ah, hon, all men are pinheaded when they're young. Hormones may be a lot of fun, but they're not very damn smart. Don't count that Davis boy out yet, Carly-girl. Given enough time, he might figure it out." She pats my cheek, then pushes to her feet. "Now quit holdin' me up. I gotta get to the dime store and buy some yarn." She whispers, "I got some baby knittin' to do."

* * *

AUSTIN

A week after my decision at the Pancake Palace to quit the circuit, I pull up my parents' U-shaped drive and shut the truck down. I thought about going to my room over the store downtown, but nixed it fast. I'm not ready to face the rumpled sheets that Carly and I left, last time we were there. Besides, when you're hurting, you want family.

The house looks the same, a sprawling adobe box, painted the color of desert sand. Home. Maybe—probably—for good. I'm usually excited to come home to Unforgiven, but sitting here listening to the ticking engine, I realize a bunch of that excitement had to do with Carly. There's a hole; like a huge chunk of "home" has been ripped away.

My brother Troy's new BMW is parked next to the house. Great. And I'd hoped to relax.

I open the truck door and slide out, making sure my right boot hits first. The left throbs, courtesy of a clumsy bronc. I reach behind the seat and pull out my travel bag of clothes; the gear bag can wait. Maybe forever.

God, I'm tired. Everything hurts: my foot, my brain, my heart.

The door opens and Mom steps onto the concrete porch, wearing slacks and a blue blouse. As always, she looks like she's off to a country club for a game of bridge, even though we don't have a country club, and no one in Unforgiven plays bridge.

"We were about to send the dogs out hunting you. Where have you been?"

She steps into the sunshine, and the silver threads in her dark brown hair light up. When did that happen? I don't remember that from the last time I was here.

"You're limping. What happened now?" She sounds worried and weary all at the same time.

I smile, take a few steps, and wrap her in my arms. "Ah, it's nothing."

She squeezes my waist, then steps back. "You say that every time. Do you need to go to the clinic?"

I know she won't be at all sorry to hear I'm coming off the road. "Just bruised. It's nothing that rest and your chili won't fix." I tuck her under my arm and head for the house.

"You can smell it all the way out here?"

"Nah. You always make it when you know I'm coming."

"I'm that transparent, huh?"

"Nope. Steadfast." I kiss the top of her head. "Where's Dad?"

"In his office with your brother, grumbling over the tax assessor's bill."

When I step in the door I *can* smell the chili: rich and spicy. My mouth waters. "Cornbread, too?"

"You know it's illegal to serve chili without cornbread in this state." She pats my waist and lets me go. "Why don't you go tell them hello? Dinner's in fifteen."

Speaking of country clubs. My brother Troy is five years older—the successful-business one. The one with the money. He's a financial advisor in Albuquerque, married with two kids and a ranch house in a gated community. And of course, that country club membership. We're as alike as alligators and assholes. I have no doubt who the asshole is.

We traveled in different orbits growing up, and he was long gone to UNM by the time I hit high school. I skipped college for the rodeo. That's not to say we don't get along; it's just that we can't seem to hold up a conversation for more than two minutes. I walk the hall to the study.

"Dad, putting bucking stock on your land is a risky proposition. What you've been doing all these years has funded your retirement. Now's not the time for risk."

When I lean against the doorframe and clear my throat, Troy looks up. "Oh, don't let me stop you. As Dad's financial planner, you get a say. But just so you know, none of Dad and Mom's money is funding this 'risky venture.'"

"Welcome home, son." Dad stands and comes around his desk to shake my hand.

"Hey, Austin. No offense meant." Troy sits on the desk, his tie dangling from the pocket of his suit jacket and the top button of his shirt undone. That's as far as he unwinds.

I know he didn't mean it personally. Troy is all business, all the time. He always was intense, but his butthole has tightened considerably over the years. "None taken. But I think you ought to know the facts before you start throwing your opinion around."

"I've looked into it. You're looking at a good five years to prove out a good line of horses, much less bulls. Then there's the extra costs: stouter fencing, more bills, and a string of horses means a farrier, and—"

"And, they'll earn three times what beef cattle will. Not only the fees and payouts, but in semen and brood stock sales." I step into the room.

"And the added expense of trailers and trucks to haul them. Insurance, and—"

"Boys, if you're going to have a pissin' contest, take it out back. Let's have a drink, eh?" Dad opens the fridge below the bar behind his desk, pulls out two Lone Stars, and hands one to me, then pours a Dewar's for Troy, because my brother can't even drink a beer like normal folk. "Time enough for business later."

I pop the top and take a long pull, then sigh.

Dad tips his chin at my leg. "Did you get stepped on again?"

"Yeah, damned mud-fest arena."

Troy shakes his head. "You rodeo cowboys have a death wish."

"Nope. Just want to live while I'm still breathing."

He snorts a laugh and takes a sip. "There are other ways to live, brother."

"And I'm going to find out what they are."

They stare at me.

"What?"

Dad settles into his big leather chair. "This is where you say, 'Next year.'"

"Nope. Starting tomorrow."

"Seriously?"

"Yep. I'm your hired hand, if you still want me."

A huge grin spreads across his long face. "Hell yes, I want you."

"About time." Troy stops swinging his foot. "Now maybe Mom and Dad can finally retire."

"I'm in no hurry to retire," Dad says, but the grin hasn't dimmed.

"Dinner's ready." Mom's voice gets stronger as she comes down the hall. "Come on, before I feed it to the prairie dogs."

"Come in here, darlin'."

We all stand when she walks in the room.

Dad walks around the desk and claps me on the shoulder. "Austin is home. For good."

She spins to me. "For really, for good?"

The hope on her face makes my gut burn. Have they been waiting for this? How long have they put off retirement, so I could do what I want? "Yep."

She takes the few steps to hug me. "Home safe, for good. My prayers have been answered."

Troy raises his glass in a salute. "Better late than dead. Welcome home, brother."

Mom herds us to the dining room. There's a table in the kitchen, but she wouldn't dream of serving a dinner there. Even though it's just us, the table has a cloth and placemats and matching everything. Weird that I grew up here, and none of this stuff rubbed off on me. Troy sucked it all up first, I guess. He's welcome to it. I sit.

Mom brings in the tureen of chili and the cornbread and after Dad says grace, we dig in. Mom's chili is the best in town and she's got the county fair blue ribbons to prove it.

"Well"—Mom puts her cloth napkin in her lap and shoots me a smug smile—"I guess this means we'll be planning a wedding soon."

A gut bomb goes off that has nothing to do with jalapeños in the chili. I knew Mom would bring this up, but hoped it'd be one on one. I put down my spoon. "Um. No."

Troy pats his mouth with his napkin. "What'd you do now?"

Mom's face is all downturned lines. She can read me—she knows it's serious. "Oh, Austin. What happened?"

No one is hearing it from me. "Oh, you know me and my bronc-for-breakfast manners."

"She always forgives you, son." Dad reaches for more cornbread. "Carly is a sweet girl. She'll be back."

"Yes, she is, and no, she won't."

Mom pushes her plate aside. "Tell me what happened, Austin. Maybe I can help work this out."

I knew that wouldn't appease her. But I can't do this now—talk, or eat. "Thanks, Mom, but I just want to settle. Okay if I go do that?"

"You go on, son," Dad says.

I blow out of there before anyone can say anything else. I retrieve my bag from where I dropped it by the front door and head down the hall.

My old room is a time capsule of how great my life used to be. Rodeo posters on the wall, the one of Lane Frost, sticking it on Red Rock over my pine log bed that's covered in the quilt Carly made me for Christmas two years ago. The buckle display case, full of shiny silver. Worthless silver. How empty all those wins are, without someone to be proud, someone to share them with. Why didn't I realize that? All the excuses I made. All the years I wasted. All gone.

I know I'm going to have to move on. She made it clear that she's not my Carly anymore.

We used to be in lockstep. I could've told you her opinion on anything because, most often, we shared the same one.

But she's changed. Or, more likely from what she said the last time we talked, she's always had different opinions, and just kept them to herself. How was I supposed to know that?

I understand a woman's brain about like I do quantum physics.

The walls close in. No way I can sleep in this grave tonight. I shoulder my bag, open the door, and retrace my steps.

Mom is loading dishes in the dishwasher.

"I'm going to go to the homestead house. That okay with you?"

She turns, hands dripping water, her look dripping concern. "Oh, Austin."

"I'll tell you about it later, okay? I just need some time alone."

"I understand." She walks over and gives me a hug that makes me want to crawl in her lap like I'm two again.

I pull back. "I'll stop by. Soon." The weight of her worry follows me as I slam out the front door into the night.

I'm backing out when my lights hit Troy's fancy car, covered for the night. Normally, he's rushing to get home to Albuquerque. I wonder about it for a nanosecond, but I've got my own problems.

Ten minutes later I pull in the dirt yard. In the headlights, the old house looks even more haunted than my room at Mom's. I shouldn't be surprised; ghosts from your past aren't left behind that easily. I drag my duffel and sleeping bag up the steps and across the porch. When I open the door, I have the strangest feeling, like voices cut off mid-whisper. I skirt the middle of the parlor, where Carly and I made love the last time we were here. I glance to the stairs leading up. I know if I had a light, our footprints would be undisturbed in the dust.

I should have stayed in my old bedroom. At least the memories there aren't fresh wounds. I limp to the dining room and roll out my sleeping bag on the floor. We never made love in here.

Carly's known me for twenty-five years. How could I have been all that, for twenty-five years, and now I'm dog meat? Feels like she's grown away from me. Or past me?

Then there's the baby. If only it were ours, life would be so different. Funny how an unplanned pregnancy six months ago would have meant giving up so much. Now, it would be the only way for me to keep so much. Maybe it shouldn't matter who the father is. But it does. Deep down in my core, it matters.

So: I'm not enough for her, she's carrying someone else's baby, my rodeo career is over, and my dream of a rough-stock business, even if I decide to go through with it, may be nixed by my dad's financial planner.

How did life implode so fast? Or had it been on a long, slow slide, and I just refused to see it?

I kick out of my boots and clothes, then lay on my back and stare into the dark, listening to the whispers telling me I'm a fool.

CHAPTER 16

AUSTIN

My stomach wakes me with a growl, complaining about the bowl of chili I skipped last night. I roll over and groan. Another thing I'm too old for: sleeping on a hard wood floor. I struggle to my knees, and remember my bruised foot when I try to stand. "God*damn* that hurts." I hop around until it stops bitching.

Wishing for coffee, I glance to the funky old gas stove in the kitchen. I could probably get it to work if I cleaned out the lines. I add a store run to my list of things to do today, dress, and head for Mom's for food and coffee. When I pull in, Troy's BMW is still covered and in the same spot. That's odd.

I stand on the porch a moment, undecided. Knock? Ring

the bell? Walk in? What is the etiquette when you return to the house you grew up in? I'm not a kid anymore, but I'm not a guest, either. To cover my bases, I knock and open the front door. "Hello?"

"I'm in the kitchen, Austin."

Mom is sipping coffee and reading the paper at the kitchen table. "I'll bet it was musty and drafty over there."

"Yeah, but I figure if I'm living there, it'll give me incentive to get it weatherproofed by the time winter hits." Not her fault this house makes me feel like I walked into a happier-time-warp. "Why is Troy still here? Where's Dad?"

"They're out feeding cattle." She stands and walks to the fridge. "You must be starving. How about some bacon and eggs?"

"That'd be great." I give her a hug. "Have I told you lately how much I love your cooking?"

"Flattery will get you breakfast. Pour yourself some coffee."

"Yes'm." I like coffee in the morning, but I've never needed it for my existence, like Tig. *Stop.* If I'm going to move on, I've got to quit relating every everyday thing to a Carly memory. I grab my mug from the cupboard, the one with UNLIKE GOLF, BULL RIDING REQUIRES TWO BALLS, that Carly got me—*Stop.* I pour from the industrial-size coffeemaker on the counter. No Keurig here—it'd wear out in a few months. I lean against the counter and watch Mom work.

When the bacon is spitting in the pan, she wipes her hands on her apron and turns to me. "Hon, what happened?"

"I messed up." I pace from the island to the door and back. "Tig told me she wanted me to come off the road so many times I figured it was just our yearly fight, and went on with business." I run my hand through my hair. "I took for granted that she'd always be here, waiting. How can it be so clear you're an idiot after, and not before?"

"Oh, honey, y'all have been through this before. She loves you. It'll work out." She forks bacon out of the cast-iron skillet and cracks three eggs into the grease.

The fact that she dodged the Troy question reminds me that Mom can keep a secret. Besides, if you can't trust your mother, you might as well hang the trust thing up. Carly's secret has been eating me up inside. Maybe it'll help to let it out. Maybe Mom will have some woman insight. "It'll work out. Just not the way anyone expects."

She turns at my tone, the spatula in her hand dripping grease. "What is it? Just tell me."

"It's my fault, really. Don't you dare think bad of her for it—"

"Austin, I've known that girl almost as long as I've known you. You couldn't tell me anything that would make me think bad of Carly Beauchamp."

"No one took her seriously, that we were broken up. Not me, not the town. She took it for a month, then headed to Albuquerque, to blow off steam."

"Not alone?"

"Yeah." Insight hits in a starburst. "You know, it just occurred to me. She couldn't see it was dumb until it was too late. Just like me."

"This story is not going to end well, is it?" She's standing looking at me, and can't see the smoke signal of overdone eggs.

I step around her and flip off the burner. I'm starving, and what the hell—they'll only be black on the bottom. "You go sit. I'll be right behind you." I push them onto the plate with the bacon, then carry it and my coffee to the table.

"She's pregnant, Mom. With some other guy's baby." The

blunt-force fact smothers all sound, save the ticking of the clock in the kitchen.

She makes a strangled sound in her throat. "Does she love him?"

"The guy?" My hand fists on the tablecloth. "She doesn't even know who he is. Where he is. And she's not looking, anyway."

Her fingers feel their way to my fist and unravel it, then twine with mine. "Has she decided what she's going to do now?"

I can't look at her. "She's keeping the baby."

Her fingers tighten. "Good for her."

"I don't know how she can just forget who fathered that baby, and love it anyway."

"It's not who made it; it's an innocent soul, Austin."

I feel as small as a scorpion, and about as nasty, but I can't lie. I just shake my head.

Mom's fingers let go. "Austin Patrick Davis, surely if that girl can bear this, you can..." Her face falls to disappointed lines, and her hand retreats to her lap. "No, I can see that you don't get it, do you?"

"Even if I could get past the fact that she slept with someone else, what if the baby doesn't have red hair and freckles?" I look up. "What if it looks like him? The only thing worse than not stepping up would be to be resentful of an innocent child. To resent Carly. To turn the beautiful thing we had into a twisted, ugly freak show that we'd both be sorry for, then have to live with forever."

She sits a moment, thinking. I know that look. She's waffling between a lecture and a sales job. When she clasps her hands on the table, I know she's decided.

"You and Troy are grown men. It's hard for me to accept that I can't paddle your butts and send you to the corner to think about your actions." Her knuckles go white. "But you make me want to go cut a switch, I swear to God." Her eyes narrow. "All this time, I thought you really loved that girl. Now it's clear that you're not capable. And that makes me so sad."

That dart hits, and the poison that spreads under my skin feels familiar. "There's more problems than that, Mom. Carly's changed."

"Well, of course she has. A baby changes everything."

"Her and me, we used to be two halves of one whole. Now, I don't know what is going on under all that hair." I give up trying to be all mature, and drop my head in my hands. "She doesn't want anything to do with me." Except sex, apparently. This isn't helping. It feels like fire ants are crawling under my skin. I can't do this anymore. I stand. "I gotta go, Mom."

Her voice follows me out the door. "What about your eggs?"

Remembering a bag of jerky leftover from the drive home, I retrieve it from the floorboard of my truck and chew it as I head for the barn behind the house.

The barn is cool, shady, and full of the smells of my childhood: hay and horses, manure and leather. I find Dad spreading fresh straw in a stall.

I step into the stall and hold out my hand. "Give me that. Why are you doing the scut work?"

"I'm not too good, or too old to be taking care of the animals." But he hands it over. His shoulders started sloping a couple years ago. They're now downright stooped, his hands gnarled, the knuckles swollen with arthritis from a lifetime of hard work out in the open.

"No, but I'd say you've put your time in." I take the fork and start spreading straw. "Where's Troy?"

He glances out the breezeway, past the paddock, to the golden plain beyond. "He went for a ride."

"What's up with him, anyway? He usually blows back to the big city before someone asks him to get his hands dirty." I move to the next stall.

"Ah, don't be too hard on your brother. He's hit a rough patch." He follows and puts his boot on the lowest stall slat.

I break up a flake of straw from the bale on the floor and shake it into the corners. "What kind of trouble?"

Dad avoids my look. "He's bedding down with us for a while."

"Trouble at home?"

Dad moves the toothpick he's working to the other side of his mouth.

"Whoa." Troy and Darcy always went together like diamonds and platinum. Darcy is an Adriano, and the Adrianos were as close as New Mexico gets to royalty. Their ranch covers over a hundred thousand acres, thanks to what's rumored to be a shady land grant back when we were still a territory.

Another unshakable relationship bites the dust.

"A lot of that going around lately."

"What?" Dad asks.

"Nothing, just talking to myself."

Dad heads back to the house, and his breakfast. I finish with the stalls and saddle my old buddy, Cochise. I got him as a colt for Christmas my freshman year of high school. The name came natural, since he's a black-and-white paint, and because I watched *way* too many *Bonanza* reruns as a kid. Troy's mare, Smooth, is missing from the paddock.

I tie some wire to the saddle skirt, put the pliers and stretcher in the saddlebag, and a ten-minute lope later, I spot them in the far end of the farthest corner of our land. Even out here, he's immaculate: creased jeans, white broadcloth shirt, clean straw hat, and spanking-new ostrich boots. He looks like he stepped off the cover of *Western Horseman.* If I had a doubt Troy was avoiding me, his pinched face would have killed it.

"What do you want?"

"I need a reason?"

"Nah, I guess not."

I pull Cochise alongside and fall to a walk. A hawk's piercing hunting cry, the swish of grass, and the jingle of bits are the only sounds. Troy and I aren't real close, but we never had a problem talking before. "Peaceful out here, huh?"

"Yeah." He keeps his gaze between his horse's ears.

We continue in awkward silence until I pull to a stop at a place in the fence where the wire's bent over and trampled down. "Goddamn bulls are assholes."

Troy stops his horse and leans his forearms on the horn. "Nah. Just horny."

I step down and untie the wire from the saddle. "What, you gonna sit and watch?" I pull the leather gloves from my back pocket.

He puts out his hands, palms out. "No gloves."

"Pussy." I reach into the saddlebag and toss him a pair.

"I didn't come out here to be a hired hand."

"You'd rather leave it for Dad to do?"

That gets him moving. In no time, his new boots are grass-stained and we're both sweating.

"Here, hold this." I hand him the one side of broken wire, while I lock the crimper on the other piece. "Why are you out here, anyway? Why aren't you in Albuquerque?"

"Why are you baching it in the homestead house?" He hands over the wire.

The stretcher clicks, pulling the wire taut. "It's easier if you use the pliers, instead of your hands to make a loop."

"You always were a girl. Shit!" I pull off the glove and suck the puncture in my thumb.

"Told you."

"Yeah, you always were a know-it-all, too."

"What's that supposed to mean?"

I put the glove back on and give the wire another twist. "Why are you telling Dad it's not smart to run some bucking stock?"

"Because it's not."

"You don't know what you're talking about."

"It's what I do for a living, Austin. It's not a smart business move." He grunts, and pulls the stretcher one more click.

One click too far. Barbed wire whistles past my ear, and the stretcher falls on my knuckles. "Son of a bitch!" I shake my hand and sit back on my heels. I pull the glove, and touch my earlobe. My fingers come away bloody. "You trying to take me out?"

"Serves you right." His growl comes from between clenched teeth.

"Why the hell are *you* mad? I'm the injured party here."

He throws his hands up. "If I'd wanted to be a cowboy, I wouldn't have gone to college. I don't *belong* here, damn it."

"Oh, I see, as always, you're the smart one, and I'm a grunt for using my hands to actually work for a living."

"It's always about Austin, isn't it? The whole world doesn't revolve around you and your rodeo-star life. I was talking about me." He steps to his horse and retrieves the reins. "See you later, little brother. I've got real work to do." He mounts and lopes off.

Forgetting my glove, I grab the stretcher and a barb digs

the length of my forearm. God*damn* city boy. I yell after him, "You're not good at *that* job, either."

* * *

CARLY

I'm on refill patrol Wednesday morning when Austin comes through the door. He's limping, his clothes are wrinkled, and his face is set in the kind of tired that sleep doesn't fix. He looks like a train wreck. That magnetic pull tugs, and my heart pumps sympathy. I set the pitcher of coffee on the table so as not to drop it.

The breakfast crowd goes silent, like there's going to be a shootout or something.

"Carly." He takes off his hat and holds it at his side. "Could I talk to you for a second?" He looks around, meeting the stare of every mother's son in the place—the daughters, too. "Alone?"

When that last word wobbles just a bit, I know what it took him to walk through that door.

"Of course." I pat the high-schooler closest to me on the shoulder. "Patsy, make the rounds for me, will you? I'll just be a minute."

Eyes big, she nods and stands.

I tip my chin to the door. He follows me and opens it. Dang railway station is just a big glass fishbowl, with windows all around. The diners even look like goldfish, with their eyes bugging and their mouths opening and closing with gossip. I keep walking, but not too far. I don't want people to think...whatever they're going to think. I duck down the alley past the dime store, turn, and wait to hear what was important enough for Austin to run the breakfast crowd gauntlet.

"I wanted to let you know, I'm home for good. Well, not home, exactly. I'm staying at the homestead house. I'll be fixing it up while I settle in, working for Dad and looking around for some good cows to have inseminated, and..." His blush shoots up from the collar of his shirt.

"Sorry, didn't mean to blurt. I guess I'm kinda weirded out about all this."

"Tell me about it."

"I am telling you." Our old joke brings only a weak smile to his lips. "Look, the way I figure it, the only way for people to stop staring when we're in the same room together is if we're okay *being* in the same room together. Eventually, they'll move on to juicier gossip."

My hand steals to cover my apron-covered pooch. "Yeah, I've got an idea about what that'll be."

His blush gets a mottled red tinge. "Aw, hell, Carly. I didn't think. I'm sorry."

"Stop it. Now you're making me nervous." I take his arm and shake it. When his rock-hard bicep jumps under my hand, I drop it. "We've been friends since we were getting sand in our diapers. Surely we can get past this...awkward stage."

We look at each other, separated by a wall of words that we can't say. "We'll act normal, and someday, it'll *be* normal." My brain whispers a bad word about cattle by-products. I ignore it, and extend my hand.

He steps in and gives me an awkward man-hug, complete with patting my back. Air rushes out of him in a huge sigh. "Oh, good. Because I really don't want to eat grease down at the Lunch Box."

"Why didn't you go to your mom's?"

"I'm a little old to be parking my boots under Mom's table every meal." He lowers his head to watch his fingers work the brim of his hat. "Discovered I'm too old for a lot of things, lately."

It sounds like I'm not the only one doing some deep soul-excavation lately. I knew he had come off the road, of course. Gossips were more than happy to impart that juicy tidbit.

Isn't it funny how the mind works? It shields you from the hardest lessons, giving you time to get ready for the truth's ultimate blow. Looking back, I can see that pushing him to come home all these years, and our eventual breakup, was me, testing a theory my brain hadn't fully let me in on yet.

That what he wanted would always come first. And I followed along, because that's what I always do. I hoped he loved me, like I love him. Even now, I can't hate him for it—he isn't withholding it from me—he's just incapable of that kind of love. But now that I know the difference, I realize I'm not willing to settle for anything less than the all-out, love-you-down-to-the-nasty-parts, kind. I push my lips into what I hope is a smile, but probably isn't. "I'm happy for you, Austin, truly. I hope you're a huge success."

He glances around. "Well, prob'ly be best if we walk in together, huh?"

I act like I don't see his arm hanging out, waiting for me to take it. One thing to wish him well—another to take a step down a dead-end road that I've been down before. There're enough mistakes to be made, without going back and making the same ones over again. I'm going to be a parent. I need to be responsible.

I won't have much face to save soon, anyway. I follow him out of the alley.

We walk into the diner. Austin heads for a seat at the counter, and I snag the coffee pot from Patsy.

The room is in freeze-frame—no kidding—forks have stopped halfway to open mouths. "Just so you know? Austin and I may inhabit the same room, breathe the same oxygen, maybe even—ohmygod—exchange a pleasantry now and again. Y'all are going to have to get over yourselves."

It's quiet enough that I can hear Fish chuckle in the kitchen.

I put a hand on my hip. "People, deal." My words bounce off the windows.

Tentative conversations start up, and I nod to Austin and resume refill patrol.

It'd be humorous if I didn't know the next boom to hit. Our breakup is a firecracker compared to the Surface-to-Air Missile of my not-Austin's baby. How long can I keep the secret? Three weeks? Surely not much more than a month. I'm going to have to figure out how to handle that.

I steal a glance over at the bar. He needs a haircut. I used to love trimming it: running my fingers through the clean, wet strands. There's just something so personal about that. So sexy. *Stop it, Carly.*

Guess he'll have to head down to the Pit Stop Barbershop from now on.

CHAPTER 17

CARLY

Carly Beauchamp, you little brat, you've been home for three weeks. When were you going to call me?" My best friend, Jess, stands in the middle of the aisle of O'Grady's, one hand on her cart handle, the other on her hip. I know every shade of her expressions, and the wrinkles in her seashell-pink lipstick tell me she's put out.

One more thing to feel guilty about; I've been avoiding her. And my whole high school posse. "Dang, Jess, you're in maternity tops already?" I stop my cart beside her.

She's wearing leggings, a blousy top, and blingy sandals. "Don't you change the subject." She points a dragon-red nail at me. "You owe me all the poop, and you're going to give it, right now."

"Jeez, Jess, right here in the aisle?"

"Ha, ha. I'm serious." She gives my basket a stern look. "You got ice cream in there?"

"No, but—"

"Then follow me." She marches down the aisle, heading for the deli section, where there are tables for those wanting a quick sandwich.

"Make mine iced tea, will you?"

"No coffee?" She arches a threaded brow. "I think I just felt the earth move. If you'd have asked for decaf, I'd be really worried."

I thought about calling Jess, more than once. But something held me back. When she fishes money from her wallet, her wedding ring flashes in the lights, and I suddenly understand why. She and I have more in common than she knows, but instead of feeling closer, I feel like there's a wall ten feet high between us, tagged all over with "*unmarried*" in spray paint.

I park my basket beside a table, then go back for hers. By the time I sit, she's there with drinks. She slides in the other side and squints at me. "You look different. What's going on?"

My stomach clenches. I may not have been sure before, but I know now, down to the ground—I'm not telling her about the baby. It's not that I worry she'd tell; she wouldn't. Not on purpose, anyway. It's not that I'd think she'd judge; she wouldn't.

It's that Jess is living the life I'd planned. The life we'd all planned, back in high school. I'm now on a different path.

And if I'm having this much of a problem telling Jess, how in happy hell am I going to tell the whole town? There's something that's been bothering me like a sticker in my sock, poke-poke-poking me. Maybe this isn't about what the town will think about me. It's about what I think of myself. Am I hanging on to the town sweetheart title because I want to go back to the old Carly?

No. Not the bad parts, anyway. I don't want to be the stereotypical country girl, up on the seat of a cowboy's truck. I have my own opinions, my own beliefs.

But Austin didn't force me into that role; he never knew it was a role—because I never told him. I'm going to need to spend some time thinking about that.

But right now, Jess is waiting for an answer. I know when she finds out about the baby, she'll see my holding back as a betrayal. And, God knows, I could use a friend. I open my mouth to try to push out the words, then close it when I realize the words wouldn't get through that wall. It just doesn't feel right. "I'm sorry I didn't call, Jess. I've been running like crazy, trying to catch up at the diner."

"I hear Austin is coming in for breakfast some days. How weird is that?" She takes a sip of coffee.

"Not too bad, actually. We talked, and decided the town was too small for us not to be in the same room together." I hold up a hand. "Do. Not. Say. It." Jess was on team "Austin forever."

She sets her cup down. "Okay then, I want to hear all about your trip. Every single detail. Was it fun, being on the circuit again? Did you run into Austin there, too? What was it like, riding the motorcycle? Dish, Carly. I'm living vicariously here."

"Why? Your life looks pretty exciting from where I'm sitting."

She pats her six-month belly. "Hon, trust me. By your third baby, the excitement has worn off. I just got Caleb out of diapers, and now I get to start all over." She blows her bangs off her forehead.

"But being married must be great." I sigh.

She rolls her eyes. "Just more underwear to wash. Don't get me wrong. I love the man to death. I do. But it's bad enough picking up after kids all day. If I have to pick up one more wet towel of his, I'm heading for the knife drawer, I swear to God."

I don't know what my face looks like, but it makes her laugh. "Carly, that is married life. You have brief flashes of greatness, long stretches of everyday, and the occasional knock-down-drag-out."

I don't want to believe that would have happened to Austin and me (my dream Austin—not the real one). Maybe I've been unrealistic all these years. But especially now, the grass looks greener on the married side of the fence.

"I'm telling you, Carly, motherhood can drive you to an early grave. The diapers, the whining, the clean-ups. The constant *neediness* of kids. Do you know I haven't had a private trip to the bathroom in seven years?"

She leans in, a glint in her eye. "But enough of my boring life. Tell me *everything*."

I tell her, embellishing the motorcycling and the fun parts, skipping the Austin-in-the-truck details.

After a half hour, I tell her Nana's waiting for her groceries and we part, her to the cashier, me back to the shopping. I stop in the cereal aisle, trying to decide between the real Nutty Buddies or the generic.

Jess makes motherhood sound like indentured servitude… and she has a husband to help. Did I make the right decision? What if I get six months into being a mom, and I flat-out can't handle it? Yeah, there's Nana and Papaw, but they're elderly. I can't expect them to—I freeze. Something's happened. Something between a twitch and a butterfly brush below my stomach. What the…I put my hand there, but nothing else happens.

My heart fills first, then my eyes.

Is that you, Bean?

My jitters melt away. I don't care how hard motherhood is. I can't wait to see my baby. The world settles on its axis, and I know down to my soul that I've made the right decision.

You and me, kid.

* * *

AUSTIN

I take one last look around my old bedroom. Sad that it only took two trips to the truck to pull out anything I'll want at the homestead house. But what's left hurts too much to have it underfoot: Carly's Rodeo Queen sash, photos, tickets to the movies, school yearbooks. I look down at the shoebox of winner's buckles on my bed. I know where they are, if I need them. Better to focus on making a future than to haul around the past. I turn off the light and head out.

A chair squeaks in the office as I pass. Troy is tapping away at a laptop. "All you do is work."

He leans back in the chair and puts his hands behind his head and stretches. "You sound like my wife. I've still got to take care of business."

"Whatever you say. Where's Mom and Dad?"

"They went into town."

He looks pathetic. Sleep-deprived and ragged around the edges. "Can you take a break? I could use some help."

He frowns. "Does it involve wire stretchers?"

"Are you kidding? I'm not letting you anywhere near a potential weapon. Follow me."

"Where are we going?"

I don't answer until we're buckled in my truck and up to speed. "To move my stuff out of my apartment in town."

"Shit. More grunt work." He leans his arm on the open window. "Now I remember why I left this place. Nothing but grunt work."

"Just doing my part to turn you into a man, brother."

"What's that supposed to mean? If I'm not a hair-on-fire bronc rider, I've got no balls?"

"Just saying."

He reaches over and slaps the back of my head. "Just because some of us were born with a brain bigger than a walnut, isn't any reason to be jealous."

I pull onto the town square.

"I do kinda miss this funky town." He points. "Remember when we got banned from the Civic for putting horny toads under the girl's seats at the Saturday matinee?"

"It was worth it to see the girls scream." Carly hadn't, though. She'd gathered as many as she could, to keep them from getting trampled in the stampede. I take the turn and cruise past the Chestnut Creek Café.

Troy checks it out. "Weird to think that you guys are broken up. So used to seeing you together."

"Weird on this side, too." My heart squeezes to a small hard fist. That has to stop happening sometime, doesn't it?

"You going to start dating someone else?"

I can't imagine it. "Someday." I turn right off the square, and down the alley behind the shops. "Here we are."

Troy eyes the old wooden stairs that lead to the apartment over the store. "You didn't tell me it was on the second floor."

I turn off the ignition, turn to him, and wink. "Not bad for a walnut brain, huh?"

We grab empty boxes from the truck bed, and he grumbles all the way up the stairs.

When I open the door, I catch a tiny hint of her perfume, then it's gone. The big room has always held only the basics: an end table, card table, and chairs. And a bed. The rumpled sheets lay where we kicked them off, the last time we were here. The vise in my chest ratchets down. Wish I could step back in time. I'da done things so different.

"How the hell are we going to get that bed down the stairs?"

"Same way it came up." I slap him on the shoulder. "Cheer up, this time we'll have gravity on our side."

He shakes his head. "I'll start in the kitchen."

Might as well do the hard part first. I peel a trash bag off the roll, step to the bed, and hold my breath while I tear the sheets off. If I reacted to stale perfume, the smell of these sheets would probably take me to my knees. I dump them in the trash bag, pull the drawstring closed, and toss the bag to the door. The rest should be less lethal.

In an hour, everything is loaded in the back of the pickup and we're on our way out of town. I wouldn't trade my past for anything, but that's gone now. It's time to buckle down and get to work on the rest of my life.

I've looked around, but rodeoing isn't great experience for many jobs that pay more than chasing cows. And I don't want to work under some other man's thumb, if I can help it.

Hey, I have a financial expert riding shotgun. I've got nothing to lose but a little pride, and if I don't like his advice, I can always ignore it. "Why do you say I shouldn't go into the rough-stock business?"

"I never said you shouldn't. I said *Dad* shouldn't."

"Why not?"

"Dad's at retirement age. That's not a time to take risks.

He needs to be in low-interest, low-risk investments." He glances at me. "The time for taking risks is when you're your age."

The clouds of worry that have been sitting on my head lighten a bit. "No one better at risk than a rough-stock rider."

"Yeah, you've got the opposite problem. You can't just jump in. You have to consider the risk, and put thresholds into place to minimize it."

"Okay, so tell me."

We talk business until I pull into the dooryard of the homestead house, questions and ideas dancing in my head.

Troy steps out of the truck, grabs a box from the bed, and looks up at the porch. "I've always loved this old house."

"It's going to be even better when I'm done with it." I pull out another box and head for the stairs.

"What are you planning?"

We walk inside. "Put that down and I'll show you." I take him on a tour, pointing out what I'll refurbish, and what gets replaced entirely. I end in the kitchen. "This room has to be totally gutted. Old-fashioned may be in, until you try to cook on fifty-year-old appliances. I'm going to sell this stuff to an antique dealer. They've got some great stuff out there now, like a kitchen faucet that looks like an old hand pump, hammered copper sinks, stuff like that."

Troy leans in the doorway. "This all sounds great, but it's going to cost a fortune."

"I'm going to do the work I can myself, to save money. I've got nothing but time."

He looks around the room. "You know, Mom and Dad are great to put me up, but Mom tiptoes around with a worried look, like I'm a hand grenade without the pin. Dad tries to act normal around me, but can't, quite."

"Totally get that. Part of the reason I moved out."

"How about I move out here, with you?"

I'm beyond surprised. First, I figured his banishment was short-term—like a week, short. Second, he's not exactly the "roughing it" type. Both of which show me that I'm not the only "lost boy" in the Davis clan. "What the hell happened between you and Darcy?"

He walks over and, hands in pockets, stares out the window over the sink for a minute. Probably deciding if he can trust me far enough to tell me. He doesn't turn. "It started out about the kids."

Their two kids, Natalia and Nate, are six and eight. Or wait, is it seven and nine? I see them only a couple times a year, so it's hard to keep track.

"You know Nate's always been crazy for the rodeo." He shoots me a laser glare. "Which I totally blame you for."

"Me? He's never even seen me ride."

"Tell me. He bugs the crap out of me to take him. He follows your rodeos on the internet. And you did buy him a rope and that roping dummy, last birthday."

A coal of pride warms my chest. "Well, what's wrong with him doing a little mutton-busting? There's worse things."

"Not according to Darcy. If she had her way, his school uniform would be made of bubble wrap."

Yeah, I forgot. Public schools aren't good enough for Darcy's kids.

He shrugs. "But really, it's more than that. The crack opened between us a long time ago, but I didn't see it until I fell smack into it."

"Y'all always looked like the perfect couple from the outside."

"So did you and Carly."

"Ah, tit for tat."

"Yeah, and it's your turn." He crosses his arms.

I feel like we're crossing something else, here. The gulf between us, maybe. Well, looks like we're going to share the same doghouse, so I tell him. Not the pregnant part. I give him the important part. "She got tired of waiting. She dumped me. Forever."

"Ah, bullshit. She'll be back."

"See? That's where everyone was wrong. Especially me." I shake my head. "Stupidity cost the best thing that ever happened to me."

He gives me the side-eye. "Why not go prostrate yourself? Grovel? Beg for forgiveness? Carly's a good-hearted girl. She'll give you another chance."

"It's more complicated than that. She's changed. Seems like neither of us have any more chances to give."

"So, she finally realized what I always knew. You're a cur dog."

I glance over. "You'd better smile when you say that."

"I'm as out of smiles as Carly is chances." A muscle works in his jaw. "So how about me moving in?"

I want to know more about him and Darcy, and about how long he's banished for, but I've pushed enough. For now. "Well, I don't know." I hike my butt onto the counter. "How about some bartering?"

When his eyes narrow, I know he's remembering when I traded him my BB gun for his arrowhead collection. I forgot to tell him the seals were cracked. "What?"

"You help me write a plan for my business, and you can have the master bedroom." No way I could stay in that room anyway. That was going to be Tig's and my bedroom.

He thinks a minute, looking for a catch. "You throw in Wi-Fi, and you've got a deal."

"And I might need your help with some of the repairs around here."

"You always were a negotiator. Maybe you'll make a good horse trader yet."

We meet in the middle of the room and shake on it. "Now, let's get the rest of this stuff unpacked."

He raises his hands. "Not part of the deal, bro."

I shrug. "Your choice. Walk three miles to the house, or help me, then we'll go get your stuff."

He sighs. "Told you. Unforgiven is nothing but grunt work."

* * *

CARLY

I swipe curls and a drip of sweat out of my eye, then go back to flipping burgers. Fish took the afternoon off to testify for a friend in a custody battle. The other cook doesn't come in until three, so I'm it for the lunch hour rush.

Business has been better than usual. My guess is that Dusty Banks, down at the Lunch Box Café, raised his prices again. I just hope our business doesn't fall off with my news.

"Table six said their french fries were cold." Lorelei pushes a plate of fries through the window.

"Crap, fries!" I pull up the fryer basket, and hot grease spatters my hand. A little dark, but they'll have to do. I throw salt on them and leave them to drain. I reach under the counter and lift the five-gallon jar of hamburger dill chips to refill that bin.

"Order up." Sassy stuffs a ticket on the crowded wheel.

"Buggers in a basket, I'll never catch up," I mutter.

"Scoot over." A deep voice comes from behind me.

I turn to see Danny Jorgensen, my wholesaler, pulling an apron over his head.

"Get out. I can't let you help. It's against my insurance codicils."

He bumps my hip with his. Actually, his hip hits my waist. He's a huge Swede, with blue eyes and white-blond hair. He would look at home behind a horse-drawn plow in Wisconsin. "You can tell them I overpowered you. Go on, read the orders to me."

"You know how to cook?"

"I know how to sew buttons on, clean house, and change a diaper. My mother believed that a man needed to be able to do anything."

"Wow. A unicorn." I want to argue, but I'm too tired. I have a hard time getting through a normal day, much less an on-your-feet/stressed-out/grease-fest like this one. "You are an angel, Danny. I owe you a huge order."

"You're going to need one, at this rate." He drops a basket of onion rings, then preps the plates like a pro, and slides burgers onto the buns.

I carry them to the window, dump the cold fries, and hand Lorelei a fresh plate of them.

She eyes it. "Well, they're hot, anyway." She slides all the plates onto a tray, then tips her head at Danny, and mouths *He wants to ask you out* and swishes away.

I glare at her back and start reading off orders.

I've only been out with one guy in my life, and that was a natural progression...Do I *want* to go out with Danny? With anyone? I can't imagine it. But I've got to find a way to ease into my future somehow. Not to get involved—I don't see that happening—but to go out on a date. It would be a start.

An hour later, the order wheel is almost empty, and I swear we've fed two-thirds of the town. "Okay, Jorgensen, you're fired." I turn, and he's right there, smiling, a plate of fish and chips in his hand.

"Here. And don't tell me you already ate, because I know it'd be a lie."

I can feel my ears get hot. Am I that transparent?

He looks down at me. "You look pale. Why don't you sit down to eat that?"

"Only if you let me fix you something. Even angels have to eat sometime."

He steps to the grill and lifts a plate full of triple cheeseburger, with fries falling off the edge. "Already did."

I put my head through the window. Lorelei is chatting with April Hollister, who works at the drugstore. "Hey, Lorelei, will you hold the fort for ten, so I can eat?"

She winks. "You take all the time you want, Carly."

I shoot her a laser glare, then lead Danny to my office. His shoulders barely fit through the door, and the chair disappears beneath him. He balances his plate on his knee until I clear a spot on my desk. "Sorry."

"No need to be sorry."

His gaze lands on me and sticks. I hold myself still, though inside, I'm squirming like a kid who needs to go to the bathroom. I know male interest when I see it.

I push another pile of paper to the side so I can put down my plate. "Thanks so much for helping. Seriously. I was in trouble."

"It was my pleasure. It's not often I get to rescue a damsel in distress."

That rankles. I was in a bind but I'm hardly the distressed damsel type. "Eat. You earned it." Finally, his tractor-beam gaze slides away, and I can move.

There's no room in here. There's no air. He takes it all up.

We eat in silence for a few.

He pats his mouth with his napkin, a prissy move for such a big man. "I wondered if you'd like to go to the movies with me one night. Either at the Civic, or in Albuquerque."

Danny's a good guy. He's polite, makes a good living, and is good-looking. Then there's Bean. It's going to need a daddy.

God, am I that calculating? That cold, looking at a guy for what he can offer me? No. I get to decide who I'm to become. If I go out on a date, it'll be because I'm interested in a man. I can recite all the reasons why I should be interested, but the fact is, right or wrong, I'm not ready.

"I'm sorry, Danny. I'm—"

"Not over Austin." He shakes his head.

"Oh, I'm over Austin. I'm just not ready to date yet." Until my secret is out, Bean has made dating a bit…sticky.

His white-blond eyebrows furrow. "I get that. But I reserve the right to ask again, later."

"Fair enough." I dip a forkful of fish in my tartar sauce. "Friends?"

He smiles at me. "For now."

I smile back. Maybe, given enough perspective, I can be fair to him, myself, and my baby. After all, my dreams haven't changed: a man I love in bed beside me every night, our kids sleeping down the hall. All I need to do is find the guy who matches the picture in my head.

It'd be easier if that picture still didn't look a lot like Austin.

CHAPTER 18

AUSTIN

Two weeks after Troy's moved in, I walk into the dining room to find him, laptop perched on the card table, working. "Shit. Do you ever do anything else?"

He doesn't even look up. "I seem to remember spending half the day tearing out walls upstairs."

"Yeah, but every other waking minute you're on that computer." I pull out a chair and settle carefully. They're kind of spindly. "No wonder Darcy—"

"Don't say it." He holds a hand in front of my face. "You've been ragging at me about my work since I moved in. I'm sick of it. And my wife is none of your business, either, so fuck off." Though he hasn't taken his eyes off the computer screen, his face is red and scrunched up like a little kid, fixing to pitch a fit.

"Hey, I'm trying to help you."

"Well, you're not helping. Why don't you focus on your own pathetic self?"

"At least I'm trying to move on, instead of hiding out with my head buried in work."

"Seriously?" He looks at me over his reading glasses. "How are you moving on?"

"I'm working on the house. We're going to get a plan together for the business."

"There's a great future. Living by yourself in the middle of Nowhere, New Mexico, with a bunch of animals for company." He lifts a thumb. "Score, bro."

I reach over and slam the laptop closed.

He jerks his mushed fingers out. "What the—"

"Okay, so we're both pathetic. Question is, what are we going to do about it?"

"If I knew that, I wouldn't be bunking with your sorry ass."

"So, why are you?" But after living with him for two weeks, I know. "Darcy threw you out because you work all the time, didn't she?"

He flinches, and I know I've hit a bull's-eye.

"Hey, I've built a successful business here. I'm managing a combined portfolio of tens of millions of dollars. I've got to be up on the latest in the stock market, the bond market, trends in gold, and economic forecasts. I've got to be available for my clients." His tone is even, but his coloring isn't.

"Why?"

"What do you mean, why? Aren't you listening? I've got to make a living."

"Why? I mean, Darcy's rich in her own right."

His face gets redder. "So, I should just mooch off my wife's money? Is that what you're saying?" He's out of his chair.

I hold up my hands in truce. "I remember wondering, when you two started dating, how you had the guts to ask her out. I mean, we never wanted for anything, but our family isn't in their league. Did any of them look down on you?"

His eyes slide away. "Nothing blatant. You know, whispers that stop when you come in the room, stuff like that." He drops back into the chair. "Her dad had a 'talk' with me, when I asked for his permission to marry Darcy."

"You have more guts than me."

We sit for a minute in silence.

"Relationships are only easy on Netflix."

"Yeah, unless it's *House*, or *Six Feet Under*, or *House of Cards*, or..."

"Maybe relationships just aren't easy."

"Mine used to be."

He snorts. "Sorry, but that's because you were the big man, and she followed you around like a puppy."

That stings. "How the hell would you know? You're never around."

"Doesn't take long to see. Sounds like Carly grew up, and wanted equal billing." He studies my face, and nods to himself. "Good for her."

"You know what?" I stand, and the chair falls behind me. "I've had enough armchair analyzing for one day."

"Hey, you started it."

"Well, I'm finishing it." I slam out of the house.

Troy may be full of shit, but his words sound familiar. Carly, Mom, and now Troy, who knows me least of all. I grab the bucket of nails I left beside the front door. The steps are wobbly, and banging nails would feel good right about now.

Did I expect Tig to tag after me? Not consciously. But looking back...maybe. I always meant for us to be a team, but then I dictated terms like I was the leader, leaving her to wait. And wait, for me to do what I'd promised.

I put a handful of nails in my mouth, and start pounding.

She must have felt like I did, when I realized she hadn't even thought of my feelings that night in the truck: used, unappreciated, taken for granted. And she must have felt that way for *years*.

I told her that I was afraid of failure, and that's true. But it's also an excuse a boy uses, not a man. Scared or not, a man takes care of those he loves. I was so wrapped up in me I didn't see *her*.

I smack my thumb, and almost swallow the nails. *Shit, that hurts.*

Now, Tig's facing the hardest time of her life, and I've let her down. Again.

If only she hadn't gone to Albuquerque...

I imagine her sperm donor as the nail, and it's flush with the board in one bang.

I can't let go of Tig. It's impossible. I love her still and always. I also know the baby is the only innocent in all this mess.

* * *

CARLY

I told Jess I wanted to take a trip to Albuquerque, to pick out my present for her baby at a real live baby store, instead of finding something online. My second reason was to tell her, in private. I look out the window of her SUV and try to pull in a full breath. I don't know if I'm more afraid of her reaction to the news, or her anger, for not telling her earlier. Doesn't matter, though; it just has to be done. "Jess."

"Yeah, Chiquita."

Jess's pet name for me washes me in a warm wave of comfort, and BFF memories. Why did I think I couldn't tell Jess? The reason now seems as thin as the cardboard evergreen freshener tree swinging from the mirror. "I'm pregnant."

The car swerves. "What?"

I grab the wheel. "Pull over. You don't want to die before you hear the story, do you?"

She takes her foot off the gas and steers to the side of the road. Luckily, this early on a Saturday, I-40 isn't busy. The wheels thump off the tarmac, and we skid in the gravel when she slams on the brakes.

I know that WTF look. But as I open my mouth to start the story, her expression softens. "You little minx. When? How far along are you?" Her eyes go wide and she squeals, "We've got a wedding to plan!" She grabs my hands in hers. "Oh, we're gonna make this one hell of a—" Her perfectly plucked brows come together. "What? Why are you crying?"

I squeeze her hands, then pull away. *Think of this as practice. If you can do this, you'll be strong enough to tell the town. To give birth. To cut a future from a black hole.* "I should've told you. That day, in the grocery. I-I-I'm so messed up. No, I *so* messed up."

"Honey, it's okay. We'll just . . . what?"

I know my face isn't right. Normal. "It's not Austin's."

"Shut up. That's not funny."

I snort and I slap a hand over my face. She hands me a tissue and I honk into it. "I can't think of anything less funny, but that doesn't make it not true."

She looks poleaxed. "I think you better tell me now."

So I do. In fits and starts and to the ruination of several tissues, I tell her the whole sordid tale, sparing no stupid move, no mistake, no idiotic decision.

"Holy chaos, Batman. That's one hell of a story."

"It's the truth." I sniff.

"Oh, I know. You couldn't make that shit up." She twists her mouth to chew the edge of her lip, like she does when she's thinking. "Okay. Austin knows, your grandparents know..." She shoots a razor-sharp glare at me. "And don't think I'm forgetting you're just getting around to telling me. The only reason you're still alive is because I feel sorry for you."

Saved by pity. "I'll take it."

"How are you going to break the news to the town? Do you want me to? I could just let it slip that—"

"No."

"I could put a spin on it. Save you the—"

"No, Jess. I mean it." I force my jaw muscles to loosen. "I love you for wanting to make it easier, but I don't want that. I've taken the easy way most of my life, and this is where it got me. It's time I grow up, and speak up for myself."

"You haven't had it easy. You've worked in that danged diner your whole life."

"No, I mean I took the easy way. Instead of saying what I thought, I let Austin make all the decisions. I followed like a little puppy, wagging my tail. It's no wonder he didn't think I had an opinion in my head—I never told him."

"Well, why the heck didn't you?"

Jess has always spoken her mind. Anyone who doesn't like it can go hang. I've always admired that about her. I look down at my hands, clasping and unclasping in my lap. "Because then, if things went wrong, it'd be my fault. There, I said it. I'm not proud of it, but there it is. I didn't want the responsibility. It was so much easier to drift along, being the good girl, letting everyone else take the risk, do the trailblazing."

I'm surprised by my words. It seems my subconscious has been chewing on this, and is just now letting me in on it. "And that worked out great, for years. But I guess I changed, along the way. It happened so slowly that I didn't realize it, until Austin and I had that last blowout." I put my hands over my little pooch. "But now I'm going to be a mother myself. You can't get much more responsible than that, huh?" I give her a watery smile. "I'm going to be the best danged mother anyone's ever seen. I'm going to raise her strong, to make her so sure of my love, and so sure that I'm always going to be there for her that..."

"Aw, come here, hon." Jess wraps her arms around me and I'm crying again. "You will make a great mother, Carly Beauchamp. You're the most steadfast, loyal woman I know."

"I think Austin would disagree."

"Stop beating yourself up. Growing up doesn't come with a timetable, or a manual. Everybody is allowed a few mistakes in their lives. Doesn't mean you're not a good person. We *know* you, Chiquita. The town will get over it, and if Austin doesn't, he doesn't deserve you."

I so hope she's right. Not about Austin; he's gone. But about everyone else. But I know how judgmental I was, before Albuquerque. Why would other people be any different?

She pushes me upright and reaches under her seat, pulls out a packet of baby wipes, and hands them to me. "Clean yourself up, girlfriend. We're going shopping for *two* babies!"

* * *

"Oh my gosh," Jess squeals in the next aisle. "Come look at this!"

I put down the breast pump and walk around the endcap

display. Jess is holding a little stuffed giraffe with legs splayed and little red hearts for eyes.

"Adorable."

"No, wait, listen." She pushes a button on its belly, and "Can You Feel the Love Tonight" from *The Lion King* plays. "I'm buying the Bean this, and you can't stop me."

"That's too much, Jess. You're insisting you're buying a third of the stuff in the basket."

"I know, but how often do I get to be a godmother?"

I asked her in the parking lot. If something happened to me, I can't think of anyone who'd do better for my baby. She'd raise it to be strong. I survey the contents of the cart. "Seems such a shame to pay full price for all this. I know at least five women who have baby stuff their kids have grown out of." I sigh. "But I can't very well ask them."

"This baby deserves better than hand-me-downs."

"Tell that to Papaw. I think half his profits last month went to the crib we bought online. Not to mention the new swearwords I learned, watching him put it together."

"Are you kidding? I'll bet he's more excited than anyone about this baby. He only acts tough on the outside; inside, he's got a marshmallow heart."

A massively pregnant woman waddles by. Her gaily striped top is big enough to have been a circus tent in a past life.

"Funny, I always imagined I'd be wearing pregnancy clothes before I even needed to, just so people would notice and ask." I run a hand down my stomach, my small bump unnoticeable under my too-big boyfriend shirt. "Instead, I'm trying to hide it."

It's more than maternity clothes, though. I never expected to do this alone. I pictured Austin buying drinks for the bar when he announced it to his friends. Warm nights, Austin curled around me us protectively. Austin, with his big hands, cradling a tiny bundle the day it was born. I miss him with an ache I feel in my teeth.

We walk into the furniture department. It's a pastel explosion, with cribs done up in adorable matching bedding.

"Oh my gosh—"

"Nope. You're not buying another thing."

"But here, feel this."

Jess takes my hand and puts it on a throw that's draped across the back of a rocking chair. It's soft as a snuggle. "You know, if you'd have told me last year I'd be unmarried and pregnant, I'd have thought it was the worst thing that could happen."

Funny how this baby worked its way into my heart, as well as my body. I don't even know the sex yet, and we've already been through so much together that I can hardly remember when it wasn't a part of me. I sit in the rocker, pull the throw in my lap, and pet it. "I can't wait to hold my baby. To give it all the love I have bottled up." I look up at her, blinking back the surge of happiness. "Whatever happens, I'm not sorry. How could I be?"

* * *

CARLY

The diner is in the 10:30 dead zone—after the breakfast rush, but before lunch—when Austin walks in the door.

And, as always, my world stops for a nanosecond.

He settles in a booth at the window beside the door. The neighboring booth is empty.

He watches me all the way across the floor. I lift the carafe. "Coffee?"

He flips his mug upright, and I fill it. "You all right, Carly? You look kinda peaked."

My feathers ruffle. He should try being pregnant and on his feet, ten hours a day. "You're one to talk. What happened there?" I nod at the bandage on his hand.

"Ah, it's nothing. Troy and I are replacing drywall, and the knife slipped."

"I heard he moved in with you at the homestead house. How's he doing?"

"He's a pain in the ass."

"You two always got along like ducks and alligators. I hope everything works out okay with him and Darcy. They always were such a cute couple." Realizing I want to slide into the booth and spend an hour catching up, I straighten and pull the order ticket pad from my apron. "You want a menu?"

"Just coffee, thanks." He looks around the room. "Can you sit, just for a minute? I need to ask you something."

I look for a reason to say no, but my orders aren't up yet, and the two patrons don't need a refill. "I guess." But my heart is pounding a drum roll in my ears. What could he want? I slide in across from him and his cologne drifts over me in a cloud of nostalgia that loosens my muscles. It would be too easy to slip into old habits like a well-worn pair of slippers.

Be careful.

He turns his mug, precise quarter turns, one after another. He stares at it, frowning like he's going to be graded on his performance. "Do you think we could be friends, Tigger?"

My old nickname is a sucker punch to my solar plexus. Day to day, you just move forward and try to forget how much you left behind. But that word brings it all back with the vivid technicolor of a deep bruise. "Can you do me a favor and not call me that? And we are friends."

"Sorry." His mug takes another pirouette. "I mean friends, like we used to be." He appears to chew his words before he spits them out. "See, there's this huge hole in me. I keep shoveling in fill dirt, but it's not making a dent. Something'll happen, and before I think, I've got my phone in my hand to tell you about it."

"You've got tons of friends, Austin Davis."

"Yeah, but not like you." For the first time, he looks at me. *Into* me.

I'm caught like a spotlighted deer, and my heart is beating just as fast. It would be so easy to tip back into him. "I miss you, too." The words are out of my mouth before my brain can filter.

He smiles. That warm, sexy, Austin-smile that always made me feel like we were in a bubble—just him and me.

The bubble pops. Being with Austin is like when Papaw's sister had Alzheimer's. It was so hard going to see her, because she looked just like my great-aunt. But she wasn't. My Tante Nell had left the building, leaving her face and body behind. Austin looks just like the guy I fell in love with (and to be truthful, I still am in love with *that* guy). But he's not. This is the guy who's in love with the old Carly. He's rejected the flawed, opinionated, pregnant, *Now*-Carly. Yet still, I'm in danger of forgetting every time I see him.

And that's dangerous. There's more at stake now than just *my* heart.

I make myself hold his gaze. "We can be friends—like we're friends with everyone else. But the way we used to be?" I shake my head. "I'm sorry, but nuh-huh."

"I guess I knew that. But I had to try." His gaze falls back to the full mug in front of him. "I still love you, Carly." It slips out on a whisper.

I have no doubt he does. As much as he can. But I need

a man who has enough room in his heart for a package deal. Austin already told me he doesn't have that kind of capacity.

The cowbell on the door clangs, and Lorelei breezes in, arms full of bags. Austin jumps up and takes them from her. "Where do you want them?"

Eyes on me, she points to the counter, and when he walks past her, she mouths *What the heck?*

I shake my head, a *you don't want to know*, and heave myself to my feet. Another afternoon to get through, and now my heart hurts as much as the rest of me.

* * *

AUSTIN

A week later, Troy and I are sitting in the dining room, putting together a first year's budget for my rough-stock business.

"Okay, that's the bull side of the equation. How much for broodmares?"

I quote him a number. The name at the top of the pad is "Davis Rough Stock." It's uninspired, but I don't have the heart it would take to come up with something clever to put in place of the "C&A" initials. If I'm honest, I don't have the heart for any of this. But it uses my knowledge, and even if I didn't need something to stay occupied, I need money.

He adds a column of figures. "Since you're going to operate at a loss for the first five years, you're going to have to—"

"Even with the stock that's ready to buck?"

"Startups always take huge capital investment." He holds up his mechanical pencil. "But after that, if your estimates are right, you're in the black."

I tighten my muscles, then ask, "What's the bottom line—total net cash outlay for the first five years?"

He names a figure more than double my savings.

I wince. "And that doesn't figure in the money I'll need to get this house into shape."

"I warned you."

"Thanks. 'I told you so' is so helpful."

"Hey, I've gotta admit, this looks more profitable a venture than I thought. I think your numbers are conservative." He leans back and drapes one arm over the back of his chair. "You could make a decent living at this, eventually."

"'Eventually' doesn't count when you've gotta eat in the meantime." Shit. One more dream gone. "Looks like I'm gonna be seeing a lot of the south end of dad's northbound cows."

"Giving up that easy?"

"Well, short of robbing a bank, I don't see any alternative. I don't own the land. You know a bank that's going to loan me money before I have assets?"

"Nope."

My mood drops to the bottom of a well. At least it has company—my future is there, too.

My phone rings in my pocket. I don't recognize the number. "Hello?"

"Davis, you mangy old coyote, how you doin'?"

"Jimbo? Jimbo Jones?"

"Yeah. Heard you were back in town, and thought I'd call."

Jimbo and I used to run around on the circuit before he retired three years ago. He's got a ranch on the other side of town. "Hey, didn't I hear you got married?"

"Yeah, about a year ago." A little girl's voice asks something in the background. "Hang on, honey, I'll be right with you."

"Was that a kid I just heard?"

"Yeah, my Annalise and her two kids came as a package deal."

"Wow. For a guy who was never getting married—"

He chuckles. "What can I say? Man plans, God laughs."

"No lie." I rub the ache below my breastbone.

"You miss rodeoing?"

Among other things. "Feels like every Friday I should be loading up the truck and hitting the road. You still miss it?"

"Oh, hell yeah. But I found a way to fix that. In fact, that's why I'm calling. I need some help."

"Help with what?"

"NMYRA. Youth Rodeo."

"You're involved in that?"

"Yeah, I have kids out to the ranch to practice, and I host local events once a month."

"I don't know, Jimbo. I'm fixing up the homestead house, helping Dad with the cattle, and trying to start my own business. Doesn't leave a lot of time—"

"Aw, come on, four hours on a Saturday once a month isn't going to kill you. Rodeo was good to you. Least you can do is extend a hand back, to help some local kids."

I do miss rodeo. "When is it?"

"This Saturday. All you need to do is help run stock in, and maybe fight a couple of calves. Think you can handle that, old man?"

"Maybe. Just barely. Tell me more."

CHAPTER 19

AUSTIN

Saturday morning, I'm pouring coffee when Troy bounces down the stairs, fresh-shaven, in a suit and tie. "Where are you going?"

"Albuquerque. Business." He walks into the kitchen, grabs a mug from the cabinet, and holds it out. "Hit me, will you?"

A fog of cologne envelops me. I wave a hand in front of my face. "Bullshit. Not with all that skunk juice." I pour. "You're going home."

"I have a business meeting. And no, I'm not going home." He takes a sip. "We're meeting at Natalia's ballet recital, then we're all going out to dinner."

"Good on you, Troy." I am happy for him. It's my problem

that the excitement sparking off him illuminates the hole in me.

I only allow myself breakfast at the diner a couple times a week. Seeing Carly is torture. Blessed, exquisite torture. I walk in and it feels so much like before, it's everything I can do not to reach out, to touch.

But then she sees me, she freezes a beat, before her face rearranges into an "I don't care" mask. That look is like the thud of a bullet to the gut. It's her remembering I'm not the man she thought I was. She couldn't have been clearer the other day. She's got concrete barriers up, and dogs patrolling the perimeter. I'm not getting in.

But I decided last night, when I couldn't sleep, I'm done beating myself up about it. That gets me nowhere but miserable. I'm going to focus on becoming that man she loved. Because, even if we never get back together, I've discovered that he *is* the better man—the man I want to be.

Troy tips back his mug. "Today is the beginning. I've laid out a five-point plan to get Darcy back."

That pulls a chuckle from me. "You're trying to fix your marriage with a PowerPoint presentation? Bro, you don't get it."

"Oh, but I do." He flashes a confident smile, and tweaks his tie. "I'm not working any more than ten hours a day, and no weekends, unless I have an unavoidable meeting."

He reels off the rest of his talking points, but I stop listening. I never have been able to watch a train wreck in progress. Besides, who am I to say? Maybe it'll work.

But I doubt it.

"What're you doing today?"

"I got roped into helping a bud wrangle a bunch of kids who want to learn rodeo."

He raises one brow. "You were always good with kids.

You may like it." He sets his empty cup in the sink. "I'll be back when you see me coming." He pats me on the back, and strides for the door. "Wish me luck."

"Good luck."

The door clicks closed.

"You're gonna need it." I rinse out the cups, turn off the coffeemaker, grab my keys, and head out.

Jimbo's ranch is down a dusty dirt road, five miles outside of town. I pull up to his outdoor roping arena. Kids are swarming. They look to be from five on up to high school age, girls and boys, black, white, red, and brown. The only thing they have in common is their dress: Wranglers, cowboy hats, and boots.

Makes me tired just thinking about trying to herd kids all day, but the adults are severely outnumbered. I open the door of my truck and step out. A promise is a promise.

A piercing whistle blasts my eardrums and freezes the kids. Jimbo's bulk towers over the height-challenged crowd by the chutes. "Hit the benches!"

The pack heads for the three-step bleachers at the side of the arena.

He waves me over. "Austin. About time you showed up."

"I'm here. Where do you want me?"

"Mutton-busting is first, because the little ones don't have much patience or stamina. You stay in the arena and pick up the kids who fall off, okay?"

"I think I can handle that."

"Kids!" He claps his hands. "We've got a long day, so let's get started. Wool Warriors, front and center." He waves to the cowboy standing at the other end of the arena. "You ready to haze sheep, Joe?"

The man waves.

Two cowboys bring in a plunging, nervous ram lamb.

"Oh, that's a biggun'." Jimbo looks around at the ten waiting riders. "Denny, you're up. Come on over here, and I'll help you with your helmet."

The biggest of the bunch saunters over, buckling on a helmet that looks way too big for his little head. "I can do it myself."

"I know you can. Next year, it'll be calves for you." Jimbo slaps the kid on the shoulder, hoists him by the belt, and lowers him onto the struggling sheep. "Ready?"

The kid wraps his legs around the animal, digs his fingers into the wool, and the helmet nods.

"Let 'er rip!" Jimbo and the cowboys all let go at the same time, and the sheep bolts for the other end of the arena.

I take off after them. The kid hangs tough at first, but with every jump, slides down the left side. Just as I come even, he hits the point of no return. I reach for his collar but the sheep veers away and I miss. The kid lands with a thump in the dirt and lays like a turtle on his back, gasping for air.

I drop to my knees beside him, and he looks up at me, panic in his eyes. "You're okay. You just got the breath knocked outta you. Give it a minute; it'll come back."

I yell to Jimbo. "He's okay."

"I'm not a baby. Had that happen a'fore." Still wheezing, the kid crawls to his feet, then walks away, smacking dust off. That one's sure enough gonna be a bull rider. He's already got the swagger down.

Next up is a little girl in pink boots and a tiny pink vest, blond hair spilling out the bottom of her helmet. God, she's adorable. Jimbo picks a small lamb for her, and to the cheers of the crowd, she hangs on like a burr, to the end of the arena.

By the time the last kid goes, I'm sweaty, breathing like a buffalo, covered in red dirt and sheep shit.

And I'm having a blast.

Next is Pee-Wee pole-bending, followed by several age heats of barrels, goat tying, breakaway roping, and calf riding. I'm done in.

"Okay, last event." Jimbo yells from the calf chutes. "Ribbon ropers, grab your muggers and come on down!"

"What the heck is that?" I raise an eyebrow to the dad who's the other arena helper.

"You'll see." He takes off his hat and wipes sweat. "It's a hoot."

"Austin," Jimbo yells, "need you down here to run the chutes."

Before I know it, I'm tying a pink ribbon on the tail of a bawling little calf. The kid on the palomino in the next chute looks to be around thirteen. When the gate opens, he takes off, ropes the calf fast, dismounts, and holds it, while the little pink mutton buster I saw earlier snatches the ribbon and hauls boots for the finish line.

"Thirty-two and a half seconds!" The announcer blares. "I do believe that's an arena record, folks. Joanie and Brian, you just made your daddy Jimbo proud!"

The record stands through the remaining contestants, and the kids come into the arena to accept their blue ribbons.

Jimbo hugs the boy, and kneels in the dirt to hug the girl. Then he takes the mic and announces that the barbecue is fired up at the house, and there'll be hot dogs and hamburgers for everyone.

He sure has changed. Besides being a passable steer wrestler, Jimbo was easygoing and jovial. The peacemaker, when drink and disagreements mixed. But he was also a confirmed bachelor, with no interest in marriage, or kids. We never discussed why, but something told me there was crap in his childhood that influenced his opinion. I head for the truck. Halfway there someone grabs my elbow. I look up to Jimbo's sweaty face.

"No way you're getting out of here without me feeding you."

I want to stop in at the diner. Carly may not want to see me, but I need to check on her; last time I stopped in, she didn't look so good. "It's okay. I'll just—"

"Nope." He pulls, and I have no choice but to follow. "Least I can do. What do you think about our little goat rodeo?"

"Gotta admit, I had fun. These kids crack me up."

"Yeah, it's a lot of work, but when you see the look on their faces, when they come to get their ribbons, it makes it all worth it."

We join the crowd in the backyard of the ranch house. The barbecue is smoking, and one of the dads is laying a dozen hot dogs on the grill. A mom is passing out juice boxes and sodas.

The screen door opens, and a slim blonde in a gingham shirt tucked into Wranglers steps out, a bowl of pasta salad in one hand, coleslaw in the other.

We walk over, and Jimbo takes the bowls in his big hands. "Annalise." He bends down to plant a kiss on her cheek. "I want you to meet a bud of mine from my rodeo days, Austin Davis. He's not bad, for a rough-stock rider."

She smiles and offers me her hand. "Welcome, Austin. Did this guy conscript you to help?"

"More like, bulldogged me."

Someone calls Annalise's name, and she excuses herself.

The older kids are bunched in groups. The little kids chase each other around the yard.

"I'm exhausted. Where do they get the energy?"

He slaps me on the back, almost driving me to my knees.

"Come on, I'll buy you a beer. No one lets me help with the cooking anyway."

The cooler closest to the back steps is full of ice-cold longnecks. We each grab one, find lawn chairs, and sit.

I put the beer in the cup holder on the chair arm. "Annalise's boy is a heck of a roper already, and her daughter is a heartbreaker."

"Yeah, they're pretty special." He smiles.

I wonder if he knows he looks smitten.

"But they're mine, too."

"Yeah, I just meant—"

"No, literally. The adoption went through the Monday after our wedding."

"Wow. What man gives up two great kids like that?"

"One who's in prison for spousal abuse." He screws the top off a beer and practically drains it in one swallow.

"Jesus. Special place in hell for men who hit women." I tip back my beer.

"Tell me about it. I'm hoping when he gets out, he'll stop by. I have a few things I'd like to 'say' to him. But he probably won't. Assholes like that are cowards at heart."

I tip my hat back and squint at him. "Could I ask you a question, without you getting pissed?"

He squints back. "Depends. You gonna insult me?"

"Hell no. I just got healed up from my last rodeo." I take a fortifying slug of Lone Star. "Don't you worry about how the kids will turn out? Especially the boy...I mean, what if he turns out like his father?"

Jimbo starts up out of his chair, and I raise my hands. "I got reason to ask, okay?"

He settles back, but his frown doesn't ease. "Cuz I'll raise him better, that's why. He'll learn how to treat women by the way I treat his mother."

"I know you'll treat Annalise right. And he seems like a good kid. But there are genetics, right? What if—"

"Damn, Davis. That happens, you deal with it. Just like you do all the other shit that happens that you can't control." He shrugs. "I love their mother with everything I've got. They came as part of the package, so I fell in love with them, too." His eyes roam the yard, and pause on each one of his small family. "If Annalise and I decide to have another kid, I couldn't love him or her more than I love these two. And that child could be genetically messed up, too." He looks over at me. "What, you looking for guarantees? Kids don't come with them. You take a leap of faith, love them, and hang on tight. It's as simple as that."

Could it be that simple? I've got the courage to get on a pissed-off bull, but I'm not sure I have the guts for the leap he's talking about. Eight seconds is easy compared to a rest-of-your-life commitment to trouble. Do I have that kind of stamina?

But Carly is the other half of that package, and Tig has always been the best part of my future. How can I not try? If I could find the asshole who hurt her and beat him into the ground, maybe I could let go of the anger I'm carrying on my back like a shrieking-pissed monkey. But Carly won't even tell me what he looks like.

And even if I can do all that, she may not take me back.

It's like I'm caught in quicksand, and flailing around is making things worse. But if I sit here and do nothing, I'll be dragged under.

Either way, I'm screwed.

* * *

CARLY

"Um, Carly, please don't think I'm being critical." Ann Miner talks over the morning babble. She's sitting beside me at the counter, sipping tea, a plate of barely touched chicken salad in front of her.

She looks me up and down. Ann is the head of the Un-forgiven Historical Society (such as it is), a reporter for our local paper, and is the self-proclaimed purveyor of critical. I tug at my oversized shirt, to be sure it's not snagged on my bump.

She smiles and bats her eyelashes to show that she's only trying to help. "You may want to take it easy on the carbs. An eligible bachelorette needs to watch her figure."

I drop my eyes to my plate of fried chicken with all the fixin's, and blink back the sting of tears. I'm so danged emotional lately, I'm crying at commercials. And I'm hungry all the time. Nosy old biddy. But if I gave her a piece of my mind, it'd end up in her "Buried Truth" column in the paper. It's supposed to be about Unforgiven's collective past, but she manages to sprinkle in current gossip, which is probably the reason it's so popular.

And if I showed up in that column, Nana would snatch me bald.

"I'll take it under advisement, Ann." I haul myself to my aching feet, lift my plate, and head for my office to eat where I don't have to worry if my belly is hanging out. My secret is growing every day, and not likely to keep much longer.

Would it be better to just blurt it out? Or wait for someone to ask, point blank? Danged if I know. I haven't been able to come up with any scenario that seems at all possible. Which is probably why I haven't done anything about it. Yet.

Two minutes later, Lorelei is at my door. "Honestly,

Carly. We stay this busy, we're going to have to hire more help—oh man, you don't look good." She steps in, lifts the catalogs from the spare chair, looks around, and drops them in the corner. Then she pulls the chair around and points. "You put your feet up."

"Stop fussing." But I toe out of my tennies and put my feet on the chair. "Ahhh. Thanks."

"Seriously, Carly. I don't know if it's so hot that no one wants to cook, or if this is still the revolt against the Lunch Box Café, but we can't keep up lately."

"I know." I shovel in the last forkful of mashed potatoes. "But the minute I hire someone it's going to fall off again, and you know I can't stand to lay anyone off." Besides, we're going to need the extra money. Babies are expensive.

"What about high school kids?"

"They only want to work from three to five. By the time we hit the dinner rush, they go home."

"Maybe it'll lighten up when this heat wave breaks." She sweeps the wet stragglers from her neck and tucks them back into her bun.

"The end of August is always the worst. It should break soon."

"I hope so, for your sake. Don't get mad, but you look like a flogged cart horse."

"With you and Ann Miner around, who needs critics?"

She crosses her arms and frowns down at me. "I'm serious, Carly. Why don't you hire someone part time, and take every other day off? Or go to half days? You know I can handle the ordering and everything."

I catch her hand and squeeze her fingers. "I know you can. And thanks for worrying. But Nana says we're 'breeders.' Tells me stories of how her grandmother gave birth to her mother in a wagon and walked most of the next day."

"I'm just saying, if you're this tired this early, you'd better make some arrangements." She squeezes my hand, then lets go. "Gotta get back and feed the teeming hordes."

"I'll be out in a minute."

"You, sit." She points a finger. "And stay, for at least fifteen. I can hold them off that long." She blows her bangs off her forehead, turns, and leaves.

This isn't the way it was supposed to be. In my dream, by now I'd be comfortably ensconced in the homestead house, nesting. Bustling around, making it a home, cooking hearty meals for when Austin came in tired from working stock all day, to find the house smelling luscious, and me, pink-cheeked and waiting for him.

When I close my eyes, a tear rolls down my cheek. Damned hormones. I wipe it away.

Time to stop wallowing. I pick up the phone and hit speed dial.

"Carly." Cora's gruff voice resurrects my smile. "How are you? Nevada and I were just wondering about you."

"Not me!" Nevada's yell echoes in the truck. I can picture them, bustling around, getting set up for the day.

There's a click, and I'm on speakerphone.

"Yeah, well, tell her the article about the rattlesnake butt-strike is coming out in our local paper this week."

There's a commotion, and Nevada's voice booms. "Tell me you didn't do that. Seriously, Beauchamp, tell me you didn't." She's breathless and intense.

"I'm kidding, Sweet. Calm down." She's awful het-up for someone who doesn't care about what people think of her.

"Thank God," she mutters and walks away.

"Carly." Cora clicks me off speakerphone. "How are you feeling? Tell me the latest."

I cross my feet, skootch back in the chair, and fill her in.

* * *

AUSTIN

Two weeks later, I'm watching the sun blazing overhead, kicked back in a lawn chair on the porch, sore from tearing out walls upstairs all morning. These old houses are great, but the rooms are tiny.

Troy's fancy car pulls in the yard, raising a cloud of dust. He steps out, looking like a puppy who just got whacked with a rolled newspaper.

I pull a beer from the cooler. "Looks like you could use this. Date night didn't go too well?"

He drops onto the top step, twists the top off, and drains the beer. The fact that he didn't ask for a glass shows just how down he is. Not to mention, he's sitting on the filthy porch in his best suit.

"Wanna talk about it?"

"No." He holds his hand out for another.

I oblige.

"We're having a romantic dinner at the club. I even snagged her favorite table, the one at the window overlooking the golf course. We're talking, sipping forty-year-old cab, the candle-light is in her eyes, and she looks like the college coed she was when we first met. She's smiling, and I lean in…" He twists off the top and polishes off half the bottle in one go.

"And?" But I already know.

"And then my phone rang."

I roll my eyes to the porch ceiling.

"You don't understand. It was the culmination of a deal I've been trying to put together for months. You just don't keep Rory Bitterman waiting."

You do if you want your wife back. "What happened?"

"I couldn't very well take the call at the table. I stepped into the hallway. When I came back, she was gone."

"No shit."

He puts down his beer and drops his head in his hands. "I know, I know. But am I supposed to give up my living? How much better would she feel about an unemployed loser, living off her family's money?"

"Maybe you should find out."

His head snaps up. "What?"

I'm following the trail of my thoughts, nodding. "You should quit."

He's looking at me like a mouse eyes a snake. "That's what I get for listening to a guy who gets stomped into the dirt for the hope of a cheap belt buckle."

"They're not cheap. And I'm serious. You want her back, right?"

He nods.

"Trust me; this mistake, I'm way too familiar with. You've ignored what she's been trying to tell you for so long that when you tell her it'll be different, she doesn't believe you. And tonight, you reinforced why."

"Maybe, but—"

"She needs to know that she means more to you than money. There's only one way to do that. Stop earning money."

"Yeah, but—"

"Hey, I clearly have no woman skills, but even I could'a told you your five-point plan was garbage." I lean forward in the chair. "Talking isn't going to cut it. You have to *show* her that she's worth more to you than money, prestige, and your own ego."

"I get that. I do. But that's like asking me to quit being a man. You grew up in the same house I did. It's the man's job to bring home the money."

There's something for me in my words, but I'm on a roll. I'll think about it later. "She doesn't need money." I hold up a hand. "Look, you did it once. You built a business from nothing. I've seen what you can do. You're good. If this doesn't work, and she divorces you, you can start up your business again."

There's sheer terror in his eyes. But under that, longing. And maybe a spark of hope.

I sit back and lift my beer. "Desperate measures, bro."

"Frankly, the idea scares the hell out of me." He swipes a hand across his forehead. "But so does losing Darcy. I'm going to put some serious brain cells to this."

"It's weird. You and I went totally different ways, only to end up at the edge of the same cliff. Our problem is, there's been a whole lot of talking and not much walking. You know what I mean?" My chest pocket rings. I pull out my phone. A local number, but one I don't recognize. "Hello?" I can hear excited babble in the background.

"It's Fish."

The diner. My heart triphammers against my ribs. "What is it?"

"Austin," he whispers, but I hear his panic. "You'd better get down to the diner. Now."

Click.

CHAPTER 20

CARLY

It's been a crazy Saturday morning. Lorelei called me early to tell me, between dry heaves, that she had food poisoning. I called Sassy Medina to come in early but she has traffic court, so she can't work more than her normal shift, from eight to one. Which means I'm working from open to close.

At one thirty, Fish pushes open the door from the kitchen and takes the tea pitcher from me. He hands it to Betsy Brandywine. "Here. Make the rounds, will you?"

His hawklike eyes land on me. "You." He grabs my arm. "You're sitting down for ten minutes."

"But I—"

He leans in and whispers, "You look like pregnant roadkill. Go. Sit. Down."

Shock stops dissent. If Fish noticed, the rest will know, soon enough. I sit on a stool at the bar. The moment of truth is almost here, and I'm still not ready. I don't have any tactics, any tools, any *ideas*. No backup plan for a nonexistent original plan.

I glance around the room. I know every person here: high school teachers, friends' mothers, local farmers, fellow shop owners. Manny Stipple is on the stool beside me, talking to Moss Jones, who is slurping soup like a thirsty dog. A whiff of Manny's booze-tainted sweat washes over me, and my stomach rolls in a greasy wave. I'm suddenly shaky. The babble of talk recedes to the sound of bees, humming, getting louder. I turn the stool to see where it's coming from and the room keeps spinning off kilter.

Spots dance on the edge of the room. The humming gets louder. A flush of heat spreads up from my chest. I'm hot. Sweating hot. I can't breathe. Gotta get out of here.

When I stand, I'm looking down the wrong end of a telescope. "I'm not…"

The dots get bigger, blotting out the lights one by one.

Blackness.

Sound comes back first. The buzzing of bees, which morphs to hushed voices. Something is squeezing my arm. Faces hover over me; the closest are Fish and a guy I don't know. There's a tier of others above them. "Wha—"

"Lie still now. Eighty-five over fifty."

The pressure cuff releases my arm.

The unflappable Fish looks flapped. "You passed out, Carly. We called an ambulance."

I try to sit up, only to be eased back by the EMT. "Stay down. Your BP is so low you'll pass out again."

I focus on the next circle of faces. My customers. "Let me

up. I have work to do." My head is full of cotton. I need to remember something. But everything is happening so fast I can't catch the thought.

"I'm starting an IV." The EMT glances to someone I can't see. "Get the gurney. We'll transport her." There's a crinkling of plastic, and cold on the inside of my arm. "There'll just be a little stick."

"Wait!" I jerk my arm away. "You can't give me anything. I'm pregnant."

The room goes still; the only sound the *whoosh* of my customers' indrawn breaths.

Fish says, "Somebody call Austin."

"Don't!" My voice is loud in the quiet. "It isn't Austin's."

"How far along?" The EMT asks.

"Eighteen weeks." I grab his arm. "Please. Is my baby okay?"

He moves a stethoscope over my belly. "Heartbeat's strong. But, you're bleeding."

"What?" I try to sit up, to see, but terror melts my muscles to a useless quiver.

The circle above me is broken, and a gurney rolls up.

"Let's get a move on. I want to get her to the clinic."

Many arms lift me onto the gurney and they strap me down. "Please, someone call Nana and Papaw." My voice cracks. Bean and I have come such a long way. God wouldn't take my baby just because I didn't want it at first, would he? I snatch at the EMT's arm. "Please. Save my baby."

"You just relax. We'll get you to a doc fast."

As they roll me out, I realize that I could give a flying fart about what people say about me. There's worse than people gossiping about my being pregnant.

Lots worse.

* * *

AUSTIN

Carly! Adrenaline spurts into my blood and I vault off the porch and run for my truck.

"What's going on?" Troy yells.

"It's Carly. I'll call you when I know."

I exceed every speed limit by 40 mph on the way to town, frantically hitting speed dial: Fish, Carly, Lorelei, Nana. They all ring then go to voice mail.

I blow around a tractor lumbering down the highway. The farmer's eyes are huge, then he's in the rearview. The fear in Fish's voice has turned my blood to a slurry of ice, making my heart and lungs labor. "Where the fuck is everyone?" I start dialing again. Fish, Carly . . .

I take the turn onto the square with a squeal of tires that sends pedestrians running. Shit. I forgot it's market day. I ease on the brakes. There's a crowd in front of the diner, just standing around talking.

No parking spots. I pull up behind the cars parallel-parked in front, hit the flashers, and get out. A truck behind me lays on the horn and eases around me.

Moss is at the outermost edge of the crowd. I grab his arm. "What's going on? What's wrong with Carly?"

He looks up at me with alarm, then his gaze slides away. No, slinks away.

My panic redlines. "Someone tell me—screw it. Get out of my way."

The quiet crowd parts before me, but no one is meeting my eyes.

Heads turn when I slam through the door. The booths are

full, with a dozen people standing, but the room is silent as if it were empty. Fish is standing behind the counter, talking on the phone. In five steps I'm there.

He ends the call, concern in every line of his long face.

"What? What's happened? Where is Carly?"

"She passed out. I called an ambulance. They're taking her to the clinic. I just called her grandparents. They're heading down there." He shoots a look around the room and lowers his voice. "She was bleeding, Austin."

The baby. She must be freaking out. *Oh, Tig.*

I need to see Carly. See that she's okay. Help her deal with . . . whatever she's going to have to deal with. I drag my fingers through my hair. But I'm not even sure she'd let me in. Even if she did, we're not like we used to be. She may let me in the room, but she wouldn't let me *in.* "Shit, shit, shit."

Doesn't matter. I need to go. I'm halfway to the door before it hits me. Something doesn't feel right. I turn back to the room. Fish is the only employee I've seen. "Where's Lorelei?"

"Home sick."

"And that little girl, what's her name?"

"Sassy. Traffic court."

Something niggles. I don't know what it is, but I can feel the shape of it enough to know this is the exact wrong thing. *Stop. Think.* That's when it hits me. I'm thinking about what I want, not what she needs. This is what she's been trying to tell me—that I think of things in terms of myself, and how it affects me.

Double shit with whipped cream. She's right. Carly doesn't need me at the clinic. Her Nana will be there.

If I'm to help, it has to be help that *she* needs. And what she needs now is for someone to take care of her other baby: the diner.

But still, I have a silent talk with my feet, that want to run for the door. I force them to turn, and keep walking until I'm around the counter. I scan the shelves, see white cloth, and pull out a half apron and tie it on. "I'm going to need your help finding stuff, Fish. I'll have a million questions."

"There's hope for you and your black soul yet, Davis." He grins at me. "Let's do this." Then he turns and walks through the door to the kitchen.

I pull out a book of tickets, drop it in the pocket of the apron, then pick up the coffeepot and the iced tea pitcher. I look up at the packed room. "Okay, people. If you're eating, have a seat. I'll be with you as soon as I can." I look around at the bystanders. "If you're not eating, show's over. Go on outta here."

A few people leave, but most stay. Standing room only. Great.

I tuck a pen behind my ear. "Y'all are going to have to be patient with me. I'm better at spurring beef than serving it."

That gets a laugh.

Old Mrs. Simmons walks over and takes the pots from my hands. "I'll do this. You get the orders."

"You're an angel, ma'am." I bend down and kiss her cheek.

"*Pssssht.* I've known you and Carly since the day you were born. Least I can do for all the entertainment you two have given me over the years." She winks at me, then totters off to do refills.

I head to the first booth, pad out and ready to write. "What can I get y'all?"

It's half the Historical Society Committee. The mean half. Ann Miner looks like she's been drinking unsweetened lemonade. "Are you aware that Carly Beauchamp is *pregnant*?" she hisses like the snake that she is.

Carly doesn't deserve the slime this woman's words are dipped in. But hell, didn't I pretty much do the same thing, when I found out? And I was her guy. Face flaming, I look down at the order pad in my hand, and speak loud enough for the room to hear. "Carly is at the hospital, in trouble. Maybe you oughta think about cutting her some slack."

If Ann Miner's nose got any higher, she'd tip over backward. "Well. I never."

I'm pissed, and so damned worried about Carly that the words fall out, unfiltered. "Ma'am, maybe if you had, just once in your life, you wouldn't be so quick to judge." I stare her down until she blushes and looks away. "Now, what do you want to eat?"

Six hours later I'm covered in sweat, grease, and too many stains to name. My feet are killing me, and I have a newfound appreciation for every waitress who has ever served me. How do they do this, day after day? The grumpy diners, the slippery plates, the kids finger painting the tables in catsup.

I ring up Booger Rothchild, the last customer, and one of Unforgiven's three city cops. "Y'all be sure to come back, now." I hand over his change.

"Tell Carly I'm pulling for her, won't you?"

I follow him to the door. "You bet. 'Night."

The bells tinkle when the door falls closed. I turn the key in the lock.

"Not bad for a cowboy." Fish has come up behind me and takes his keys from me.

"Today, I found another profession I can't handle." And how has Carly been doing this, *pregnant?*

"Not tough enough, huh?" He smiles.

"Not by half." I untie the apron and empty the pockets. "Got some good tips, though."

"Ha. Pity tips."

"Hey, I earned every dollar." I stuff the apron under the counter and hand the bills to Fish. "These are Carly's."

He claps me on the shoulder. "You go on. I'll take care of cashing out."

I'm almost to the door when his voice comes from behind me. "You tell Carly we've got it under control here. She doesn't need to worry about a thing."

"I will. Thanks, Fish."

I did what needed to be done, but now I'm doing what *I* want, and no one is going to stop me. I unlock the truck, fire it up, and head for the clinic. The hospital doesn't normally give updates if you're not family, but I know everyone there, and I called so often they eventually told me that Carly and the baby are both stable. They're keeping her overnight for observation.

I stop on the way and pick up some flowers. Nothing massive, just a simple bunch of ones that remind me of Carly— daisies and something yellow, and fragile little white things the clerk called baby's breath. *Fitting*, I thought.

Unforgiven's not big enough for a hospital, but the clinic can handle most of the small-town medical emergencies. Bonnie Carver, who was a few years behind us in school, is manning the desk, and directs me to Carly's room.

Carly is lying in bed, pale as milk, an IV in her arm, the green lights on the stand displaying her vitals. In the harsh overhead lights, I can read every shade of emotion on her face: fear, anger, exhaustion, but over them all, a layer of crushing powerlessness.

A protective snarl rises in my chest. I choke it back, but I can't stop my feet from taking me to her side, or my hand from taking hers. I lean in. "How can I help?"

Just for a fraction of a second, I'm sure she's been waiting for me. The relief is there in her eyes. When she blinks, it's gone.

But in that nanosecond before she turns away, it slams into me—what it's like having Carly love me. Depend on me. Like a smell, or a song—it put me back there, back when I had it *all*, and was too stupid to know it. It throws into sharp contrast the difference in my life, before and after. Makes me realize that my life is more precarious than it ever was when I was riding bulls.

This is my future, lying here in this bed.

She pulls her hand away and looks over my shoulder. "You didn't need to come."

That's when I realize we're not alone. Her Nana and Papaw are sitting in chairs on the other side of the bed, watching my every move. Papaw looks like he longs for his shotgun.

I straighten, take a step back, and take off my hat. "Mr. Beauchamp. Miz Beauchamp."

"Oh, I'm not Nana anymore, eh?"

My face is on fire. I stand there, flowers in one hand, hat in the other, feeling like a naked man in a bull pen.

"Nana, don't give him a hard time." Carly turns to me. "Are those for me?"

"Oh, yes, sorry." I look around for somewhere to put them and she points at the water pitcher on the stand beside the bed.

"Thank you."

I drop them in and look down, working the brim of my hat. "I just came by to set your mind at ease. The diner is closed up, safe and snug."

"What . . . how—"

"I now can add 'waitress' to my résumé." I look down at my boots. "Not that I'm ever going to take it up. I'm not tough enough."

"That's a fact." Nana cackles.

Carly smiles. "Man, did anybody take a video? I'd pay money to see that."

"Well, you won't. I confiscated all cell phones when they walked in. It'd ruin my reputation."

"Seriously? You really waited tables?"

Her tender look has my knees going soft. "Well, I figured there was nothing I could do to help here, so…"

"Thank you, Austin." She's smiling, but her brows are frowning. "That was the perfect thing to do. I'm grateful." The smile slides from her face. "The diners. I blurted out my news…How did they take it? They didn't harass you, did they? Because I—"

"It's fine. You have more important things to worry about."

But she is worrying. She chews the corner of her mouth just like this when she's worried. I can't help myself. I take her hand.

Nana jumps in. "Me 'n Papaw will go down there in the morning and straighten things out."

"No!" Carly and I say together, her voice louder than mine.

"No need, Miz—Nana. Fish is managing it."

"You plannin' on settin' a spell, Austin?" There's a challenge in Nana's blue eyes.

"All night, if they're keeping her."

She stands. "Come on, Leroy. We're goin' home."

Carly slides her hand from mine. "Nana, you don't have to go. And you"—she glares at me—"are not staying."

"Here." Nana pats the chair closest to the bed. "You just set right here."

"Nana." Carly's voice is a clear warning.

"Come on, Leroy, I'm tired." She lays her hand on her

husband's forearm. He stands and, with a warning glare at me that speaks volumes, they walk out.

I step to the door and flip off the fluorescents. The lamp by the bed softens the harsh, industrial lines of the room.

"That's better." I walk to the other side of the bed, settle in the chair Nana vacated, and drop my hat in the other. I lean forward, elbows on my knees. "Tell me. What happened? What does the doctor say?"

"Do not think I'm letting you off the hook. I want to hear everything that happened. What people said."

"Okay, but you first."

She sighs and looks up at the ceiling. "Low blood pressure caused the blackout, but the more serious part is that I have what the doctor calls a 'low-lying placenta.'"

"That doesn't sound good."

"Most often, it resolves itself. If not, it means a C-section. Bean is okay, but..." She looks down and plays with a torn cuticle. "That's what I call her."

"Her?" A picture flashes, of Carly as a little girl: red curls, green eyes, and freckled, wrinkled nose, squinting to find me in the bright sunlight. My heart takes a few heavy thuds before stumbling back into a normal gait.

A tender, lopsided smile spreads on her face. "Yeah, they told me after the ultrasound."

Will she look like Carly? Or the sperm donor? A burst of anger flares, but I beat back the flames. The past won't help now. I have to consider the future. "I'm so glad she's okay."

She looks down at her hand, on her belly. "The doctor isn't putting me on bed rest, but he says I have to take it easy. No strenuous activity, or the bleeding could start again." When she looks up, her eyes are tortured. "God, I was so scared. The thought of losing her..." Her voice thickens, then clogs entirely.

I reach and take her hand. "You're not going to lose her. I'll help you."

"Nana, Papaw, and I have it covered." She slides her hand from mine. "But thank you for helping out today. You were right. I was worried about the diner." She gives me a wobbly smile. "You're a good friend."

The word rips into me like shrapnel, shredding everything in its wake, leaving gaping, bleeding holes. "Carly, we have to talk."

She knows my expressions as well as I know hers. Her head drops onto the pillow. "I'm tired, Austin. Too tired."

"You're right. Now's not the time. You sleep." I lean back in the chair and cross my ankle on my knee. But the time is coming when we'll talk. About a lot of things. I can only hope she'll listen; that she'll forgive me for being such a bumbling, macho asshole.

"What are you going to do? Watch me?"

"Only until I fall asleep."

"Oh." She thinks about arguing, but then closes her eyes. "Okay."

I spend the next hours thinking about babies and Tig and how to somehow show her that I am the man for her. Her and her baby.

It's a tall order. I sit and think, watching dreams dance across her eyelids.

CHAPTER 21

CARLY

I jerk to wakefulness, my hands cradling my belly. The sun is just peeking over the windowsill. I'm at the clinic. Bean is safe. The nightmare of losing the baby slinks back to the darkness it came from.

There's a squeak of a chair, and Austin's face is over mine, his knuckles skimming my wet cheek. "Bad dream?"

"Yeah. I'm okay now." I force my head away from the soft comfort of his touch, but it doesn't cost anything to look. He's soft and sleep rumpled, with a two-day beard shadow. In a word: adorable. My mind takes me to the last time I saw him like that; in the apartment over the square on a very different morning. It seems a hundred years ago. Back when I was free to touch, and taste, and delve, and...*Stop it*.

He hooks the toe of his boot around the leg of the chair, pulls it over, and sits. "Tell me about it."

"It's nothing. You didn't have to stay all night."

"I wanted to. I got more sleep here than I would have at home, worrying."

The door opens and a nurse comes in. "Good morning. How are you feeling, Carly?" She walks around Austin and checks the green stats.

"Fine."

"Your blood pressure is back to normal. If Doctor Simmons agrees, we'll see about getting you out of here." She gives me a cheery smile. "In the meantime, breakfast is on the way." She's gone as fast as she came, and I'm left with Austin's furrowed brow.

"I want us to talk, but I know now isn't the right time." He studies me as if to verify, and he nods. "Tig, I—"

The door is pushed open and Jess steps in with a tray of covered food, a bouquet of flowers, and a too-big smile. "I wrestled this from a candy striper down the hall." She sees Austin and stops dead.

"We'll talk later," he whispers. He straightens, takes his hat from the other chair, drops it on his head, and walks to the door. "Hey, Jess." And he's gone.

"Okay, I want to hear all about *that*." She looks over her shoulder as the door snicks closed. "But first, you're going to eat breakfast." She walks over and slides the tray onto the tray table, and uncovers the plates, one by one. Scrambled eggs, toast, and orange juice.

"God, I miss coffee."

"Hey, don't complain. I can't even stand the smell of bacon, and you know that's a major food group for me." She drops the flowers with the others in the water pitcher. "Do you need help?"

"I think I can handle a fork, Jess." I'd ask how and why she's here, but it's apparent she's bursting to tell me.

"Good, because I may need my hands to gesticulate." She plants her fists on her hips. "Have we not been friends since Home Ec in junior high? Were we not Girl Scouts together? Cheerleaders? Homecoming court? How many sleepovers have we had over the years at my house? At yours?"

"Are those rhetorical questions? Because they're coming too fast for me to—"

"For cripe's sakes, why didn't you have someone call me?"

I lift the plastic fork, so I won't have to look at her. "I've been a little busy, Jess. Sit down. I'll tell you the story."

"I already know the story."

I wince. "The jungle drums are beating early?"

"Oh, it's all over town."

I drop the forkful of egg. No way it could get past the wad of dread in my throat. "I can just imagine." I'm going to explain at the diner about the baby and soon.

"You know you'll always have me." She backs up, and fans her face. "Enough of that. I'm hormonal, too, and I'm going to ruin my mascara."

We laugh, and it helps banish the tears.

She snatches a piece of toast from my tray. "Now, settle in, because I want to hear everything that happened yesterday."

* * *

AUSTIN

I hold the door to the clinic open for a woman pushing a stroller with a pair of squalling twins. "Ma'am."

I walk out into a gorgeous morning. I don't know if it's

me, or the light, or the cooler air, but I'm antsy; way too jacked up for sleep. I head for my truck. I came up with a plan in the quiet hours of last night. Time to put it into motion.

Go big or go home.

Before I can change my mind, I head for Coop's Hardware.

A half-hour later, I'm standing on the porch of the Beauchamps' farmhouse. I shift the cans of paint to one hand and knock on the screen door with the other.

"Austin, that you?" Nana's reedy voice comes from the shadows. She comes to the door in slippers and a ratty robe and opens it. "I just got off the phone with Carly. Get yourself in here. What brings you here this time of the mornin'?"

"I'd like to talk to you both, if I could." I step in.

Leroy looks up from his paper.

"Sir."

"Come sit." Nana takes my elbow. "I'll pour you some coffee."

I set the paint down by the door. "If it's all right with y'all, I'd like to paint Carly's room. To get it ready for the baby."

Leroy growls, "Is that your business now, son?"

I stand at attention, hat in hand. "I hope to make it so, sir."

He looks me over. Close. "Sit."

I let out the breath I've been holding since I stepped onto the porch.

Nana puts a chipped mug of coffee on the table and holds out a chair for me.

I sit on the edge of the seat. "I'm stubborn, and not the smartest pig in the poke. I spent a lot of time thinking last night. It took me realizing that I could've lost Tig—lost them *both*..." I'm blowing this. Not even making sense. "See, I've been so angry about what happened, I couldn't get past it. To see that Tig's baby..." God, I sound like a cretin, but I stumble on, because it's critically important that they understand what's in my heart. "It's not a by-product. It's not *his*. It's a tiny little girl, and she'll be a person in her own right. With all the strengths and weaknesses that any of us have." I shake my head. "I'm sorry to put this so badly, but I need you to know how much I love your granddaughter. I want to do right by her, to make up for—"

"We already know that, child." Nana pats my arm, her eyes full.

"Did you come here to ask me for my girl's hand?" Leroy hasn't moved—hasn't changed his somber Mount Rushmore expression.

"No, sir. That's not my place. Not yet. Not until I can convince her that I've grown up. That I can be the man she wants." *If that's even possible.* I put my hands around the mug. "I just thought I should let you know my intentions."

Leroy nods, slow and thoughtful, watching me the whole time. "Momma, get the boy some breakfast." He pushes out of his chair. "Come on, I think I got some drop cloths in the barn."

* * *

CARLY

The doctor pulls off his gloves, then checks the fetal monitor readout.

"Is she all right?"

"She should be fine. It shouldn't be a problem for you bringing this baby to term, if you're careful. But"—he holds up a finger—"you have got to slow down. No working double shifts, lifting anything over ten pounds, or any other strenuous activity. No working out, no jogging or running."

"No worries there. I never run unless a bear is chasing me."

"I mean it, Carly. If you care about your health, and your baby, you're going to have to take it easy."

I rub my belly. "I will, I promise. But how easy is easy? I have a diner to run. My family depends on it."

"I'm not going to put you on full bed rest, but you can't be waitressing. Sitting in your office with your feet up; I see no problem with that."

"Okay, I can do that." Looks like Lorelei is going to get her new waitress after all.

He flips a few pages in my chart. "In that case, I'll let you go home."

"Great. Thanks, Doc." I probably should stop by the diner, but all I want to do is get home and take a nap.

"I'll get the nurses working on your discharge paperwork. You should be set to go in about an hour, if you want to call someone to pick you up."

My first call is to the diner. "Lorelei?"

"Oh my God, Carly, I'm so sorry."

My heart thuds. "What's happened now?"

"Oh, nothing. Everything's fine here. I meant I'm sorry to have missed yesterday. I feel like this is all my fault."

I chuckle. "You weren't home eating bon-bons, and dry heaves don't make for good restaurant sales."

"Ugh. Don't talk about food. I may never eat again. Now, tell me everything."

"No time. They're letting me out of here soon. I'm fine, but the doctor says I need to take it easy, which means no waitressing. We're going to have to hire another waitress after all." More money out the door that I can't afford. But I don't have any choice. Bean comes first.

"We don't need to."

"What do you mean?"

"Um. Never mind. I have it under control."

But I've known Lorelei for seven years. There's bad in her voice. "Just tell me. I'll worry more, if you don't."

"It's kinda, um...quiet here."

"Quiet, as in ghost town?"

"As in, Fish and I are playing Spades."

Crappoli. This is my worst fear. The town has voted with their feet. Nana and Papaw, the baby, the hospital bill—they're all going to take money. Money I won't have without the diner.

The other line rings, and I say good-bye to Lorelei to answer. "Hello?"

"Carly Beauchamp. What the heck is going on?" Cora sounds frantic. "I do a 'find friends,' and it shows you at the Unforgiven Medical Clinic."

I forgot to cancel that when I got home. "I'm okay. I was just fixin' to call you."

"Really? When? After you're dead? What the heck is going on? Is the baby okay? Tell me this is just a doctor's visit."

"Right now, yes, and no." I give her a quick sketch of the past twenty-four hours.

"Oh my God, Carly. Do you need help at the diner? Because I can spare Nevada, if—"

"No." From the sounds of things, I don't need the employees I have now. "No, we're fine here." A nurse comes in with a clipboard. "Cora, can I call you when I get home? They're here with discharge papers."

"Hang on, Nevada. I'll fill you in in a minute. Okay, Carly, but see that you do call me. I want all the details."

"Promise. Talk to you soon, Cora. Be sure you ride herd on that mustang, now."

"I can only try. Bye."

Despite my protests that I can walk, they put me in a wheelchair and roll me out to where Papaw waits in Fartito. I've only been in the clinic overnight, but the hot sun on my skin is welcome. I look over the tarmac parking lot to the mountains that rim the horizon. I long for home like a kid on his first time away at camp.

Papaw holds the passenger side door open, and takes my elbow to help me in.

"I'm not spun glass, Papaw. I can do it."

"You jest set there and relax, missy." He closes my door gently, and walks to the driver's side. "I'da brought the Camry, but your Nana had other plans."

"I like El Fartito better anyway."

Papaw cranks the truck, which starts after only a little grinding. He heads for the exit and pulls out onto the road that leads home. I hang my arm on the hot metal door and lean my chin on it. I'm tired, and just want my own bed.

"You oughta give that Davis boy another look, you know."

That pulls my head around. My grandfather doesn't involve himself in matters of the heart. "Are you feeling okay, Papaw?"

His heavy gray brows come together. "Fitter'n a bean in a toe-sack. Why?"

"I always had the feeling you just tolerated Austin."

"It's my job to not like boys who date my granddaughter. None of 'em are near good enough. But things have changed. You're fixin' to have a baby. You need a husband. Of the sorry lot, I believe he'll do."

Clearly, the world has gone off its axis while I was in the

clinic. "You don't get to choose a man for me, Papaw. Did he ask you to talk to me?"

"You think we're a couple of those metro-sexu'ls like on TV? Men don't talk about sech things."

And yet, here we are, having a chat about my love life. This conversation is studded with land mines, and it's not one I want to have with my emotion-constipated Papaw to begin with. So, I collect my wild hair in one hand, stick my head out the window, and let the hot wind fill my head with the smell of home.

Papaw pulls up in the dooryard, and Nana steps out. "Welcome home, darlin'."

"Good to be back, Nana."

Papaw ambles for the barn.

Nana comes to put an arm around me. "I've got a pot of beans on for dinner, and I made a dump cake for dessert." She busses my cheek. "Gotta go. They can't start the noon trifecta without me."

"May the cash ball be with you, Nana." I totter for the house. My bed is calling Bean and me. I pull the screen door and step into the kitchen.

Austin is sprawled in a chair at the table, a sweating glass of sweet tea in front of him. "Hey, Tigger."

Like opening the screen door has activated a time machine, I'm back in high school. It must be sleep deprivation, because my insides turn to peanut butter, and I feel a silly smile spread on my face.

Bean flutters below my belly button, reminding me that there's been oceans of water under that bridge. In fact, the bridge washed out a couple of months ago. "What are you doing here?"

"I knocked, and they let me in."

"I smell paint." I follow my nose down the hall.

The kitchen chair squeals, and Austin comes up behind me. "Um. You may not want to."

I open the door to my bedroom. The furniture has been pulled away from the walls, and is covered in old sheets. The walls are a warm, understated yellow that seems to pull in the light.

It's beautiful. I turn. Austin's chest is two inches from my nose. I take a step back. "Did you do this?"

He gives me a crap-eating grin, and tucks his thumbs in his belt loop. "Yeah."

He so doesn't get it. He's doing it again; taking charge like he knows what is right for me. "Did I ask you to?"

His smile falters. "No."

"Did Nana or Papaw ask you to do it? Did they hire you?"

"No. Don't you like it?" He steps to the wall and touches it. "Good, it's dry."

"I love it. Bean will love it. But, the point is—"

"I wanted to." He turns to me with a little-boy half-smile, then he pulls the paint-spattered sheet off the bed.

First Papaw talking marriage, then Nana letting him in (and I have no doubt it was Nana). "You have to stop this." I'm too tired. My thoughts are a whirling jumble, and I can't pull an argument out of the mess. I close my eyes and put my hand to my forehead.

"Whoa, now." His hands come around my elbows. "You need to go to bed."

"Why didn't I think of that?"

"Here." He leads me to the bed and pushes my shoulders until I sit. Then he kneels to untie my shoes.

"Stop. I'll do that."

He pulls off the first, then the second. "Already done. You lie down."

My bed wraps me in warmth and comfort. And paint fumes. Luckily, they've never bothered me.

"Close your eyes."

"There you go, pushing again."

"Shhh, Tig. You're out on your feet." He takes Nana's quilt from the iron footboard and spreads it over me. "Now, you get some rest. We'll talk later." He grabs my toes through the quilt, shakes them, then he's gone, closing the door behind him.

My last thought, before sleep catches me, is that he's been painting from the time he left me until now. He hasn't slept at all.

CHAPTER 22

AUSTIN

I roll onto my side on the camp cot I bought at the sporting goods store and clamp a pillow over my head, but it's no use. Between the light streaming into the new dining room windows and Troy talking on the phone in the next room, sleep is impossible. When I hear him end the call, I yell, "Shutthe-hellup, willya?"

He walks in the room, phone in hand. "What the heck are you doing still in bed at noon? Are you sick?"

I drop my feet to the floor and scratch my head. "No. I stayed up all night."

"You were here when I came down, so I assumed... Where have you been?"

"Watching Carly sleep at the hospital most of the night, then I painted her bedroom."

He squinches up one side of his face. "Huh?"

"To get ready for the baby."

"What? What baby?"

I look up at my big brother, who has told me everything that matters about his relationship. I've told him hardly anything that matters about mine. At first, I didn't trust him. But now? I feel like a shit. "Um. Carly's."

"You ass. I've been spilling my guts—"

"I know, I know." I hold up a hand. "I'm sorry. I thought about telling you a bunch of times, but..." I struggle off the cot to my knees, then stand.

He just watches, arms folded.

"I'll tell you everything. But first, I need coffee."

For the next half hour, I do. "I know you always looked down on me and my career. If you'd have judged Tig, I'da had to kill you, and I didn't want to spend the next twenty years in jail."

"Shit, Austin, give me some credit."

I raise one brow. "Remember our fight over the barbed-wire fence? You were a snob."

"And you were a bad-old-boy."

"I doubt either of us is going to change, at this point." I put out my hand. "How about a truce? Living with you the past weeks, I've found you do have one or two good points."

"Jeez, don't go all sappy on me, brother." He shakes. "What are you going to do now?"

"I'm going to try to get to know this new woman that I've known all my life. If she'll let me close enough."

"Well, it'd help if you start over."

I squint at him. "I don't recall asking for advice."

"Oh, and I did? Didn't stop you from jumping into my business. So just shut up and listen."

I can't argue with that logic.

"You assumed, all this time, that you knew her, just because you've known her so long. Y'all met when you were kids. You've grown up." He looks me up and down. "At least she has."

"I can get abuse almost anywhere—"

"Shut up and listen. Carly's changed. And from what you've told me, you have no idea how. You're only going to find that out by listening."

"I'm listening."

"No, I mean like you're on a first date kind of listen. Don't make any assumptions."

I nod. "That's not a bad idea, for a guy who wears a suit to work." I remember the few words I heard of his phone conversation. "Did you do it?"

"Take your advice?" His grin falls off. "Yeah. That's why I've been on the phone all morning, referring clients to other investors." He rubs his forehead. "Getting on a bull would be less scary."

"Trust me. Way less." I put my empty mug in the sink. "That means you'll have more time to help with the renovations here, right?"

"Short term, yes. If this plan doesn't work, I'm going to have to get a job. A shit-shoveler, grocery-sacker, 'do you want fries with that' kinda job. That should impress my by-then ex-wife."

"Nah. You can just start over in the investing business."

"Right. It took me ten years to build my client list. And somehow, I don't think I'll be invited to charity golf tournaments once Darcy hates me. Hell, I won't have the money to belong to the golf course, much less afford to play a round."

"Oh, the horror." I squint at him. "You'll look pretty good in a Whataburger paper hat. Good chance for advancement, right there."

He punches my arm, but he's smiling.

I snatch my paint-spattered T-shirt from a corner. "Let's get to work. They're delivering the new kitchen appliances today, and if we don't fix the back steps before then, they're going to go right through." The new slate floor we laid in the kitchen looks great; old and new, all at the same time. My body is dragging, but my spirit is floating on a cloud of hope.

The work will give me time to plan.

* * *

CARLY

"I don't know why you're draggin' your feet." Nana stirs oatmeal at the stove, then pokes at the popping sausage in the frying pan.

I pour coffee. "It's just that I've kept the baby a secret so long, it seems strange that everyone will know. People can be—you know." I don't have the guts to tell her that business has fallen off at the diner.

"It's gonna be fine." She turns and points the spatula at me. "And if it ain't, you let me know. I'll straighten 'em out."

Yeah, that'd make things better, for sure.

Papaw stomps his boots on the mat outside, then pulls the screen open. "Could come a gully-washer today."

I glance out the kitchen window. The pewter clouds seem to squat on the barn roof, and the wind is thrashing the trees and stirring little tornadoes of dust in the yard. "Be a nice break from the heat."

Nana pours out oatmeal, and I blot the sausage with paper towel, then carry it to the table.

We sit, and Papaw clasps his hands and bows his head.

"Lord, make us thankful for the food, and all the other bounties you've given us. Thank you for our home, our health, and our family." He hesitates a moment, then adds, "And for taking care of missy, along with her little baby. Amen."

"Amen." My voice comes out thick, and I sniff. Could be the hormones, but I don't think so. Sometimes, love just comes out liquid. The two papery, weathered faces at this table are so precious. "I can't wait for Bean to meet her great-grandparents."

Nana squints at me. "Bean? What kinda name is that for a baby?"

"Dumb, that's what." Papaw shovels in a spoonful of oatmeal.

My face heats. "That's just what I call her. Guess I'll have to be thinking of a real name soon."

"They're sure it's a little girl?" Nana sips coffee, a dreamy look in her eye.

"That's what they said. I'll be happy, either way."

"You oughta be more worried about givin' her a last name," Papaw says.

Oh, I see where this is going. "She's got a perfect last name already. Beauchamp."

"Hmph."

And that's the end of that conversation.

I reach town as the sky lets loose. Water is bouncing off the pavement, making it hard to see. Fartito's wipers can't keep up. When I turn onto the square, every parking spot is taken for two blocks. Dang, I didn't have this problem when I'm in early. I pull around back and squeeze my truck in next to Lorelei's little roller-skate Smart Car. I can barely open the door enough to squeeze out. In another month, I'd be stuck like a cork in a bottle. Pulling up the hood of my poncho, I dodge puddles to the back door.

I step into a warm-as-toast kitchen, pull off the poncho, and hang it on one of the hooks by the back door. "It's a real frog-choker out there."

"There she is." Fish puts down his tongs and spatula and comes over to wrap me in a hug. "I'm so glad you and the baby are okay."

"Thanks to you." I hug him hard.

"Carly!" Lorelei squeals through the serving window. She disappears, then bolts through the swinging doors. "You scared the bejeezus out of us." She hugs me, then kisses my temple and releases me, all except my hand. "Come on. People have been asking after you all morning." She tugs me toward the swinging door.

"I, um. I have work to do in my office."

"Nope." She shoots a General Patton look over her shoulder. "The quicker you get this over, the better you'll feel. Let's go."

She pulls me through the door.

Only a quarter of the booths are occupied. Moss is all alone at the bar.

People halt, mid-chew.

Thunder cracks overhead. A strong storm is building, outside, and inside my chest. They all know that Carly's no longer the good girl. It's time to show them the real Carly Beauchamp. I tighten my muscles and my courage. "I need to talk to y'all. Not that I owe you an explanation. But rumors get bigger with the telling, so I want you to know the truth. From me."

I look around. Expressions range from happy to worried. Several people's faces are closed; painted in disapproval.

"Yes, I'm pregnant. It's a girl. She and I are both fine. No, it's not Austin's. Yes, he knows." I raise my chin, and straighten my spine. "I made a mistake. A bad one. But I can't be sorry. I didn't plan this baby, but I've discovered that love doesn't care about that." I cradle my belly. "I'm going to have her, love her, and be the best mother I know how to be." I stop. Funny, how I worried so much about this speech, built it up in my mind; it seems like it should be longer. But there's really not much left to say. "You judge me however you want. I've got a life to lead, and a future to find." I turn and push through the door to the kitchen. Only time will tell how the townsfolk will treat me, but no matter what they choose, I know I'll press on, regardless.

Because that's what strong women do.

* * *

CARLY

Two days later, I'm driving Fartito home with the window down, grateful for the break in the dragon's-breath heat. Things are falling into a "new normal" at work. No one will let me lift as much as a tea pitcher, and most of the time, I'm relegated to my office with my feet up. Not that they need me much; the diner is half empty most of the time, and if this keeps up we'll be lucky to break even.

Some people have gone out of their way to be nice, to talk to me, and let me know they care. Others won't meet my eyes. No one's crossed the street to avoid me yet, but from their sour looks, it's a near thing.

In spite of all that, I wake every morning, light, optimistic, grateful.

I'm free.

Funny thing about carrying a secret. After a while, you get used to it. Like a too-heavy purse, you sling it over your shoulder every day and haul it around, never thinking about it, until the strap breaks. It feels so good when you put it down, vowing to buy a smaller one next time.

It's freeing to be able to talk about the baby. Bean is more real, because I can admit, out loud, that she exists. It's so nice to not have to choose the day's outfit based on hiding my bulge. Jess and I are going maternity clothes shopping this weekend. Oh, and Jess. She and I are closer than ever, comparing pregnancies and sharing tips.

I feel like any other pregnant woman.

Well, except the no-husband thing.

The sharp pang that hits below my belt has nothing to do with Bean. I should be resigned by now. My old dream is gone, and even the dust of its passing has settled. No matter what Austin says, change, even change you want, isn't easy. I should know. You can pretend for a time, but true spots can't be covered up forever.

I'll find another guy, eventually, someday (maybe). In the meantime, I'm thankful for the blessings I do have.

And I have a bunch.

I turn in at our long drive, rolling up the window to keep out the billowing dust. There's a suspicious black spot in the yard that has no business being there. As I get closer, it comes into focus. Austin's truck.

The little girl in my head claps with glee. But the older, wiser me knows this is dangerous. I can't afford to fall into the old Carly, being second place in Austin's world. I have a baby's future to think about.

This might be a good thing; Austin Davis and I need to talk. We need boundaries. *I* need boundaries.

I pull up beside the house and wait until the truck blats its last fart, push down the irritation, and head for the O.K. Corral.

Austin is sitting in the same place as last time, drinking coffee at the table as if he belongs there. Nana is bustling around like Julia Child on crack, cooking his favorite meal, spaghetti. Complete with from-scratch garlic bread, and there's an apple pie cooling on the windowsill.

The irritation I pushed down rises like Nana's bread. This is not high school. I'm not that girl.

"Hey, Tigger."

I see worry beneath his good-ol'-country-boy smile. He knows he's pushing. Again.

"Fifteen to supper, hon. Why don't you take our guest into the parlor?" Nana's innocent face doesn't fool me, either.

Oh, it's a parlor now? My jaw is so tight I can feel the muscles in my jaw bulge. "Guests are invited."

Nana's wrinkles go hard. "I invited him. And you'll keep a civil tongue in your head, missy. I taught you better."

Austin abandons his coffee and the casual pose and stands. "Shall we?"

"By all means." My sarcasm drips onto Nana's clean floor and she harrumphs as I walk by her.

The *parlor* is uncharacteristically neat. The pile of newspapers is gone from beside Papaw's chair, probably stashed in the closet along with Nana's knitting and her Bingo magazines.

And next to the front door sits a small wooden rocking horse, with a rope mane and tail, and a big smile that tugs at my heart. "Oh, my gosh, how adorable."

Austin beams like he just won the bareback finals. "I saw it and had to get it for the little one."

"Thank you." Tenderness smacks into my wall of No. I always knew he'd make a great dad. If he *was* the dad. "We need to talk, Austin. You've got to stop. This isn't for you to do."

"Why don't we sit on the couch?" His hearty tone belies the misgivings I know are there.

"You sit, I'll stand." I tighten my muscles, my stance, and my resolve. I know I sound like an ungrateful witch, but I can't afford risks anymore. I have more than my heart to lose. *You and me, Bean, you and me.*

He doesn't sit. "Look, Carly. I just came by to talk, and Nana—"

"Oh, I know. She's on your side."

"Sides? There are sides?"

"I appreciate that you saved the business when I got taken to the hospital. Truly. My room is pretty, thank you. And the horse is adorable, the perfect gift. But that's enough. The hard sell isn't going to change anything."

"Whoa. Hard sell? What is this, a slow month at Floyd's Used Cars? I'm talking about our future here."

Seeing a hard man go all tender does things to my insides. It always has.

He still loves us.

Shut up, traitor.

He's changed.

And you know this, how?

Those damned green eyes. They're melting my resolve like the Wicked Witch in a waterfall.

"If you'll just loosen that Cajun stubbornness a notch, you'll see what's real. *I'm* real. Our future can be real." He pulls the first two snaps on his dress shirt, exposing his considerable pecs, and my name in ink, on his smooth skin. "I love you more now than when I had your brand put over my heart, Tig."

I cross my arms to shield my own. "Yeah, except the not-your-baby thing."

He winces. "I was wrong. I was just so mad about what

happened. You were lost, and I couldn't do a damned thing about it." He looks down at his boots. "I don't do helpless very well. But once I had time to think…hell, as many mistakes as I've made, for so many years, what kind of hypocrite would I be to hold your mistake against you? After all, a decent part of what drove you to Albuquerque was me, and my concrete skull. I wanted to talk to you; to tell you. But you kept me at arm's length—I couldn't find an opening.

"But when I heard they carried you off in an ambulance, saying that you could lose the baby, things changed. *I* changed. I stopped looking at your pregnancy as some horrific outcome, and realized…" A look of wonder comes over his face. "You're going to have a little girl."

Emotion gathers behind the bones of my face. I know this man. This is the man I've loved all these years. I close my eyes, slamming the door on the feelings. I know he means it. But he said we were getting married "next year" for ten years, and he meant that, too.

"You said once that what I wanted was a sidekick, someone to share my adventures. You were right; that's what every kid wants. But I've grown up. I want a partner. Someone to argue with me when I'm full of crap. Someone to run a business with. Someone to lean on, when things get hard."

He takes two steps, and my hands.

"And I want to be there for you to lean on. For the baby to depend on, when she gets older. See, I'm not the badass bull rider anymore. My own ignorance bashed up and burned that guy down to nothing. What's left is what's standing in front of you. I'm not cool, not suave, not proud. I can't even promise that I'll be successful."

His fingers run over the back of my hand. His gaze searches my face. "All I'm asking for is a chance."

I want to step into his arms, to relax into him so bad,

it's a physical ache. It's exhausting, being on my own, making all the decisions, not knowing if they're right. Knowing more than just me will pay for mistakes. God, how wonderful would it be having someone trustworthy to lean on? It'd put the ground back under my feet.

But I did that before, that incredible night in his truck. And I hurt him. Much as I want to, I'm not stealing comfort again. I've got to be honest.

Austin is still fixing me with those radar-love eyes, reminding me of every other time I've seen that look of dogged devotion on his face. When he saw me in my prom dress. When I won Rodeo Queen. When I learned to ride his dirt bike—above me, every single time we made love.

He loves me. That's never been in question. I know it, down to my DNA.

I'm still in love with the guy I thought I had, all those years. Question is, are the guy I love and this guy the same guy?

But it's bigger than that. I'm afraid. Of losing my heart again, to be sure, but more afraid of old familiarity. That's why seeing his boots under Nana's table put my back up. What if the old Carly comes back with the old relationship? I already know from the night in the truck how weak I am. How easy it is to fall back into Austin. I've fought so hard to change. What if change reverses faster than a good cutting horse?

The words are in my mouth, I've only to open it and spill them. Even though I don't want to. "I can't."

The pain on his face eats through me.

He's bared his soul to me. I owe him the truth. "You know me. I love hard. I love forever. I've been in love with one man, my whole life. But I'm not the same woman. Lots of our problems were my fault. I didn't open my mouth and tell you what I thought, and why. I went along." I reach out and touch his cheek. "I want to grab onto hope and hug it to my torn-up heart. But I'm not that innocent little girl anymore. I've had hard lessons, too. Soon there'll be a tiny helpless human depending on me. Mistakes I make are going to hurt her." I cradle my belly with both hands. "I'd gladly risk myself, for just a chance of having you again, Austin. But I won't risk her."

He takes a deep breath and nods. "You're right. I don't really know the new Carly. And the way things are, you have no way of knowing who I am. And all the presents I buy and all the rooms I paint aren't going to show you that. So, I have a solution." He puts out his hands. "Will you go out with me?"

"What? No." I take a step back.

"How are either of us going to know who the other is, unless we try to find out?" He takes a step forward. "If you meant it, about wishing, don't you owe it to us—the us we've been, all these years—to find out, before you throw us away forever?"

Maybe another woman could tell him no, but I'm not her. I miss him so bad I wake from dreams in the small hours of the morning, my body aching, my lips missing his touch. Odds are, he's not that man in my dream. But how can I let go until I know for sure? "I have opinions now. I'm saying what I think. You may find you don't like that me."

"Well, that's what we'll find out, then." He holds out his hand. "Now, let's go eat your Nana's spaghetti. We'll figure the rest out as we go."

* * *

AUSTIN

I take the steps to the porch of the homestead house in one bound, throw open the door, and yell up the stairs. "I have a date with the best girl in town!"

"Seriously?" Troy's head appears at the top of the steps.

"How did you go gray in the three hours I've been gone?"

He walks down the stairs, scrubbing a snowstorm of white out of his hair. "I'm plastering the master bath, you idiot. Tell me what happened."

I head for the kitchen. "I'll get the beer. Meet you on the porch."

While we drink beer and admire the rising harvest moon, I explain the night's events. It's warm, but the smothering heat is gone. Maybe fall is finally on the way. "So, there I was, my boots under her Nana's table, eating spaghetti just like we're still in high school and all the years between never happened."

"I'm glad. Even a bumbling fool deserves a second chance."

"And I'm not going to screw it up this time." I raise my beer in a salute. "Hey, did you tell Darcy yet that you're an unemployed loser?"

"Yeah." He stares out at the grassy plain.

"Well, what did she say?" *Please tell me I didn't give him bad advice.* How awful would it be if my life is finally floating, and his hit an iceberg of my making?

He turns to me. "She thought it was the most romantic gesture in the history of man."

"Not bad for a walnut brain, eh?"

He smiles. "I'm not out of the doghouse yet, but at least we're talking. And we're going out tomorrow night."

I point my finger at him like it's a gun. "No business talk."

"The only business I'll entertain is funny business."

"I knew you had my genes in you somewhere."

He throws his bottle cap at me. "Oh, and so you know, I put out feelers to get you an investor in your business."

"Wait. I thought you closed up shop."

"It was the last thing I put out there."

"Wow, thanks. But how does this work? I don't need a partner."

The full moon makes it easy to see his head shake. "That's not how it works. They're just investors. They're looking for a return on their money. They analyze your business plan and decide if they want to invest. Then they move on to the next. They'll give you the five years you need to show a profit, but they'll want quarterly reports."

The roll of barbed wire that's been living in my gut dissolves. Five years. If things go well, by then, C&A Contractors could be cranking, Carly and I could be married with two kids, and another on the way. Maybe the dream isn't dead. It could just be beginning. A wad of gratitude lodges in my throat. "Damn, Troy. I don't know what to say…"

"Don't thank me until someone bites."

We sit in silence for a time.

"You know," Troy says, "it's a strange kind of alchemy, that both our lives have the potential to change from shit to gold."

"I sucked at chemistry, so I'll take your word for it." I raise my beer bottle. "But here's to science."

"Amen, brother." He clinks his bottle with mine. "Where are you going on this date?"

"Don't know. At first, I thought about taking her to a nice restaurant in Albuquerque. But that might bring up bad memories. Nowhere around here is special enough."

"Where was the best date you two ever had? You could go there."

"I thought about that, too. But taking a pregnant woman up on top of the water tower probably wouldn't be smart."

"Jesus, Austin."

"Hey, you asked." I tip my head back and watch the moon, enjoying the buzz that isn't from the beer. "I'll come up with something."

CHAPTER 23

CARLY — A WEEK LATER

I'm not the first at work anymore; doctor's orders. I sleep in, eat a leisurely breakfast, and wander in around ten.

The bells on the door tinkle when I walk in. I look around, dumbfounded, afraid to believe what I see. There isn't a spare seat anywhere.

Lorelei beams from behind the counter, where she's taking orders from the line of guys picking up sack lunches before work.

"Hey, Carly." Pat Stark raises his coffee mug in salute. "How you feelin', darlin'?"

"What...why...where have y'all been?"

Moss Jones turns on his bar stool. "Ah, Dusty, over to the Lunch Box, lowered his prices. But over the weekend he jacked them back up again, so we're back."

That's so not what I expected to hear. A tidepool of emotion opens in my chest, swirling and churning. "You mean it wasn't because I'm the unmarried pregnant girl who let you all down?"

Quad Reynolds frowns. "Carly Sue, I'm surprised at you. Do you think that everybody loved you for being Homecoming queen? For all those barrel ribbons? It ain't." He scratches his head, and dandruff drifts onto his black T-shirt. "It's 'cuz you're our Carly. You're one of us, and we wouldn't trade you for nothin'. And when you have that baby, we're gonna love it, too, 'specially if you teach it to cook good. Right?" He looks around.

"Darned straight," says my third-grade teacher from booth three.

"Dusty Banks's food is so greasy I had the runs," Moss Jones says.

"I hope that baby looks like her hot Nana," Manny Stipple slurs from the bar.

Something inside that was wound tight loosens. I hadn't let myself know how much I was worried about this, in case it hurt the bean. I swipe my cheeks, walk over to Quad, and lay a big old kiss on his cheek. "Thank you, Quad. I think that's the nicest thing anyone's said to me, ever."

He blushes to the roots of his hair, but when his arm tightens around me, I sidle away. Don't want to give him the wrong idea.

"I love you all. There's nowhere else I'd want to raise my baby but right here in this town." I have no idea how the town got the name Unforgiven, but I can attest that it's a lie.

I put my head down and truck for the kitchen, before I blubber all over the floor. "Y'all are the *best*."

* * *

CARLY

I check myself in my dresser mirror one more time, smooth my new peach plaid maternity top over my bump, and push down the butterflies partying in my stomach.

Get a grip, Carly. It's not like you haven't been on a date with Austin Davis before.

All the facts and stats aren't helping. The butterflies crank up the music and rock out.

Thanks to all the rest I'm getting, at least I don't look like Night of the Living Dead. I may even have a bit of that pregnancy glow the blogs talk about. I try to tuck my hair behind my ear, but it springs out. I thought about pulling it back, but Austin likes it down. He likes to slide his fingers through it. He likes to fist his hands in it when . . . *Stop.*

I sure have that glow now. I shake a finger at the mirror. "You are keeping a tight rein on those wild hormones tonight. No. Sex."

Hell, I can't even ride herd on a bunch of butterflies; how am I going to make it through the night without jumping his bones?

I glance to the crib. *Because, Bean.*

Now if I can remember that, when he does that thing with his tongue . . . Okay, no kissing. I'll be safe, then.

"Missy, your date is here," Nana bellows down the hall.

I glare at the mirror. "No. Kissing."

I fluff my hair, turn, check my butt in the mirror, and the butterflies carry me to the door. I kiss my fingers and touch them to my parents' photo in the hall on my way by. What would my mother have told me, if she were here? Probably to keep my knees together. Good advice, Mom.

Austin is standing, hat in hand, in the kitchen.

I think Nana is more nervous than I am. She's flitting

around like a hummingbird on speed. "Now, you two go have fun. Do you have your key, Carly? Don't worry about rushing home. Where are you going? Oh, never mind, you can tell me later. Y'all get on out of here. Go do what young people do."

Austin turns for the door, and she smiles and winks at me. I mouth, *Behave*.

He holds the screen door open for me and I walk out on a butterfly rave.

Austin hands me up into his suspiciously shiny truck. "Where are we going?"

"I thought we could run down to the Rowdy Rooster. The Squeaky Wheels are playing tonight. Is that okay?"

Him and me, walking into the Unforgiven watering hole on a Friday night? Uh, no. I've been in the white-hot spotlight of gossip enough lately, thank you very much.

But he's standing in the open door, looking so hopeful, I can't find the heart to crush him, this early in our first date. "Sounds fun."

His bright smile in the cab light is my reward. He shuts the door and jogs around the front. It's not like our dating would be a secret long anyway. Not in Unforgiven.

I pull in the smell of Austin's truck and hold it in my lungs. His cologne, dust, and the pine tree air freshener hanging from the mirror spark so many memories. Many of them starring me, naked. I take a moment to appreciate; I'm somewhere I thought I'd never ever be again—on a date with Austin Davis. My nerves settle a bit.

I'm going to party with the butterflies tonight.

But no kissing.

Austin hops in, fires the truck, and we head for town. "So, how are you feeling? Is the baby okay?"

"I'm great. No worries."

"Good."

"How are you doing?"

"Finer'n frog's hair."

"Good."

The only sound is the hum of the road. We *never* run out of things to talk about. But we don't really know who we are now. But we know who we were. Maybe old memories will help. "Hey, remember that time Bubba Belkins got drunk and tried to rope that coyote?"

He chuckles. "He'd a done it, too, if he'd had his heeler with him. Remember when..."

Our memories melt the ice all the way through town and down the lonely stretch of highway on the other side. In a few minutes, the neon lights of the red, ragtag rooster atop the bar appear on our right. The parking lot is full.

We're still reminiscing as we walk in. Austin is laughing. I'm not saying the bar comes to a standstill; of course it doesn't.

It goes to slo-mo. Beers hesitate on the way to open mouths. Conversations stop mid-word. People either stare or studiously avoid staring. But when I look down, I can feel their eyes crawling all over us.

"Come on." Austin takes my elbow and leads me to a tiny table in the corner, whispering, "Sorry. I should have thought..."

"It was bound to happen. Let them get their ogling over with, and things will go back to normal."

Patty Pederson, the waitress, flounces over. "What can I get y'all?"

"A Lone Star, and..." He looks at me.

"Iced tea?"

"Sure thing. Be right back."

We sit, trying not to look around. Which narrows our choices to each other. His face has changed. It's subtle, but it's there. As if the last of his youth is gone; hardened to a man I'm not positive I know.

His eyes are soft on me. "I always knew pregnancy would look good on you. You look like a Christmas Madonna."

I shift in my seat, tickled and embarrassed at the same time. "Um. Thanks. How's your business coming?"

He lights up. "It's looking up. Troy is working on getting me some investors that could move up my timeline. And in case it comes through, I'm getting in contact with a couple of contractors to buy stock, and scouting out semen."

Patty arrives in time to catch the very end. "Well, you go, Austin."

His turn to blush.

She drops off our drinks, winks, and walks away.

"Good for you. It was always your dream."

"Part of it, anyway."

I don't want to see the longing in his eyes, but I'm unable to look away.

The band starts up with the Friday night clash of sound you'll find in any country bar in America, but it hits my ears like the scream of a train wreck.

"This was a bad idea." Austin throws down a twenty. "Let's go somewhere else."

Between the noise and the scrutiny, I don't care enough to ask where. I stand. "I'm ready."

* * *

AUSTIN

I steer onto the road back to town, my fists tight on the wheel. What now? I should've realized the bar would be the last place we should go. People around here need to get a life. I wanted to punch every eye that wandered down to her waist. But what now? Albuquerque is out and everything in Unforgiven is buttoned up tight.

Carly's looking out at the moonlit plain through the window. So odd, to see her way over there. She's always fit best right beside me. Maybe, someday—

"Have you ever thought about leaving Unforgiven?"

"No." Surprise makes the word bounce off the windows, and I lower my voice. "As big a pain in the ass as this place can be, it's home. Have you?"

"Yeah." The word has the melancholy of a distant train whistle at night, and it's another reminder that even though this Carly looks the same, she's not the same.

"What made you stay?"

"Same as you. This is home." But her glance tells me way more than her words.

It's me. Hope holds for a heartbeat, until I recognize the sadness in her tone. Something deep inside me tears, and the liquid released rises to my eyes. "Ah, Carly. Do you know how sorry I am?"

"I do." She turns a bit and leans her back against the door. "And I'm sorry, too. Instead of talking to you about how I felt, I just whined and nagged at you. No wonder you thought I wasn't serious—why the entire town didn't think I was serious. You're not the only one who had growing up to do."

Suddenly, I know where we're going. Where we need to be tonight. I turn at the junction and follow the railroad tracks to the high school.

"Why are we stopping here?"

"You'll see." I park in the student lot, right in front of the sign:

Unforgiven High—Home of the Fightin' Billy Goats

"Man, this brings back memories." Her voice still sounds of deep blue sadness.

I step out and pull the sleeping bag I never unpacked from behind the seat. Then I walk around and hold her door, so she can slide out. I take her hand, and our boots crunch on the gravel until we reach the grass of the football field.

"Where are we going?"

"You'll see." Certainty spreads the closer we get. Luckily, tonight is an away game—we're alone, and the gridlines shine ghostly in the light of the full moon. At the thirty-yard line, I stop, unroll the sleeping bag, and invite her to sit. The night is windless, warm, and the scent of crushed grass rises when I settle. "Do you remember?"

Looking out over the field, she wraps her arms around her knees and nods.

"We rode the float right onto the field for Homecoming. Right about here, I looked over at you, in your gold dress, crown, and red velvet cape. You smiled up at me, with your eyeshadow and freckles—you were the most beautiful thing I'd ever seen. I'd known it for a long time, but that was the first time I told you that I loved you."

She turns to me. "We've sure changed from those naive kids."

"Maybe, but I don't think you're giving yourself enough credit."

"How so?"

"Look at where you've been the past months. The things that you've been through. Would that Homecoming Queen have been able to do that?"

She smiles out at the darkness. "No way."

"I have no doubt that no matter what, you'll keep that

baby safe, and raise her to be a strong, amazing woman. Just like her mother." I wrap my arms around my knees. "A friend of mine was telling me a while ago that sometimes, all it takes is a leap of faith. I'm starting to believe he's right."

"I always stunk at broad jump." She looks down at her bump. "And now..."

"Com'ere." I put my arm around her, to try to get her to lean into me.

She resists.

"Look, Carly, I won't get the wrong idea. You've been up front about how you feel. Can't you trust me this far?"

She holds tight for the space of a few seconds. Then she relaxes against me, but I can still sense the tension in the line of her back. She may trust me this far, but not much further.

I drape my hand over her shoulder. "You know, I think we did this all backward."

"How so?"

"Most people are single, growing up. They get to know themselves, and what they want. Then they meet someone who fits their grown-up selves, and it clicks. We met in kindergarten, and were together ever since. It's like we had to be apart, to discover who we were, by ourselves. Now we need to see if the people we are now still fit together."

She looks up at me. "When did you get so wise?"

I snort. "Me? I'm just a broken-down cowboy."

"You remind me of my Papaw. You always did know more than you say."

"So did you. I just never asked." We sit quiet for a time, looking over the sporadic lights of our hometown.

"What are you going to name the baby?"

She starts a bit. "I'm not sure. Why?"

"I know what I'd name her, if it were my choice to make."

"What?"

"Faith."

"Really? Why?"

"Because you had faith, the whole time, that keeping her was the right thing. In spite of me, and the entire town, you knew what the right thing was."

"I've been so scared."

I want so bad to tell her she doesn't have to be, any longer. But they're only words, and I've thrown words at her for years. "I have, too."

I'll have to be content to sit for now, inhaling the apricot scent of her hair. It's going to take time for her to see that I've changed. That I am the man she and the baby need.

CHAPTER 24

CARLY

I open my eyes to sun streaming in my bedroom window. A bloom of panic slams into my brain until I remember. I'm not working today. I stretch and smile. My sunny walls smile back. I cradle my getting-bigger belly. *Mornin', Bean.*

"Faith?"

I whisper it out loud, trying it out on my mind, on my tongue. I kind of like it. The fact that Austin spent time thinking about the baby does things to my insides. Good things. Traitorous things.

Sitting in the quiet dark last night, I couldn't help but see differences in him. Before, he'd have chattered away, filling the holes in conversation with stories of him at his last rodeo, him on his last escapade . . . him. But instead, we talked about me. About life. About Faith. He's no longer so sure of who he is, and what he believes. I like that.

Not that I want him to be tentative, or insecure, but if you only deal with what you know you know, how do you ever learn anything new? If you don't test your beliefs, to stir them up now and again, they set like wet cement in August. I don't want someone who tells me what I think because it's what he thinks. I want someone I can discuss ideas with. Someone who *wants* to know what I think.

Like the guy who sat with me in the dark last night.

I discovered something else. Austin was right. He exposed a lie I didn't even know I'd told myself. I'll see that my baby is safe, no matter what. I'm not risking her.

If Austin and I get back together, I'm risking my own heart.

I should be brave. From the stories I've heard of my mom, she would have jumped in with both feet. But I don't feel brave. Let's face it; I didn't handle heartbreak well the last time. How much worse would it be now, if things didn't work out, *knowing* what lies ahead?

But if it did work out, I'd have my dreams back. Nothing grand or original, just a simple small-town country girl's hand-me-down dreams: love, a home, a family.

I'm caught between two irresistible forces, like a metal bar between two magnets. Both have a push, and a pull.

How do you decide?

"Daylight's burnin', missy." Papaw's gruff voice booms through the door.

"Coming." I throw off the covers, grab my robe at the foot of the bed, and cram my toes into my slippers.

My mom smiles down at me from the wall. I miss her especially, today. I'm conflicted, confused, and sure could use a mom to talk to.

"What're we doing today, Papaw?" He's already got a pot of coffee on the stove, staying warm. I take out Nana's cast-iron skillet from the oven and open the fridge.

"I'm makin' product. And afore you ask, you can't help. I don't want you anywhere near that stuff, in case it could hurt the baby."

I pull out eggs and bacon, and get to work. "Nana sleeping in?"

"She stayed up waiting for someone to come in last night."

Prepping the pan allows me to keep my back to him and hide my blush. "I hardly think she needs to wait up. I'm twenty-nine."

"I think she wanted to know what happened."

I turn, but he holds up a hand. "Didn't say I did. Save it."

Nana shuffles in, her hair in a cloud of spun sugar around her head. "Spill it, missy. I wanna hear everything."

If we were alone, Nana and I, I would. But expose tender feelings around Papaw? Not happening. "Later. Do you need my help around here today, Nana?"

"No. You go have fun." She steps to me and fluffs my rat's nest hair. "That's an order."

I hug her tight. Damned hormones have my eyes leaking again. "You sit. I'm cooking this morning."

An hour and a half later, I'm showered and dressed, and Nana's done grilling me about my date last night. The only spots on the kitchen counter are the worn ones, the living room is straightened, and there's nothing left to do. Nothing anyone will let me do, anyway.

I'm sick of the war being fought in my head. I need outside input. I fold the rag over the sink and take Fartito's keys from the hook by the door. "I'm going out, Nana. You need anything?"

Her voice comes from the living room. "Nah. Papaw will

need the truck late afternoon, though. He's got a delivery to make."

"I'll be back way before that."

I swear I didn't have a destination in mind, but before I know it the truck steers himself to the Davises. Mrs. Davis and I had a good relationship, back when. She treated me like the daughter she hadn't had, and I was as comfortable at her table as I was at Nana's—I was there just about as often.

But I haven't been in touch since the breakup. I know I'm taking a chance—she may be mad at me. After all, she has a dog in this hunt. But I sure could use a mother's advice, and she always happily filled that space as best she could.

I step out of the truck and force my feet to the front porch, and lift my hand to knock.

The door is opened, and after a moment of startled hesitation I'm wrapped in Mrs. Davis's hug. "Oh, Carly Beauchamp, I can't tell you how many times I've picked up the phone to call you."

I'm suddenly so aware of how much I've missed her. Hormones clog my throat. She sees, takes my hand, and pats it. "You get yourself in here. We'll have coffee and a long chat."

In two minutes, I'm in a chair at the glass-topped umbrella table on the patio, a cup of coffee and plate of Danish at my elbow. "I—I didn't know how you'd feel about everything."

"My heart hurts for you both. That's how I feel." As she studies me, her eyes narrow. "You didn't come here for me to tell you what to do. You're capable of working that out for yourself."

"I know. I was just so missing having a mom this morning. I'd've called, but I ended up here before I realized I was coming."

She sits beside me, doctoring her coffee with a generous

dollop of cream. "Did I ever tell you the story of how Bob and I met?"

"I don't think so."

She takes a sip, then sets the cup down. "We fell in love over a microscope in chemistry class."

"Aw, that's sweet."

"Except things were different then. The spur had shut down, and times were hard. The town pulled in on itself, and if your daddy hadn't fired grapeshot at the Yankees you were on the outside, and his mother was from Detroit. Add to that a single-wide trailer on the south side of the tracks, and her never being married…let's just say my parents were not fans of Bob Davis." The corners of her mouth rise in a soft, but so-sad smile. "The day of graduation, we eloped. I lost the baby three weeks later."

My hand flies to my open mouth. My chest tightens to hold the swirling rush of sympathy.

"It could have torn us apart. He could have gone home. After all, he had no reputation to lose. But I couldn't—my parents made it clear when I left that I wouldn't be welcome. That's when I truly saw the man I married. The experience forged him into someone the same, yet different. He was stronger, truer. He put on his best clothes, marched down to the bank on the corner, and talked them into giving him a job. That was the beginning."

I knew that Austin's dad had retired the head of Unforgiven Bank & Trust, but I had no idea what that said about him, until now.

Her soft gaze finds me, and her hand covers mine. "I won't be one to judge you, Carly. I'm proud of you. Despite the heavy responsibilities on those fragile shoulders, you've grown to be a strong young woman. You're going to be a wonderful mother."

I use the napkin under my coffee cup to blot my eyes.

"But I'm getting off the point of my story. I learned not to count a man out until he's been forged in fire. That's when you'll see what he's really made of." She sits back, and the lines on her face clear.

I would have never guessed what was hiding behind that smile, all those years. I'm so glad I know now.

"Enough of that. So, tell me all about that baby. What are you going to name her?"

I realize that sometime in the past hour, I've decided. "Faith. Her name is Faith."

* * *

CARLY

"Jess, what are you doing tonight? Want to hang out? Got any bathrooms you need cleaned?"

"Holy Lysol, Carly. You *want* to clean? Are you sick?"

Sick of thinking. "No. Just bored." I plop onto my bed. "I'm off today, and no one will let me do anything. If I sit around much longer, I'm going to start cleaning out our junk drawers."

"Oh man, you need help. Okay, hold tight, I'll be by to pick you up in a half hour."

"Oh good. Where are we going?"

"Do you care? It's bound to be better than heading for the junk drawers."

"Good point." I end the call and get ready for wherever. Luckily, nothing in Unforgiven is dressy, so I'm safe in my can't-button jeans, blousy maternity top, and my Fightin' Billy Goats ball cap, my ponytail pulled through the hole in the back.

Forty minutes later, the sun is almost down when Jess pulls into the yard in her mommymobile, with her oldest, eight-year-old Travis, in a booster seat in the back. The window rolls down, and Jess yells, "Travis said it was okay if you come, but it's going to cost you."

I pull the door open and slide in. "Travis, your next Mickey D's is on me."

He glances up from his iPad. "Score, Dude."

Jess glares into the rearview mirror. "We've got to work on your gender slang."

" 'Dude' is unisex, Mom."

I love all Jess's kids, but Travis always was the smart one. "He's going to be a lawyer when he grows up, mark my words."

"What, and break his daddy's heart?" Jess turns the car around in our yard and heads down the long dirt drive. "Jake is determined he's going to be a major-league second baseman."

"Jake is dreaming. Luckily, you have a spare. Maybe little Beau will like baseball."

"We can hope."

"So where are we off to?"

"To do what this one *really* loves—"

"Rodeo!" Travis throws his fists in the air.

Jess rolls her eyes. "Jimbo Jones has a kid's rodeo school. Travis drove us nuts until we signed him up."

"I'm a goat-tier, but only 'til they let me ride the mini-bulls."

Jess shoots a look in the mirror. "If, son. If."

"How did I not know about this?"

"You were off having adventures, girlfriend."

"Yeah, despite a disastrous beginning, there have been lots for the highlight reels." I pat Bean—Faith. "And the real adventure begins in a couple months."

Jess chuckles. "You don't know the half of it, Grasshopper."

I chat with Travis about the finer points of goat tying, until we pull in and park at the side of a floodlit arena.

Travis is out of the car like he's been shot from a grenade launcher.

I peer through the windshield at the lambs, mini-bulls, ponies, and goats milling in the arena. "It's like somebody took a rodeo and miniaturized it." A few men are trying to sort out the menagerie.

"Ruh-roh." Jess turns to me. "I swear, I had no idea."

I squint at the men, but I don't need to see their features. I recognize the loose-hipped roll of that tight butt. A burst of adrenaline fires down my nerves. "It's fine." I unsnap the seat belt. "I'm fine." But I'm not.

And from her look, Jess knows it. "Let's go sit in the bleachers with the other parents."

When we get there, I tell Jess to go on ahead, and I hang back in the shadows. I'm not sure why, but I don't want Austin to know I'm here.

The sorted animals are being hazed to different pens when the loudspeaker crackles to life. "Howdy, folks, and welcome to the Monthly Unforgiven Youth Rodeo!"

The parents cheer. The kids mill in a group that's no less chaotic than the animals'.

"We're going to open with Ribbon Roping. The teams are queued up and ready to go. First in the chute is Hazel Montoya and the ribbon girl is her little sister, Brandy."

The little calf is released, and Hazel, who looks to be around thirteen, comes out of the chute on a pretty sorrel, spinning her loop. Her little sister takes off on stubby eight-year-old legs, trying to keep up, and to haze the calf toward the horse. With perfect form, Hazel releases and the loop settles over the calf's head. Hazel does a flying dismount, runs down the rope to the struggling calf, and tries to hold it as her little sister runs around, trying to pull the ribbon off the calf's tail.

The crowd screams encouragement.

When Brandy has it, she takes off for the finish line.

"Twenty-four and two-tenths. The Montoyas have set a blazing speed, but Randy Belcher and Raye Cameron will try to match it. They're up next."

Austin stands in the squeeze chute, tying a pretty pink bow on the next calf's tail. The rough-stock-riding cowboy I knew a year ago wouldn't have been caught dead doing that.

The events tick by, and Austin is right in the middle of everything, putting kids on sheep, setting up poles for pole bending, picking up the mini-bull riders when they fall off. He dusts red dirt off each, dispensing high fives or words of encouragement. I'm trying to hold tough, but I'm awash in cuteness. And old dreams.

It's clear from his face he's enjoying it all. I always knew he was good with kids. He would stop everything to sign an autograph, or talk to the kids at the rodeos.

He says he's changed his mind about Faith. I believe he believes it. But what if she doesn't look like me? What if she has black hair and ice-blue eyes? Would he see a sweet baby, or the guy I slept with?

"Folks, Sub-Junior goat-tying is up next. Contestants, report to the squeeze chutes, pronto. You've got bedtimes, remember."

I step out of the shadows to scan the bleachers until I find Jess on the lowest bench, her knees bouncing in the nervous-mom dance. When I sit beside her, she grabs my hand and squeezes hard enough to make me wince. "I've been sitting here praying. Travis is so little, and the horse they're putting him on is so big. What if he falls off? What if it bolts? What if—"

"Jess. Take a breath. Travis is a strong rider. I taught him, didn't I? And his dad has been working on his roping skills. He's going to be fine, you'll see." I peel my hand from her grip and put my arm around her shoulders. "Now buck up. If you show you're scared, he's going to be."

"You're right. I know you're right." Her knees hammer like pistons. "Why didn't he like something sane, like football?"

The chute opens, ejecting a large, bawling goat. He sprints for the other end of the arena, with a bay quarter horse in hot pursuit. My heart squeezes. Jess is right. Travis looks tiny up there. But he's spurring and spinning his rope like a pro.

"Get him, Travis!" I yell.

"Hang on, son!"

The loop settles nicely and the horse squats in a pretty stop that catches Travis leaning forward. He's ejected, does a perfect somersault, and lands on his back pockets in the dirt.

Jess is up and heading for the pole fence. I just manage to catch her arm. "He's okay! Look at him go!"

The parents yell encouragement as Travis gains his feet and runs down the rope to the thrashing goat. He grabs it, and despite the fact that it weighs more than he does, dumps it in the dirt and scrambles to collect its feet to tie them.

One of the goat's flailing back feet gets free and smacks Travis square in his face.

He freezes, stunned, then falls on his back in the dirt, his mouth wide open as he sucks in enough air for a gale-force wail.

Several men run into the arena but Austin beats them to

Travis's side, where he pulls the kid's hands away from his bloody face to inspect the damage. He tips Travis's head forward and pinches the bridge of his nose.

Jess bolts into the arena and drops onto her knees in the dirt beside her son. I follow, but I stand behind Austin, to be out of the way.

"Travis! Talk to me, baby. Are you okay?" Jess tries to gather him in her arms, but Austin stops her with a hand.

"Let him be, Jess. He's just got a bloody nose." He looks down at Travis, who's now just snuffling, trying not to cry. "You can't be a cowboy without a few bloody noses. Everybody knows that. Right, Travis?"

"I'b okay."

"I broke my nose, twice."

"You did?" It comes out like he's talking through cotton.

"Sure did. Feel this." He takes Travis's blood-smeared hand and runs his fingers over that cute bump that I always thought saved Austin from being too pretty.

"Wow." Hero worship replaces the tears in his eyes. "I'b okay, Bom. Cowboys are tough." He sits up.

"You dizzy?" Austin runs his hands down the boy's limbs. "You hurt anywhere else?"

"Nah, I'b okay."

Austin takes Travis's hands and lifts him to his feet. "You're going make a bada—I mean good cowboy, Travis."

Jess takes her son's hand. "Maybe, but that's enough cowboy-ing for one day. We're going home to put some ice on that." Holding the pressure on his nose with the other hand, she heads for the stands.

The crowd cheers. Travis waves.

Austin turns and walks right into me.

"Tig!" He grabs my arms to steady us both.

"Austin."

"I didn't know you were here. Did you come with Jess?"

"Yeah." I glance to the stands. Jess is gone. I look to the parking lot, to see her van back up and pull out. In full-on momma-bear mode, she's totally forgotten me. Not that I blame her. I'd've done the same. "There goes my ride."

"I'll give you a ride home, but it'll be a bit. This is the next-to-last event, but I have to help shut down after that."

"No rush. Thanks." I'm unaware of the last rounds, lost to my thoughts. Seeing Jess and Travis tonight brought back my old dreams. That could be me in a couple of years. I realize, watching Austin with the kids...everything I ever wanted, somehow, miraculously, is still possible. Austin has put out his hand, and all I have to do is be woman enough to take it.

It's time to cowboy up, or sit in the stands.

I still want Austin. I want our dream. I want that wreck of a homestead house. The babies he promised. C&A Rough Stock. I want all the hardships, heartaches, and happiness a future with Austin could bring.

But if I want it, I'll have to take a chance. That long-leap-over-a-deep-chasm chance he spoke of last night. Trust that the new Carly is strong enough to step into the old Carly's life, and not become her.

I loved Austin my whole life, but the road forked at Albuquerque, leading me here, to this bench, feeling a butterfly kick of the baby in my womb.

I'm not blaming him for decisions I made. But I'm no longer blaming myself, either. Stuff happened. I've learned a lot since that naive young woman fled to the big-city lights for the oblivion of booze and music.

I've learned that I can live without Austin Davis. I can face down the whole town, if I have to. So what am I afraid of? If I've learned anything the past months, it's that I can bear a lot more than I thought I could. I'm a Beauchamp woman, after all. I can pick myself up, dust myself off, and move on.

I can do that again, if things go bad.

But if they don't...oh, if they don't...

Austin has changed, too. After watching him the past weeks, and especially today, I know it, deep down.

My lighter-than-air heart lifts, floating on the helium of hope.

Austin yells just before the arena lights go out, "Stay where you are, Tig. I'll come get you!"

I sit in the dark with my uncertainty, my nerves, and whatever courage I can muster. Only my entire future, and the future of my baby, depend on my ability to articulate. And I failed speech in high school.

No pressure.

But beneath the jitters is bedrock that wasn't there three months ago. One thing about surviving the worst thing that can happen to you—you have a rain gauge to measure *bad* by.

It's like swimming in a deep lake; you always wonder what's down there, and because you don't know, you're afraid. Once you've sunk to the bottom, you find the bottom is useful, because you can use it to push off from. When your head breaks the surface, you'll never be that afraid again, because you know where the bottom is.

"Blacker'n the inside of a bat's butt out here. Tig?"

"Right here." I slap the bleacher to give him a homing beacon.

His hand finds mine. "Ah, there you are. You ready to go?"

I pull his hand. "Can we sit for a bit? I need to talk to you, and if I put it off, I'm going to chicken out."

He sits beside me, and I hear him take a deep breath. "Okay, I'm ready."

"You sound like you're going before a firing squad."

"Am I?"

"I deserve that. It seems lately that if you say it's dark, I'm going to point out some spot of light somewhere." I take my own deep breath. "I'm sorry for that, Austin. I've been thinking and thinking, and other people have been trying to tell me, but I've just figured it out."

"What?"

"I cruised through the beginning of my life. I worked hard, but lots of stuff just came to me: popularity, horsemanship, grades...you." I turn, rest my leg on the bleacher between us. I can't see much of his features, and I'm good with that; it's easier, this way. "Then, when you didn't take me seriously about wanting to get married, instead of explaining until you understood, or we came to an agreement, I stomped my foot and threw a fit. Heck, the patrons in the diner even told me that I did that every year. It's embarrassing."

"Tig, I shouldn't have needed a boot upside my head to—"

"There's enough blame to go around, Austin, but I'm not going there. It's time for us to forgive; ourselves and each other. I'm trying to explain what I've learned from all this."

"Shutting up now."

I squeeze his hand. "Then I made that trip to Albuquerque. Looking back now, I see every mistake along the way. Because things came easy to me, I thought they always would. I never understood the most basic thing that most people learn way earlier. If my life isn't the way I want it, it's up to *me* to change it." Saying it out loud resonates through me like the tolling of a bell. "You were right last night. I think we had to be apart to grow up—to discover the people we want to be."

He squeezes my hand. "Tig."

"Shhh. I need to finish." Now I wish for light, so I could

see his expression. His hand shudders in mine; a thrumming of nerves that my body picks up like a tuning fork. "I've learned that I'm strong enough to stand alone. That's an invaluable lesson. But I also learned that I don't want to.

"You're my dream, Austin Davis. You always have been. Can we start again? See if—"

He puts a finger over my lips. "I'm sorry to interrupt. But would it be okay if I kiss you now?"

My leap of faith ends in Austin's arms. His lips find mine in the dark, and he pulls me to him, like he's afraid I'm going to run. No chance of that. I pull him tighter, trying to show him I'm all in, with my hands, with my lips.

His kiss is the same, dear and sweet and warm as the kiss of the sun. But there's also a change. Not a hesitancy, exactly, more a waiting, letting me take the lead if I want.

I want. I drink him in like cold well water on a hot day, and just like that, we click back together. Different, maybe, but I feel the strength of the bond surging through me.

I open my eyes to the black-velvet heavens. "Thank you, God," I whisper against Austin's lips.

"Amen to that," he whispers, pulls the ribbon out of my ponytail, and buries his hands in my hair. "I'll always love you, Tig." He tips my head to kiss me again.

EPILOGUE

THE UNFORGIVEN PATRIOT

Goings On About Town
January 12

Carly Beauchamp, granddaughter of Nancy and Leroy Beauchamp, and Austin Davis, son of Marguerite and Robert Davis, were finally married on January 12, in a beautiful ceremony at the First Baptist Church of Unforgiven, with Rev. Scooter Schmidt officiating. Two triple rings were exchanged, representing the commitment to each other, and their unborn baby. The bride was attended by her best friend, Jessica Bowmain, and Troy Davis, the groom's brother, was the best man. The bride was resplendent in an empire waist beaded bodice gown of pale yellow chiffon. The reception was held in the basement of the church following the ceremony, after which the couple flew off to a honeymoon in Galveston, Texas. When they return, they will settle into the Davis homestead house.

We wish our hometown favorites the best, and hope this isn't the end of their escapades; they're just too entertaining.

* * *

APRIL

CARLY

I wake and reach across the bed for Austin, to touch cool sheets. I check the alarm clock on the nightstand—two. At the cooing and whispers from the baby monitor, I relax. I've got a minute.

The moon spills in the window, illuminating our huge master bedroom in soft gleam. Being a mother is every bit as amazing as I imagined, all those years. Austin is as smitten with Faith as I am. She's got my red hair, but I'm betting her eyes are going to lighten to ice blue. Austin says he hopes so; says she'll be striking. He's already bought a new shotgun for when she wants to date.

At a lip-smacking sound from the monitor, my milk lets down. One more nightgown to wash. I throw aside the covers, toe into my slippers, and pad out the door.

The nightlight spotlights my loves. Austin, hair tousled, is standing in his boxers, his big hands cradling our baby to his chest. His head is bent, and he's whispering.

He turns to me with a warm, sleepy smile. My name on his chest bows like a rainbow over Faith's head. "You didn't have to get up. I'da brought her to you."

"What, and miss this?" I step over and wrap my arms around his waist, the baby between us.

He bends his head to kiss me. "I was just telling Bean that her uncle and his family are coming to visit for Easter today."

I reach for the soft drape over the back of the rocker, wrap it around my shoulders, and sit. "Hosting Easter for the first time is a big deal. I've got statistics homework, but it'll wait." Who'd've guessed I'd like accounting? But when I get my associate's degree, it's a job I'll be able to do from home. Austin wants me to get my bachelor's and sit for the CPA, but my dreams are smaller; a part-time accounting job, working from home while raising babies, suits me to the ground. He hands Faith to me. "I still can't get over that Troy was the 'consortium' who gave us the money to jump-start the business."

I settle her in my arms. "Your brother is a good man. I'm so glad it's worked out for him and Darcy."

"Yeah, I never thought my brother would be a 'kept man,' but he sure seems happy, so I'm not knocking it." He leans back against the crib.

I lower my nightgown, and Bean latches on. She's such a good baby. I run my fingers over her softer-than-down cheek. "Your grandma and great-nana will be here today to spoil you spitless."

We talk about everyday things until Bean is dozing in my arms.

"Tig."

I look up. How can a smile be tender, sleepy, and sexy all at the same time?

"Do you know how much I love you? The woman you are is so much more interesting than the girl—even when we disagree." His smile is soft in the moonlight. "I'll never forget that I'm the luckiest guy in the county."

"If you help me get your princess back to bed, you might just get even luckier, cowboy."

He rushes to take her from me.

I smile, knowing in my heart that no one could get luckier than me.

ACKNOWLEDGMENTS

This Book. It didn't come easy. Huge thank-you to those who helped carry me across the finish line. Critters Kimberly Belle and Orly Konig. Beta readers, Fae Rowen and Jenny Hansen. Head cheerleader, Miranda King. Double thank-you to my plot-angel, Orly Konig. And as always, thank you to my friend and lay-editor, Donna Hopson. Oh, and Lorelei Lynn Frank, for letting me use her name.

Thanks to my super-agent, Nalini Akolekar of Spencerhill Associates, and my saving-grace editor, Amy Pierpont.

A big thanks to Carly Simon, whose song "Jesse" was the original inspiration for this book.

Nevada Sweet's spent nearly her whole life running away from trouble. But when trouble turns to danger, Nevada heads to Unforgiven, New Mexico, which seems about the last place anyone would ever find her. And when she meets Joseph "Fishing Eagle" King, Nevada discovers a whole new kind of trouble, the kind she most desperately needs.

SEE THE NEXT PAGE FOR AN EXCERPT FROM
Home at Chestnut Creek.

CHAPTER 1

A wooden sign blows by the bus window:

WELCOME TO UNFORGIVEN, NEW MEXICO
HOME TO 1,500 GOOD NEIGHBORS
AND A FEW OLD SOREHEADS.

I knew Carly lived in the toolies, but damn.

The bus turns onto an old-fashioned town square, with a peeling gazebo plunked in the middle of a bunch of dead grass. Most of the store windows are covered in butcher paper. Snowflakes drift from gray flat-bottomed clouds to melt on deserted sidewalks.

This place is the back-end of civilization. A good place to hide.

The bus turns, and I see it: an old train station with the sign CHESTNUT CREEK CAFÉ above the door.

I pull the cord, lift my backpack, and stumble down the aisle as the bus comes to a halt.

The driver watches me in the long rearview mirror over his head and the door opens with a squeal.

I step out into three inches of slushy water and the bus pulls away with a roar and a choking cloud of diesel. My tennies are soaked, and the wind whips right through my denim jacket. Cora tried to get me to buy a heavier one before I left, but that would've been just one more thing to carry. I don't need the weight.

Warm light from the café spills onto the cold sidewalk. There are people inside. It looks welcoming. Yeah, like I'd fall for that.

Besides, I could give a crap about a welcome. I need a job.

My shoes squelch all the way to the glass door with old-fashioned gold lettering. Metal bells jingle against the door when I pull it open. I step into a hug of heat and the smell of grilling beef. Shaking off the shivers, I wipe my freezing feet on the mat and look around.

Red vinyl booths, mostly occupied, line the windows on three sides, and in front of me, a counter with round stools covered with the butts of locals. Behind it, a serving window with a long chalkboard above, declaring the daily special. Hmmmm, meatloaf. My stomach snarls, reminding me I skipped breakfast *and* lunch.

The room is full of voices and laughter. I walk across the old black-and-white-patterned tile floor to take the last open stool at the counter.

A tall blonde in jeans, a checkered blouse, and a food-spattered apron steps up, holding up a steaming pot of coffee. "Cold night for a light jacket. Want some?"

"Oh, hell yes." I flip over the mug in front of me and she pours. I'm about to ask about Carly when the bells tinkle behind me.

In walks Austin Davis, in a Marlboro man shearling coat, one arm weighted down by a carrier full of blanket-wrapped, kicking baby. Carly follows, laughing and shaking snowflakes out of her crazy red curls.

Patrons call to them.

"Hey, Austin."

"There they are!"

"Carly!"

A frail old lady with fire-engine-red lipstick bleeding off her thin lips waves bony, talon fingers. "Austin Davis, you bring that baby over here right now. I need to give her some sugar."

"Yes'm." Austin stomps off his boots then walks to the booth and sets the carrier on the table.

Carly sees me, and her mouth drops to an O of surprise.

She rushes across the floor and wraps me in a hug. "Nevada Sweet, I hardly recognized you! Why didn't you tell me you were coming? What did you do to your hair?"

My fingers go to my new pixie cut, and I untangle myself. "Back up off me, Beauchamp."

"Davis."

I look down at the small rock on her hand. "Cora told me he finally made an honest woman of you."

A lightning flick of pain crosses her face before her smile amps again.

Damn it, I always say the wrong thing, even when I mean well. Not that I often mean well, but I wouldn't hurt Carly on purpose.

"Why didn't you call?"

"Because, if I owned a phone, I'd have to talk to people."

She laughs. "Same old Nevada." She looks around the room. "Where's Cora?"

"Wintering in Oregon, same as always." I know Carly from when she ran away to the rodeo, preggers and scared. Cora went to visit her newest grandkid, and left me and Carly to handle the food truck. It was rocky, but in the end, we didn't kill each other.

"I thought you were going to stay with her until the rodeo circuit starts up again."

"Hang around a bunch of squalling kids? Not hardly." That's at least partly true. The other part, she doesn't need to know about. "Thought I'd stop in and see if you had any work."

I can read her face like the *Houston Chronicle*. Her lips turn south, and one cheek lifts in a wince. "I don't—"

"No problem. Just thought I'd check before I headed to Albuquerque." I push off the stool.

She frowns, studying my face. "No, wait. Let me see what I can do…" She waves at the blond waitress.

"Hey, forget it, okay?" I knew this was a mistake. I'd fit in this cozy place like a coyote at the kennel club. I shoulder the strap of my backpack and reach in my pocket for a couple bills to pay for the coffee.

"Dang it, Sweet, would you stop being so stubborn?" She nods to the kitchen door when the blond waitress walks up. "You. Sit." She glares at me and points at the stool. "Stay."

"Marriage made you even bossier." Might as well sit. Maybe my feet will warm up before I go out again.

I take a sip, and the coffee burns its way down, warming me from the inside out.

Austin is now in the middle of a crowd of people wanting to pet the baby. The cowboy I saw last summer would have never put up with not being the center of attention, but he looks as proud as if he pushed that baby out himself. She has her hand around his little finger, but it's clear from the sappy look on his face that it's really the other way around.

I order the meatloaf from a young waitress who stops by. When she brings it, I dig in. It's not just that I'm hungry—I know good cooking when I taste it. Green peppers, jalapeno, and some spice I can't quite name make it the best meat loaf I've eaten. I look through the serving window. A tall, thin, broad-shouldered guy has his back to me at the grill, a long black braid trailing to his waist.

I'm mopping up gravy with a piece of homemade bread when Carly and an older blonde come through the swinging door.

"Nevada, this is Lorelei, our manager. Lorelei, Nevada Sweet."

I nod.

Carly looks around until she finds her husband, and a smile lifts the corner of her mouth. "What with Faith, and our new business, I don't get in here much. Lorelei would be your boss. But you need to know, we've already got a cook—a good one."

"Yeah, I found that out." I wave at my empty plate. "That's okay; I'll just—"

"But we *do* need a busboy, and someone to waitress in the busy times," Lorelei says. "Carly vouches for you, so that's good enough for me."

Carly hasn't stopped looking me over. "I know you can do better, but I want you to stay. Will you take it?" She names an hourly rate that's better than the job deserves.

I don't do charity. But I'm tired. Tired of running. Tired of worrying. And I'd be near invisible here in the armpit of America. Besides, it's too cold to be on the road. Maybe I'll stay 'til spring, when it warms up. I hold out my hand to

Lorelei. "Okay." I can't meet Carly's eye, but I pull the word from my gut and spit it out. "Thanks."

"Come with me." Carly clamps on the sleeve of my jacket and pulls. "I want you to meet Fish."

"I just ate. And I'm not a fan of tuna."

She laughs that tinkling laugh I remember. "No, silly." She pulls me through the swinging door to the kitchen. "Nevada, this is Joe 'Fishing Eagle' King. Fish, to his friends."

The name makes sense when he turns around. He's obviously American Indian: long burnished face, raven-black hair, with a prominent nose. His eyes...it's like they see *into* me.

"Fish, this is Nevada Sweet."

He takes his time, looking his fill.

"What, do I have meatloaf on my chin?"

He smiles like he knows something I don't. He's got a mouthful of startling white teeth. "Welcome, Nevada."

I lift my chin. "Thanks." That's two "thanks" in five minutes. Gotta watch that.

Carly says, "Nevada's going to be bussing tables, and helping out cleaning up in the kitchen, and waitressing when we're short. But she's a heck of a short-order cook by trade, so if you want to take some time off for a change, you can."

"We'll see." He turns back to the grill. "Nice to have the option."

Carly tows me back through the swinging door. "You'll come home with us for tonight."

"I'll just get a hotel room."

She stops, and puts her hands on her hips. "Did you see a hotel anywhere around? The closest one is five miles down the road to Albuquerque, and how would you get back for your shift in the morning?"

"Hitch a ride." I don't want to be the flat spare tire in their home-sweet-home.

"Oh, shut up, Sweet. You're coming home with me. You look beat. Austin will bring you back in the morning."

I don't have anything to say to that.

"Come on, we'll rescue my husband and baby, and get home."

It's too cold to sleep outside, and she's not letting go of my arm, so I follow.

"I'm sorry, everyone, but we've got to get this princess home. Past her bedtime." She touches his sleeve. "You ready, Babe?"

"Ready, Tigger." He looks down at Carly, smug as a dog by the fire.

The massive snake in my chest wakes, writhing, making me queasy. I'm *not* jealous. I'd never get married, much less have a baby. But the reminder that I'm alone in the world...it gives me a lonesome ache sometimes. I shove it down, and the snake goes back to sleep.

"Nevada's spending the night. She'll start work in the morning. Thought you could bring her in when you go to the hardware."

"Sure thing." But from his corner-of-the-eye look, he's not thrilled.

Well, I won't bother them long. I'm not taking the chance of bringing trouble to their door. Besides, I'd probably have a blood sugar problem from all the sweetness flying around. I follow them out the door between good-byes and blown kisses from the diners.

Turns out, they live a ways out of town in a big rambling old house with a shake roof and a porch all around. Austin opens the front door for Carly and me, then carries the baby in.

"You forgot to lock the door." I glance around to see if the furniture is gone.

"We're in the country, silly." Carly unzips her ski jacket and hangs it on a hook by the front door. "No one locks their doors out here."

I shrug. If they don't care about being robbed, I don't.

"Come on. I'll show you the guest room." Carly hefts the sleeping baby out of the carrier and leads me through the kitchen—a modern room with shiny appliances, made to look like old stuff—through a hall, to a small room behind the stairs. She snaps on the light. "Here you go. We have more bedrooms upstairs, but if Faith cries, it'll be quieter here."

The room has a whitewashed dresser, a rocking chair in the corner, and an iron bed covered in one of those old-fashioned nubby bedspreads. "This is nice." I drop my backpack right next to the bed.

"Oh, you're going to need blankets. Here." She hands over the sleeping baby. "I'll be right back." She walks out.

The baby frowns in her sleep and squirms, so I settle her in the crook of my arm before she starts yelling. Doing the math from when I met Carly, the baby is around eight months old; all legs and head and she weighs a ton.

Her eyes open. Seeing who's holding her, two little commas form between them. Shit, this is going south.

I walk and bounce her. Where the hell is Carly?

The baby's lower lip pops out and she pulls in a breath.

"Hey, hey little girl."

Her look shifts to undecided.

"You got nothing to complain about. I'm bouncing you. You're warm. You have people who think you're the bomb. You have a nice house, and all you can eat. What's the problem?"

Her face clears, and she looks up at me with wise eyes, waiting to hear what else I have to say.

"There's not one rat in this house, and I'm fairly sure your dad's drug of choice is a longneck on the weekend."

She reaches a pudgy hand up and pats my face.

"Trust me, kid, it doesn't get better than this."

She grabs my nose and squeezes.

"Ow, ow, stop!"

Carly rushes in, dumps a heavy American Indian–pattern blanket on the bed, and pulls the baby's nails from my nose. "Sorry. I should have warned you. She's into noses this week." She takes the baby and lays her on her shoulder.

"Kid's got a grip."

"Yeah, wait 'til she gets hold of your hair." She rubs circles on the baby's back. "Nevada, what happened? Why did you leave Cora?"

I shake my head. I can't tell her I'm on the run. Not yet. Maybe not ever.

"Hey, you can tell me. I've seen your butt, remember?" She smiles.

Carly probably saved my life that day, riding me down the mountain on the back of her motorcycle. "That was your fault. How'm I supposed to know to look for rattlesnakes when I pee in the woods?"

She winks. "But you know it now, right?"

"Hell, now I watch in a bathroom."

She snorts. "Okay, you're tired, so I'll leave it for tonight. But tomorrow morning..."

"Yeah, yeah, so you say."

She turns and walks away. The baby's face is soft in sleep, her fat lips puffing a little on the exhale, relaxed, trusting that Mom's got her.

Lucky kid. I close the door, kick off my wet shoes by the old-fashioned floor grate, unbuckle the ankle sheath that holds my knife, and strip out of my jeans. Mom's NA Welcome chip falls out of the pocket. I pick it up and rub my thumb over the Serenity Prayer on the back. It's cheap plastic, more like a Vegas poker chip than something special. They probably give out better ones to people who go to more than one meeting. I tuck it back in the watch pocket.

The door is old-fashioned, with a hole for a tiny key. I dig through the dresser, but there isn't one, so I pull the rocker over and shove the top under the door. I'm pretty sure I'm safe here, but taking chances isn't what's kept me alive so far.

I fall onto the bed, pull up the blanket that smells of cedar, and drop my head on the feather pillow. It's good to get off the road, to be warm and safe.

I'll decide in the morning if I'm going to stay.

* * *

FISH

"Come on, Awee. You move like a *tsisteeł*." I slow my steps until I'm abreast of the fourteen-year-old girl who's lagging. The rim of the horizon is the color of a dove; sunrise is minutes away.

"Who're you calling a rat, Fishing Eagle?" She pants.

"I called you a *tsisteeł*."

"What's that?" She picks up the pace a bit.

I smile. "You'll have to look it up."

She groans.

I run on ahead on the path my feet have trod hundreds of times. "Only a half mile left to go. Pick it up. Do you want the Zuni girls to beat you in the Wings Competition?"

The girls in the front of the pack sprint away. They may not be fluent in Navajo yet, but they have tribal pride. And I have pride in them.

The reservation itself is one hundred twenty miles from here, but a good percentage of the county population is Navajo. I do what I can to teach our young ones the old ways, as I was taught. It's not easy when we're fighting for attention with the rest of the world on their phones. But the ones who stay, and the ones who return disgusted and disillusioned...they want to know.

The sun tips over the horizon just as we reach the cluster of old hogans and trailers. I'm breathing hard, but not sweating. I gather the girls in a group as the last stragglers run in. "It's always a good day when you get to greet the gods in the morning. *Yá'át'ééh abíní.*"

"You have a good day too, Fish."

I get in my battered truck and head for my place, and a shower. If I don't hurry, I'm going to be late for work.

A half hour later, hair still wet, I pull up behind the café. I unlock the back door, flip on the lights, and when I walk to the dining room to raise the blinds, I see Austin and the new girl, Nevada, arguing on the sidewalk. I open the front door.

"You're not carting me back and forth every day."

"Just until you find something. It's not a problem."

"Not happening."

"Okay, then at least..." He reaches in his back pocket, pulls out his wallet, and pulls out some bills.

Nevada puts her hands on her hips and gets in his face. "I don't. Do. Charity."

When Austin backs up a step, I grin. Spunky little thing, backing up a rough-stock rider. "You want to continue this inside? I'm freezing here."

"We're done here." She flips a hand to wave Austin off, and pushes her way past me.

"Damn." Austin watches her stomp her way to the kitchen. "I was just trying to help."

"The proud ones are the prickliest."

"Don't matter to me, but for some reason, Tig has a soft spot for that girl. Damned if I see why." He shakes his head and dons his cowboy hat. "See ya, Fish."

"Later."

I close the door and lock it.

"What do you want me to do?"

She's standing behind me in one of my extra-long aprons that almost brushes the floor. But doesn't cover the slogan on her T-shirt: SARCASM: IT'S HOW I HUG.

Not going there. I'll let Lorelei deal with the dress code. I reach to lift the apron strings.

"Hey!" She backs up, her face mottled red.

I hold up my hands. "I'm trying to show you how to tie that so you're not tripping over it."

"Oh."

She allows it, but I can see from the taut muscles in her forearms she doesn't like it. I pull a horizontal pleat in the apron, cross the laces in the back, and reach around her sides to hand them to her. "Tie them in the front, or you're going to be stepping on those, too."

H ad down, she pulls it tight and ties a bow. "I just don't like people touching me, that's all."

"Noted." She reminds me of a Chihuahua my grandmother had when I was a kid. It snarled at everyone but her, and even bit my ankle once. When I threatened to kick it, she said, "Be gentle, *ghe*. It is not angry. It is afraid, acting the big dog to cover it up." Man, I miss my *amá sání*.

"You want me to fire up the grill?"

Easy to see the job she really wants. "Why don't you pull up the shades, sweep, and then come back and unload the dishwasher? Our early waitress will be here in a sec." There's a knock at the back door.

Sassy Medina bounces in, pink cheeks and all. "Hey, Fish. Nice day, huh?"

"A beautiful day."

"I think today should be—" She stops when Nevada steps in.

The two couldn't be more different. Sassy's all curves and bouncy blond hair and enthusiasm while Nevada's rectangular, athletic frame and short brown hair are as sharp as her snark.

"Sassy Medina, meet Nevada Sweet. She's our new busboy...girl...person."

Sassy's face lights up. "Oh, good. The high school boys we had bussing were gross."

Nevada rolls her eyes. "I'll get to work."

I glance through the serving window. A couple people are standing on the sidewalk, stamping their feet to stay warm. The day has begun.

* * *

After the lunch rush, Lorelei says through the window, "Nevada, why don't you take your lunch break?"

Nevada pulls the silverware tray from the industrial dishwasher. "Nah, I'm good."

"You have to eat. Meals while you're working are on the house."

"Oh. Okay." She sets down the tray and wipes her hands on her apron.

"What'll you have?" I ask her. "I'm making a BLT for myself. Want one?"

"I'll make my own lunch."

I am about to object, but the look of longing on her face when she steps to the grill stops me. She looks like a little kid, looking through the window of an ice cream parlor. "On second thought, I need to check inventory. You mind making mine, too?"

"Sure. You want fries?" A not-quite smile dances around the edge of her lips.

"Heck yes."

"Then move."

I watch her out of the corner of my eye as I pretend to go through our stock.

Not a wasted movement, she drops in a full fry basket, puts bacon on the grill, and cracks two eggs, then scrambles them. "You need some music in here." She glances to the order wheel, then at me.

I shake my head. "They can sit for a couple minutes. You need to eat."

"Like I'm going to starve in the next ten minutes?" One last longing look at the wheel, then she pulls up the fry basket, gives it a practiced bounce to shed oil, while scraping eggs off the grill with a spatula.

"Where'd you learn to cook?"

She shrugs, and pulls bread out of the toaster. "Here and there. Why?"

She looks at me as if I've asked if she was wearing underwear. Lots more to this prickly girl than she shows on purpose. "Just wondering. You clearly know your way around a kitchen." I pull out two plates, and she fills them; mine with a perfect BLT and fries, hers with a breakfast burrito and fries.

We lean our butts against the counter to eat.

"You know, I probably shouldn't tell you this, but the Lunch Box Café, down the square, is looking for a cook."

Her brows raise, and her eyes light. Then the scowl that seems to be her normal expression falls again. "They've got to be the competition, right?"

"Yeah, but—"

"Not doing it." She shakes her head and brushes a crumb from her mouth with her little finger. "I owe Carly. I pay my debts."

"Yeah, I heard about the rattler butt strike."

She whirls to me, face red. "It wasn't my butt. It was the back of my leg."

I smile. "I know. I'm just teasing you."

She slaps her hand on the stainless counter. It sounds like a gong. "Why don't we have a few chuckles at your expense, then?"

My face heats. I, of all people, know what it's like to be the brunt of jokes. "You're right. Sorry."

A glacial silence fills the kitchen, dampening sound like a heavy snow.

My grandmother's Chihuahua has nothing on this stray.

ABOUT THE AUTHOR

Laura Drake grew up in the suburbs of Detroit. As a tomboy, she's always loved the outdoors and adventure. In 1980, she and her sister packed everything they owned into Pintos and moved to California. There she met and married a motorcycling, bleed-maroon Texas Aggie and her love affair with the West began. Her debut Western romance, *The Sweet Spot*, won the coveted RITA Award for Best First Book.

In 2014, Laura realized a lifelong dream of becoming a Texan and is currently working on her accent. She gave up the corporate CFO gig to write full-time. She's a wife, grandmother, and motorcycle chick in the remaining waking hours.

You can learn more at:
LauraDrakeBooks.com
Twitter @PBRWriter
Facebook.com/LauraDrakeBooks

Looking for more Cowboys?
Forever brings the heat with these sexy studs.

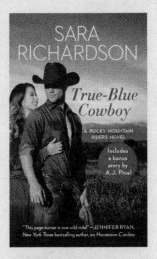

True-Blue Cowboy
By Sara Richardson

Everly Brooks wants nothing to do with her sexy new landlord, but when he comes to her with a deal she can't refuse, staying away from him is not as easy as it seems.

Tough Luck Cowboy
By A.J. Pine

Rugged and reckless, Luke Everett has always lived life on the dangerous side—until a rodeo accident leaves his career in shambles. But life for Luke isn't as bad as it seems when he gets the chance to spend time with the woman he's always wanted but could never have.

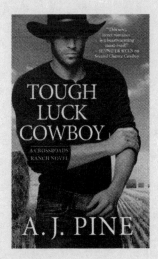

Be sure to follow the conversation using
#ReadForever and #CowboyoftheMonth!

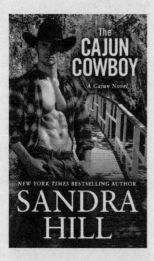

The Cajun Cowboy
By Sandra Hill

With the moon shining over the bayou, this Cajun cowboy must sweet-talk his way into his wife's arms again...before she unties the knot for good!

The Last True Cowboy
By Laura Drake

Austin Davis never meant to put his rodeo career before Carly, and this cowboy will do whatever it takes to win her back. But Carly's hiding a secret—one that will test the depth of their love.

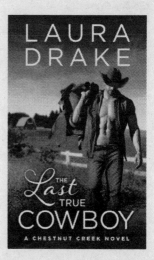

5449

Look for more at: forever-romance.com

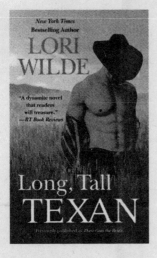

Long, Tall Texan
By Lori Wilde

With an altar to avoid and a cop to dream of, Delany Cartwright is a runaway bride who hopes a little magic will unveil the true destiny of her heart. But be careful what you wish for... (Previously published as *There Goes the Bride*)

Cowboy Brave
By Carolyn Brown

After meeting a handsome cowboy who literally sweeps her off her feet, Emily Thompson starts to wonder if the way to fix her broken heart is to fall in love.